This book is due for return on or before the last date shown above: it may, subject to the book not being reserved by another reader, be renewed by personal application, post, or telephone, quoting this date and details of the book.

REG GADNEY

Immaculate Deception

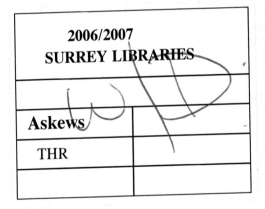

faber and faber

First published in 2006
by Faber and Faber Limited
3 Queen Square London WC1N 3AU

Typeset by Faber and Faber Limited
Printed in England by Clays Ltd, St Ives plc

This paperback edition first published in 2007

A CIP record for this book
is available from the British Library

ISBN 978-0-571-22690-0

2 4 6 8 10 9 7 5 3 1

For Fay with love

As I was going up the stair
I met a man who wasn't there.
He wasn't there again today.
I wish, I wish he'd stay away.

HUGHES MEARNS

Contents

Leaving Home

I want to spend the rest of my life with you.
I love you.
Please will you marry me?
   Alan Rosslyn's marriage proposal to Mei Lim

On the day she left him, he hid the envelope in her jewellery box.

The sealed envelope was addressed:

With all my Love to MEI –
Please Open On Arrival in Hong Kong ALAN

By no means certain that she would accept his offer, he added another note: *Answer me before we're together again at Christmas. I love you.*

She had explained the reason for her departure:

'You need breathing space. I'm the reminder of the phantom that haunts you. I make your obsession with Terajima worse. If we're to make a life together, you've got to get him out of your mind. You're the only person in the world who still thinks that animal's alive. He's dead, Alan. He's dead and gone. Forget him. For your

3

sake. For my sake. It'll be easier if I go away for a while. Don't stop me. Please don't even try.'

He wasn't able to prevent her leaving, just as he wasn't able to exorcise the phantom of Klaas-Pieter Terajima.

Nightmares of the violence in the South China Sea plagued him, even though more than a year had passed since he had so nearly succeeded in ending Terajima's infamous career.

The Kowloon Flying Services Puma helicopter lowers towards the surface of the ocean near the position where Mei's father, Winston Lim, had lost his life, where we will drop the bouquet of flowers in his memory. The sea is beautiful. Turquoise. Sparkling tips of tiny waves. Mei, safe at last, is in the seat beside me and we are holding hands.

Then the horror when I realise that Terajima is at the controls of the helicopter he hijacked from Hong Kong International Airport.

Burning smoke fills the cabin.

We'll be burned to death.

The rush for the emergency exits.

We jump. The deafening whistle in my ears.

White spray claws the eyes. Everything's white. Then it all goes black.

The helicopter hits the sea and vanishes in a cloud of white spray.

It's a mercy we've survived. Or is it? Is survival really worth the nightmares?

Flashes blind me. It's like looking at the sun. Fir of yellow, red, blue and white.

The ocean's on fire. There's the stench of burning

4

Back in London the days went by and the nightmare continued. He'd wake up soaked in sweat and Mei would hold him in her arms telling him everything was all right.

It isn't. Everything's very wrong.

Mornings would offer some release until he felt his limbs turn leaden and exhaustion got the better of him. For reasons he couldn't understand, he'd find himself unable to stop weeping.

There was the blank in the story between the moment when he lost consciousness and the rescue in the ocean.

Some people reasoned that Terajima couldn't have survived the crash without injury. But along with Rosslyn, other people had survived.

Others argued that even if Terajima had jumped for his life before the helicopter collided with the ocean, he couldn't have made it to the shore. But they hadn't reckoned with Terajima's strength and fitness and the beautiful way he swam.

The inescapable fact is no one's found Terajima's body.

The obsession that Terajima is still alive and determined to kill us leaves me floundering. Sometimes I look in the bathroom mirror and it's Terajima's face I see.

He told Mei:

'I want him brought to justice. He murdered your father. What he did to you deserves a hundred years in gaol. He's still alive. I know his mind. He's pathologically jealous. He wants you and me dead. I blame myself. I should've gone after him. Mei, I'm sorry. I'm really sorry. I just can't live with myself until I see him dead.'

5

'Listen, Alan. You know how much I love you. I always have. I always will. That's why I can't take this obsession with Terajima. Of course, he abused me. But, I've managed to deal with all of that. Why can't you? It's very strange to me that you're mentally and physically stronger than me, and yet you're the one who's been defeated. Why allow him to win? He's dead. Believe me. Now you must rebuild your life. Please, Alan – for me.'

He didn't know where to begin.

'Call in some favours,' she told him. 'Talk to Grant Feller at Virtus. See your friend Ron Costley at Allegiance. He's always been the one person you've trusted without question. He thinks of you as a son. He won't shut the door in your face, will he?'

There was some sense in Mei's suggestion that he turn to Virtus, the Anglo-American private security and intelligence firm he worked for. He could also ask Ron Costley, who worked for Allegiance, Virtus's rival, whether he might help. He doubted either firm would look at his request with favour. Or he could wait until Terajima showed his face and made his next move.

Right up to the day of her departure he begged Mei to stay with him: 'I'll miss you. Falling asleep in your arms. The sound of your laughter. All of you. Please tell me you'll stay. I need your help, Mei.'

'Alan – the only person who can help you is you. You'll do it. And when you have, I'll be waiting for you.'

It occurred to Rosslyn that he might confide in another friend, a colleague at Virtus: Grant Feller. Rosslyn wondered why Feller wasn't returning calls. He seemed to have gone to ground.

6

2

BRIGHTON

Grant Feller was in Brighton. 'Please hurry,' he said to his father.

'The train will leave late,' his father said. 'It always does.' The old man was taking an age to gather up the letters that had arrived for him during the past few weeks. Many of the envelopes bore foreign stamps and were variously postmarked Antwerp, Tel Aviv, Rio de Janeiro, Mumbai or New York. Grant had tried, and failed, to persuade his father to have post forwarded to Verdant House, the old people's home on the Finchley Road that was his father's current place of residence.

'I don't want those old stiffs poking into my business, thank you very kindly,' said Grant's father.

Books in many languages filled the shelves of the secretive and obstinate old man's Brighton flat: bound volumes of the proceedings of the Gemmological Institute of America, and the Society of Jewellery Historians, London; catalogues from Sotheby's and Christie's. On the walls were the pre-war photographs of Budapest, and several portrait photographs of his late

7

...e and his granddaughter Anna. Large illus-
...books about diamonds lay strewn across his desk,
including Ian Balfour's distinguished study *Famous Diamonds*.

On a table by the window of the sitting room, on fine cloth dustsheets, stood small weighing scales, blocks of brilliant white paper, microscopes and single eyeglasses – the *loupes* or magnifying lenses that were the working tools of the *diamantaire*.

Grant's father was celebrated in the world of gems as a diamond cutter *sans pareil*: the equal of the legendary Joseph and Abraham Asscher and William Goldberg. Perhaps the only item that struck an incongruous note in the flat was the black-framed three-inch length of rusted barbed wire. The inscription in Hungarian beneath it showed he had spent time behind the wire – but for how long he had been a political prisoner of the Soviets no one was quite sure.

The profession he no longer practised suited his nature. Diamonds fire the imagination. Their brilliance affords the *diamantaire* a kind of hiding place. It's said a great *diamantaire* can think himself inside a stone and see the finished diamond in his mind's eye. He can imagine how best the light ought to enter the stone; how it should dance inside it. There are, of course, still great *diamantaires* in New York City, and others in Antwerp, Tel Aviv and Mumbai. However, the older generation will tell you that none had the insight or breadth of experience to match Pieter Feller, *diamantaire sans pareil*.

The old man stuffed the unopened correspondence into a Waitrose carrier bag and still he dithered. 'Grant, I don't want to leave here.'

8

'Father – please.'

Finally the old man gave in. 'Oh well, I suppose it's time to go. *On y va?*'

Grant helped his father on with his canvas backpack. Then he triple-locked the steel-reinforced door of the flat overlooking Brighton's seafront. To the best of their knowledge no one saw them leave.

They headed for the railway station to catch the early train to London. Their purpose, like their final destination, was secret. They would make no mention of it on their journey to the city.

This explained why, when they bought their tickets for London Victoria, the old man faced the kiosk slightly sideways to give no hint that beneath his greatcoat he carried a loaded handgun in a holster.

Though his father had no idea quite who was planning to do him violence, Grant Feller knew his father's instinct for mistrust was correct. The old man could hide, but nowadays he was too frail to run. What with one good eye, the livid scar across his cheek and his conspicuous height, disguise was out of the question. But even at his advanced age, he believed that with his experience he could survive whatever attack his enemies might launch against him and still preserve his secret. 'Why, *they* don't even know of its existence.'

Feller senior, born in Budapest before World War Two and veteran of the anti-Soviet uprising of 1956, had that year fled Hungary with a death sentence on his head. He crossed into Austria, taking with him one of the world's greatest cache of diamonds. He and he alone knew its present whereabouts.

Today he would hand the secret hoard of diamonds to

his son to sell for the benefit of his granddaughter, the ten-year-old Anna whom he adored and who would never want for money in the years to come.

As they boarded the London train that morning, neither Grant Feller nor his father noticed the two well-groomed men behind them in fashionable coats. They could have been dealers in antiquities – the profession listed in their bogus German passports.

3

At about the same time that morning on another train, the voice over the intercom was advising the passengers that they would arrive at Victoria Station in thirty minutes. Among the passengers seated in First Class who had boarded the train at Gatwick was an attractive oriental, Dr Elizabeth Pereira. She was wearing a beret, black suit and dark glasses, she was slim and wore a ring of rubies and diamonds.

Her expression betrayed none of the strain you might associate with the weeks of intercontinental travel from Beijing via Antwerp and Luxembourg to the mountain landscape of Greece where the sun had darkened the skin of – the temporarily gender-changed – Klaas-Pieter Terajima.

There had been other changes too in the life of the man whose new-found friends in Greece knew as Takashi Sakamoto.

True, there remained the observation of strict self-discipline in work and prayer, the good manners and the rather feminine delicacy of movement he exhibited as he took his solitary walks in the Taigetos.

Even from the hidden remoteness of Greece, Takashi Sakamoto's *guanxi* – 'useful personal connections' – with the authorities in Beijing remained intact. In Beijing he was known as Pastor Leung, and his *guanxi* went some way towards explaining the arrival at the door of his Beijing apartment of the officials and foreigners who had visited him during the past few years.

Of those who had beaten a path to Pastor Leung's door in recent times were two German dealers in antiquities and a South African with a gingerish crew cut. These visitors had several things in common. Each of them, like Pastor Leung, was one of the four most wanted criminal fugitives on earth. Pastor Leung, who was proposing they do business together in Europe, had warmly welcomed all of them to Beijing and they left the city happy to be awaiting the call to action.

As for Pastor Leung's immediate – and mostly elderly – neighbours in Beijing, they liked him, and reckoned that the gentle pastor was a man of rare wisdom.

There had been one or two occasions when a neighbour had been bold enough to ask the pastor about his past and family. He would reply that he was an orphan who'd been educated by women. 'Virgin nuns,' he called them. An aunt in The Hague had provided him with an inheritance and, God be praised, the money had been enough for him to devote his life to private scholarship and the study of Confucius and the *Analects* for what he called the benefit of mankind's future generations.

The truth was less salubrious.

Raised in Amsterdam and The Hague, Terajima had a

Chinese father and a mother, Kasuko Terajima, who was part Dutch and part Japanese.

The young Klaas-Pieter's dentists frequently commented upon this combination of race.

Secretive by nature, the growing boy became the subject of some academic interest among Amsterdam's dental surgeons. As a result, he had suffered acutely at the hands of orthodontists. The problem was that the physical form of his mouth's interior was essentially Japanese. It was round and small. But his teeth were Caucasian and too large for the mouth; thus, the eruption of his second teeth caused havoc with his jaw. His parents, bourgeois and conservative, spent a fortune on surgeons' fees in Amsterdam and London. The ministrations of the Dutch and British dental surgeons did nothing to alleviate the child's continual headaches. He was rarely without small pads of cotton wool, soaked in some newfangled painkiller, between his swollen gums and cheeks. Later on in life, he took up the habit of placing *snuss*, Swedish snuff, between his gums and cheeks to gain a rush of adrenaline.

The boy was given to violent outbursts that disturbed his father, a Lutheran theologian. The fits of anger also frightened the instructor from the Amsterdam Staff Band of the Salvation Army who had been hired to teach the boy to play wind instruments. The lad became proficient as a flautist. An outcast among his peers, the solitary Klaas-Pieter haunted the canal sides of Amsterdam. He played his flute and was known as 'the wandering minstrel'. His performances soon made him friends among the sex workers, who petted him and early in life – some might say too early – satisfied his precocious sexual appetites. The prostitutes regularly allowed him, unseen by clients, to watch them in pursuit of their profession. He became an obsessive *aficionado* of the arcane sado-masochistic acrobatics of what, even in those days in Amsterdam, were considered perverted sexual practices.

'Career choices', as his father called them, were endlessly discussed at home. Klaas-Pieter, the precocious teenager, wanted to be a doctor, a gynaecologist. The neurological mysteries of extreme pain, its infliction, control and remedy, enchanted him.

At some stage – quite when it is hard to fathom – he rejected his medical studies and joined the merchant marine in Bremerhaven, taking his flute with him. He enjoyed the company of German sailors and visits to brothels from Alexandria to Bombay and further east in Penang, Tokyo and Yokohama. He experimented with drugs, mostly opium or heroin, during the periods of rest and recreation he enjoyed in South-East Asia. He also assuaged his appetite for sexual intercourse accompanied by violence.

When he was accused of murdering five prostitutes in Seoul, he jumped ship and a few months later began dealing in drugs and trading in Thai gemstones and antiquities lifted from temples throughout South-East Asia. He lived according to what he called one-word maxims. *Calculation. Observation. Organisation. Control.* His was, you might say, life lived to the full.

As to death, he said: 'I laugh at it. And death smiles back.'

His instincts were animal. Or perhaps it is fairer to say that his animality was tempered by a longing for the world of spirituality. It is fairly easy to understand why he first developed his fascination with Confucius and the *Analects*. Confucian thought seemed to offer a diversion from pragmatism. It seemed to satisfy his driven mind. This, combined with his receptive memory, his demonic energy, his attention to his own security and his inside knowledge of the workings of police forces and law enforcement agencies on several continents, led him to what he called 'the professional life'. Professional in the sense that he earned money in vast sums and studied the best methods available to protect it in European banks and offshore investment set-ups whose rules of secrecy he admired.

He felt he had much in common with the neat little men and women he dealt with, especially those in Luxembourg.

They took their commission for re-diverting his cash, which flowed – indeed, flooded – into Middle East asset management syndicates and American property investment portfolios.

He treated these dull, reliable and secretive officials with calm and that certain air of arrogance he also showed to the people who commissioned him to plan extortion strategies and to carry out murder, robbery and illicit arms transportation. After all, he maintained, conspiracy fuels legitimate business as much as it does criminal activity. With hindsight, it seemed inevitable that the pursuit of maritime terrorism would eventually attract him.

Maritime crime suited his temperament to a T. It was quick to carry out and it was virtually impossible to trace the booty.

He had grown rich. But the expansion of his fortune

created a certain problem. In the past decade or so, it had become easier for the authorities to follow the movement of capital investment. The possession of money in different currencies along with shares, however disguised, had become something of a risk. Sooner or later it could be followed. It was for this reason that Terajima had turned his attention to investment in diamonds.

Trim and fit, he was now approaching middle age. He reckoned he was still the most virile of men, his mind sharper than that of most men of his age. He had a great deal to be thankful for. It was, however, a thankfulness tinged with regret: the loss of his lover – the woman above all others he adored in body, mind and spirit. Mei Lim. He wanted Mei back and he wanted to kill her present lover, Alan Rosslyn. He had the means; he had the motive; all that remained was to create the opportunity to destroy his rival: *the pink Caucasian penis*. He loathed pink skin. *One fine day I will sever it from the root and make him swallow it.*

In order to create the opportunity, he discreetly removed himself to Greece. He savoured the irony that his choice of sanctuary was no great distance from a house that Rosslyn had occupied with a former lover in the Peloponnese a decade before, when Rosslyn had foiled the plot to return the Elgin Marbles to Athens.

He had settled upon a remote monastery in the Taigetos Mountains. It was a perfect place, far removed from the hurly-burly of the outside world. Here, as Buddhist monk, he became a stalwart among the followers of Tzu Yin.

He spoke the languages of the brothers and sisters at

the monastery. He understood their culture. He was, as he put it, a citizen of the world, without national or racial prejudice. During summer he would sit in the olive groves and play his flute for the benefit of the followers of Tzu Yin. He played what he called 'laments': cod versions of Salvation Army hymns in the style of Mozart.

He relished his different identities, the ease with which he could assume the male or female role. How, he thought, could any police force in the world, bogged down in local customs and failing systems of criminal justice, hope to catch up with him? Such systems were pathologically committed to lumbering concepts of democracy. The ideas of citizenship that his father had tried to imbue in young Klaas-Pieter had quite simply evaporated in the mind of the mature Terajima: the man who considered himself to be the unsung genius in the fight against humanity.

As he would say: *'Huo xi fuo suo yi. Fu xi huo suo fu.'* ('Good fortune lies within bad. Bad fortune lurks within good.')

Take, for example, the successful killing of Mei's father, Winston Lim.

He had waited patiently for Winston Lim's obsession to get the better of him; to strike at the moment Lim was off balance.

It had sometimes disturbed him that Lim must have understood him just as he had understood Lim. Now his was the victory and the pleasure.

Naturally, he would have preferred Lim's ending to have been, as he phrased it to himself, 'more Terajima-friendly' – that is, 'more terrible'. There had really been no alternative other than to dispatch his adversary with the lethal injection of diamorphine. Terajima was disappointed that his victim had finally floated towards his maker riding high and painlessly on clouds of adulterated diamorphine. He would have liked Lim to have died in agony and fully conscious of his suffering.

'More Terajima-friendly' was what he had in mind for Rosslyn. *Rosslyn's death will be my masterpiece and render the name of Terajima immortal.*

Mind you, things weren't all bad. For example, there was much satisfaction to be gleaned from his meeting in the Grand Duchy with his Vansburgische Landesbank personal banker.

Entertaining Dr Pereira over dinner, the gnome-like banker had told 'her' that her accounts were in a very healthy state indeed.

'You are', said the gnome, 'the glittering star lighting my raft of clients.'

'Why, thank you.'

'In what way will your next income be paid?'

'I can tell you that my next fee is to be paid in diamonds,' Dr Pereira told him. 'What is your view of that?'

'Very sensible,' said the gnome.

Dr Pereira had felt his hand press and explore her thigh.

'Later,' she said. 'We can go to my hotel suite later.'

'I can arrange', the gnome said, 'for whatever quantity of diamonds you receive to be stored in our vaults in conditions of the utmost security.'

Dr Pereira asked if he could arrange for the export of the diamonds from Antwerp.

'With no difficulty whatsoever,' said the gnome, eager

to switch the subject to his impending conquest. 'Tell me, Elizabeth, all about Beijing. What sort of quarter do you live in?'

'In the university area of north-west Beijing.'

'A busy modern woman with little time for pleasure?'

'On the contrary. I am translating the *Analects* of Confucius and composing a new critical commentary upon the philosophy of the Master.'

'You must tell me more,' the gnome said. 'Shall we retire now to your hotel suite? I can call for cocaine.'

'That's very generous of you,' Dr Pereira said. 'But as well as men who need to pay for sex, I also hold in contempt those who take drugs to enliven their senses. I have an active imagination and a satisfying sexual life. My companion will enjoy meeting you.'

'Your companion?'

'Also a scholar of Confucius.'

'Lucky man,' said the gnome with a sigh of disappointment.

'My lover is a woman,' said Dr Pereira. 'A Somali of aristocratic descent.'

The gnome's face blanched. 'She's very fortunate in having you.'

'The good fortune is mine. She's a lover of the greatest sexual expertise. She is waiting for me, black and naked, in a silk robe of sheerest white.'

Beads of sweat formed on the gnome's forehead.

The Somali was, of course, a creature of Dr Pereira's imagination. Dr Pereira placed her fingers on his hairy hand. 'Now you tell me', she said, 'about your children and your wife.'

'Another time,' the gnome said.

Dr Pereira had not finished yet. 'You have a small nose,' she said. 'You know what we Orientals say a small nose indicates in a white man?'

'Not really, no.'

'Think small. Small is not beautiful.'

Seeing the gnome's reaction Dr Pereira said, 'I have upset you? Never mind. I did not intend to show you a racist front.'

Dr Pereira finished the last of her home-made breakfast – fresh greens inside an omelette wrapped in a pancake, plus a bowl of *jianbing guozi*, green tea – and inserted a tab of *snuss* between her lower lip and gum.

Within a few hours she would demonstrate she was the mistress of her chosen science: the execution of the innocent.

The train drew into Victoria Station. Dr Pereira collected her leather bag and joined her fellow passengers heading for the barriers.

4

Gesucht!
*Vermutlich noch am Leben**

said the poster outside the Bundeskriminalamt (BKA) headquarters in Wiesbaden. It featured mug shots of the two Germans now lurking in a private car park in Belsize Park.

They saw that Feller senior was moving slowly, apparently discomfited by the straps and buckles of his canvas backpack. He was obstinately refusing to let his son carry it. The backpack contained a change of clothing, a torch and the loaded handgun the old man had surreptitiously transferred towards the end of the rail journey up to London. Skirting around plastic rubbish bags, Grant followed his father as he marched across the car park to the narrow steel door marked 'Strictly No Admission'. Here the father paused and looked around. Tears of cold streamed from the old man's eyes. There were a few cars

* Wanted! Missing Presumed Alive

21

parked close together, along with a windowless white van and two abandoned cars with their doors hanging open. There was no sign of anyone else about. A burglar alarm rang in the distance. If stalkers were watching, none was visible.

Grant stared at his father, who seemed rooted to the spot in front of the steel door.

The old man was muttering to himself: 'I've taken two days' leave from the residential home. I told the nursing staff I was going to Oxford Street. I told them I'll be returning by ten at night in time for Last Post. But I won't. I WON'T.'

'It's okay, father. You're okay.'

'I know I'm okay. What are you talking about, Grant?'

'The staff accepted your little story without question. You're a trusted inmate.'

'I'm not an inmate. I am a resident.'

Grant looked at his watch. 'Soon you'll be back in the warmth of your quarters. Please, father, let's start.'

This wasn't how it was supposed to happen.

Maybe I should never have agreed to it.

Father should be back in the home.

Suddenly the old man's mind seemed to regain its equilibrium. He gestured at the heavy mortise locks securing the steel door. The first lock was level with their eyes, the second with the tops of their shoes. Water was streaming slowly from a broken gutter close above. It made the unlocking of the door awkward. Once the door inched open, they slipped inside, closed the door behind them and locked themselves in.

'Darkness is my friend,' the old man said. 'Let me tell

you about this place. This is where the most beautiful diamonds you will ever see in your life are safe and sound.'

'Where, father?'

'Remember this. This door was once the exit to one of seven deep-level shelters constructed in London during World War Two. There are two parallel tunnels about twelve hundred feet long. Look at that. The shelter against the Nazi flying bombs.'

Grant followed the direction of his father's out-stretched hand. He read a notice above the exit:

'Only To Be Used In Emergency

London Passenger Transport Board.'

They were standing on a small steel platform. The beam from the old man's torch illuminated the arched brick corridor leading to the lift shaft and emergency spiral staircase.

His father said: 'The tunnels are a hundred and forty feet below.'

He removed his gloves and carefully unwrapped the handgun. Gripping it firmly in one hand, lighting their way with the torch in his other, they began the descent, picking their way gingerly down the steel stairs, pausing every few moments to wait, watch and listen.

There was the sound of dripping water, the scurrying of animals – rats perhaps – and the distant rumbling of the tube trains.

Slippery stair by stair, down they went. The odour of faeces and sulphurous city sewage was hard to bear. Both of them grew short of breath.

Finally, they reached a passageway at the base of the lift shaft and paused.

'This is the most awful place I've ever seen.'

'I've seen far worse. Look to your right.'

Grant looked. To his right, just past the disused extractor fan mechanisms, was a room containing switchgear.

'Over there', said his father, 'was a steel thing housing a 1940s mercury arc rectifier. Gone now. Beyond that, if you want to know, there's a short tunnel housing a sewage tank. It reeks of corpses.'

'Whose corpses?'

'Drug addicts and vagrants come down here and sometimes starve to death. I've seen their bodies. They die and the addicts' dogs start howling. You want to know more?'

'I don't want to know more, father, thank you all the same.'

'I want you to admire me for finding this place.'

'I do admire you for it, father, I do sincerely.'

'You don't sound sincere to me, Grant.'

'I am sincere, father. It's just that I want to get on with it.'

'You should've inherited your mother's patience.'
They passed several empty rooms. The old man said, 'There's another tunnel ahead.'

'How many more?'

'What?'

'I said, *how far to go?*'

'How far to go?'

'That's what I said, father.'

'Not far.'

They reached a derelict stairway. It seemed to lead down to a lower level.

'Almost there,' the old man said. 'Look. That's the stairwell to Belsize Park tube station. Stop here.'

Grant watched his father remove some loose bricks from the wall. The old man reached into the hole he had made and withdrew a bunch of keys. 'Follow me.'

Grant followed him towards an alcove where his father kicked aside the debris covering the floor. The alcove was at the edge of a trench filled to the rim with stagnant water. It smelled repulsive.

'Careful,' his father said. 'The water in that drain's very deep.'

He exposed a small, square trapdoor in the floor. The old man carefully inserted one of the keys into the lock and released it. With a great effort he then raised the trapdoor.

Grant looked down into the hole and saw two oblong steel trunks.

'Here,' his father told him. 'Lift –'

Grant helped him to lift the trunks out of the hole. Then his father unlocked and opened them. One by one he removed the plastic sheets wrapped around the cloth bags.

'Look.'

Grant looked inside the bags and, by the light of the torch, found himself staring at some of the most beautiful pink diamonds he had ever seen.

His father removed the canvas backpack. 'This is where they've lain in secret since I fled Budapest.' He took out the handgun and released the safety catch. 'Keep me covered.'

Grant was transfixed by the sight of the remarkable hoard.

'You're looking at a fortune,' the old man said. The sight of the diamonds seemed to restore the old man's energy. 'But don't look at it,' he said. 'Look about. Keep me covered. I won't be long.'

The old man had perhaps three or four more cloth bags to stuff into the canvas backpack when the savage lights came on. There were beams like searchlights and they were directed straight into Grant's eyes. They blinded him. Instinctively, unseeing, he stepped between the beams and his father.

His father was shouting, 'Shoot, shoot', when the solid object struck Grant's head. The force drove his jaw downwards to his chest, trapping his tongue between his prominent front teeth, filling his mouth with blood. The lights went out and the gun slipped from his hand. A second blow slammed his head against the brickwork, his glasses shattered and a harsh light swirled in his bloodied eyes and then went out.

5

Thynne was the chairman of Allegiance, one of Europe's premier private security firms. Relishing the power that private security and intelligence could wield, Thynne had masterminded his firm's expansion. In hours of need, industrialists, entrepreneurs and the very rich sought the services of Allegiance. Thynne's managerial skills included the presentation of an honest front to a dishonest world. He was respected, sometimes feared.

For some time, Thynne had lived alone, fending for himself. The Thynnes, who had a childless marriage, were separated but not divorced. There had been private heartache when his wife left him for a civil servant in the Home Office, a voluble gay rights activist young enough to be her daughter, but no public fuss. The Thynnes had told their small circle of friends that the parting had been amicable and some benefit would be derived from pitching their tents apart.

Thynne's fellow directors at Allegiance were accustomed to the chairman's sudden and often unannounced absences. Their highly profitable and clandestine work required the senior executives to leave London at a moment's notice. Thynne was also known to be a man of religious conviction. He was a *nomen* of MondoDei, a senior functionary of the secretive Anglo-American religious society.

Whereas the executives would tell Thynne where they were going and why, the chairman himself was not required to inform anyone. In any event, Frances Verity, his personal assistant, could always reach him on his mobile phone or by e-mail whether he was away on business or at some MondoDei gathering in Washington or Rome. And she well knew that Thynne preferred to be the one to initiate contact with home.

Thynne had been missing for the last ten days.

No one had a clue where he was or what might have happened to him.

After the first week, since there had been no word from him, even Verity began to worry. And it was only then, at Verity's request, that Zhilin, deputy chairman of Allegiance, alerted the police to Thynne's disappearance.

6

Two police officers called at the house in Onslow Road, Richmond-upon-Thames, that same day. Verity was waiting for them on the front steps. She had a set of house keys and showed them in. Thynne seemed to have forgotten to activate the burglar alarm and his telephone answering machine was switched off. Otherwise, they found nothing untoward.

The police officers said everything seemed to be in order. They nonetheless suggested it might be a good idea to employ 'the resources of Missing Persons'.

With slight embarrassment, Verity explained Allegiance's line of business and suggested that, in the first instance, it might be best if Allegiance began a search of their own. With that, the police left her alone in the house.

It was her first visit to the chairman's house and perhaps it was natural curiosity that led her to conduct a more detailed inspection. Flowers had mouldered in large crystal vases in the drawing room, milk had soured inside the kitchen fridge. She thought the house could do with a breath of fresh air. Otherwise the place was neat and tidy. *But quite so neat and tidy?* It had been tidied to the point of obsession. Cushions on the sofas were aligned in ranks. Magazines lay in neat piles. Polished pebbles had been laid out on the veranda with the vacuous intensity of some contemporary art installation. It was as if Thynne retreated here seeking a sanctuary of tidiness to escape the strains of his professional life.

Verity crossed the spotless grey Wilton carpet of the drawing room to the tall french windows and parted the curtains. She stood looking at the view of the manicured garden spotted with autumn leaves. A pergola stood beneath the trees. Beyond it was a garden shed.

To one side of the drawing room a door opened into what seemed to be Thynne's private study. Like everywhere else, this was the epitome of tidiness. On the desk lay a journal in a spiral-bound folder. She was drawn to the familiar typewriting on the open page. Thynne was the only person Verity knew who still used an old-fashioned typewriter. The entries were undated. She read the last page:

We occupy a frightened and sinful world.

I confess I have never been easy with our targets. Suspects. Conmen. Fraudsters. Gangs. Organised Crime.

I live in a world that pries into other people's. I look at people who try to be or are acting the part of others. People who try to

live up to a grand image they have
of themselves. They live the lie
with a front.

Perhaps I should forgive them in
His Name.

We set up pretext companies with
offices and bank accounts to attract
money. Then we make the bump. The
bump's the moment we offer services
such as money laundering or the
elimination of rivals through scandal, exposure, even killing in a
discreet manner. The accidental car
crash. The overdose of medication.

I have heard my people say: Let's
face it, everyone's either At It or
Going To Be At It.

Then there is Green Slime. There
is Green Slime at Allegiance.

I am frightened of Green Slime as
I am frightened that my shield is
too weak to fight the Devil.

There is Green Slime at the bottom of the world in the Garden.

May He in His Mercy protect me.

Tempted to take the journal with her and read the rest,
Verity thought better of it. It would be an invasion of privacy and it was not in Verity's nature to snoop. Mind you,
she thought, the chairman had a point about the state of
things within Allegiance. Some of the events of the last
few months at Allegiance had disturbed her. For example:

One of their best investigators had been found dead in Poole Harbour. She had apparently taken an overdose of crack cocaine and drunk the equivalent of half a bottle of vodka.

Ivan M had been shot in the head in Moscow by a man with a shotgun. She had seen the photographs. Where there should have been a head there wasn't one. Just blobs of bloodied flesh and bone like you'd see in the slop bucket at the local butcher's at the end of a busy day. It had upset her badly.

Two young women, former police officers, had been tortured and raped in Shoreditch, their laptops stolen and the identities of confidential informers taken.

Men and women, nominally from the Foreign and Commonwealth Office, had called on Thynne. Verity knew enough to realise they were from MI6. None of the visitors knew how to stem the violence. There seemed no end to it.

Indeed, morale had sunk so low at Allegiance that Thynne had called a general staff meeting. He had tried in vain to reassure everyone:

'There is a war on. A war of the detectives, you might say. The competition gets rougher by the day. My new deputy chairman, Mr Zhilin, tells me our Russian friends are understandably showing great concern. We here are good and honest people, friends and colleagues believing in integrity in this increasingly dangerous world of ours. You may rest assured that Anatoly Zhilin and I will continue to do whatever's needed to strengthen the security of our firm and all who serve it.'

Thynne had delivered his address with the quiet passion of a believer. People wondered privately whether he had it in him to succeed. A few went so far as to say that the world of the private security agencies was populated by the Devil and that it was the Devil they were fighting.

Verity told herself she must do something about Thynne's absence from the office.

She asked for a confidential and personal interview with deputy chairman Zhilin. The jovial Zhilin had apparently been a Soviet diplomat. As chance had it, the Russian was a neighbour of hers in Mill Hill. There was something old-fashioned, dependable and almost fatherly about him. She thought him, as Thynne had put it, to be a Safe Pair of Hands.

Zhilin closed the door to his office and told her to make herself comfortable. It was plain she was a very worried woman.

She told Zhilin roughly what she'd read in Thynne's journal.

He spoke fluent English, with the accent of a BBC radio announcer of older generation. 'What's your view?' he asked her.

'Not perhaps what you'd think,' she said. 'I think something terrible might have happened. Only a feeling, you understand.'

Zhilin looked at her with sympathy. 'Tell me what you feel.'

'I don't expect you to take my feeling terribly seriously, Mr Zhilin.'

'I will take it very seriously.'

'I think Mr Thynne's dead.'

'What makes you think so?'

'There are, well I mean, many people . . . I mean, he's

33

not without enemies, is he? . . . There may be people who would prefer to see him –'

'Dead?'

'That's what I've been feeling.'

'These enemies . . . who do you have in mind?'

'The people at Virtus for a start,' she said.

'Well, it's true we are, so to speak, rivals. But are we to believe they might resort to violence?'

'I hate to say it, Mr Zhilin, but we do, don't we? I mean, we all know that various opponents of ours have, shall we say, come to very unpleasant ends. So have a few of our own.'

'But you see,' said Zhilin, 'if a rival, an opponent, call such people what you will, sought to kill Mr Thynne . . . don't you think his body would've been found by now?'

'But no one is looking for it, Mr Zhilin.'

'There would seem to be no motive. I can't think of one, can you?'

'A motive might be known only to Mr Thynne, and he isn't here to explain it to us, is he?'

'True,' said Zhilin.

'Mr Zhilin, no offence intended, but I think we should do something. I mean, for a start, you should at least come with me to his house. He kept a private journal. It's rather disturbing.'

'He kept a journal?'

'I saw it in his study.'

'What did you find in it?'

'I'd rather you read it for yourself.'

'As you wish.'

'His house is in Richmond. I have the keys here in my bag.'

34

Zhilin watched her searching the contents of her shoulder bag and then glanced at his watch. 'Very well, I'll take a look. Come along with me. We must do things correctly. I'll need a witness to my search.'

Within the hour Zhilin and Verity arrived in Richmond and unlocked the front door of the house.

It was all much as it had been on Verity's previous visit. Zhilin had brought a small tape recorder with him, and once the door had closed behind them, he began to record his observations in the tone of the tourist guide who's seen it all a thousand times.

Together they walked through the house. The only sound was the drone of Zhilin's voice. Mostly he spoke in English; sometimes adding Russian phrases which Verity was unable to understand. She noticed that, like a police officer, he was very thorough in his search.

He produced a pen torch and looked right to the back of wardrobes, felt beneath shirts on a row of shelves, even poked about beneath Thynne's bed. He spent a long time searching a bathroom cupboard full of medicines.

'Must have high blood pressure. 10 mg Zestril. No sign of a safe anywhere.'

He left the study and Thynne's journal until last. He read the most recent entry while Verity watched him.

'*Green Slime. Green Slime.* What does that tell us?'

'I've no idea.'

'Me neither.'

Flicking through the pages his eye was caught by the mention of his name:

35

Anatoly Zhilin has brought us
invaluable gifts. He understands
the business.

I've confided in him that I am
keen to recruit our Ron Costley's
friend Rosslyn from Virtus, along
with one of their investigators or
administrators, such as Grant
Feller, who comes from the family
of the Feller Diamond Company, one
of the long-established diamond
dealers in Hatton Garden. We could
do with an investigator covertly in
place in Antwerp. The time does not
quite seem ripe at present to make
the approach to either man.

Costley is of course extraordinarily adept at gaining intelligence. He is also a MondoDei <u>nomen
iunior</u> and to be trusted.

Costley has already assembled a
vivid account of the Russian oligarchs, especially the Ilyushenkos
with whom I am all too familiar
already.

Ostensibly engaged in a close examination of the shelves
above Thynne's desk, Zhilin was mesmerised by what he
had just read.

*He must have been out of his head to write that down.
I have to get the thing out of here and far away.*

'How much of his journal did you read?' he asked Verity.

'Only the last entry,' she said. 'There's something rather upsetting about it, isn't there?'

'There is,' said Zhilin.

On the shelves above the desk lay stacks of papers in neat ranks, each tightly tied with red ribbon like a barrister's papers.

'Would you go to the kitchen, please?' he said. 'Bring me a plastic bag and tissue – a length of kitchen roll will do.'

When she returned he held the journal gently, his fingers protected by the tissue, and lowered it into the plastic bag. 'I'll read this later. Let's take a look at the garden. *Green slime in the garden.* You never know. Anyway, I like gardens. Do you?'

'Yes. I could do with some fresh air.'

'Me too,' said Zhilin, leading the way to the french windows. 'Let me have the keys.' He stooped down and looked at the lock. 'Tip: if you need to find a key on a bunch like this, always look at the lock first.' He handed the keys back to her.

'I'll remember. Thanks.'

He opened the doors on to the garden. 'It's a lovely day.'

'Chilly though,' she said. 'You have heavy shoes.'

'You don't,' he said. 'Be careful not to slip.'

In the winter sky, lowering *en route* for Heathrow, an aircraft's engines whined. There were patches of frost in the shade beneath the trees. Thin ice sparkled on the lawn. Blackcaps were on the bird table, along with some greenfinches and great tits. Zhilin admired the shrub roses, the apple trees, the clematis and honeysuckle climbing over the pergola. 'Must be a picture in spring,' he said. He stared up at the sky. A watery haze blurred the sun. 'What a perfect English winter's day,' he said.

He turned to his right, then to the house, then to his left, then ahead. Three hundred and sixty degrees.

'Hand me the keys, please.'

She did as he had asked and followed him to the garden shed. He tried the handle to the door.

He turned on his tape recorder. '*No windows to shed. Shed is relatively new in construction. Say a year or so. Strongly built of brick and green painted wood. No sign of electric power link. Door to the shed is locked. Yale.*'

She watched him examine the lock. Then turn through the keys on the metal ring.

'*No Yale key. None that match either.*'

Once again he tried the door handle. He leaned against the door. 'Shed is locked against me. It's well built.'

'*Stand aside a moment,*' he told Verity.

He took a few paces backwards on the grass and then, after two strides, raised his right leg and gave the door a kick at the height of the lock. Zhilin was a powerful man and the force of his kick splintered the wooden frame so that the door opened inwards a few inches and then stopped suddenly as if it had been barricaded from the inside.

Zhilin peered through the gap. 'Okay. We have some bad news here. Would you mind walking back up the lawn, please?'

'What is it?'

'Please do as I say.'

'What's in there?'

'A body.'

'Oh, no,' she whispered and, frozen to the spot, she covered her face with her hands.

With some difficulty, Zhilin eased his way inside the shed.

'Body blocking entry. Man hanging from roof support beam with twisted ligature around his neck. Feet a few inches above brick floor. Feet are naked. Shoes and socks folded beside upturned chair. A usual step-off. Facial features bloated. No suggestion of auto-erotic or unusual sexual practice. No signs of rubbed flesh or scrapes under cord.'

He edged his way out of the shed. 'I'm afraid it's Mr Thynne.'

She stared at him, shivering violently.

'Would you mind going back into the house and bringing me two or three pairs of his shoes from the bedroom closet? See if you can find me any that haven't had the laces untied. Think you're up to that?'

'Shouldn't we call the police?'

'Yes, Verity, we'll do that in a minute. Can you get me the shoes please? And one more thing. Two actually. Bring me two of the packages of papers tied with red ribbon. You know, the ones on the shelves in the study above his desk?'

'Yes, of course.'

'Sure you're okay?'

'I feel sick, Mr Zhilin.'

'There's nothing we can do for him. Breathe evenly. Take it easy. Take your time.'

'The shoes – the red ribbons.'

'Yes, please. I'll be here.'

'Oh, don't leave me –'

'No, I won't. Take it easy.'

Zhilin returned to the interior of the shed.

Thynne's features were puffy. A few flies were hovering around dry mucus at the sides of the open and distorted mouth. '*He's been hanging here for several days. Hard to judge how many. Post-mortem autopsy will reveal. Body hasn't, as far as I can tell, been interfered with. There's no sign here of a suicide note.*' He thought of Thynne's journal. *To take it – or not to take it? There may be a note of intention in it. Either way it'll have to be lifted without being seen. Decent citizens sometimes forget the policeman learns the villain's ways.*

'Sorry,' Verity said on her return.

Her hands were shaking so much she almost dropped the shoes and packages of paper tied with red ribbons.

'You've done well,' he said. 'Now walk away, please.'

'I want to see him.' She tried to push past him. But he grabbed her by the wrist. 'Let go of me. I need to see him.'

Still he restrained her. 'Look, Mr Thynne sure as hell would never have wanted you to see him like this. Respect his right, my friend. Do as I say.'

She backed away from him and began to sob.

Zhilin returned to the shed, taking with him the shoes and the packages tied with red ribbon. Using the beam from his pen torch, he examined the knots on the cord around Thynne's swollen neck. He compared them with the knots in the shoelaces and red ribbons. Someone had tied them all in precisely the same way: left-handed. If Thynne was left-handed, then it was a fair bet he'd tied the slipknots himself. If he was right-handed, then within a very short space of time a murder investigation would be under way. He left the shed and relocked it.

'I'm sorry, Mr Zhilin,' Verity said.

'I appreciate your calm. These situations are the very worst. Believe me. Let's go back to the house. We have to call the police.'

They returned to the kitchen.

Zhilin told her he needed to use the bathroom and excused himself.

On the way to the bathroom he returned to the study and removed Thynne's journal from the desk. It fitted neatly inside his overcoat. Then he found the bathroom and washed his hands.

Finally Zhilin dialled 999.

First Quarter

7

The chairman murmured: 'Please stand.'

Alan Rosslyn got to his feet, along with the four men seated opposite him at the conference table.

The chairman said: 'I want to observe one minute's silence in remembrance of Thynne. Those of us here like me who take pride in our faith may pray for the peace of his soul in heaven.'

'I didn't know he was dead,' said the man directly opposite Rosslyn.

'He's taken his own life.'

'I don't believe it,' another said.

'What did he do?'

'Hanged himself.'

'Well, I'll be darned.'

'He was a soldier of the Almighty. Thynne fought the good fight.'

'Thynne?' someone muttered.

'Gentlemen. *Please*. Remain upstanding for one minute. In God's name we pray for the soul of Thynne.'

45

Apart from Rosslyn, the men standing in silent remembrance of Thynne were the London directors of the Virtus Security Corporation, one of the USA's most formidable private security agencies.

The four Americans formed what was known as the DCG or Damage Control Group, the most secret committee within the firm. The DCG only assembled when the chairman personally decided the firm was facing a major crisis. Such a meeting could be called at any time of day or night, whenever the chairman signalled the red alert.

The chairman had summoned the DCG to meet in the apartment overlooking Queensgate, well away from the head office in Fitzroy Square.

The chairman and his co-directors, among the most feared people in the world of private-sector security, were often sneered at by their detractors as glorified private detectives hell-bent on profit. Rosslyn rated them highly as professionals, men skilled and experienced in the art of getting other people to do dirty work in the interests of their international clients. Control freaks, steady hands, they knew how to sail close to the wind, steering a course on the cusp of good and evil. When subordinates were called to a meeting of the DCG it invariably meant trouble.

'May the Almighty bless his soul,' the chairman said. 'Amen. Will one of you guys open the door? The caretaker's waiting. We have a tight schedule.'

The caretaker of the Queensgate apartment set a thermos of coffee on the table, a jug of cream, a bowl of sugar, small bottles of mineral water and a selection of chocolate candies from Garrison Confections of Providence, Rhode Island.

The sweet-toothed chairman of Virtus London, Lincoln Bausch, turned over some papers in a folder. He waited until the caretaker had left the room and then came to the point. 'Alan,' he said, 'we have a problem with Grant Feller.'

Before Bausch could continue his introduction, his mobile started ringing. He took the call and, getting to his feet, paced slowly round the room.

Bausch cut an imposing and rather pious figure. Beneath his head of silver hair, he had a broad face, sun-burned from weekends entertaining Britain's Great and Good aboard his yacht moored off the Isle of Wight. The former United States Navy captain had, by his own account, come a long way since gaining a place from high school in New Jersey to a senior appointment at the Annapolis Naval Station in Maryland. He had a prac-tised way of smiling falsely, with bared teeth and dead-ness in his bright blue eyes. Within Virtus he was known unsurprisingly as the Captain.

The others, each of senior rank in Virtus and known as Masters, waited for Bausch to finish his call. Across the table sat the chief executive officer, Eduardo Valente Jr, who slowly steered an open bottle of mineral water in Rosslyn's direction. Slim and very tall, Valente had the look of a balding eagle. He had earned the sobriquet of the Hound because he was a Joint Master of Foxhounds of the military hunt affiliated to Fort Leavenworth in Kansas. Virtus operations permitting, Valente returned to Kansas twice a year to hunt foxes and coyotes with hounds in the prairie grasses of the Flint Hills at the Mulvane Ranch.

Born in Ohio, chief operations officer Montana

Bogaart, pug-faced and overweight with a bullying manner and foul mouth, had a degree from the University of Toledo College of Law. He was rather proud of the fact that the Virtus juniors called him the African Queen.

Chief finance officer Dick Shepperfeld, or the Bad Shepherd, was the youngest of the quartet. His flamboyant blue shirt from Mark Christopher of Wall Street emphasised the redness of his face, so fleshy it almost buried his narrow eyes.

Bausch completed his call and returned to the table. He closed the file in front of him and stared directly at Rosslyn. 'We have to decide what we do about Feller. That's the problem we're facing, isn't it?'

Without so much as a goodbye, Grant Feller, Dick Shepperfeld's accounts man, had gone missing a week ago. A married man in his thirties, with a fine head for figures and fluent in Russian, French and German, Feller was mild mannered with an owl face. He was the last person you'd imagine to vanish without a word of explanation.

Like Rosslyn, Grant Feller was one of the minority of British employees at Virtus in London.

Whereas Rosslyn had originally been a Customs and Excise undercover agent and was headhunted from a smaller security firm, Grant Feller came from the security department of a City bank. They had joined Virtus at about the same time and the Masters had welcomed both of them with open arms. Both were familiar with the shifting world of Anglo-American conmen, fraudsters and organised crime syndicates. These were the sub-species of civilisation Virtus called Foxes, Prey or Vermin. Like Rosslyn and Feller, the firm's investigators

48

worked in secret, mostly for leaders of industry, or Royals as they were known. Some of them were quite nice guys who nonetheless thought nothing of digging up dirt or even fabricating some to smear reputations before a major corporation take-over. Only on the face of things did integrity and fair play appear to govern Virtus's dealings.

'The fact is,' said Bausch with exaggerated reasonableness, 'he seems to have transferred a substantial sum of money from his special operations budget allocation into his private NatWest bank account and he withdrew it the day he left without authorisation.'

'Without authorisation,' Shepperfeld emphasised.

Rosslyn was astonished at the revelation. Leaving aside Grant's manic nature, his addiction to conspiracy theories, he found Grant to be straightforward, reliable and scrupulous with money to the point of fussiness. 'How much money exactly?' Rosslyn asked.

'Between a quarter and a half million pounds sterling,' said Shepperfeld.

'I can't believe it,' Rosslyn said.

'We don't want to believe it, Alan,' Bausch said quietly. 'Believe me. This is painful.'

'Is there any trace of authorisation?' asked Rosslyn.

'Nil fuck,' said Bogaart.

Bausch winced. '*Mister* Bogaart. Please.'

'What's in the computer data?' Rosslyn asked.

'That a sum's missing,' said Valente. He was smiling, his skin tight about the eyes where, like his wife, he had undergone elaborate plastic surgery. 'It seems that you, Alan, authorised the withdrawal.'

Rosslyn stared in silence at the remains of Valente's

49

drooping eyelids. Valente's long right hand, spattered with liver spots, slid inside his jacket and he withdrew some sheets of paper.

Rosslyn looked at the requisition orders signed by Grant Feller with convincing versions of his own signature on the dotted lines as approving officer.

'Take a look, Alan,' Valente said. 'The payments weren't made all at the same time. Your pal Feller may look like a barn owl but he isn't clumsy.'

'I've never seen these before,' said Rosslyn. 'These are not my signatures.'

Bogaart cleared his throat. 'C'mon, you say you never saw your Daddy's dong? Feller's clawed ours for nearly half a million.'

'And we're anxious', Bausch interrupted, 'that you, Alan, use your best endeavours to get the money back. Feller has to be found and soon. This is a Level Red operation.'

'For the first time in our corporate history,' said Bausch, 'a Level Red operation will involve one of Virtus's finest.'

'Follow the money,' said Shepperfeld. 'Talk to the family. Feller's people are in the diamond trade. I guess they'll not want the son and heir arrested. The Feller Diamond Company's stock is up thirty-four per cent since it went public last spring. Feller has a five per cent stake. That makes him a rich man. They won't like him being accused of larceny.'

'Neither would we welcome court proceedings,' said Bausch. 'It'd be, not to put too fine a point on it, the beginning of the end of Virtus as we know it.'

Rosslyn looked briefly at each of the Masters in turn.

It fell to the oleaginous Valente to break the silence.

'There exists the bond of trust. It has never, never been broken, Alan. That is, until now. Think morale. Think the more senior investigators. Our Silverhairs and Hunters. Recall how much secret intelligence on former clients, covert contacts and informers their files contain. Feller had access to the archives.' Here he paused. 'We might never see their like again if there was a rumour, even a rumour of a rumour, that we had haemorrhaged internally.'

'Ed has it right,' Bausch said. 'I don't have to remind you . . .' He laid his hands flat on the table. 'We don't want your friend Feller ending up in gaol. Or you.'

Bogaart's bovine nostrils flared. His fists clenched. 'Because if we don't get the money back, we'll come down on you like a heap of . . .'

'I can try to find him,' said Rosslyn. 'God knows where he is. I may need some outside help.'

'You'll use no other agency,' said Bausch. 'No mention of the A word.'

It had already occurred to Rosslyn that Grant Feller might conceivably have defected to the arch rivals, Allegiance. In the closed world of private security agencies, by far the most powerful were Virtus and Allegiance. Virtus was to all intents and purposes American. Allegiance was basically British, but no one was quite sure who its main backers were. The two agencies were locked in a struggle to destroy each other, to become the premier agency. If Grant offered Allegiance inside knowledge from Virtus, the rival firm would welcome him with open arms. The only rule was survival of the fittest. But why would Grant have needed money to jump – why did he need so much money?

'Turn over the mess of his life,' said Bogaart. 'Get into the dirty laundry. Maybe Mr Feller likes whores. Find shit.'

'Grant has a settled family life,' Rosslyn said.

'Go get it,' said Bogaart.

Valente interjected, 'You could, I suppose, use a junior Blood to help you.'

'I'm a professional investigator,' said Rosslyn. 'I do my job to the best of my ability. When it comes to Grant Feller, I'd like to search for him alone. I have to say I find it impossible to believe he had his hand in the till. But I take your word. You have mine that I'll find him.'

'That's good,' said Valente. 'Prove us wrong.'

'I want you to give me a progress report daily,' said Bausch. 'Nine each morning. Oh yeah, one more point, Alan. The call I took at the start of the meeting was from Michael Das Gupta.'

Rosslyn knew of Das Gupta, the sharp lawyer they employed.

'We need a forensic report on those signatures of yours. Das Gupta recommends that for the time being you stay clear of the office and colleagues. If you bump into any of them by chance, simply say you're working directly for me. If need be, I'll put the word around about your changed circumstances. Das Gupta also made an important point. He's building a close relationship with the legal aid attaché at the US Embassy. Do you know him?'

'No, I don't,' said Rosslyn.

'He's FBI. A man called Bernal Schiff.'

'I see no reason why I should've crossed his path,' said Rosslyn.

'He may cross yours,' said Bausch. 'Let me know if he does.'

Rosslyn made a mental note of the name of the FBI man. He wondered why Bausch had mentioned him.

Bausch continued: 'Montana here will arrange for your pending cases to be taken on by others. And no mention of Feller's disappearance to anyone in the business. If I haven't said so already, remember that the Allegiance vultures are hungry for our flesh. If they smell weakness they'll attack. But now that the asshole Thynne's fucked himself, well, things may be that much easier. We'll say Feller's on indefinite leave. Family reasons. Meanwhile, Alan, you have to find the guy.'

'And if I can't?' Rosslyn asked.

The Masters stared at him in silence.

'If you can't,' Bogaart said finally, 'you're dead meat. Call me if you need my help. Any time. You have my number.'

'I have your number,' Rosslyn said.

The Masters clocked his tone of challenge and Rosslyn sensed he had made an enemy of his American bosses.

As he headed for the door he caught snatches of their excited conversation: 'Thynne – we've won.'

'Show respect, gentlemen, please,' Bausch was saying.

He heard Bogaart break into song:

Have yourself a merry little Christmas . . .

8

Known to his neighbours as the Basement Man, Rosslyn occupied a lower ground floor flat in Claverton Street, as a sitting tenant. The landlord had allowed the house to run gradually to seed with a view to encouraging the residents to leave.

The front room of Rosslyn's flat had a window just below the ceiling. The heavy iron bars set into the outside sill had rusted. A layer of moss covered the sill itself. The exterior hadn't had a lick of paint in years. No one bothered to collect the litter tossed into the stairwell by passers-by. The lock to the gate from the street to the stairwell had been broken and occasionally Rosslyn would find syringes discarded by the addicts who mostly used the place at weekends to shoot up.

Shortly before Mei left for Hong Kong, she had made a fair job of redecorating the interior of the flat. She painted it a light, almost luminous grey. Rosslyn's 'golden welcome handcuff' to Virtus had allowed Mei to have a flooring firm lay what would have passed as a squash court floor of plain wood. There were still signs of rising damp. A Polish builder had told Rosslyn there was little point in fighting it. It wouldn't be long, the Pole had observed, before the Thames rose to a dangerous level. 'Then you'll be in a sea of love,' the Pole told Rosslyn with a smile. He seemed to have learned his English from pop lyrics. 'But you have your love to keep you warm,' he observed, gazing wistfully at the striking photographs of Mei above Rosslyn's bed.

Mei had made no mention of Rosslyn's letter containing his proposal of marriage.

Rosslyn decided, at least for the time being, not to press the matter further. Was it, he wondered, something to do with his previous lovers? Though Mei had never mentioned the fact that previous loves had occupied his bed, Rosslyn had changed the mattress and bought expensive new sheets, pillows and a new duvet.

When she e-mailed him to tell him of her intention to do a degree course at the University of Hong Kong, he was careful not to dissuade her. He would let her be.

Still, her silence on the matter hurt. When he watched her diminutive figure walk through the barrier at Heathrow, he broke down in tears. It seemed that the only thing he had to cling on to was her response to the proposal. Either yes or no. The odds were fifty-fifty.

The Claverton Street flat, the scene of happiness, now seemed empty. Sometimes the emptiness was hard to bear.

They had, of course, arranged to spend Christmas together in Hong Kong. Rosslyn counted the days like the prisoner in solitary confinement scratching off the dates on the walls of his cell. In a farewell exchange of presents they had given each other laptops and promised to keep in touch by e-mail. They agreed one rule: no phoning. It would be too upsetting. Their e-mail communication went some way towards compensating for her absence.

Unlike some pairs of lovers, there were areas of conversation to do with their pasts that, as Mei put it, were strictly no-go. More especially those concerning her former lover: Klaas-Pieter Terajima.

Terajima, who had murdered Mei's father Winston Lim, a senior Hong Kong police officer who had also been one of Rosslyn's greatest friends.

Terajima had seduced Mei with calculation. To say she had fallen under his spell would be too easy a way of describing what had happened. Terajima had introduced her to drugs. She had become an addict. He had sexually abused her with violence. Some might say she had become his slave. Again, that would be too simplistic a view of things. With Rosslyn's help, perhaps because of the love she knew he felt for her, she had abandoned drugs and been clean ever since.

If there was a shadow over their lives, it was Terajima's.

As he promised Mei, Rosslyn tried to dismiss the phantoms. When they returned he sank into a depression. He had to see Terajima dead. But at present he had no idea how to translate the wish into action. So when Rosslyn had watched Mei leave he felt both disconsolate and worried for her safety. *God knows where Terajima might be*. If God knew, He had so far given no clue.

When Rosslyn returned to his flat after the meeting with the Masters, the first thing he did was to telephone Grant Feller's wife Viktoria.

The Feller family lived in a terrace house overlooking

the Thames at Hammersmith. Rosslyn said he'd like to call on her later in the morning.

She suggested they lunch together at her house in Hammersmith.

He made himself a mug of coffee and opened up his e-mails. Nothing from Grant. The owl was silent.

Mei e-mailed Rosslyn:

> Alan
>
> I wish it was ME you were looking at and holding in your beautiful hands and not this e-mail. I'm writing this in a corner of the University Library.
>
> I've gone in for a photography competition. The Canon EOS Photo Contest Student Division. I am going to make a self-portrait and then I will send it to you.
>
> What have you been doing? Tell me EVERY-THING. Write soon.
>
> I love and adore you
>
> Mei
> ❤❤❤❤
>
> PS What do you want for Christmas? Tell me.

Rosslyn replied:

> Mei
>
> Thanks for your e-mail. It really lifted my spirits.

I can't wait to see you at Christmas. Only about three weeks to go.

Grant Feller's still missing. It's very worrying. Someone's forged my signature on a series of cash requisitions he made. God knows who did the forging or why. Can't have been Grant. I've been asked to find him as soon as possible. Meanwhile, I've been banned from going to the office. Can you believe it? But you can reach me here as usual.

I really look forward to seeing the photo you've done for the contest. I know you'll win. What's the prize?

What I want for Christmas is to spend all of it in bed with you.

I love you

Alan

Rosslyn called a minicab to take him to Hammersmith to see Viktoria Feller, then collected a miniature tape recorder and a small device for copying computer files.

He switched on the tape recorder. 'Testing . . . I have to get Viktoria to show me the route to Grant . . . And one more thing . . . The time's ripe to call in a favour . . .' He replayed the test. 'Fine.' Then he dialled a number he knew by memory.

The voice at the other end said: 'Costley. Allegiance.'

'You on your own, Ron?'

'I am. Go ahead.'

'I'm sorry about Thynne.'

'Me too.'

'What happened?'

'He topped himself.'

'I'm sorry.'

'It was bad. Depression. Stress. A lonely man. Things just got too much for him.'

'Is there any family?'

'A wife somewhere. They were separated. Had been for quite a time.'

'No one else – children?'

'No one.'

'When's the funeral?'

'We buried him yesterday. He was a devout Catholic. A leading light in MondoDei. It was very moving.' Costley cleared his throat. 'What can I do for you then, young man?'

'Ron, I need to see you urgently.'

'Not today.'

'Then tonight. It's urgent, Ron.'

'What's so urgent you want to speak to the opposition?'

'Forget opposition. I need a whereabouts.'

'On who?'

'Name: Grant Feller. Age: late thirties. British. White. Virtus. Lives in Hammersmith. Married. One daughter.'

'Why?'

'He's done a runner.'

'Okay, I'll take a look.'

'Can you get me something by tonight?'

'Maybe. I have a reception to attend in Kensington Palace Gardens at seven.'

'One of your Russian oligarchs?'

'You guessed. The people who pay my salary. I could make dinner with you, say, at nine?'

'Usual place?'

'Usual place. I'll do what I can for you.'

Former Detective Inspector Ron Costley, the man he trusted above all others, was now working for the opposition, Allegiance. He too was under orders not to speak to the opposition. Rosslyn imagined that with Thynne gone, Ron Costley would be looking to his future.

9

The combination of fog and a security alert had brought traffic in west London to a standstill and it was three o'clock before Rosslyn eventually arrived at the Fellers' home in Hammersmith. He asked the minicab driver to drop him off at the end of Verbena Gardens.

There was a chill in the air and the smell of decaying leaves. Not far from the Fellers' house a down and out sat cross-legged in the doorway beneath the sign 'House For Sale'. A face with the blistered features of a gargoyle turned to Rosslyn with pleading eyes from beneath a khaki blanket. The man's spaniel was licking a bloodied paw next to some cardboard boxes and a notice saying 'Homeless'. An upturned baseball cap lay by the man's shoes. Rosslyn put a five-pound note into the baseball cap. 'God bless you' echoed as Rosslyn rang the doorbell.

Viktoria Feller opened it. Of Russian parentage, she was a tall woman with a wide smile, dark eyes and a long mane of blonde hair. She wore faded jeans, a white shirt open at the neck and one of her husband's blue cashmere sweaters. Gold chain bracelets dangled from both wrists. When she held out her hand to Rosslyn in greeting him, her fingers felt very cold.

'Come in,' she said. 'You must be cold. Let me take your coat.'

He removed his coat himself. He didn't want her to discover he was carrying a miniature camera and tape recorder, as well as the small device for copying material from computers.

She led the way up to the living room on the first floor of the narrow house. A published children's book illustrator with a growing reputation, Viktoria worked under the professional name of Larionov. She was also a collector of original works by Kate Greenaway and Edmund Dulac. Piles of books and catalogues from book dealers lay strewn across the faded carpet.

'Excuse the chaos,' she said over her shoulder.

The mantelpiece above the fireplace was stacked with her illustrations and photographs of her daughter Anna. A dozen or more cod versions of Van Gogh's *Sunflowers* covered the wall opposite high windows that afforded a view across the grey river at low tide. The family furniture had seen better days. A variety of worn embroidered cushions disguised the lumps in its sagging upholstery. The scent of lilies filled the room.

Viktoria lit a cigarette, inhaled and coughed. He followed her into the kitchen.

'Don't look too closely at the mess,' she said. 'I have to collect Anna in an hour. Everything's a bit of a rush round here. What did the people at the firm say to you?'

'They want me to find Grant.'

'So do I. Anna isn't sleeping. Neither am I. We're exhausted. I'm getting scared, Alan.'

He sat at the kitchen table. 'I'll find him somehow.'

'But where are you going to look?' she said. 'He's never done anything like this before. It's so bloody unlike him, isn't it?' She set two bowls on the table and filled them with soup. 'Help yourself to bread and cheese. Some wine or something stronger?'

'I don't drink in the middle of the day.'

'Me neither,' she said. 'Well, not until now.' She stubbed out her cigarette in an ashtray overflowing with cigarette butts. 'I'm going to have a whisky.'

The truth of the matter was that Rosslyn had no idea quite where to begin the search for her husband. He told her that he had tried calling Grant's father, even the father's housekeeper, with no success.

'The old man no longer has control of his faculties.'

'Do you know where he is?'

'He was in an old people's home in Finchley. Apparently he told the people there that he was leaving and going home to Brighton. I've tried calling him. He's not there either. His cleaning woman hasn't seen him for weeks.'

'How does the cleaning woman get paid?'

'I imagine there's a standing order with the bank or something.'

'When did Grant last see your father-in-law?'

'I've no idea. The old man and I never got on. The old man doesn't care for Russians. He had a bad time during the uprising in 1956. His paranoia has increased with age. Secrecy runs in the family. You know Grant. Like father, like son. There's no point asking them questions. You won't get any answers.'

'Viktoria – I need answers from you. Is there something you haven't told me?'

'Like what?'

'I don't know. Say, perhaps, Grant may be seeing another woman?'

'Oh, for heaven's sake, Alan. Don't be absurd. I'd be the first to know.'

'Except his work?'

'Work doesn't count. You know I'm not actually terribly interested in his work.'

She toyed with her bowl of soup. Only the whisky seemed to satisfy her hunger.

Rosslyn asked: 'Has he ever said he wanted out?'

'If you mean does he want out of Virtus – well, yes, he does. To be exact, he's told me he wants to do whatever I want him to. You know what a softie he is. What he means is that he no longer wants to be tied to those awful so-called Masters of yours. Don't you sometimes feel the same?'

'I sometimes feel that, yes. But I have a living to earn.'

'Surely,' she said, 'you must have discussed *something*?'

'The senior people at Virtus have discovered something. I'll be frank. They're saying he's taken a whole lot of money out of the firm.'

'That's ridiculous.'

'They say he transferred between a quarter and half a million pounds into his own bank account and withdrew it the day he left. On top of that, they think he faked my signature on the requisition orders. Or if he didn't, someone else did. I haven't a clue who it could have been.'

'Oh God, this really is getting to be a nightmare.'

'The only way I can refute the allegation is if I find him

and have him prove that what they're saying is lies. That's why I need you to be completely open with me. And if you've no objection, I'd like to have a word with your daughter too.'

'Look, Alan, Anna's not old enough to understand what's going on. She's only ten – a vulnerable ten at that. She's going through a really difficult emotional stage. She's not eating. The doctor's worried. So am I. If you don't mind, I'd much prefer it if you didn't involve her.'

'As you wish.'

'Anyway, surely you should be asking questions of the Virtus people. All these minor public schoolboys talking about – what is it now? – Bloods, Prey, Vermin and Masters. Why don't they grow up?' She stubbed out her cigarette and immediately lit another one.

'Questions have already been asked at Virtus, Viktoria. There were no answers.'

'Then what are you going to do about it?'

'For a start, I need to search through his papers here. Bank statements. Diaries. Correspondence. I need to get a picture of his state of mind before he left. Can you help?'

'Manage on your own,' she said. 'I've got to collect Anna. The only gift she seems to have is for playing the flute. If you wouldn't mind doing whatever you have to do without me. You'll find Grant's study on the top floor.'

Looking flustered and irritated, she pulled on a coat. Giving him a rather theatrical wave, she hurried from the room.

Rosslyn heard the front door close. He made his way up the stairs. On the stairs to the top floor he passed the open door of what was obviously Anna's room.

Unlike the rest of the house it was very tidy. There was a desk beneath the window with a computer on it, an Apple Mac like Rosslyn's. A digital clock showed the time: 16.10.

Before he began his search of Grant's study he photographed the room from different angles. The study was also very tidy. Like daughter, like father. There was a bowl of apples on the windowsill and one or two of them were turning mouldy. Then he spoke softly into his tape recorder as he made his search.

'16.12 hours. Grant Feller's study. A small room with a view overlooking the Thames. Either Grant tidied everything up before he left or someone else has tidied the room.

'There are framed photos of diamonds on the walls, some cut, some uncut. No mention of what they are. Grant knew his diamonds, didn't need reminding. A wedding photograph of Grant with Viktoria. Several of Anna as a baby. A small washbasin in one corner. Clean, unused hand towels on a steel hanger beneath it. Basin doesn't seem to have been used for some time.

'On the desk a pile of NatWest bank statements. Personal account. No mention anywhere of a substantial payment in. Nothing anywhere near a quarter of a million pounds. No big sums going out. Next to the bank statements is a pending file. Some references to an investment account. No big sums in there either. No unusual expenditure.

'So problem number one. Virtus says he made a big payment into his NatWest account. But there is no record. He has a personal banker. A Mr John Hagan.'

What would his personal banker say? He took a risk

66

and dialled the number. A woman answered and Rosslyn recorded the call:

'Is Mr Hagan available, please?'

'Who is speaking?'

'Grant Feller.'

'Yes. Hello, Mr Feller. This is Sara speaking. I'm afraid Mr Hagan has left for a meeting in Ealing. Is there anything I can do to help?'

'Yes, if you wouldn't mind, Sara. I have a question concerning a payment or payments made to my personal account during the last two to three weeks or so. It's a big sum. Nearly half a million pounds.'

'Very good. What's your account number, Mr Feller?'

Rosslyn read out the number.

'Yes, Mr Feller. Would you mind holding the line for two minutes? Bear with me –'

She came back on the line sooner. 'I can find no record of any sum of that amount.'

'You're sure?'

'Yes. Would you like to call Mr Hagan in the morning?'

'No, thank you. I appreciate the trouble you've taken.'

'You're welcome and thank you for banking with NatWest.'

So there has been no payment made. What the hell are these accusations about? Grant, where are you? A letter from his private medical insurance company says he's completely fit. Doesn't smoke. Doesn't drink. Also similar letters about Viktoria. Doesn't smoke. Doesn't drink. Someone's got that all wrong.

Desk drawers contain holiday snaps. Another drawer has old family photos in it. Grant with a couple who look like his mother and father.

Now the shelves. Not many books. I've checked between each book. Nothing hidden. Nothing.

I have lifted the desk and moved it. Nothing beneath it. I have rolled back the rugs. Nothing. Boards creak.

What's odd about Grant's hidey-hole is that there's nothing hidden.

An ordinary enough life ordinarily enough lived.

He made his way back down the stairs. When he reached Anna's room, he paused.

I am going to have a look in the daughter's room.

He drew down the blinds and turned on the lights.

The chest of drawers is full of kids' stuff all neatly folded. Nothing extraordinary. There's a line of dolls and teddy bears on a shelf. A CD player. A rank of CDs. Flute music. A music stand. A Miyazawa flute. Several framed photographs of Grant. One of Viktoria. Grant's the favourite by five to one. There's an Apple Mac on the desk. I have switched the Apple Mac on. On the screen are several folders variously entitled Anna Maths, Anna English, Anna French, Anna Names & Addresses and AF's Bank Account. I've opened these. No mention of any big payments in or out. He didn't use his daughter's account. He could've had one with another bank. But why did the Masters mention NatWest then?

There's also a folder entitled D. I have opened D. Now we have, under D, a JOURNAL marked PRIVATE. I have inserted the Cruzer micro SanDisk. Copied the whole JOURNAL. Am copying everything else on the hard disk. Folders marked FAMILY HISTORY and GRANDAD.

Checked I've left no easily accessible trace of copying. Digital clock says 16.40. Expecting Viktoria back with her daughter shortly. I hope it won't be necessary to interview the girl. I have something then. Not much. I don't like the look of Grant's hidey-hole. Too tidy. Someone, probably Viktoria, has been through it. I don't believe Grant was ever that tidy. Daughter might be. Who's to say it isn't her mother who tidies up after her? It's been a cold trail. End of recording: 16.42.

IO

Former Metropolitan Police Detective Inspector Ron Costley was a generation older than Rosslyn. Rosslyn had first met him at a transnational police conference in Hong Kong. In those days investigation into money laundering was what they had in common. Costley gave a paper to a working group entitled 'Freeze and Seize: International Co-operation in Confiscation and Partnerships with the Private Sector'. More recently they had led the hunt for Klaas-Pieter Terajima. It was some time since Rosslyn had last met his friend face to face over dinner. It was good to see him again.

They were seated at a table in the corner of the restaurant of the Goring Hotel in Beeston Place near Buckingham Palace. An elderly couple whispered to each other at a window table. They seemed to be bickering about answers to a crossword in the evening paper.

Rosslyn commiserated with Costley at the loss of Thynne.

'I suppose I should've seen it coming,' Costley said. 'But he must have made his mind up some time ago. He

70

was a very religious man. It's totally out of character that he could have resorted to suicide. Sort of thing he'd have considered sinful.'

'You don't think of it like that, do you, Ron?'

'You know me, Alan, I keep my religious beliefs to myself. Tell me about this Feller.'

Rosslyn reviewed Feller's background and brought Costley up to date with his search.

'Tell me what you saw on the girl's computer,' Costley said.

'Personal stuff. It turns out that when Grant's away on Virtus work Viktoria has a friend in the house. He sleeps over. A guy by the name of Mikhail Ilyushenko. Mean anything to you?'

'Go on.'

'The daughter's been eavesdropping on them. Viktoria wants to divorce Grant and marry this Ilyushenko.'

'Is that what the daughter imagines?' Costley said. 'Or is it fact? And the fancy man, same for him. He wants to marry her?'

'If you believe the daughter's journal. Here.'

I wish Daddy was here. I love it when we sing together. I hate it when the Man visits Mummy.

I have seen them in Mummy's bed with nothing on.

I wish Daddy would come home and kill the Man.

MIKHAIL ILYUSHENKO. I Hate You.

He's a Russian. He's hairy and big and ugly with a white body. I've seen her taking the photos. It's horrible, horrible.

They speak a lot in Russian so I don't understand what they're saying. But I can hear his voice through the floorboards. He's usually monged. Then he laughs and Mummy says Shush you'll wake up Anna.

He says I AM AN OLLY-GARCH. He's gross. He asks a lot about Daddy's diamonds.

I think that Daddy knows about this man. There have been rows between them.

I said to Daddy You won't D Mummy?

He said No I won't. I love Mummy.

One day Mummy pushed Daddy down the stairs. He had a bruised elbow and cut his face. Mummy said it was an accident. Just an accident.

Once when Daddy came back he turned on his CD player and this is what he played. It's a song by Leonard Cohen. And it made me cry.

> Everybody knows that the dice are loaded
> Everybody rolls with their fingers crossed
> Everybody knows that the war is over
> Everybody knows that the good guys lost

He played it over and over again. So I went downstairs and hugged him and told him I loved him and he cried too. I thought he would never stop crying.

Costley handed back the printout. 'Tell me, Alan, what, if anything, you know about this Ilyushenko?'

'The name's familiar,' Rosslyn said. 'What do you know?'

'In the first instance, your Grant Feller applied to join

Allegiance. He speaks Russian. What with a Russian wife, I suppose you'd expect he would. I don't have to tell you that he's a very bright accountant. He knows his way around the private sector security business. Maybe not as well as you or I. But he knows how things work. As for Ilyushenko – up to two, maybe three, years ago no one outside Russia knew very much about him. He and his brothers Grigory and Pyotr are three very rich men. I mean rich. The Ilyushenkos were among the first to seize the opportunities afforded them when Gorbachev removed the prohibition on free enterprise. Think raw materials. Oil. Think the advantages to be gained by the people who were in with Yeltsin. Think aluminium. Currency exchange dealings. Banks. Then when the going got really tough, the Ilyushenkos shifted their investments overseas. Mind you, they still operate in Moscow. One of the more favoured of the reclusive oligarchs left there. A financial empire needs protection against organised crime syndicates. They need security. They need intelligence. So, if you were in their shoes, what would you do? I'll tell you. I'd buy into a premier British agency like Control Risks or a global set-up like Kroll. Any of the big international firms. I'd make it my own. Use it as a kind of iron curtain.' Costley was toying with the glass of water beside his plate. He was looking uncomfortable. 'There's a lot more besides I can't tell you, Alan. Believe me.'

'I believe you.'

'Shall I tell you what you don't know? Two months ago Grigory Ilyushenko bought into Allegiance. Grigory, Mikhail and Pyotr personally have the controlling interest. They're the people who pay my salary, Alan.

Ilyushenko and one of his right-hand men, Zhilin, together with Thynne saw Feller in private at Ilyushenko's mansion in Kensington Palace Gardens. Then there's Viktoria. You look back at the files you nicked from her daughter's computer and you'll see the dates fit. Because it was after Ilyushenko saw Feller that he asked Feller to start supplying us with Virtus intelligence. Jumping ship, treachery, call it what you want, but it's common currency. And let me tell you this: under its new Russian ownership Allegiance will declare war against its rivals. What with Virtus being American, they are going to fight with everything they have.'

'Who's taking over from Thynne?'

'No one's decided yet.'

'You think it'll be a Russian?'

'Maybe, maybe not.' Costley paused to take a sip of water. 'They'll take no prisoners, Alan. They deceive to survive. That's how the Russians work. They don't jump up and say, Hey, boys, we're at war. No, that's not their style. They simply remove the obstacles in the way of their getting richer. And if the obstacles are human, why then they hire a hit man to do the job. There are dozens, if not hundreds, of professional killers just aching for a job in Moscow. Feller won't have stolen that money, Alan. Could be someone set him up. Anyone'll jump if the money's right and the mindset geared up. Anyway, Allegiance have been the beneficiaries.'

'He's opened up the Virtus books?'

'What do you think?'

'I think he didn't have it in him to go so far.'

'So Feller's a calculating grafter,' said Costley. 'What investigator isn't? Anyhow, I quite liked the guy.'

'You say "liked" – past tense?'

'However you want to put it. Listen, Alan, I know the guy's done a runner. I don't know where the game's taken him now. Do you?'

'No,' said Rosslyn. 'Other than that a lot of money's missing. And I've been asked to find him.'

'And his marriage is in serious trouble,' Costley said. 'I think you have to find him before you report back to your so-called DCG. They may have their suspicions about him already. What if you don't find him?'

'I guess it's goodbye, Rosslyn.'

'Well, if they show you the door,' said Costley, 'there's always a place for you with us. That's if you don't mind working with me, young man. Would Mei like that?'

'At least she likes you, Ron.'

'I think of her as family. Send her my love. She in Hong Kong still?'

'She is. I'll send her your love.'

'What do you think about working for me, then?'

'It's good of you, Ron. Really good. Meanwhile I want to clear my name with the Masters over those faked signatures.'

'They won't do anything about those,' said Costley. 'It isn't worth their time chasing after a man with your experience. Feller will probably turn up. People like him are full of surprises. Like you, Alan.' He signalled the waiter to bring the bill.

'This one's on me, Ron.'

'No, thanks all the same,' said Costley. 'I've learned a little more than I'd bargained about Ilyushenko. I didn't think he was a marriage breaker.'

'He sounds a tough bastard.'

75

'And proud of it,' said Costley. He drained his cup of coffee. 'I've enjoyed this evening. It's been like the old days.'

'Without, thank God, Terajima.'

'You think he's still out there?' Costley asked.

'I do,' said Rosslyn.

'Still give your eye teeth to nail him?'

'Wouldn't you?'

'Given the chance,' said Costley, 'I'd give everything I've got.'

Rosslyn paid the bill.

'Next time on me, then,' Costley said. 'I've got my car outside. You want a lift home?'

'Fine, thanks. I'll get a cab.'

'In this weather? You'll be lucky.'

'I can walk.'

'Whatever. But take my advice, Alan. There's going to be a bloody war. If I'm wrong, there's still going to be a bloody war. Watch your back, young man.'

'Thanks for the tip,' said Rosslyn.

'Call me whenever you need me to help out,' said Costley.

Rosslyn saw Costley to his car. Then he asked the Goring Hotel concierge to call a minicab firm. Costley was right. There were no cabs to be had. It was a foul night.

I I

Rosslyn, eyes narrowed against the wind from the river, headed along Millbank for the roundabout by Lambeth Bridge, following the bend of the Thames. Bleak lights shone from the barred windows of Thames House, head-quarters of MI5.

He had walked the route alone countless times, alert to shadows: the figure in the dark sent to watch him by enemies known and unknown – or nowadays, hooded muggers ready with a blade and the demand for his mobile phone and cash. He welcomed the anonymity of the darkness.

He had a meeting with Bausch at nine in the morning at the Virtus main office. He wouldn't have much to tell the chairman, unless he revealed the contents of the teenage daughter's journal or passed on what Costley had told him. He decided against mentioning what he'd learned. Grant Feller's marriage was his business. And to bring up the matter of Grant and Allegiance would most likely compromise Ron Costley. Bausch would demand to know Rosslyn's sources.

He marvelled at Costley's calm. If Costley of all people said that war was breaking out between the investigation agencies, then that was what was happening and he didn't want to be on the opposing side to Ron Costley.

On the other hand, he had no intention of abandoning the search for Grant. He wanted to find Grant for his daughter's sake.

The darkness pressed in hard. He needed to resolve the Feller issue as soon as possible. The Virtus people could demand he postpone his Christmas trip to Hong Kong and he had no intention of letting Mei down.

He passed Dolphin Square, then the entrance to the restaurant Pomegranates, Mei's favourite, where the proprietor, jovial, trusted and discreet, was a friend of hers. Rosslyn walked up Claverton Street.

He peered into the stairwell of his flat. He could make out a package wrapped in Christmas paper; a pair of tubes wrapped in golden foil protruded rather absurdly from the gift box. He stepped back into the street and called Costley on his mobile.

Costley arrived within the hour.

'A pipe bomb,' said Rosslyn.

'We have three choices of action,' Costley said. 'One: we call the Yard and get the bomb disposal boys here. Two: we just walk away as if we've never seen it. Three: one of us disarms it.'

'Give me the torch,' Rosslyn said. 'Follow the beam, Ron. We're looking for a trip wire.'

Costley passed it to him and he shone the beam on to

the package. Then, slowly, he surveyed the rest of the stairwell space, the concrete paving slabs covered in grey slime, the black iron railings and the lock of the gate at pavement level.

'See anything?'

'No trip wire,' Costley said. 'Could be using some wireless trigger.'

'Have you seen anyone in the street since you arrived?'

'No.'

'Then I don't think radio is involved,' Rosslyn said. 'What've you got in your car repair kit?'

'The usual.'

'Pliers? A Stanley knife?'

'There should be a pair, yes.' Costley hesitated. 'Alan, are you sure about doing this?'

'Ron, I would rather, much rather, call the bomb disposal guys.'

'You realise the risk?'

'You think I don't? I'm not leaving the thing down there for some other poor bastard to detonate. And think of the opposition, Ron. Am I going to give them the advantage of knowing that I'm scared shitless because they're showing me they're trying to kill me? That way they win. Or, if we get the bomb boys in, then there'll be the usual fart-arse investigation taking for ever and the word's out that I'm a target, all of that. I don't need it, Ron. But what I do need is to see if the construction of the bloody thing tells me something about the bastard who built it. I want the bomber's signature. I want his mind. I also want the fucker's neck.'

'You think you can do it?'

'I know how to build one. Taking one apart is a matter of doing the same thing in reverse. If I win, I win. If I lose, I won't know anything about it.'

'I don't like this, Alan.'

'You think I do?' said Rosslyn. 'Would you mind fetching me the pliers from the car? And one more thing. Do you have a tape recorder?'

'In my briefcase.'

'Bring that too.'

Costley left Rosslyn peering down at the package.

The disposal of conventional munitions – say, grenades, anti-tank rockets or mortar bombs – is never easy. But it's made easier because the arms manufacturers work to a set pattern. You know in advance how much explosive each device contains and what the likely dangers are in rendering them harmless. With an improvised explosive device like the one Rosslyn was looking at, you don't know anything until the thing has been defused. There are dozens – some say hundreds – of different ways to construct a home-made bomb. To make matters worse, the men who manufacture them, and they are mostly men, sometimes fit a booby trap or attach an anti-handling mechanism.

Costley returned with the pliers and the tape recorder.

'You're going to have to take a risk too, Ron. You're going to move into the doorway there and stand against the door. I am going to be talking and if you can't hear me, you say so. I want you to make sure there's a record of everything I see down there. If the fucker goes up, then at least forensics will have some sort of head start. Okay, move to the doorway.'

'Take it easy, Alan.'

Rosslyn unlocked the gate to the stairwell and slowly

and steadily picked his way down the steps one by one. His mind raced with calculations about the possible extent of the bomb's risk level and destructive force. Even if the quantity of explosive was relatively small, this was without doubt a Level One risk.

This was the worst moment. Too far away to be killed cleanly and know nothing. Near enough to be maimed. Never to see Mei again. To see nothing.

He took the last two steps across the paving stones and looked down at the package.

Sweat dripped from his forehead. He tasted salt.

'You hear me, Ron?'

'I hear you. Tape's running.'

Rosslyn cleared his throat. *'It's about the size of a cardboard wine box for a half-dozen bottles set down on its side. It's been wrapped . . . untidily with industrial adhesive tape.'*

He widened the beam of the torch and set it on the windowsill, wedging it against the sill and one of the security bars so its beam shone directly on to the package. Then, inch by inch, he nursed the tip of the Stanley knife blade through the tape, gently unpeeling it.

His mouth was dry. *'I've peeled back the adhesive tape – first cut completed.'* His mind raced, seeking to unravel the procedure the bomb maker had followed. *'It's a semi-skilled job. Seems to me the tape is of foreign make. Could be German or Spanish. There's a manufacturer's label. Ekhart or something. Looks to me that the current is from a battery. A relay connection. Switch is electromagnetic. There could be a real danger of a circuit here collapsing. Could be a short. I'm going silent a minute . . . wait out.'*

He spent the next sixty seconds looking and listening. His eyes itched. He blinked, stretched his neck, looked at the mechanism, wondered whose fingers had last nursed the wiring, wondered what degree of fear the bomb constructor had felt. The seconds ticked away. He heard the sound of his own breathing and felt the throbbing of the muscles in his chest. His fingers were moist and when he shivered he dislodged droplets of sweat which stung his eyes. When he leaned close to the device, he felt certain he could hear the faint sound of clicks. *Tk-tk-tk-tk.* There was a moment when he sensed that enough was enough: *I want to live. One false move and –* Then he felt a flash of anger followed by the twitching of a nerve in his temple. He straightened, summoned up an effort to breathe slowly and regularly, and felt the cold air in his lungs. He thought he could hear the crunch of footsteps. Perhaps Costley was shifting from foot to foot. He cleared his throat.

'*Okay, it's a small timer. Maybe . . . an adapted alarm clock.*'

Doubt plagued him. His hands were shaking and he cursed. He brushed sweat from his eyes and wiped the palms of his hands against his coat. *What is the bloody thing?*

His voice sounded detached: '*Could be a kitchen timer.*' He clenched his hand. Massaged his fingers. Opened and closed the pliers. '*I'm going to cut the wire.*' Very slowly he moved the cutting edges of the pliers towards the wire. He held his breath. Then he squeezed the pliers. He heard the click. The wire came away and he gently, millimetre by millimetre, turned and nudged it away so no further contact could be made. His voice was shaking. He said hoarsely: '*Wire's cut.*' For a few moments he stood staring at the package. It contained a great deal of explosive. Quite enough to have blown him to bits and most of his flat as well. He began to breathe jerkily. His body was shaking even more violently. He was staring at the pattern of the construction. 'I've narrowed the choice of bomb artist down.' He wiped the salty sweat from his lips. 'All done, Ron.'

'Say again.'

'I said, all done. I'm coming back up.'

Rosslyn raised the package, cradling it in his arms like a newborn baby, and carried it up the steps and out on to the pavement.

Costley approached him from the shadows. His face looked ghostly. 'It's a long time since I saw that done without the use of protective gear.'

'You're old, Ron Costley – I've *never* seen it done without the gear. Here, these are yours.' He handed Costley the pliers, torch and Stanley knife.

Costley stared at the package in Rosslyn's arms. 'Well done,' he said again.

'Thanks,' said Rosslyn. 'I'm going to get some essentials from my flat. Then I want you to take me to your place for the night. I need a safe house.'

'I know a safe one,' said Costley. He was pointing at the package. 'What are you going to do with that?'

'I want a DNA test on it,' said Rosslyn. He punched the keys on his phone. Waiting for the number to answer he asked Costley: 'Where's this safe house you know?'

'My daughter's place. Border of Marylebone and

Euston. She's on her gap year. I'm looking after it. You can have the spare room. It's safe.'

Finally there was an answer to his call. The woman's voice said: 'Ann Chisholm.'

'Ann, this is Alan. Have I woken you?'

'No, I'm on night duty.'

'Are you alone?'

'No.'

'Okay then. Just answer me yes or no.'

'Go ahead.'

'This is urgent. Are you in the University Street lab?'

'Yes.'

'Could you have someone deputise for you? Say for an hour or so?'

'I think so, yes.'

'I'm outside my place in Claverton Street. If I were to tell you I have a disarmed explosive device here, could you get here fast, I mean, right now?'

'Yes.'

'You'll have to bring the right transport to collect it.'

'That may be difficult.'

'But can you do it?'

'Yes.'

'I need tests on it.'

'What sort?'

'DNA for a start. Construction patterns. Searches on your database. The usual things. Can you do them fast?'

'Yes.'

'See you in, say, twenty minutes.'

Ann Chisholm, thirty-nine-year-old divorcee, is senior analyst at the Defence Science and Technology

Laboratory (Dstl). She has an office deep within the heavily protected and secret Emergency Outreach Unit (EOU) far below ground at the Gower Street end of University Street.

Rosslyn first encountered her during the Terajima/Zhentung brothers murder investigation. Passionate about her work, she shares Rosslyn's love of Greece, the Mani and Peloponnese. A few people reckon she has a romantic interest in Rosslyn. Most of her affection is directed towards her dog Rufus, a spaniel and retired sniffer dog, the gift to Ann from a grateful Commissioner of Police. Rufus is the only pet allowed access to the EOU. The majority of Chisholm's colleagues are her appointees and women. The EOU, over which Chisholm presides, is known throughout Dstl as 'the beehive'. The beehive in which Chisholm is Queen uses highly sophisticated sensors and systems for the round-the-clock detection of chemical and biological (CB) agents and explosives. Since the 7 July London bombings the EOU has never closed. If you need to unravel the life and times of an explosive device, Ann Chisholm is your woman.

Driving an unmarked white van, she arrived at the entrance to Rosslyn's flat within thirty minutes and spent some time looking at the package, wiring and explosive charges. Costley kept watch down the street for unwanted witnesses.

Rosslyn explained to Chisholm what had happened outside his flat.

'You really should have had me disarm this, Alan,' Chisholm said.

'I did a bomb disposal course with Customs and Excise,' Rosslyn replied.

'Makes no difference,' she said. 'I'm the professional. Not you.'

'I won't argue,' said Rosslyn.

She gave him a flirtatious look. 'What do I get from this?' she asked. 'Dinner? A weekend in Paris?'

'One day, Ann.'

'I'll hold you to it. Okay, I'll take this crap away with me for safe keeping. I'll check the database. It may take a few hours. We're talking MoD, maybe Geneva, and I can have a look-see via my people with the FBI in Quantico. I presume you're wanting the assembly patterns linked to known IDs?'

'Very badly.'

'I can tell you now that this is a professional assembly. At any rate, let's say semi-professional. Someone's fairly experienced handiwork. The actual explosive and detonator looks interesting. It's not all that common.'

'Do you think you'll be able to give us a name?'

'Probably not a single name. But names, yes, most likely. I assume this is confidential?'

'Yes.'

'But you realise that sooner or later I may have to hand the findings to the powers-that-be.'

'Yes. Can we agree on that later? I'm really grateful, Ann.'

'Don't mention it.'

'You want to come in for a drink?'

'No, thanks. If I'm not back in University Street very soon and there's a terrorist attack, that's the end of Ann Chisholm's career.'

'The end of all of us.'

'Which is the most sensible thing you've said all night,' said Chisholm. 'Call me.'

Then, after the remains of the device had been properly secured in the rear of the white van, she hesitated, one hand on the rear door locking system. 'I should tell you my initial hunch. We have seen elements of that construction before. I'm only saying elements. And this is a hunch, not a professional analysis. The configuration suggests Klaas-Pieter Terajima.'

'Except he's dead, Ann.'

'That wasn't what you told me last time we met.'

'I will have told you that I *think* he may be dead.'

'My intuition is strong.'

'There's been no sign of him in the UK.'

'But with a psychopath like that there wouldn't be, would there?'

Rosslyn looked at her blankly. It was just what he hoped not to hear.

'I'll put out some feelers with Quantico. Let's see what the Yanks have to say.'

'You'll let me know?'

'Of course,' she said. 'And if you need further help you might do worse than have a word with my friend at the US embassy outreach, Bernal Schiff, the legal aid attaché. He's a veteran. You can trust him.'

'Right now I don't want anyone else involved.'

'You have to keep a cold mind with a man like him, Alan. Take care.'

'You too.'

Chisholm left and Rosslyn went into his flat to collect clothing, his laptop computer and photographs of Mei.

Costley was saying it was time to go.

He felt no sense of relief, just a quiet anger. He thought of Mei. Mei would have said: 'Search for calm.' The quiet place in the mind, but his heart was telling him: *find Grant – get Terajima.*

Full Moon

Gedda Immaculata DaCeption (c'mon)
Snow moon in de ol grey sky above (c'mon)
Is the land of make de love wid K-P T (c'mon)
Wanna spaz out de gaz (c'mon)
Give me your hand you lustashus He/She (c'mon)
Gedda Immaculata DaCeption (c'mon)

12

Before dawn in Greece.

The temple bell clangs four.

It is two hours before the sun rises above the ridges of the Taigetos Mountains in the Peloponnese.

Takashi Sakamoto wakes from a contented sleep beneath the cotton blanket on his hard mattress in his monastery cell. Four hours' sleep a night, maintains the master Tzu Yin, is all his followers need. Most of the monastic brotherhood sleep for six hours, but Sakamoto is a strict adherent of the Master's rules.

Sakamoto wrapped a towel of rough grey linen around his waist. Then, to the accompaniment of the barks of the monastery guard dogs, he made his way barefoot across the courtyard to the shower room. A cat followed him: one of several who gathered together, as they did each morning, to watch the naked Sakamoto shower under the jet of cold water.

Without flinching, Sakamoto let the water hit his shaven head and course down his slim, olive-coloured and powerful body. Sakamoto was a Eurasian, his blood a mixture of Japanese, Chinese and Caucasian. He was equally well able to pass as Chinese or Japanese. Unless you considered the soft eyes with their feminine eyelashes, the attractive boyish smile, the perfect teeth or the exquisitely manicured fingernails unusual, you would not have found his appearance out of the ordinary.

Once he had finished showering, he returned to his cell and dressed in his saffron robe of cheap cloth. He folded his cotton blanket in a neat square and then knelt in homage on the bare stone floor beneath the iconic image of the Master, Tzu Yin.

Homage completed, he swept his cell with a stiff broom and then, still watched over by the cats, the outside courtyard. The housekeeping task completed, he returned to his cell and sat in the half-lotus position, his eyes closed in meditation.

Dawn broke slowly across the mountains and wild gorges, the sun edging the snow crests of the mountains with gold and crimson. It brought a strange and ethereal beauty to the wilderness of this secluded part of Europe. Some called it the forgotten territory.

Few people visited the followers of Tzu Yin, who practised the Master's refined and arcane form of Buddhism in this part of Messinia.

At the end of miles of twisting and precipitous mountain tracks, inaccessible by cars or off-road vehicles, the monastery had been constructed out of an ancient ruin. The stone buildings were low and hidden from view by giant rocks, scrub, cypresses and pine trees. They looked out across the wilderness of the rocky gorges to the Messinian Gulf in the far distance. Until you came across the monastery, after a long curve in the last of the steep and stony tracks, you would hardly have realised it existed. None of the groups of avid mountain walkers from Scandinavia and the Low Countries who came to the Taigetos Mountains in spring and summer ever got this far.

The brotherhood had its own crystalline springs, a small herd of goats, some donkeys, hens, a vegetable garden, beehives, vines and olive trees. Priding itself on organic food production, it was entirely self-sufficient. Heating, and there wasn't much of it, was supplied by solar heaters, which had been bought with donations made to the brotherhood by patrons from Scandinavia, Holland, the United Kingdom, Germany and Russia.

The Spartan regime of living meant that the two dozen men and ten women stayed remarkably healthy. If any of them required medical treatment the brotherhood could provide it. Among the followers of Tzu Yin at the monastery were a German doctor from Stuttgart and a Swedish woman dental surgeon from Malmö. The majority of the brotherhood consisted of so-called 'former professional people'.

The brothers and sisters had no regular contact with the outside world. If relatives needed to meet, then the brother or sister would make the journey of some five hours down the mountains by donkey or on foot, then onwards by bus or taxi to Kalamata.

There was no web site, no e-mail facility, only an unreliable landline telephone link over which the members of the community could make contact with the sympathetic Papas, or priest, some miles below. The Papas, unusually for the region, spoke almost fluent German and passed on messages in an emergency. In return for these favours, the community made an annual donation to the Papas's church funds. Appreciative of their generosity, the Papas put it about that the 'quiet people up the mountain' could be trusted and, as they wished to be, left to their own spiritual devices in peace and the worship of their God.

In the thin light of early morning, Sakamoto attended to the gathering of food from the vegetable patches. Barefoot, he walked in silence with downcast eyes, gathering winter greens into a straw basket with the cats watching him from a discreet distance.

After breakfast at seven-thirty, he resumed meditation until about eleven. Then, along with the rest of the community, he ate his second meal of the day, finishing it, as Tzu Yin's precepts ruled, before noon. The meal, excluding drinks of water or herbal tea, would be the last nourishment of the day.

That afternoon he returned to his cell alone to read the *Dhammapada* and practise chants.

It was almost five in the evening, just before the bell summoned the brotherhood to devotions at the *vihara*, when Brother Søren, the Dane who acted as glorified caretaker and managed telephone communication with the Papas, came to Sakamoto's cell. The Papas had an urgent message for him.

Sakamoto walked in silence with Brother Søren to the small room that served as the administration office. Brother Søren watched Sakamoto take the call. When it was finished, Sakamoto told Brother Søren that his sister had been taken critically ill in the Netherlands. His brother had told him that she was in hospital in

Amsterdam and he had asked that Sakamoto go to her bedside as soon as conceivably possible.

'You must go,' said Brother Søren. 'You will of course need money and so forth. Passport and perhaps other things.'

'Yes. I will need my passport,' said Sakamoto. 'Nothing else. I have adequate funds in your safe. Enough for the bus to Kalamata and another onwards to Athens. My brother can arrange whatever further funds I need. He has made the necessary arrangements with my bank in Athens.'

'Well, dear Takashi,' said Brother Søren. 'I'm very sorry to hear the news. Be brave. You are a man of spirit.'

'Let's hope my sister recovers soon,' Sakamoto said. 'But it sounds unlikely. I will leave in the morning.'

'We shall miss you,' Brother Søren said. 'I wish you well. The Master will speed your safe return. We look forward to interviewing the pilgrims you have recommended to join us in retreat. I trust you will tell them the conditions they may expect in the guesthouse in due time.'

'You can leave them to me, Brother Søren. They will not impinge on our routine.'

'Given that you will, alas, be away from us for a few days, maybe longer, could you perhaps give me their names?' Brother Søren said. 'Just in case any of them wish to get in touch with us before your return. There are to be three, are there not?'

'Three,' said Sakamoto. 'Two Germans and a South African.'

'I hope the trio will be happy with us. I trust they will come equipped for the winter weather.'

'All are very fit,' said Sakamoto. 'They will cause us no hardship. They will keep themselves to themselves. And they will, naturally, contribute funds to the communal purse.'

'That will be deeply appreciated by the brotherhood,' said Brother Søren. 'Bless you, brother.'

With that, the two men retired to their respective cells for further meditation.

Before going to sleep, Sakamoto wrote a note to Brother Søren:

My dear Brother,
The names of our guests for retreat are:

Gunther Reincke
Rudolf Berben
Robin de Gray Pienaar

With respect
I remain
Yours truly

Takashi Sakamoto

Each name was an alias. So too was Takashi Sakamoto.

At three o'clock next morning, in the darkness, Sakamoto prepared for his journey down the mountain.

He carried a cloth bag containing a water bottle and money for the bus fares to Kalamata and on to Athens. He let himself through the gates set in the monastery's low stone wall and headed along the track in a north-westerly direction.

The mountain air was cold and moist. His footsteps

were the only sounds that broke the silence. He walked at a steady pace and for the first hour made slow progress in the darkness. The sense of solitude made up for the trickiness of the path he was negotiating. A goat watched him and did not move. A fox dashed for cover in the shadows. Otherwise the landscape was still.

An austere man, Sakamoto relished solitude. The life of the monastery fulfilled the requirements of his complex spirit. Today's journey beyond the confines of the monastery was one of several he had taken since he had first been received into the community of Tzu Yin a few short years before. He visited London for short periods. Sometimes he was away in Moscow, in Luxembourg and Milan. Sometimes, for extended periods, he was in Beijing. Brother Søren always showed understanding when he requested absences to help friends in need or to undertake selfless missions similar to the one that had given rise to his present journey.

None of his companions following the monastic life had enquired about the state of the outside world. Theirs was the life of the inner world and its demands of denial were considerable. With very few exceptions his companions had maintained mental and spiritual equilibrium, perhaps each of them had found a way to what some called 'the inland sea of peace'.

Like Sakamoto, most of the members of the community kept their pasts to themselves. But to the best of Sakamoto's knowledge, in no case did their past life intrude upon their present life in quite the way that his did, however shrouded in discretion it might be.

What balanced his formidable intellect and appetites, like equal weights upon the platforms of a scale, was self-denial on the one hand and homicidal mania on the other.

With the strength derived from knowing he would carry his secrets to the grave, Sakamoto had come to terms with his innermost desires. The more he practised self-denial, the more extreme the savagery of the killings and calculated executions he carried out and the larger the fee he demanded for their commission. Like extreme solitude, murder induced the spirit of ecstasy *in extremis*; ecstasy was something he could not live without.

It was, he reckoned, inevitable that sooner or later the last encounter he had with the Russian arms-dealer in northern France would result in his being contacted.

Sakamoto relished the memory.

I can see the Russian Nurmukhan at the bar of the Café St Omer. He might have been offering low-cost cigarettes for sale.

'I can get you cut-price guns,' Nurmukhan had said. 'My friends also have explosives. I can do all of this for you and more. You have to believe me.'

'I believe you,' I said, watching the bubbles in my glass of Perrier. 'When are they coming?'

'When I tell them to come,' Nurmukhan said. 'Some time tonight.'

'Cool,' I said. 'Who are they?'

'They don't have names I can spell out to you. Remember we're talking asylum seekers UK-bound. I don't know who the Indonesians deal with. Maybe people in Moscow. Who knows?'

'My people like to know who they're dealing with. Seems like you have too many people involved. They might give trouble. I don't want trouble.'

'I know that,' Nurmukhan said.

I searched the faces of the other customers in the café, which had seen better days and nights. These days sullen truckers from eastern Europe favoured the place. Most had hard faces. The Café St Omer specialises in sausages and boiled vegetables. The price of vodka is rock bottom. You can hire a cheap upstairs room with a shower for a few euros. A girl for a few hours costs not much extra. There's always an illegal immigrant willing to turn a trick at the Café St Omer, and the local gendarmes or plainclothes British immigration snoops rarely visit.

I don't come here for sex. I have my Mei. She's always on my mind.

Thinking of Mei naked, I gazed through the haze of cigarette smoke at the TV showing a mindless French quiz show. The TV set filled the café with shrieks of mindless laughter. 'These are desperate people. You should know. You told me you're Taiwanese. I heard you were a dangerous man. You don't look dangerous to me.'

Nurmukhan talks too much. I speared the slice of lemon in the glass of Perrier. I wondered how much Nurmukhan really knew of my identity. I wondered, if it proved necessary, how easy Nurmukhan would be to kill. He has a bulging vein behind his right ear. A jab of the fingernail.

'I have to tell you,' I said, 'I don't like dealing with desperate people.'

'These are desperate times,' Nurmukhan said. 'There are many needy people in the world.'

'I am not among their number.'

'You may not be.'

'Are you?'

99

'Look, you know where you are with desperate people. They're in need of getting into the UK no matter what. They've got this far. They sell guns. I get a pre-sale with someone like you. I buy the guns. I sell them to you for pounds or euros or US dollars cash. But you know, there's all sorts in the world. They're not all so desperate that they're unreliable. Do you understand?'

'I'm not sure I understand anything you say.'

'Put it this way,' Nurmukhan said. 'I trust you, Liu Jin, if that's your real name.'

'That's my name,' I lied. 'You did what I suggested?'

'Sure I did, yellow face.'

'You called the German?'

'Of course I called him. He says: "Any friend of Liu Jin is a friend of mine. You can do business with Liu Jin." That's good enough for me. You're clean. And there isn't anybody for five hundred kilometres that can get you goods as I can get you. Don't you believe me, Liu Jin?'

'Maybe I believe you,' I said.

'And something else besides,' said Nurmukhan. 'The German said that maybe you could deal me some ID for one or two of my friends out of Indonesia. They're hospital nurses, highly qualified.'

'You're talking passports?'

'More than passports,' said Nurmukhan. 'Money's not a problem. You have a British passport.'

'Sure.'

'You can get me two or three?'

'For why?'

'Say I have a client who's three months pregnant. She and her man want to get into the UK.'

'Is the husband running guns?'

'He could be. The problem's with his pregnant wife. She's wanted for procurement and racketeering and murder in Taichung. Sweetness shines out of her ass. But you wouldn't want to make an enemy of her.'

I thought: She sounds a likely candidate for me. I said: 'Maybe I could make a friend of her.'

Nurmukhan rubbed his cheeks. They were scarred from acne. 'You're weird,' he said with a smile, showing two front teeth that looked as though they'd been made of steel. 'Maybe you could make a friend of her? Maybe I could deal for both of them?'

'You're talking passports?'

'You read my mind,' Nurmukhan smiled. 'You know something? Nothing surprises me any more. I think you need drugs. I think you need guns. Now here we are and you're saying you can sell me passports for a pair of wanted killers out of Taichung.'

'I could be.'

'Everybody in this goddamned place needs passports.'

'That I know.'

'How long would you take to get them?'

'Passports? Maybe a week. Maybe longer. Who knows? I'll need photographs and the usual sort of information.'

'I know,' said Nurmukhan. He scratched his cheek. 'Who do you use?'

'Who do I use?' I was thinking of the cat-loving English forger known as Martin in the Rue de Cels, Montparnasse. 'Never mind who I use. Maybe I could use the Indonesians.'

Nurmukhan pushed up the collar of his leather jacket. 'What do you need them for?'

'I can give them some legitimate work in London. Find them a room. Let them find their feet.'

Nurmukhan laughed. 'You run a charity?'

'You could call it that,' I said. 'Shall we talk the money?'

'Let's do that thing,' Nurmukhan said.

'First I have to find the men's room,' I said. Someone badly wants to hire me. They'll have to pay me more money than the Russian pinko-grey Nurmukhan has ever dreamed exists. I took my mobile and waited in the locked toilet, for what seemed an interminable time for the German to take my call.

I stared at myself in the stained mirror, through the graffiti.

The German answered. He was cautious. 'They need a professional,' he said.

I said, 'I don't like the Russian here.'

'He's not paid to be liked.'

'Neither am I. But he has a low forehead.'

'What?'

'He is not very intelligent. I'll need a million down. Expenses. A million on completion.'

'Pounds or dollars?'

'In diamonds.'

With that I returned to the weasel Russian at the bar.

'A deal?' Nurmukhan said.

'No go,' I said.

'You serious?'

'One day in the future,' I said. 'Here's how you contact me. Via Amsterdam.'

'An answering service – whose?'

'Mine. I own it. Oh, and in case you're thinking you

might just go visit that answering service, don't even think about it. It's locked in a safe, my friend. And the safe is linked to an explosive device that'll blow you to God's kingdom come.'

'I don't believe in God.'

'Now that you mention it, I doubt He believes in you.'

'What do my people say?'

'They send me a message. Your sister's ill. I'll take it on from there.'

'Your sister's ill?'

'Your sister's ill. Your people know how to reach me.'

'How do they pay you?'

'I'll tell them. I run the operation. Me. Alone. No one else.'

Nurmukhan's eyes flickered. Something about me chilled him.

Good. Very good.

I leaned forward to Nurmukhan, so close his face almost touched mine. He stank of fear.

I warned him. 'If you talk to anyone – police, informers – your people will put a bullet in your head. If not –' I showed him a small steel nail file with a finely sharpened tip. 'If they don't, I will remove your eyes.'

And they came back. They always do in the end. The murder drive is stronger than having the cramp in your dick. They have to let it out. They can't help it.

So what was agreed?

This.

Nurmukhan's people agreed to pay the lot in diamonds. The stones will be available to me in Antwerp. Now it's up to me to make contact in Moscow.

I will choose the method of execution.

You don't give technical instructions to perform surgery on the one you loathe. That's my responsibility and I earn more, much more than the President of the United States for carrying it out.

Unlike him, I only answer to myself.

The winter sun warmed his shaven head. After the long walk it raised his spirits higher still.

He knew his mind and body were in peak condition and before other passengers showed up at the roadside bus stop, Sakamoto sang snatches from the anthem composed and dedicated to him at the monastery by the American-German rap musician he had tutored in the techniques of deep hypnosis:

> *Mei lügt doch, Mann*
> *Ein geiler Plan, Mann*
> *Jetzt kommt's drauf an, Mann*
> *An K-P-T lutscht Du, Mann*
> *Du lügst doch, Mann*
> *Du hast 'nen Steifen, Mann*
> *Willst doch Mei vögeln, Mann*
> *Ich lüg nich', Alter*
> *Rosslyn is'n Killer, Alter.* *

---

* Mei not true to yooz I say
  Gedda Immaculata DaCeption I say
  Wanna gook da crunchtime I say
  Watchu suckin K-P-T I say
  You not true to me I say
  Goycha feelin hard on I say
  Yooz wanna lay Mei on de old brass bed I say
  Call me DaCeption if you willing I say yeah yo
  This Rosslyn he da one true killing I say yeah yo

He was the only passenger to board the bus at the remote stop. Village by village it filled up on the zigzag way through the mountains to Kalamata.

The other passengers looked at him with curiosity. Several of them bowed their heads in his direction and he gave each a slight smile of what might have passed as a benediction. They must have realised he was a holy man.

The bus arrived in time for him to transfer to the bus bound for Athens.

13

He spent the rest of the day in preparation, first presenting himself at the branch of the NatWest Bank on Kifissias Avenue, and asking to see his personal banker.

The personal banker's name tag read 'Nicos Karayannis'. Mr Karayannis asked Sakamoto to identify himself. Sakamoto did so with quiet courtesy and asked Mr Karayannis for the envelope that had been forwarded to him from Amsterdam. Whilst he waited for the envelope, he withdrew enough cash to pay for his initial preparations with cash in hand. Enough to make various purchases of women's clothing. Enough to meet the bill for one night in the Grande Bretagne. Enough for the round trip airline ticket Athens–Moscow–Athens.

Karayannis completed the formalities for the handing over of the envelope.

'A small parcel of clothing will be delivered to you later,' Sakamoto had told him. 'If you would be good enough to store it for me in the usual way until I next return to Athens.'

Karayannis said there would no problem.

Once Sakamoto was outside on the street, he removed the contents of the envelope: the passport he had requested from the cat-loving English forger known as Martin. It was an immaculate forgery. There was also a tourist visa for a Japanese to enter Russia. His new identity was Mitsuko Furyawa. What is it in their blood, he wondered, that makes the English the best forgers in the world? Meanwhile, there was the parcel of clothing to be made up – the parcel Karayannis would keep for him at the bank.

On his way to the small clothing shop near the Al Salam mosque on Galaxia Street in Neos Kosmos, he told himself that Russian security officers familiar with the violent culture of the Moscow streets would protect his target. Given the network of corruption, the near certainty of some informer having prior knowledge that a major hit was likely, he wanted to be in and out of Moscow fast.

Minimise the risks. He would make only the single reconnaissance trip to the killing zone. *Maximise efficiency.* The layout of the area would determine the means of execution. *Be certain of escape routes. Time spent in reconnaissance,* as the man said, *is seldom wasted.*

As to the method of execution, he most often favoured strangulation or the slicing of the victim's throat with his fingernails. He enjoyed the feel of splitting a man's Adam's apple. When it opened, it made a noise that was remarkable: like knifing a pomegranate. There was that click as the blade punctured the skin – the squeak – the sudden burst of blood. It was always something of an added bonus to smell the sweetness of fresh blood. *It's such a pure smell – like no other. Isn't it extraordinary that more human beings don't relish the niceties of disposing of their fellow beings? And to be paid for what one most loves doing? Death's administration.*

In the Galaxia Street shop, he bought a burka and metal faceplate and had them packaged. He arranged for the assistant to have the parcel delivered to Karayannis.

To complete his transformation – Takashi to Mitsuko, he to she – he headed for Kifissia and the Raxevsky clothing shop on Kyriazi Street.

'I am purchasing items for my sister, whose baggage has been mislaid by British Airways,' he told the assistant, who showed no inclination to disbelieve the monk. 'My sister is confined to her hotel,' Sakamoto added.

There was a short discussion about sizes and fabrics.

'My sister is a professional woman. I need something elegant. Suitable for the office and the evening. Why, she has even lost her winter coat.'

'Raxevsky clothes are of specially chosen fabrics which are easy to clean,' the assistant explained with pride. 'I'm sure we can supply everything your sister needs. We also stock some new lines in silk lingerie and shoes.'

The monk said that he would prefer the assistant to select the latter on his sister's behalf. He would, if it were not too much trouble, like to choose one of the Raxevsky berets that were displayed in the main window. His preference was for the black one. Within fifteen minutes his purchases were complete.

Using the telephone in the clothes shop, he booked a suite for two at the Grande Bretagne. He had, he explained to the reservation clerk, lost his credit card at Athens airport. Perhaps the hotel would be good enough to accept cash payment. He would be pleased to put down a deposit on arrival. The reservation clerk said there would be no difficulty providing a room with a view of the Acropolis. He preferred to be among people he didn't want to know. The privacy afforded by the Grande Bretagne was worth the price.

Before checking in, he made his way to the ground-floor lavatories and slipped into the women's unnoticed. He locked himself into a cubicle, stripped naked, made a bundle of his robe and sandals and shoved them into one of the Raxevsky carrier bags.

He stuffed the carrier bag into the lavatory bowl. Then, for good measure, he squatted down and emptied his bowels and bladder. Hotel lavatory cleaners are not, he believed with good reason, inclined to examine such malodorous deposits in great detail.

Having dressed in a conservative black suit with matching shoes, he set the beret at an angle he judged to be demure. He would see to what little facial make-up he needed later to match the photograph in the passport.

The transformation gave her satisfaction. This was she: Mitsuko Furyawa, the guest of Brother Sakamoto. And very attractive she was too.

Next, she went to the nearby Attica department store on Panepistimon Street which offered a variety of women's swimwear and selected a one-piece Rosa Chá swimsuit, the better to show off her lines in the pool of the Grande Bretagne's Spa.

Mitsuko Furyawa swam freestyle beautifully: head low in the water. Pulling her hands back past her slim hips in a straight line, breathing evenly, her progress through the water excited thoughts of the mission that lay ahead. The arrow flying to the bull's eye.

She noticed another swimmer in the pool, a young woman probably in her early twenties whose style of swimming was impressive. Her flip-turns were acrobatic, her broad shoulders powerful. Sensing the woman was challenging her to swim faster, Mitsuko responded and, after several lengths, turned out to be no match for her playful rival's speed. Life in the monastery denied her the opportunity to swim regularly. She would have preferred to keep in trim with a minimum of three sessions a week. Exercise in the Taigetos Mountains had made up for some of the swimming time lost in the hotel pools of Europe, South-East Asia and Beijing.

The brief contest with the appealing stranger ended with the pair of them standing in the shallow end, short of breath and side by side.

'You're good,' said Mitsuko.

Her rival swimmer had her hair cropped and a tattoo in the pattern of a snake around her left forearm. 'I should be,' she said with an infectious smile. 'I'm a professional. You're quite good yourself . . . but you need to keep your fingers closer.' The accent was Australian and she spoke with a slight lisp. 'Like this . . .' She demonstrated the point with long and slender fingers. 'You should let me give you a lesson or two.'

'What are you – a swimming coach?'

'Mostly a personal trainer and masseuse.'

They got out of the pool and dried off.

'Where are you from?' Mitsuko asked.

'Kyoto, Japan. I'm on a sabbatical from training. And you?'

'Beijing.'

'You don't look Chinese.'

'I'm part Dutch. Part Japanese. And you?'

'Japanese-Australian.'

'We have Japan in common.'

'What do you do?'

'International finance, that kind of thing.'

'You on vacation here?'

'Mostly business. What sort of massage do you do?'

'I use techniques from both yoga and ayurveda – you know, shiatsu and traditional ayurvedic stroking massage. What's your name?'

'Mitsuko Furyawa.'

'I'm Ono, Kylie Ono. Everyone calls me Ono. Are you travelling alone?'

'Yes. And you?'

'Me too. Do you want to have some dinner?'

'Sure. That'd be nice.'

They agreed a time to meet at Milos, the hotel's restaurant where seafood is the speciality.

The waiter was attentive to the two sleek oriental women: Mitsuko dressed in a black silk suit and fine cotton shirt, Ono in pale blue T-shirt and jeans, with silver chains around her ankles. Mitsuko subtly tried to get her companion to talk about herself. Confident and assured, Ono was nonetheless evasive, and Mitsuko, who was an expert in embroidering her past, reckoned that, like herself, Ono probably had a lot to hide. Ono was left-handed, and looking closely at the tattoo on her forearm, Mitsuko noticed that the snakeskin patterns disguised a long razor scar. Maybe she too was on the run. Mitsuko wondered whether Ono was even her real name. Ono's dark eyes rested on her, while Mitsuko gazed back at her companion. Mitsuko talked about Beijing and London. Ono displayed a familiarity with London, but proved reluctant to explain why she knew it so well. When Mitsuko pressed her, she said she had been employed as bodyguard to the wife of a Greek ship-owner. 'There was trouble,' she said with a laugh. 'Her husband fell in love with me.' It was none too difficult to see why. 'That's why I'm here in Athens – he likes to see me twice a year and pays me well. Oh, not for what you may think. No, I massage him. You want to know about it?'

'Tell me –'

'Your body's the threshold of your mind. Why don't we go to your room and I'll prove it to you? I'll go to mine and bring some oils. Give me an hour. You don't mind waiting for me?'

Mitsuko Furyawa smiled, paid the bill and went up to her suite.

Good. Good. Latin *virtus.* She gave a laugh. *From Latin vir. Valour. Manhood. Moral perfection. Do the British police suspect this man Feller? Feller is Rosslyn's friend. I am coming, Rosslyn. Do I still haunt your dreams?*

Her hands were trembling. She called the hotel service for an early wake-up call, ordered a car to take her to the airport, then dialled a London number. After a few rings she heard the answer phone click into action.

She heard Rosslyn's voice saying: 'Sorry. Mei and Alan are unable to take your call at present. But if you'd like to leave a message or send a fax after the beep we will get back to you.'

Mitsuko placed a tissue over the mouthpiece and spoke softly: *'Alan, nakanai de! Mei, kawaii desu ne!'*[*]

Dressed in a bathrobe Mitsuko walked slowly to the table bearing a dish of fruit. A note of welcome from the hotel manager was attached to it. Selecting a pomegranate, she had kissed it, bared her teeth and sunk them into the fruit, allowing the juices to trickle down her body. *Your body's the threshold of your mind.*

She heard the knocking on the door. It was Ono.

'I've brought candles,' Ono said. 'Go and light them. Draw the curtains. Lower the lights.'

In the dimness, Ono told her to remove the bathrobe. When Mitsuko said she was reluctant, Ono smiled. 'Don't worry – I know your secret. I'm curious to see it.'

'How did you know?' said Mitsuko.

'It's my business and I want my pleasure.'

Mitsuko undressed while Ono removed the duvet from the bed and arranged it on the floor. 'Lie down.' She took off her clothes. 'Let me warm you.' She rubbed Mitsuko with oil. 'Relax – let me go deeper into your tissues. Feel . . . the strokes. I'm opening your muscles. The tendons in your neck are tight –'

Ono pummelled and stroked Mitsuko's shoulders, back, hips, legs and feet. Mitsuko surrendered to her. 'The stress is dissolving . . . You like the smell of the powder? . . . It's vaikahand. It lets my strokes go deeper. The pain – it's nice?' She slowly turned Mitsuko over and lay on top of her, running her hands between the legs.

---

[*] *Alan. Don't be a cry baby! Mei. Isn't she cute!*

'I can taste your juice.'

'It's pomegranate.'

'Now it's your turn. Inside me. Deeper – the threshold of my mind – my body – prove it to me. Please . . . take them – harder, hurt me – hurt –'

14

Rosslyn climbed the stairs to the top-floor flat.

'It isn't exactly the Savoy,' Costley said. 'But you'll be safe here for the time being.'

Rosslyn opened the curtains on to a view of the junction with Tottenham Court Road, where part of the traffic dives into a tunnel. Beyond was a grim backdrop of office blocks.

The two windows provided scant protection against the traffic fumes, the rumble of articulated lorries and the choruses of motorbike engines and emergency vehicle sirens. It was hard to imagine a noisier place to live – unless it were beneath the flight path into Heathrow or overlooking the tracks by one of the city's rail termini. Adding to the pollution were the smells of the street-level restaurants, one Chinese, one Thai.

The back rooms, the kitchen and two bedrooms, overlooked Warren Street. 'Who lives in the flats below?' Rosslyn asked.

'There's a Bulgarian, Silvia, who works for an optometrist in St John's Wood. Two Turkish girls, Roni and Zayn, from a dry-cleaning outfit in Cleveland Street, and a family of Indians who work in a Euston restaurant. They come and go. They're fine. I have to tell you there's a problem with some of the other residents.'

'Who are the other residents?'

'Rats,' said Costley. 'Did you know that you're never more than ten feet from a rat in this great city of ours? Four thousand rats are born in London every hour. One rat can give birth to two thousand every year. There are sixty million of them in Britain. Almost as many as there are humans.'

'Thanks for sharing that with me, Ron.'

He left Costley on his own to sift through the pile of mail he had retrieved from the broken ledge in the downstairs hallway. Some of the mail was addressed to the Bulgarian and Turkish women and the rest to Costley's daughter Kelly-Jo; Rosslyn noticed that several were addressed to Kelly-Jo from North Carolina State University.

In one of the small bedrooms overlooking Warren Street, Rosslyn spread a Chinese-patterned quilt on the low bed opposite the window. Either side of the window stood an electric heater. Judging by the books on Kelly-Jo's makeshift shelves, she was a fan of Harry Potter. She had been reading at least one of his adventures in Italian.

Another of her passions seemed to be entomology. He scanned the book titles: *Entomology and Death – A Procedural Guide*; *A Manual of Forensic Evidence*; *Common Names of Insects & Related Organisms* and a short run of the Entomological Society of America's *Journal of Medical Entomology*. Kelly-Jo seemed to have inherited her father's investigative gene; in her case, for bugs and insects.

He set up his laptop on the desk and above it hung the large colour photograph of Mei in white T-shirt and bleached jeans. She was smiling straight into the camera.

Costley put two tumblers and a bottle of whisky on the kitchen table.

'I bought this place as an investment for Kelly-Jo. It'll be here when she gets back from her retreat with MondoDei in Florence.'

'I didn't know she was a member.'

'She joined it a year ago, just after her eighteenth birthday. About the time her mother left. I think it's been very good for her.'

'Do you hear from her?'

Costley sucked his teeth. 'Sometimes. I miss her very much.' He took out his wallet and showed Rosslyn a snapshot of his daughter. Kelly-Jo had a beautiful smile but looked too thin for her own good. 'Yes,' said Costley with a sigh, 'she wants to be a forensic entomologist. She's been accepted as a special student in botany at North Carolina State University. The fees and all that will cost me an arm and a leg. That's why I like the Allegiance pay days. Aside from the king-size rats I have as colleagues, I'm grateful to Allegiance. Now – let's do the work. For starters, who are we looking at?'

'I can think of one, maybe two people. But I don't think either of them would choose a bomb to do it. There are better ways. It's not so much I represent a physical threat, unless we think of Terajima. No, it's more likely the person behind the Christmas gift believes I know something – I mean, that I know something that makes the difference between life and death. But who? If you were looking to hire a major hit man, what sort of a list would you draw up?'

'You're talking names?'

'I'm talking names. Who'd be on it?'

'I can think of a few,' said Costley. 'Theodoros Tzoumakas the Greek, for one.'

'Tzoumakas must be in his early sixties. He has to be effectively nearing the end of his career.'

'The Germans?' suggested Costley.

'Jortzig or Merkel?'

'Jortzig.'

'Jortzig's hit and run. His speciality is contract killings in southern Spain, mostly in the employ of British hard men. What about Carlos Naranjo the Costa Rican?'

'I might include him,' said Costley. 'He'd be an unknown quantity.'

'So is Merkel. He's hot on explosives.'

'So we have Tzoumakas, Jortzig, Merkel, Naranjo.'

'Makes four,' said Rosslyn.

'There's also the South African Jacques Geddes, the tranny weirdo gynaecologist. He completes the worst-case list.'

There was a long silence. Like card players familiar with each other's gambits, they sat opposite each other at the kitchen table, the bottle of whisky open in the centre. Costley fiddled with the top.

At length, Rosslyn said: 'And you're going to tell me Terajima is number one?'

'I am going to tell you that Terajima is in at one,' said Costley. 'Yes. The Number One.'

'Except one thing,' said Rosslyn. 'The bomb didn't go

off, Ron. Do we think Terajima would know I'd disman-
tle it?'

'I don't know what he thinks.'

'I do,' said Rosslyn. 'Somewhere in this there's the
stench of Terajima. I sometimes wonder how many people he's killed. I'm telling you, he'll be back and soon.'

Fully dressed, he lay down, sprawled across the bed.
Seconds later exhaustion overcame him. The next thing
he heard was the bedside alarm clock sounding 8.15
a.m.

15

FITZROY SQUARE. LONDON

When Rosslyn arrived for his morning meeting with
Bausch he was drawn involuntarily to look through the
glass partition shielding the accountants' department.
Grant Feller's workspace was empty.

Bausch's secretary beckoned him to her desk. 'The
Chairman would like to see you in the entrance hall.
Don't forget your coat.'

On his way downstairs to the ground floor Rosslyn
activated the miniature tape recorder he was carrying in
his inside jacket pocket.

Bausch was talking to Bogaart, who stared at Rosslyn
and looked straight through him. Bausch was smiling.
He looked too jovial. Not a good sign. Then, through
the main entrance door of the building, Rosslyn saw the
figure of Virtus's lawyer, Michael Das Gupta, standing
on the doorstep.

'How are you, Alan?' asked Bausch, without pausing
for a reply. 'I thought we'd take the air in the garden.'

They walked in silence to the garden entrance.
Bausch unlocked the gate. Das Gupta walked gingerly

across the wet grass, picking his way carefully, not wanting to soil his highly polished shoes. He had a mild, almost academic manner. He apologised for having what he called 'a murderous sore throat – the beginnings of Asian 'flu, I'll bet'. His manner disguised his role as Virtus's hatchet man. Rosslyn looked at him warily. Bausch raised his hand. The authoritative gesture for Das Gupta to begin.

'The Feller problem isn't going to go away, Alan. You've heard nothing more, I suppose?'

Das Gupta looked at Bausch and *vice versa*. Rosslyn sensed that they had rehearsed the conversation beforehand.

'Predators are hovering,' Bausch said. 'We believe we're being looked at by hostile people who want to take us over – even close us down, Alan. This Feller thing may be part of a strategy to damage our reputation, to relieve us of a few clients, shall we say, operationally in midstream. We don't want to rock the boat. We need to know, we badly need to know, what the opposition's thinking.'

'There's the smell of Russian money hanging around Allegiance,' said Das Gupta.

'I wouldn't know about that,' said Rosslyn.

'We thought you might,' said Das Gupta.

'I'm afraid I don't,' said Rosslyn.

'So be it,' said Das Gupta. 'In any event there are other matters we need to settle. For example, the business of your signatures on Grant's applications for finance.'

'They're fakes,' said Rosslyn.

Das Gupta gave a dry laugh. He slipped a throat lozenge into his mouth and swallowed it with apparent difficulty. 'Our people have had the lab report. It's negative. Writing not your hand.'

'I've told you that all along.'

'We needed to be absolutely sure,' said Das Gupta.

'So who's responsible then?'

'The lab's pretty sure it was Feller's writing.'

'C'mon, you don't believe that.'

'I'm pretty sure.'

'*Pretty sure* isn't good enough.'

Das Gupta put his hand on Rosslyn's arm.

'It's good enough for us, Alan,' Bausch said quietly. 'Michael here thinks we should put it to good use. Let's allow Allegiance to hear we have mattress mice in Virtus. That we firmly believe you were part of a scheme to defraud the company. Look, whichever way you think of it, your participation in Feller's scam is, as it were, not disproved. We could burn you with heat from hell.'

'You wouldn't want that, Alan,' said Das Gupta.

'I can look after myself,' said Rosslyn.

'You have no alternative,' said Das Gupta. 'You're perfectly placed, aren't you?' A fit of coughing temporarily defeated him.

'Perfectly placed?' Rosslyn asked. 'For *what*?'

'To be our man under cover,' said Bausch.

'Inside Allegiance,' said Das Gupta, breathlessly.

'We can't disguise it will be difficult,' said Bausch. 'Even dangerous.'

'The Russians play rough,' said Das Gupta. 'If you think that Virtus is, shall we say, necessarily ruthless, then bear that in mind. The Russians take no prisoners. I say again – *no prisoners*.'

'Let me be clear about what it is you're asking,' Rosslyn said. 'You want me to go under cover –'

'Deep,' interrupted Bausch.

'– inside Allegiance. And pass back what?'

'Whatever you can find on Royals, Foxes, Prey or Vermin.'

'You know that one of my oldest friends is a senior man at Allegiance?'

'Ex-Detective Inspector Ronald Costley,' said Das Gupta, with the look of the cleverest boy in class.

'Ron's my friend. He isn't someone I'm going to cross.'

'Of course not,' said Bausch. 'I like Ron. That brings us to Part Two. We want you to soften him up. When you come back to us, we want you to bait a hook.'

'What are you saying?'

'We want you to bring Costley in with you. For us.'

'That'll be entirely up to him,' said Rosslyn.

'In God's good time,' said Bausch.

'And you can dangle one hell of a lot of money in front of him,' said Das Gupta.

'That's the kind of money we'll give you,' said Bausch. 'If we break Allegiance, we can pull off the reverse take-over. Now that Thynne's gone.'

'C'mon,' said Rosslyn, 'you're forgetting the Russians.'

'Even the bear has his price,' said Bausch. 'In this campaign we're the bulls. They have the claws. We have the horns.'

'– and the balls,' put in Das Gupta.

'What's your idea?' Rosslyn asked him.

'That in the not too distant future you become chief executive officer of New Allegiance within Virtus. A powerful position. With substantial bonuses attached. Go away and think things over. Come back to either of us whenever you want. Here –' He handed Rosslyn a business card. 'Call me any time of day or night.'

'Or me,' said Bausch. 'My wife considers you one of her favourites.'

Rosslyn did not savour the compliment. He'd only met Bausch's wife once, at the Virtus Christmas drinks party, when she had held his hand for rather too long.

'Give it forty-eight hours,' said Bausch. 'Meanwhile, continue looking for Feller. The word's out in the firm that you're in charge of finding him. It's good for morale that the staff think we care about their welfare on the personal level. By the way, I don't suppose the legal aid attaché at the US embassy has been in touch with you, has he?'

'No, he hasn't.'

'Let us know if he approaches you,' said Bausch.

'Why should he?' said Rosslyn.

'His people have been showing more than a casual interest in our operations,' said Bausch. 'If you see what I mean.'

'It's a matter of routine,' said Das Gupta.

Rosslyn was sure it wasn't.

'There's no need to be concerned,' said Das Gupta.

Bausch began to walk towards the garden exit. 'One more thing,' he added, almost as an afterthought. 'No need to continue with the morning briefings on Grant, Alan. We have other fish to fry right now. If you'll excuse me, I have a meeting with our MondoDei friends.'

Das Gupta hung back a moment. 'He's getting grief from Washington,' Das Gupta said, with an air of pity. 'But he has MondoDei to make life easier.'

'He has what?'

'His belief in the Almighty. MondoDei is very power-ful. Goes all the way to Downing Street, as well as to the First Family in the White House. We can be grateful that power is in the hands of God. That's what Bausch thinks. Oh, and by the way, so does Ron Costley. He's MondoDei too.'

'His religious beliefs are his affair.'

'Of course they are,' said Das Gupta. He began to cough again.

Rosslyn returned to the flat and telephoned Ann Chisholm, only to get her answering service.

He stared across the Euston Road. Some Japanese were hurrying along the pavement to the west. He thought of Mei and Terajima.

16

In the early afternoon sunlight, just after one o'clock Athens time, the Aeroflot Tupolev T-154 began its flight for Moscow. It was scheduled to arrive at Sheremetyevo airport at about four o'clock Moscow time.

At ease in her business-class seat, passenger Mitsuko Furyawa relished the power of the Tupolev's Kuznetsov NK-82 turbofans as they accelerated. Furyawa thought of Ono. She was a wonderful lover. 'You have a lot to tell me,' she had said, kissing her lips.

Ono had lain on top with her hands around Furyawa's throat and whispered: 'You remind me of me.'

'I can see it in your eyes. How many have you taken out?'

'Three in San Francisco. One in Yokohama. Four in Monte Carlo. One in Paris.'

'You use guns?'

'Blades mostly. Some have bled to death. I like to watch. And you – how many?'

'More than nine, more than you.'

Ono laughed. 'I could so easily kill you here and now.'

'I don't doubt it. And now?'

'Now I'll be back to haunt you.'

'Good. I'll tell you how you can reach me.'

'Reach you? I already have.'

'I want to e-mail you. Okay?'

'Okay by me. Maybe we could work together?'

'I think we could.'

The plane lifted from the runway, juddered and gathered speed. *Ono will be very useful to me.*

Passenger Furyawa found no pleasure in the menu offered to her by the steward. *It's a proven fact, something learned from experience, that one's work is best served if one has an empty stomach, which generally seems to sharpen the senses.* Fewer than thirty minutes into the flight, passenger Furyawa made herself comfortable and fell into a dreamless sleep.

17

While passenger Furyawa slept *en route* for Moscow,
Rosslyn e-mailed Mei:

Mei

I still have no idea where Grant might be or
why he has done a runner.

I've seen Ron Costley. He sends his love. As
you'd expect, he's being very helpful. There
are problems with Grant's Russian wife. The
marriage is in dire straits. She's got herself
involved with some Russian oligarch.

Worst of all, when I got home I found something unwelcome, very unwelcome, lying in the
stairwell outside the flat door. It turned out to
be a pretty lethal explosive device wrapped as
a Christmas gift.

To cut a long story short, I succeeded in defus-
ing it. I got Ann Chisholm to take the device to

her laboratory – you remember Ann. She's agreed to check it out. I should get the results fairly soon.

Meanwhile, I'm not returning to Claverton Street for the time being. Ron's allowed me to stay in a flat he owns. So don't bother phoning Claverton Street – you can get me on my mobile if you need. Otherwise the e-mail address remains the same.

This business scares me. I hate to be the one to say it, but I have a gut feeling that some-where Terajima's handwriting was on that Christmas gift. Could you do me a favour? Could you give me the number of someone at HK police HQ, someone we can trust, who could give me up-to-date résumés on the fol-lowing:

1. Gunther Jortzig, German, 30s
2. Horst Merkel, German, 30s
3. Jacques Geddes, South African, 30s

Whereabouts. Colleagues. The usual. I really would appreciate it. I don't want to start making enquiries about them here.

I saw Bausch today and a man called Das Gupta, the lawyer who Virtus employs. They have some scheme that I should work for Allegiance, in reality under cover for Virtus. I don't like the idea. Ironically Costley wants me to work for Allegiance. It will be a hopelessly compromising situation.

Everything's up in the air.

Except I'm longing for you. Will be with you in Hong Kong soon. I love you more than ever.

Always

Alan

As a result of the meeting with Das Gupta and Bausch, there were matters he needed to discuss with Costley. He had the proposals Bausch and Das Gupta had put to him on tape.

After he'd sent the e-mail to Mei, he called Costley, who accepted an invitation to dinner.

He was impatient for Mei's reply.

One of these days she'll mention my proposal.

He dreaded her saying No.

Mei replied to his e-mail:

Alan

I hope you're okay. I am very worried. You must put Terajima out of your mind. God damn his soul.

I will do what you ask about those names. I might even make some enquiries at headquarters about you and those creeps you work for.

Love to Ron. He won't have told you this. I

told him to keep it secret from you. But I called him and told him to keep an eye on you for me.

I love you.

Mei

18

If Mitsuko Furyawa felt a sense of irritation at being met at Sheremetyevo by the man she recognised as Nurmukhan, she gave no sign. It was enough that Nurmukhan greeted her as a stranger and treated her with respect. She could also tell that Nurmukhan found her attractive. The sleek winter coat and matching beret suited her. Artificial eyelashes provided additional glamour.

Nurmukhan led the new arrival to the car park and held open the door of a Mercedes. He eyed her slender legs. 'Where to?' he said.

'Straight to the location. Then we talk *matériel*.'

Nurmukhan set off towards central Moscow at speed. 'You look familiar. Have I seen you somewhere before?'

'To you people, we Orientals all look the same.'

'I guess you're right.'

'To we Orientals you Caucasians all look the same,' she told him. 'Not too fast,' she added.

Nurmukhan looked sideways with a smile. 'You need a gun?'

'Maybe.'

'What else?'

'I do the recce. Then I tell you. Maybe gas.'

'I can't get gas.'

'Then I leave.'

'You can't.'

'If you can't get gas, I don't do it.'

'You're the boss woman.'

'I know. You take me to the location. Where is it?'

'Gorokhovetsky Street. In the Basmannyy area. You want to look at the map?'

'No, I know it. We're looking at a city location?'

'Yes.'

'Then I'll need explosives. A motorbike. Courier ID. Leathers. Boots. You are going to have to shop.'

'Who's paying?'

Cunning Russian bastard. You expect me to get receipts? 'What d'you mean, who's paying? Your people are paying.'

'I can get explosives,' said Nurmukhan.

'Tell me about them. I need to know sourcing and technical specifications.'

'Sourcing?'

'Where they come from.'

'What is it to you where they come from?'

'Because I make the device. You don't. All you do is drive and shop. Tell me about the explosives. Talk it through. The source please?'

'The source is the State Scientific Research Institute. The main centre in Russia for the research and development of new explosives, equipment and technologies. It's located in Dzerzhinsk. Detonators from Murom instrument-making factory.'

'What make of explosive?'

'Sibirite, registered in Sweden from an ongoing project at the Kostomuksha mining complex.'

'And initiating devices?'

'All from the Novosibirsk factory, Iskra.'

'Who's your purchase source?'

'A senior officer from the body governing state regulation and supervision in the mining industries. Her speciality is explosives. Name of Dr Yelena Voloshina.'

'You trust this Dr Voloshina?'

'I should. She's my girlfriend.'

A mist was lowering across the Basmannyy area.

Good. The mist is good.

As they neared the location for the eventual assassination, she could sense the tension in Nurmukhan's voice. 'That's the building,' he said. 'Your target leaves there at seven tonight. A chauffeur-driven Mercedes V Class people carrier.'

'Is there CCTV cover?'

'Only inside the building there. None covering this specific area.'

'Armed guards?'

'Yes. A bodyguard and the chauffeur.'

'Yes, of course. Who's the target?'

'You destroy the Mercedes.'

'Is the vehicle armour-plated?'

'It may be.'

'Okay. Then it's explosives. I need a reliable motorbike, preferably a BMW, and all the other things. And I have to make a phone call. Let's find a landline. Maybe in a hotel?'

'Okay. You want to check into the hotel to change?'

'No. I do that in this car. Out of view.'

'Where are you staying the night?'

'Who said I was staying the night?'

'I thought we could do dinner,' said Nurmukhan. 'I know some good restaurants.'

'You're very kind. I'd like that. You can be my date. I'll choose the restaurant. It'll be my thank-you gift. Now take me to the National Hotel. I want you to be there at six-thirty. I'll be waiting for you in the Bar Aleksandrovsky.'

The Royal Meridien National Hotel in central Moscow is a five-minute walk from the Bolshoi Theatre.

Mitsuko Furyawa booked herself into a luxury suite equipped with satellite television and a personal safe. She made a reservation for dinner at the Restaurant Moskovsky for later that evening. She also booked and paid for a second room. This second room, she told the reservation clerk, would be for a business colleague, a Mr Kasimir Chernikov, who would be arriving later.

From her suite with the view of the Kremlin, she put through a call to a hotel in Antwerp and booked a room at the hotel De Witte Lelie on Keizerstraat. The receptionist said that yes, there was an envelope awaiting her collection. It was secure in the hotel safe.

Furyawa asked the receptionist to put the manager on the line. The manager was pleasant. 'We have been expecting your call,' he said. Presumably accustomed to the arcane ways of international diamond dealers, he told Furyawa to identify herself. Furyawa gave him the password: 99Ac/jho/554/zxa. The manager said it would take him about two minutes to collect the envelope and read over the contents. He was as good as his word. 'Perhaps you would like to take this down,' he said. Slowly he dictated the encrypted message:

Vv54 . . . 7.+±

Furyawa asked him to read it again.

He did so. 'We look forward to welcoming you here as arranged, Ms Furyawa.'

Simply put, the message meant that the diamonds that constituted her fee had been placed in the vault in the bland Grimbergen building on Schupstraat. The diamonds would lie there secure behind the 20-centimetre-thick bomb-proof main door of the vault.

Good. It was time to go. Six-thirty and Nurmukhan would be waiting for her in the Bar Aleksandrovsky.

She looked out of the window. The winter mist had drained the colour from Moscow. It seemed like a warning that snow was about to fall.

19

GOROKHOVETSKY STREET. MOSCOW

At seven that evening Gennadi Shafranik parked the Mercedes V Class people carrier outside the Forovaz headquarters building on Gorokhovetsky Street. This was his routine:

1. Arrive at seven.
2. Report to front desk.
3. Wait for the boss to appear with his bodyguard Tikhonov.
4. Leave for the Ilyushenko family mansion just outside the city.

A creature of routine, Shafranik drew on his overcoat and plodded across the street to the entrance of the Forovaz building.

The security guards at the front desk knew Shafranik well. Even so, the chauffeur was required to identify himself. Once he had done so, he told the guards to keep an eye on the Mercedes parked across the street – not that the falling snow made it easy. Shafranik hurried off to relieve himself.

Monitoring the Mercedes was something Shafranik would have done himself, for the security of the car was his responsibility. You had to be on continual alert for high-explosive booby traps or the presence of hired hit men. Like everyone else on the Ilyushenko payroll, Shafranik knew his boss was a potential target.

Last spring, the armoured gates of the Ilyushenko mansion had been booby-trapped with an explosive device. With Grigory Ilyushenko in the back of the Mercedes only feet away, it was a miracle the bomb failed to explode when Shafranik's predecessor opened the gates.

The next person to seek the attention of the Forovaz guards was a motorcycle courier delivering three packages, which required one of the guards to sign for their receipt. There were many such deliveries to the front desk each day.

The guard told the courier to remove his helmet and gloves whilst the other guard placed them on a small ramp. The courier, who kept his balaclava on, watched the guards attend to the business of examining the contents of the packages by X-ray. Then the senior of the two guards put the packages on the floor for the sniffer dog to go through its paces and confirm that the packages were free of dangerous substances. The dog reacted favourably. The junior guard read the name of the addressee on the three packages. Marked with the label of an Italian bank, each bore the name of Grigory Ilyushenko. The guard telephoned Grigory's personal assistant on the uppermost floor and told her that the packages were ready for her to collect.

The courier muttered his thanks, drew on his motorcycle helmet and heavy protective gloves, and walked nonchalantly towards the exit beneath the icon of St Theophan the Recluse.

The doors opened automatically, then closed behind him. The senior guard followed the progress of the departing courier and watched him until the figure became a blur in the snow. He heard the muffled sound of a motorbike start up across the street. Then he peered briefly at the indistinct shape of the Mercedes parked opposite.

When he returned to the desk, his colleague told him that the Ilyushenkos were on the way down in the lift.

At the same moment Shafranik the driver reappeared with a look of satisfaction on his face. The senior guard told him that there had been a change of plan.

Shafranik would have additional passengers on board. As well as Mikhail and Grigory Ilyushenko, he would be driving Grigory's wife Tatyana and their daughter Galina to the private family compound on the outskirts of the city. Shafranik muttered some words of complaint about the weather conditions and poor visibility. His time, he grumbled, was no longer his own; tonight he was also on personal protection duty at the Ilyushenko mansion, just another pair of wide shoulders in a suit among several dozen. The Ilyushenkos were hosting a reception for graduates of the Institute of Management at the Academy of Sciences. The guests would include many of Russia's scientific-industrial elite. At about the same time Tatyana would be giving a small party for Galina's seventh birthday.

The lift brought Shafranik's passengers down from the uppermost floor. Mikhail Ilyushenko accompanied his brother Grigory. Both men wore dark overcoats.

Immediately behind them was Grigory Ilyushenko's

bodyguard Tikhonov, a large man whose bearing revealed something of his military background. Tatyana carried a bag of birthday presents that some of the staff had given to Galina, who was in a fairy's outfit complete with a diamanté crown, a red velvet cloak and magic wand.

Tikhonov gestured to Shafranik that it was time to leave. Shafranik walked a few paces ahead of the others to the exit. One of the armed guards removed a handgun unobtrusively from his shoulder holster and covered the departure of the party as they crossed the street.

Shafranik unlocked the Mercedes. He held open the rear door for the Ilyushenkos, who got into the car. Finally Tikhonov got in, easing himself into the front passenger seat. Shafranik took his position behind the wheel and turned the ignition key.

With that the bomb exploded.

Mikhail Ilyushenko found that he could not recall whether it was the roaring in his ears or the tumultuous waterfall of glass that made him realise he was staring death in the face.

The explosion threw him sideways and away from his brother in the seat next to him. The force of the bomb attached to the motorbike parked nearby seemed to suck open the car doors, and the flying fragments of the bike cut into his arm and face. Not that he remembered the savagery – the blast had knocked him unconscious.

The security guard was the only person who saw the unfolding of the horror from start to finish.

Seconds before, once he had satisfied himself that everyone was safely inside the Mercedes, he had returned his handgun to its holster and had begun to walk back across the reception area to rejoin his companion at the desk. Then he heard the explosion and turned to see the windows of the building's ground-floor façade splinter and collapse. His face was buffeted by an icy wind. He was aware of a strange silence, followed by the screams from across the road.

Wading through the debris of the office building's exit doors, he found himself peering into the cloud of black smoke and a rising wall of flames across the street. Chunks of metal, shards of glass and burning paper lay across the roadway. He stumbled through the snow towards the wreckage.

His companion joined him, running towards the smoke. It did not occur to either of them to return to the building to fetch fire extinguishers. Not that the extinguishers, at this point, would have been of any use. The two men followed the sounds of the moaning across Gorokhovetsky Street.

They saw Mikhail Ilyushenko lying several metres from the wreckage. He was sprawled on his front, his face in a pool of blood spreading across the snow. His legs were twisted beneath him. One of his arms had been partially severed. Soot drenched his smouldering clothes, and as the snow continued falling on him, the burning fabric hissed and spat.

Both of the guards thought that Mikhail Ilyushenko was dead. But he was still alive, his chest heaving for breath, blood pouring from his mouth.

Grigory Ilyushenko's legs stuck out from a section of the car at some forty-five degrees. The rest of his body, from the waist up, had been crushed. He must have died instantaneously. The hefty frame of the bodyguard Tikhonov lay spread-eagled on mounds of bloodied debris. His face was unrecognisable.

Both Tatyana and Galina were dead. Galina's costume had caught fire and she had been burned alive. Tatyana's legs had been crushed but not as severely as her head. Her hair had been burned off. Her blackened features were unrecognisable. But it was as if the greatest violence of the explosion had been meted out to Shafranik. He had been decapitated. Shafranik's head lay in the street like a punctured football.

One of the guards ran back to the building, where he was confronted by a terrified group of onlookers. He had to shout to make his pleas heard for someone to call the police and doctors.

In the panic that ensued, someone from Forovaz saw fit to put through a call to St Petersburg and tell Pyotr, the third of the Ilyushenko brothers, the news that Grigory was dead, along with Tatyana and Galina and two of the staff.

The caller was also able to report that Pyotr's brother Mikhail was fighting for his life, but reckoned it was unlikely he would survive.

Pyotr Ilyushenko left for Moscow in despair.

The death of Grigory was a hammer blow. Grigory had controlled the family fortune like a feudal baron. If Mikhail died, then control would pass to him, and his life would change for ever.

In the midst of his despair and fear, Pyotr nonetheless felt a flicker of excitement that so much power might fall into his hands.

20

Mitsuko Furyawa was well satisfied with the completion of her task.

The sophisticated radio-control device had triggered the explosive attached to the BMW motorbike. She had heard its deafening report from a safe distance and immediately left the area with Nurmukhan bound for the Royal Meridien National Hotel. Neither Furyawa nor Nurmukhan knew the extent of the damage or the number of casualties. She had changed out of her motor-cycle courier's clothing and left Nurmukhan to dispose of it.

Furyawa returned to her hotel suite and relaxed in the hot water of the bathtub in a cloud of soapy foam. Afterwards she wrapped herself in the white towel robe provided by the hotel. Lying on the bed, she filed the fingernails of both her hands to sharp points and watched television until her rendezvous with Nurmukhan in the Bar Aleksandrovsky. She reckoned it was still too soon for news of the explosion to feature on the local television newscasts. But in this she was wrong.

The state TV station RTR and the public TV station ORT both ran early reports of the explosion in Gorokhovetsky Street. There had been more than one fatality. Several seriously injured people had been rushed to hospital.

Who are the dead?

Is my target amongst them?

Or is he one of the injured?

She dressed carefully, applied some light make-up, including pale lip gloss, and splashed herself with Dioressence. *Pretty as a picture.*

It was now approaching nine o'clock in Moscow, six o'clock in London.

21

EUSTON ROAD. LONDON

Mei e-mailed him:

Alan

Good news. I've gone one better. Hope you're pleased. Jortzig, Merkel and Geddes are being sought worldwide for a whole range of crimes.

Each has very substantial financial resources. FBI offers huge sums as rewards for info leading to their arrest.

Bad news. I might have guessed – all are seriously suspected of having had recent contact with K-P T.

Alan, what the hell are you doing? Please, if you love me as much as I love you, back off K-P T.

Can't put my contact's name at Police HQ in

e-mail. You'll appreciate why. Anyway, she's very pretty. Your type!!

Mei
xxx

Rosslyn replied:

Mei

I'm really grateful. Thanks.

I'd sort of guessed at the K-P T connection. It's what I both want and don't want to hear.

I love you

Alan
xxx

He called Costley and confirmed the time of his dinner appointment at the Regent Chinese restaurant.

Costley said he would be with someone he wanted Rosslyn to meet. Rather pointedly, so it seemed to Rosslyn, Costley declined to give the person a name. All he would say was that the man who would join them was an American.

That evening, Rosslyn found Costley seated at a window table of the restaurant. 'The American will join us in the flat a little later,' Costley explained. He handed Rosslyn a copy of the menu. 'We've got time for dinner. I've already ordered. Your turn.'

Rosslyn gave his order to the waitress. He leaned

towards Costley. 'Who's your American?'

'Bernal Schiff. The legal aid attaché at the US embassy. He's meeting us with two of his colleagues. He's a worried man. So am I.' Costley was sweating. 'I have to tell you the news from Moscow,' he continued. 'Sometime after seven p.m. their time a bomb exploded outside the Forovaz headquarters in the central area of the city. The extent of the damage isn't clear yet, but it was considerable. Paramedics pronounced Grigory Ilyushenko dead at the scene. His brother, Mikhail Ilyushenko, is in intensive care. No one's certain about his chances of survival. There are other casualties. No one has any idea who was responsible. God knows where all this leaves Allegiance. My bosses are shitting themselves.'

Costley's anxiety seemed almost tangible. This was unfamiliar territory to Costley, Institutional Man, who talked of Old England, service, decency and duty. Costley understood the machinery of investigation; he was familiar with its techniques. But warfare between firms like Virtus and Allegiance and the poison of new kinds of treachery and violence in Moscow were beyond his experience.

This warfare was quite different from the internecine squabbles of the police and the government security services, even the Customs and Excise undercover investigation departments.

For the first time in the years of their friendship, Rosslyn found himself pitying Costley in his confusion and fatigue. Costley said: 'What did I tell you?'

'Seems you're right.'

'What's started is the war of the detectives. We're in it up to our necks. And what we have now is a jockeying for power and position fuelled by wealth from ill-gotten gains. Here in London. Now in Moscow. What gets me is that more than one professional killer's at work. Are they working separately or together? Who's calling the shots? Who's paying the fees? Who's providing the materiel?'

'Let's see what Ann Chisholm has to tell us.'

'She's taking too long, Alan.'

'Hang on,' said Rosslyn. 'She'll deliver. Meanwhile, first take a look at this.' He handed Costley the copy of the secret transcript he'd made of his meeting with Bausch and Das Gupta. 'I've highlighted the relevant points.'

Costley scrutinised the transcript. The veins in his hands were twitching.

The waitress set their dinner on the table along with two glasses of beer and a bottle of mineral water.

There was a long silence.

Rosslyn looked into Costley's weary eyes. 'You can't hide it from me. You're scared. What else, Ron?'

'The bomb in Moscow, Alan. Are you thinking Terajima?'

'Tell me what you think.'

'Could be,' said Costley.

'Could be isn't enough.'

Costley leaned forwards with both hands on the table. 'Don't lose your rag with me, Alan.'

'I'm not,' Rosslyn said calmly. 'If we're thinking Terajima, he'll have upped and gone by now.'

'That what you'd do?' Costley asked.

'That's what I'd do. I'd get the hell out of Moscow as soon as possible.'

'But Terajima would have had to have a Moscow point of contact.' Costley poured sparkling water into his glass of wine. 'I've found someone. If we can get a purchase on him, we may be ahead of the game. He's been in business in northern France. A man called Nurmukhan.'

22

Nurmukhan had sought solace in too much vodka in the Bar Aleksandrovsky. 'Grigory Ilyushenko is dead,' he told Furyawa. 'His brother Mikhail is wounded, probably fatally. They don't expect him to live till morning. You also disposed of his wife, his young daughter and two of his personal staff.'

Furyawa stared at his companion. She brought her sharp fingernails to her mouth and pondered.

Nurmukhan's speech was slurred. And when Furyawa suggested a minor change in the plans for the evening – namely that Nurmukhan might like to share a dinner for two in her room – the Russian accepted with pleasure. Leaving the Bar Aleksandrovsky, Furyawa took her companion by the hand. He was unsteady on his feet.

When they reached the room, dinner had been laid out on the table. Furyawa turned down the lights. 'Thank you for all you've done for me,' she said. She kissed him lightly on the cheek and he turned his mouth to hers.

'I want you,' he said.

'I want you too,' she said. 'But dinner first. Here –' She lifted the bottle of champagne from the ice bucket. 'Open it. Oh, and tell me this – who commissioned me?'

'I can't tell you.'

'Please tell me.'

'It's more than my life's worth.'

'How much do you want me?'

'I want you, yes. But please, I can't tell you.'

'You can't tell me who's behind the job?'

'You're a professional. You know I can't.'

'But I want to know.'

She took him in her arms and slid her hands beneath his left armpit.

'Take off your shoulder holster,' she said. Her hand wandered to between his legs and she toyed with him. 'Don't you trust me?'

'I don't trust anyone,' he said.

'Me neither,' she said. 'Take off that holster and throw it on the bed.'

He smiled at her. And then did what she had asked.

'Turn on the TV. There were news items about our success earlier. I'm going to have a bath.'

'You want me to run the water for you?'

She kissed him again, this time on the lips. 'Do you have a condom?'

Nurmukhan produced his wallet and showed Furyawa the packets.

'You think of everything,' she said.

'I'm getting stiff,' he said.

'Where I come from we call it *nice cramp*.'

If Nurmukhan had entertained doubts about Mitsuko Furyawa's gender they now seemed dispelled.

Nurmukhan's eyes were watery. 'We have a problem.'

'We do? Tell me.'

'You were supposed to kill Pyotr Ilyushenko.'

'How was I to know who he was, this Pyotr Ilyushenko? What's the problem? *Why* did they want this Pyotr Ilyushenko killed?'

'All I can tell you is –'

'Spit it out. Otherwise you don't get to shaft me.'

'They're holding back part of your fee. They're not paying you what you asked for.'

'They told you that?'

'Sure. They told me not to tell you. They reckon you'll find out when you take delivery of your fee.'

She thought of the diamonds in the vault of the bland Grimbergen building on Schupstraat, secure behind the twenty-centimetre-thick bomb-proof door.

'You still have those Indonesian friends of yours on standby in France?'

'Sure.'

'They're still in the same place?'

'Sure. They'll do anything for me.'

'And for me?'

'Sure. They're desperate. I told you that.'

'Yes, you did. Now I'll make love to you.'

He grinned.

'I want you . . . to tell me . . . now. Who wants Pyotr Ilyushenko dead?'

'No, please. That I cannot say. I won't survive in Moscow if I say. I have a family here, you understand.'

'You must think of me as family. Give me the name. They're people here in Moscow?'

'Yes.'

'You're lying to me.'

'No. If they weren't I'd tell you.'

She lowered her chin and ran her tongue across her lips. 'Baby, I'm going to persuade you very gently. I want you smelling sweet and clean. Let's bathe together.' She handed him the champagne bottle. 'Bring me a glass to the bathroom.'

Whilst Nurmukhan opened the champagne bottle, Furyawa went to the bathroom. 'Here –' she called to him. 'Catch.' She tossed him a towel robe. 'Undress too. I'll call you when I'm ready.'

She turned the bath taps on full. Then she stripped down to her underwear and waited for the bath to fill. Once the bath was almost full, she called out: 'Come –'

Now naked except for the bathrobe, Nurmukhan opened the bathroom door. The robe fell open at the waist. As he was carrying a champagne glass in each hand, his stiffness was exposed.

Furyawa slid her hand around his testicles and squeezed gently. 'Get in the water.'

He set the champagne glass on the side of the bath and did as she told him, sliding down into the bath.

She knelt beside the bath and put the edge of the champagne glass to his lips. 'Drink,' she said. 'Drink.' She kept on pouring until he choked on the champagne. Then she drove the glass against his teeth until it splintered and went on pressing the jagged edge down deep into his throat. His arms flayed at her as she pressed his head beneath the water. Then she released the pressure and lifted his mouth to just above the surface.

He looked at her with pleading eyes, blood and water flowing from his mouth. '*Please*. Don't kill me.'

'Who commissioned me?' she said quietly.

He shook his head in protest and then raised his hand to strike her in the face. As his clenched fist was in mid-swing she caught hold of his wrist.

'Who?'

'No.'

'Names.'

'I don't know.'

'C'mon.'

'It came from Switzerland.'

'Where?'

'Geneva.'

'What did they pay you?'

'Half a million US dollars.'

'Who paid you?'

'I don't know. It wasn't his own name.'

'Whose name wasn't his own?'

The pressure of Furyawa's sharpened fingernails against his throat was so strong he could barely speak. 'I don't want to kill you, Nurmukhan. You have to give me a name.'

'I can't.'

'You can't what?'

'I can't tell you.' Then he murmured a name.

'Say again,' she screamed in fury. Nurmukhan began to retch and seemed to be repeating names that were wholly unfamiliar to her. '*Emmmsss.*' Or '*Mmmmsss.*' His face was turning purple. His eyes began to roll. The splintered base of the glass had wedged itself sideways in his mouth. Nurmukhan was unable to cough up the glass fragments he'd swallowed.

*

154

Later Furyawa e-mailed Ono:

> You should have been with me. I used a bro-
> ken glass in the mouth.
> Makes me think of pomegranates and you.
> I want to see you.

Ono e-mailed back:

> Wish I was here in your hands.
> Make it back to Athens when you can.
> I have pomegranates.
> Want u 2

23

HOLLAND PARK. LONDON

In London, the wind was bitter as Rosslyn and Costley left the Chinese restaurant for the appointment with the American.

The woman who approached them must have been waiting for some time. She wore a muffler and dark green winter coat against the cold. 'Mr Costley – Mr Rosslyn? I'm Jana Turner, United States embassy, assistant to Bernal Schiff. We have a car waiting for you in Great Portland Street.'

'But Mr Schiff is due to meet us at our place.'

'We're sorry. Bernal would like to meet with you at his apartment in Holland Park. He has a colleague with him from Quantico. We have a car waiting for you. Is that okay?'

'If that's what you people want,' said Rosslyn.

They followed the woman to the waiting car.

The Holland Park apartment was decorated in the style of a hotel suite. There were oil paintings of Cape Cod on the walls and on the mantelpiece a small signed photograph of the President and First Lady. One of His Holiness the Pope. There was little evidence to suggest that Bernal Schiff or anyone else actually lived there.

Schiff was a tall man in his fifties. The thick lenses of his glasses magnified his bright blue eyes. 'You've already met Jana,' he said, and introduced Ron Costley to his colleague from Quantico, Sandra Holmes. Schiff had the manner of an elderly and patriarchal university professor. He was wearing an expensive British tailored suit. This was by no means a stereotypical FBI man. *God knows who you are*, thought Rosslyn. *Or who your masters are, in Washington or anywhere else.*

Holmes was a large woman with narrow blue eyes and short red hair. Her quizzical expression seemed fixed. Schiff explained that Holmes was 'attached to the National Center for the Analysis of Violent Crime (NCAVC).'

Schiff said: 'We've waited a little longer than we'd have liked to talk to you guys. We think we might now be ready to work to our mutual advantage.' He gave Rosslyn a direct look. 'May I ask you, Mr Rosslyn – perhaps I can call you Alan – may I ask you, Alan, whether any of your people at Virtus have raised my name?'

'Yes, they have. Pretty well all the Masters, as we call them, have suggested I keep clear of you.'

'They've also insisted that Alan stays clear of me,' Costley added.

'Of course,' said Schiff. 'You're rivals. That's maybe one reason why you're here. Companions in treachery.' He smiled distantly. 'That tars all of us with the same brush. It seems we have a good basis for co-operation. I think we three want much the same thing.' He turned to Sandra Holmes. 'Ms Holmes, by way of a beginning I'd like you to show our colleagues the profiles.'

'Sure,' said Holmes. She opened up a laptop on the table in the centre of the room. 'Maybe you'd like me to explain that the profiles are of men we're actively seeking on an international basis.' She hesitated a moment. 'And, Mr Rosslyn, we'd like an assessment of your friend Mei Lim.'

'She isn't involved in this.'

The anger in Rosslyn's voice took Holmes aback. 'But she knew Klaas-Pieter Terajima at first hand.'

'You don't have to tell me.'

Holmes said: 'I can explain the situation later.'

There was an awkward silence.

'I think we'd better look at the profiles,' Schiff said.

They turned their attention to the computer screen.

Holmes said: 'We're going to look at four people. First, I'll give you background. Second, I'll explain the links they have with each other. I'd really appreciate your input. Here we go –'

She played some edited video sequences of a man walking on a beach. She began her commentary in staccato tones: 'Gunther Jortzig is a German national. That's him carrying a surfboard. He's aged thirty-five.' A dog was running ahead of the muscular German. The man's posture was stiff and straight-backed. 'He's wanted for allegedly killing a judge in Munich. He's believed to work in partnership with Horst Merkel, aged thirty-three, also a German national . . . They've been known to travel as dealers in antiquities.'

The next video clips showed a prematurely grey-haired man of stocky build presiding over a stall at an antiques market.

'Merkel, you can see,' Holmes said, 'has three fingers missing from his left hand. Formerly a musician, he's fluent in Russian and may be travelling throughout central and eastern Europe. He's thought to be involved in narcotics distribution. Like Jortzig, Merkel's known to deal in diamonds.'

The third sequence of video clips showed a woman of slender build with dark hair, possibly a Eurasian, seated at an open-air café in Paris.

'We're looking at a transsexual, known as Patsy Nicholson de Thwart or Rachelle Pienaar, originally Jacques Geddes, a South African. Geddes is a gynaecologist, anaesthetist and physician. He's a career criminal and master of assumed identities. Originally a semi-professional musician, he's known to be a supplier of hallucinatory drugs. He's thought to have undergone cosmetic surgery to alter Caucasian features to Asian. Specialises in trading in body parts. So that's the first three . . .'

Schiff interrupted. 'The fourth person will be familiar to you,' he said for the benefit of Rosslyn and Costley. 'In this instance, we're looking at Takashi Sakamoto.'

'Otherwise known as Klaas-Pieter Terajima,' said Holmes. 'You know his background as well as we do . . .'

'I do,' said Rosslyn. 'So does Ron.'

The video clips showed Terajima in Hong Kong, Beijing and London. The text running across the base of the images from right to left read:

MULTIPLE MURDER | CONSPIRACY TO COMMIT MUR-
DER | RACKETEERING INFLUENCED AND CORRUPT
ORGANISATIONS (RICO) | CONSPIRACY TO COMMIT
EXTORTION |

'Erroneously reported missing by British and US law
enforcement agencies in the South China Sea.'

'You say *erroneously*,' Rosslyn said. 'Do you know
where he is right now?'

'We think he's somewhere in Europe.'

'Has he been in London recently?'

'Possibly, yes.'

'And the other three?'

'We think the Germans may also have been in London
recently,' Schiff smiled. 'We finally decided to convene
this meeting because, in our judgement, the hour has
come to act in order to prevent a wave of assassination
initiated by these men. Imagine a web. At the outer cir-
cumference are Jortzig, Merkel, Geddes. At the centre is
Terajima.' Here he paused and looked at Holmes. 'Let
me outline matters in general. If you wish to interject,
Ms Holmes, please feel free to do so.'

'Thank you, sir.'

Schiff said: 'Washington is expressing increasing anxiety about the burgeoning activities of private sector
intelligence agencies both here in London and at home in
the United States. We have a raft of concerns, such as the
crimes referred to in the profiles. But here let me empha-
sise, it is the use of such persons by premier security
agencies in London and in Moscow that's giving rise to
real worry. They are damaging our operations.
Washington wants to hit back. That's why we're here.

We're going to strike, and hard.' He drove his clenched right fist into the open palm of his left. 'You'll have already deduced that the men whose details you've studied constitute a kind of syndicate or cadre. We know that they're all dangerous, among the most dangerous of international criminals.'

Holmes said: 'They can call on unlimited funds to prosecute their endeavours. These resources, it's become clear to us, have pretty much rendered ineffective any investigation of them by police forces and specialist police units across Europe.'

Schiff said: 'Let's say, in strictest secrecy – for reasons we needn't dwell upon right now – authority's been given to bring each of these men to justice. Or, if needs be, kill them.' Still smiling pleasantly, Schiff let these last few words hang. 'I think it's time for some refreshment,' he continued. 'There's tea and coffee. Beer, wine or something harder. Bourbon perhaps?'

Jana Turner wheeled a refreshments trolley to the table.

'Shall we help ourselves, ladies and gentlemen?' Schiff said.

While the others helped themselves from the trolley, Rosslyn took Sandra Holmes aside.

'You said you want an assessment of Mei Lim?'

'Anything that might be helpful in finding Terajima.'

'She's no longer in contact with him, or he with her.'

'You're quite sure?'

'I am,' said Rosslyn. 'Yes.'

He left Holmes fiddling with her laptop and walked to the windows, looking out on to the street through a gap in the curtains. Schiff joined him.

'I want you to meet a Russian . . .' Schiff was saying. 'Name of Sergei Dmitriev . . .'

Rosslyn heard Schiff's agitated voice. Something was wrong. Somewhere he heard a door close. 'Sergei's working for us under cover . . .' Raindrops streaked across the window. A couple hand-in-hand passed by in the street outside, the wind tugging at their shared umbrella. '. . . with the Ilyushenkos in Moscow . . . Maybe tomorrow . . .'

'I don't want Mei involved,' Rosslyn said. He was staring across the street at a black car. He heard Holmes say: 'We're all involved.'

'Sandra's right,' said Schiff. He touched Holmes on the shoulder. 'Why don't you have a brief word with Mr Rosslyn in private?'

'Sure,' said Holmes.

'Use my office along the corridor,' Schiff said, hurrying from the room.

Rosslyn turned away from the window and followed Holmes to Schiff's office.

Now it was Sandra Holmes who showed unease. 'We think that Terajima will try to re-establish contact with Mei.'

'You could be right,' said Rosslyn.

'We want her to be prepared for that eventuality.'

Rosslyn disguised his fear. 'Mei can handle herself.'

'Has she been in touch with him?'

'For God's sake, of course she hasn't.'

'And she would have told you if he had contacted her?'

Rosslyn turned on her: 'What do you think?' He sat down heavily in the chair behind Schiff's desk. He noticed files open on the desk and a legal pad by the telephone. Holmes was standing by the window surreptitiously looking outside. She was saying: 'If there's more you'd like to tell us . . .'

Glancing at the legal pad, Rosslyn read the note that someone, presumably Schiff, had scribbled in a hurry. *Collection* and a time. He glanced at his watch. The collection time was two minutes ago.

'You realise that while Terajima remains alive,' Holmes was saying, 'Mei's life's in danger?'

'She's not the only one,' said Rosslyn. 'Let's go back and join the others . . .' He interrupted Schiff, who was talking to Costley about Dmitriev in the doorway to the main room. In the hallway, out of earshot, Rosslyn called Chisholm. She sounded preoccupied, her voice muffled and, unusually for her, offhand. She gave him the result of her analysis of the device that Rosslyn had disabled in Claverton Street. The pattern of the device was familiar to her. The handwriting of the assemblage pointed, almost without doubt, to the mind and hand of Klaas-Pieter Terajima. 'Or, you can be fairly certain, to one or more of his associates to whom he's imparted lethal technical data.'

Alerted by the entrance bell, Schiff came into the hallway.

'Your collection?' Rosslyn said.

Schiff gave a brief smile and opened the heavy door.

Rosslyn stared at the man in the doorway whose eyes were blank. The man showed no sign of recognition. It was Grant Feller.

24

Rosslyn e-mailed Mei:

Mei

Terajima has to be alive. There are reliable people who will give me the means to go for him. All I need is the opportunity.

I've met with a man called Bernal Schiff, some former legal attaché i.e. FBI.

Thanks to him I've found Grant. The news is bad. His elderly father has been killed. The police are dealing with it. So far the thing's a real mystery. According to Schiff, Grant was found in an abandoned tunnel in North London used by vagrants. They were the ones who found his father's body. He'd been shot dead. Grant had been shot and left for dead. He was stretchered out and taken to hospital, the Royal Free in Hampstead. The doctors reckoned he wouldn't live. But they operated and he survived. The tragedy is that he's suffered brain damage. He's lost his speech and can only communicate by writing notes. He can't remember who attacked him in the tunnel or what happened to his father and can't explain what he was doing there. I guess they thought that if Grant saw me his memory might click in. Well. It didn't. The sight of him was very sad.

Schiff's people have arranged a place for Grant in a private nursing home. Schiff took the line with me that there are things, what he calls connections, that I will never understand. He means MondoDei.

He gave me a copy of extracts from Yeltsin's farewell speech from way back and said that Russia's run by gangsters. 'You'll find out soon enough,' he said. The man speaks in riddles. 'You've no idea what the hell is happening,' he said. He enjoys keeping people in the dark.

Please will you do two more things for me? Get me anything you can on a man called Sergei Dmitriev. Background and so on.

Please also make sure your flat's secure. If you have any reason, any reason at all to be concerned, lift the phone and call me. Trust me. I know what I'm doing Mei. This is for both of us. Can't wait till Christmas when there'll be a big surprise for you!!

All my love

Alan

Mei replied:

Alan

Yes. I'll do what you ask. I've got a surprise for you! Break the rule! Call me day or night.

All my love

Mei

Rosslyn called Mei:

'Have you guessed.'
'No.'
'What do you think?'
'Tell me –'
'I'm expecting our baby.'

New Moon

This is an extraordinarily important day for me. I wish to speak more personally than I normally do. I ask you for forgiveness, because many of our dreams have not materialised, because what we believed would be easy turned out to be painfully difficult. I ask you to forgive me for not realising the hopes of all those people who believed that we would be able to leap from the greyness and stagnation of our totalitarian past into a gleaming, rich and civilised future at one attempt.

I am going. I have done all I could. I am not quitting because of my health, but because of all the problems. A new generation will now take my place, the generation of those who can do more than I could and do it better.

I have signed the decree placing the duties of the president of Russia in the hands of Prime Minister Vladimir Vladimirovich Putin.

BORIS YELTSIN
FAREWELL SPEECH

25

Pyotr Ilyushenko kept a vigil at his brother Mikhail's bedside.

The Ilyushenko family's icon depicting St Theophan the Recluse had been placed on a shelf near the bed. The air in the room was thick with the scent of lilies.

On the afternoon of the murders, no fewer than four ambulances had rushed to Gorokhovetsky Street. Mikhail, the sole survivor, was taken to the hospital known affectionately as the Sklif. Here he was stretchered into the operating theatre.

Pyotr, Mikhail and Grigory's younger brother, arrived at the hospital from St Petersburg. He was shocked to see his brother's condition. The doctors' prognosis was far from good. It had become clear that Mikhail was paralysed from the waist down. He had lost one eye and the wreckage of his left arm required amputation. The burns looked terrible. They had disfigured Mikhail's face. It was a mercy that, as far as the doctors could ascertain at this stage, no damage had been done to Mikhail's brain functions.

As four armed guards kept a twenty-four-hour watch outside Mikhail's room, numerous telephone calls interrupted Pyotr's bedside vigil. He took each calmly in turn. A senior murder investigation officer from the police asked when his men could visit Mikhail to question him.

'I don't know,' said Pyotr. 'His life is hanging by a thread.'

'What do the doctors say?'

'He's dying.'

'I'm sorry,' said the police officer. 'But you understand how urgent it is we speak to him.'

'Talk to me instead,' said Pyotr.

'We want to do that anyway.'

'Then you know where to find me. I'll be here for the foreseeable future.'

The police officer said he would show up in an hour or two.

Konstantin Krivisky, who was Grigory and Mikhail's closest associate at Forovaz, also phoned and Pyotr gave him news of his brother's condition.

Pyotr tried to think about what the unconscious Mikhail would now want of Krivisky and he heard himself say:

'Konstantin, you have to step into my brother's shoes for the time being.'

Krivisky said he would be pleased to do so. 'If there's anything else I can do, you only have to ask me.'

'I know I can count on you,' said Pyotr. 'When we know where we are, we'll have a full meeting.'

'And you – how are you, Pyotr?'

'Me? Oh, I'm fine.'

Pyotr stared at his brother's broken body. His fury

towards those responsible for what happened on Gorokhovetsky Street numbed him. His eyes filled with tears. Staring at the icon by his brother's bedside he prayed to Almighty God that 'I, Pyotr Ilyushenko, be given the strength to control my rage'.

He turned his thoughts to the organisation of the triple family funeral. It would be small and private. He dreaded the funeral as he dreaded having to tell Mikhail that they had lost Tatyana and Galina. Grigory was the only Ilyushenko brother to have married. Pyotr would have no grieving widows, parents or close relatives to console: only Mikhail – if he survived. It was a mercy his parents were no longer alive. The loss of Grigory and little Galina would have broken Mother's heart.

Of the intimate friends to whom Pyotr spoke from the hospital, two broke down in grief. The first was Mikhail's mistress Viktoria Feller, who with her daughter Anna was now in seclusion and under armed protection at Mikhail's London mansion in Kensington Palace Gardens. Viktoria had already been placed on the Forovaz payroll as Mikhail's personal assistant. Mikhail had personally made the appointment only hours before the bomb exploded in Gorokhovetsky Street. When Pyotr telephoned the news to Viktoria in London, he heard her howl in pain. The line went dead. The second woman he called was his own mistress Elke Wedemeier.

Elke's husband Jean-Pascal was a member of Switzerland's Bundesrat or Federal Council – the member responsible for finance. Elke lived her life in the shadow of the more famous and influential Jean-Pascal. With Elke working in Moscow and Jean-Pascal in Switzerland, the Wedemeiers' marriage was a strained affair. Soon after Elke was appointed a Forovaz director, she became Pyotr's mistress. She had struggled to control her weeping. 'Mikhail needs you to be strong, Pyotr,' she said. 'You mustn't exhaust yourself. You must get some sleep. Come to me tonight. I love you. Let me look after you.'

'Maybe I will,' said Pyotr. 'I've asked Konstantin to see to things at Forovaz.'

'Keep your head,' said Elke. 'Control that anger of yours. Thank God that Mikhail isn't dead. You'll have to take charge of everything now.'

'I know,' said Pyotr. 'Maybe you could help with the funeral arrangements. Talk to Konstantin.'

'Anything you want. Anything.'

'I want something special read when we bury Grigory. It's something Mother taught us. She made us learn it by heart. The lines come at the end of Chekhov's *Three Sisters*. "Time will pass, and we shall depart for ever. We shall be forgotten. But our sufferings will turn to joy for those who live after us. Peace and happiness will dwell on earth, and people living now will be blessed and well spoken of."' He stumbled over the last few words and sobbed.

'Don't cry, Pyotr,' said Elke. 'Come to me tonight.'

'Okay, I'll come to your place tonight,' said Pyotr.

He looked at his brother, who was attached to myriad wires and tubes. 'Something else, Elke. Arrange for Forovaz to make substantial payments to the families of Shafranik and Tikhonov. Have Andrei Ilyukhin or Yaroslav Dorenko arrange their funerals according to the wishes of the dead men's families. I'll see you later.'

'I'll be waiting for you,' said Elke.

Pyotr called Konstantin Krivisky and asked him if he would be good enough to arrange the triple family funeral. He told him to make sure it was kept private.

When Pyotr next answered the telephone, the caller announced himself as Oleg Chebotarev. Chebotarev was calling from his desk at the offices of the radical democratic newspaper *Moskovsky Komsomolets*. Pyotr knew Chebotarev's reputation as an astute investigative journalist. He could be relied upon to write sympathetically about the family. Pyotr made a note of Chebotarev's number and told him he would call him back later. Then he told the hospital switchboard that, for the time being, he would take no further calls.

Pyotr had never enjoyed a close relationship with either of his brothers. He shared none of their asceticism. He was heavily built, with the broad shoulders of the wrestler he had been as a teenager. Now in his mid-thirties, he was prone to over-eating and bingeing on vodka, and his muscles had mainly turned to flab. But one thing no one could deny: the family fortune had been Pyotr's creation. Watching over his disabled brother, he wondered what the future held in store. For Mikhail. For Forovaz. For him. For Russia.

He had come a long way since army service, after which he had followed the example of the entrepreneur Vladimir Gusinsky by manufacturing the copper bracelets that had been much in vogue the previous decade. The bracelet-manufacturing centre was a disused state factory outside Moscow. Discarded reels of copper were easy to come by and cost next to nothing. The bracelets cost two or three kopeks to manufacture. Pyotr sold them for five roubles each. His two brothers joined the business and watched the money pour in.

It was Grigory who charmed the bureaucrats, politicians, security mandarins and Anatoly Chubais, deputy prime minister in charge of privatisation; it was Mikhail who expanded the business into cheap jewellery and formed a co-operative to court Western businessmen with available cash who sought a foothold in Moscow. Office blocks were rebuilt, American and French technology installed. Vast profits accrued. Mikhail displayed remarkable entrepreneurial flair. He bought an apartment in Monte Carlo and the mansion in London's Kensington Palace Gardens, which had been restored by his sister-in-law Tatyana, sparing no expense as befitted a Russian oligarch. Inevitably, the brothers' increasing wealth attracted the attentions of gangster syndicates and protection racketeers in Moscow.

For the sake of self-preservation, the Ilyushenko brothers agreed that Pyotr should set up the family's own private and necessarily secretive security firm, SecurRisks. To keep criminal syndicates and opportunist gangsters at bay, Pyotr took on board a former KGB general with a record of persecuting dissidents. The general taught Pyotr the ropes. Pyotr hired staff such as the hapless Shafranik and Tikhonov.

The former general spent lavishly and assembled what amounted to a secret army.

Quite suddenly, the general decided to retire. Then, with equal suddenness, he died in mysterious circumstances. His naked body was found suspended from an electric cable in the office of a dance-hall owner. The dance hall was a notorious hangout for prostitutes and racketeers. So SecurRisks, still in its fledgling state and staffed by a small number of former KGB officers acting as bodyguards and drivers, became Pyotr's baby. Until the carnage in Gorokhovetsky Street, SecurRisks under Pyotr's supervision had successfully preserved the security of Forovaz.

With profitable property development schemes already in place, the minds of Grigory and Mikhail had become exercised by the vast financial rewards to be gained from currency speculation. It was not long before dollar-rouble speculation and second-guessing the exchange rate proved to be another source of the incomes administered by Forovaz. But whereas the more prominent Russian oligarchs then amassing fortunes – such as Vladimir Gusinsky, Boris Berezovsky, Aleksandr Smolensky and Mikhail Khodorkovsky – had sought political influence and the role of kingmakers, the Ilyushenkos remained more shadowy, reclusive and inscrutable.

By avoiding the Yeltsin spheres of influence, the brothers Ilyushenko seemed to have escaped the unwanted attentions of organised crime syndicates and the envy and hatred of a deeply divided Russian society.

This, however, was not the view taken by the senior police officer who showed up at the hospital later that afternoon. Colonel Kiriyenko seemed to be facing a challenge he was incapable of overcoming.

Colonel Vladimir Kiriyenko of the Moscow Criminal Investigation Department looked even more exhausted than Pyotr Ilyushenko. Mikhail was obviously in no fit condition to face Kiriyenko's questioning.

'The motorcycle courier is our prime suspect,'

Kiriyenko told Pyotr. 'The assassinations bear all the hallmarks of organised crime. Unfortunately, there's no sign of his body or that he's a casualty. The bomb destroyed the perpetrator or perpetrators' motorcycle but not the rider.' He gave Pyotr an accusatory stare. 'Your CCTV installation covering the reception area doesn't include a recording system and the descriptions of the courier that the guards have given are too vague to be of use. You know about the packages the man delivered?'

'I heard,' said Pyotr. 'They contained blank sheets of paper.'

'Correct,' said Kiriyenko. 'The labels on the packages were reproductions of those used by the Italian bank and not the real thing.'

'You're sitting here telling me that you people have no clue who the courier was or who might have issued the contract for the killings?'

'Correct,' said Kiriyenko.

Pyotr struggled to control his rage. 'What the hell's the point of police who don't police – what sort of retards do you employ?'

'We do our best.'

Pyotr had almost reached breaking point. He didn't bother to disguise his contempt for this police officer in his cheap suit who reeked of tobacco smoke and whose breath reeked of whisky.

'The device was attached to the motorbike,' said Kiriyenko. 'It was triggered by remote control. The extraordinary thing was that the bodies were so near the wreckage.'

'The Mercedes was a strong vehicle.'

'Even so, the bombproofing was inadequate, wasn't it? It was a colossal blast. The forensic people searched for pieces of the device. We searched a wide radius. Even the reception area of Forovaz. Searched everywhere.'

'And – *found what*?'

'We are trying to reconstruct the device.'

'From what? You can't reconstruct Grigory, Tatyana or little Galina. Reconstruct – you sound like the lamentable Putin.'

'I believe, with God's help, we can reconstruct it.'

'What God's helping you? What are you – Christian, Muslim or Jew or what?'

To which Kiriyenko made no reply. He looked at his watch.

'I need a guarantee that everything is being done to find the killer.'

'I can't guarantee anything,' Kiriyenko persisted. 'You've read the newspapers. The killings are just one more addition to the list of unsolved Moscow murders. Maybe it was the work of one of your business rivals.'

'We have no rivals who'd go that far. They wouldn't dare. You know SecurRisks has the most efficient killers of any security firm in Russia. Our rivals know there'll be a bloodbath if they attack us. What I know is that you're incapable of stemming the chaos. Be in no doubt, Kiriyenko, I am going to pay millions to the man who can find my brother's assassin. I'll have him go to the ends of the earth to find whoever thinks he can destroy our family. Do you understand?'

'Look, almost two-thirds of Russian commercial enterprises, thousands of banks, private businesses and state-owned companies still have links to organised crime syndicates. Syndicates that have gone to ground. Gone abroad to London, Paris and California. You read the statement from the Ministry of Internal Affairs?'

'Maybe I did. Maybe I didn't.'

'It pointed to the existence of some three thousand organised crime groups. Don't imagine they've happily given up their businesses.'

'Will you stop lecturing me, Colonel? I know that *razborki* * are everyday occurrences. So what's your line, then? Best not to investigate too closely the death squads using car bombs similar to the one that blew up our Mercedes? Is that it? *Tell me*.'

'You're not being fair,' Kiriyenko said.

'Any child can still buy a Kalashnikov or rocket-propelled grenade. You've only got to sign up to the Internet.'

'I'm trying to tell you that you never know when you might be a target.'

'Thanks for that,' Pyotr snarled. 'My brother Grigory was carried off in a body bag. You can't have seen the bits. So was his wife. So was his daughter. My brother Mikhail here will never walk again. What the hell are you going to do about it?'

There was a long silence.

Pyotr managed to control himself. He put his face near to Kiriyenko's. 'You're either unwilling or unable to stem the violence. The criminal justice system is inadequate, the judges corrupt. Even the so-called law to outlaw the organised crime groups is impotent. You're free to accept the blandishments of gangsters and surrender

---

* Gangster shootouts.

to their threats, and thousands do. You want to see shit? Look under any carpet in the city.'

'I can understand your anger,' Kiriyenko said. 'I don't think there's much more we can usefully discuss at present, do you?'

'It's up to you, Colonel.'

'Tell me, now that Grigory is dead and your brother Mikhail has suffered such injuries, will it be you who assumes control of Forovaz?'

'It's too early to be discussing such things.'

'It'll make you one of the most powerful men in the world.'

'If you say so.'

'I can be useful to you.'

'Good,' said Pyotr. 'Make yourself useful by finding the bastards who planted the bomb and fast.'

'That's what I want too,' said Kiriyenko. 'Believe me, I'm the friend of the Ilyushenko family. You must know that Grigory had many dealings with me in private.'

Pyotr knew nothing about such dealings. He wondered what sort of dealings the police chief meant. 'Everyone has dealings with us. Across Russia. In Washington and New York. In London. In Beijing. And we tell those people – Americans, British, Chinese – we tell them what we want them to do. It isn't the other way around. They crawl to us. We crawl to no one. No one.'

'Yes, well, I'm sure we can carry on as before. Things will be the same.'

'No, they will not,' said Pyotr. 'Do me a favour, Kiriyenko. Please get out of here before I say something I might regret.'

Without replying, Kiriyenko left.

Pyotr called Elke and said he would be at her apartment within the hour. He gave Elke's number to the senior of the duty nurses and told her to call him if he was needed.

He stooped over his brother and kissed his forehead: 'You'll be okay – you're in safe hands.' He noticed Mikhail's eye flicker. 'It's me, Pyotr.'

The dry lips parted slowly. 'I know –' Mikhail whispered.

'You mustn't talk. Just rest.'

'Yes,' said Mikhail. 'Pyotr, you talk too much –'

Pyotr was well accustomed to his brother's biting reprimands. He really didn't care about this one. His brother was recovering. He was truly the strongest of the brothers.

'Bad luck for you, eh?' said Mikhail weakly. 'I'm going to live.'

'We'll see,' said Pyotr.

'I want to see Grigory, and Tatyana, and Galina –'

This was the moment Pyotr had dreaded. He heard himself saying: 'Mikhail, listen, I have to tell you that all of them are dead.'

Pyotr reached for the bell beside Mikhail's bed to summon the nurse. He began to weep. He pressed the bell long and hard.

'It's not true,' Mikhail said.

The nurse arrived and Pyotr said: 'I'm afraid it is, Mikhail.'

Mikhail whispered: 'I want to know –'

'Later,' the nurse said, turning to Pyotr. 'I think you'd better leave now.'

Mikhail was murmuring: 'You and I will find the animals who did it, Pyotr. If we have to wait till hell freezes, we'll find them. Do you understand me, Pyotr?'

'I understand. I told Kiriyenko the same sort of thing.'

'Kiriyenko?'

'Kiriyenko's been here,' said Pyotr.

Mikhail fought for breath. 'Keep him away from me,' he said. 'Kiriyenko's a gangster.'

Still weeping, Pyotr took the nurse to one side and gave her the telephone number where she could reach him. 'Ask for Elke Wedemeier,' he said.

'Your brother is hallucinating,' the nurse said.

'He knows the truth now,' said Pyotr. 'Now we have to deal with it.'

'I'm hurting,' Mikhail said.

For a few moments Pyotr stood in the doorway watching Mikhail with the nurse standing beside his bed. He watched her slide the needle into Mikhail's forearm and squirt the painkiller into his bloodstream.

26

Elke's bed was damp with sweat. Her fingers guided him inside her, squeezing him until he arched his back and began to whimper. She pressed her open mouth against his and sucked his tongue. Then she released the grip of her wet fingers, felt Pyotr's flesh grow soft and held him in her arms until he slept. Her sweat turned cold and she left the bed without disturbing him, the candle flickering by the bedside.

Her eighth-floor apartment overlooked the Moscow Arts Theatre and the busy cafés and restaurants on the pedestrianised Kamergersky Lane, a short walk from the Okthotny Ryad metro station, Red Square and the Kremlin. Drawing on a cotton robe over her damp negligee, she walked barefoot to the kitchen, lit a cigarette and began to prepare a supper of Pyotr's favourite *pirozhki* with potatoes, mushrooms and *carp à la Russe*. Cooking helped her to forget the chaos of her life.

The murders had shaken her. Her head had been ringing with the warnings her husband Jean-Pascal had given her about working for the Russians. The oligarchs, he had told her, are infected with the slime of corruption and violence. Why put yourself in the way of so much scum?

It had been Grigory Ilyushenko who convinced her to accept the appointment at Forovaz. She had graduated with distinction from Stockholm's Institute for International Economic Studies, been headhunted by a London merchant bank and cultivated impeccable connections with European and American banks. Grigory had pursued her with the ardour of a lover. The more she refused him, the more he increased the offer of financial rewards. She accepted and was fully aware that she had more than justified the confidence Grigory had shown in her abilities.

For many weeks after her arrival in Moscow she had been unable to find herself a suitable apartment. She wearied of living in hotel suites and grew homesick. She confessed as much to Pyotr, who offered to find her somewhere suitable to live. It was he who had found her the apartment overlooking Kamergersky Lane.

She had shown her gratitude by regularly cooking him supper, and eventually they became lovers. She found that, unlike her husband, Pyotr was sexually unsophisticated. She didn't care – in fact, she rather liked it. It seemed to her a sign that she was in control of their relationship.

Once a month she returned to Jean-Pascal in Geneva. His sexual appetite was undimmed. She made out to Pyotr that her marriage to Jean-Pascal was as good as over. Similarly, she convinced Jean-Pascal that her nights in Moscow were lonely without him. Inevitably, there came the morning when Pyotr had answered her telephone while she was in the shower. It was Jean-Pascal.

She was leaving that afternoon for Switzerland, and when she got there she found that, instead of arranging their usual table at their favourite restaurant, Jean-Pascal had prepared a candle-lit dinner at home. Cooking was not his strong suit and she was not surprised to find him chain-smoking and drunk.

Jean-Pascal bombarded her with questions about Forovaz – rumours he'd heard that the Ilyushenko brothers were secretly planning to obtain a foothold in the vast profits to be gained from oil production. She told him she knew nothing about oil. They were too busy reaping profits from dealing in aluminium.

'Is that piece of scum Pyotr involved?' Jean-Pascal asked. 'I mean, he's your lover, doesn't he tell you their dirty secrets?'

'He's not my lover, Jean-Pascal.'

At first she thought her denial of her affair with Pyotr rang true enough, and Jean-Pascal fell silent. He had placed a large bowl filled with ice cubes on the table and was struggling to open a can of caviar to set in the bowl's centre. 'I thought I'd cook Russian for you. Make you feel at home.'

'I don't like caviar.'

'You don't?'

'You know I don't.'

'So what's good enough for fucking oligarchs isn't good enough for your husband?'

'I didn't say that.'

'I want the truth.'

'I've told you the truth.'

'You haven't. You even smell of Moscow.'

'You smell of Austria and Switzerland.'

'Don't you speak to me like that. Or I'll beat the hell out of you.'

It was the first time he had threatened violence. She had never believed he would inflict it on her.

His tone suddenly changed to one of reasonableness. 'Okay, let's be adults. I get to screw you here. You screw Ivan in Moscow. You're a big girl. There's room for the two of us inside you.'

'You disgust me.'

'Let's call Ivan and ask him.'

'His name is Pyotr.'

His anger rose. 'Pyotr,' he chanted, making an obscene gesture with his fingers. 'Pyotr. Pyotr.' Her nervous laugh seemed to confirm his suspicion. He strode towards her and punched her in the face.

She felt the blood pour from her lips. It was dripping down the front of her white blouse. 'Yes, Pyotr's my lover,' she spluttered, getting to her feet and colliding with a chair so that it fell over backwards on to the floor.

She ran into the bathroom, locked the door and examined her bloodied face in the mirror. Her broken lips had swollen and his fist seemed to have chipped a lower tooth. She did her best to stem the flow of blood with paper tissues. The tissues were of little help. She sat on the edge of the bath. Jean-Pascal's clothes were strewn across the floor. His jacket hung from a hook beside the door and she noticed his wallet in the inside pocket. Pressing the tissue against her mouth with one hand, she took his wallet and extracted the wad of euros. She found she had also taken out a photocopy of several mug shots with the caption 'Klaas-Pieter Terajima'. The man's face was distinctive and so was the small print:

MULTIPLE MURDER, CONSPIRACY TO COMMIT
MURDER, RACKETEERING INFLUENCED AND
CORRUPT ORGANISATIONS (RICO) CONSPIRACY
TO COMMIT EXTORTION.

It seemed to confirm her view that Jean-Pascal associated with scum. Returning the photocopy to Jean-Pascal's wallet, she took the euros and went into the adjoining bedroom. She grabbed clothes and jewellery and stuffed them into her suitcase. As she was leaving, she glanced into the dining room. Jean-Pascal was slumped over the table, whisky glass in hand, sobbing. Without looking at her, he said: 'Have you got anything to say to me?'

'Like what?'

'Like *sorry*.'

'Well, yes, I do have something to say to you. I'm expecting a baby.'

For several moments he stared at her unblinking. Jean-Pascal's voice was slurred. '*Whose* baby?'

'I'll let you know,' she said and left the apartment.

She spent the night in a hotel and the following morning took the first available flight back to Moscow.

She lied to Pyotr about the cause of the damage to her face.

She also lied to Pyotr a few weeks later when she miscarried and her doctor ordered her to rest.

The preparation of Pyotr's supper was complete.

She laid the table and lit the candles, and as she was doing so it crossed her mind that a police informer might have had a hand in the bomb outrage that had killed Grigory. Forovaz had once supplied evidence against another conglomerate that had resulted in a senior director getting a punitive jail sentence. Ordering up an assassination in Moscow was as easy as buying a bottle of Kutskova, Pyotr's favourite vodka. She disliked speculation, so she turned her thoughts to her future in Moscow and the protection to be had by remaining Pyotr's lover.

Over dinner she asked Pyotr if he thought control of Forovaz and the family fortune would pass to him now that Grigory was dead and Mikhail so severely disabled.

'That's what that shit Kiriyenko asked me.'

'You've spoken to the slug?'

'I had no option. He's personally running the murder investigation.'

'Kiriyenko?' Elke asked with a look of disbelief.

'He made out he was a friend of Grigory's.'

'He told you that?'

'Why do you look so puzzled?'

'I'm not puzzled. He was more of an associate. Someone Grigory kept up his sleeve. I mean, Grigory made payments to him.'

'For what?'

'I don't know what for. I imagined he made them for criminal intelligence. For favours.'

'What favours?'

'I don't know, Pyotr. I'm an innocent in all of this.'

'How do you know about the favours then?'

'Because I was the one who paid sums, big sums, into bank accounts in the Cayman Islands.'

'How do you know the money went to Kiriyenko?'

'Because Grigory had me set up an account with a

bank I trust. I asked my contact to let me know, off the record, who the real beneficiary of the account was. It was listed in Kiriyenko's name.'

'Have you told anyone else about it?'

'No. Not until now, that is. No wonder he was first in with questions about the future. It's his future he's thinking about. He can't have reckoned on Grigory being murdered, can he? He'll be pretty desperate to know who's going to take control. He'll have got his bloodshot eyes on you, Pyotr. I'd watch your back.'

'Mikhail said much the same thing to me.'

'I'm not surprised. You'd have known all about Kiriyenko if you'd been made more privy to the slush funds. Grigory and Mikhail kept them secret. Now, if Mikhail dies, their control will fall into your lap.'

'We made an agreement that if anything happened to one or other of us, control would pass to the survivors. In this case it's Mikhail. And me.'

'And the future – the plans for expansion? Russia needs Forovaz. Forovaz mustn't stand still.'

'I suppose Grigory will have shared his plans with Mikhail.'

'Grigory was about to embark on new initiatives,' she said. 'He had me prepare a secret strategy.'

'For what?'

'Raising investment in China.'

'He was always full of pipe dreams,' Pyotr said bitterly. 'He never told me. My job's been to protect the secrets. Not to pry into what they might be. That was Grigory's way. He worked on everything in secret.'

'He's been raising cash, vast sums of cash from China.'

'All I was told was to vet the agent in Beijing, Dr Ushi

Jiang. What the hell do our people know about China? Grigory knew nothing about China. Neither does Mikhail.'

'They don't have to. But if you want new funding, then China's the key that unlocks the loans. It attracts investment. Just as those gigantic oil deals attracted Berezovsky and Abramovich. When they planned to take over the Omsk refinery, the director Ivan Litskevich blocked the move. Then Litskevich was found dead in the Irtysh River. He'd drowned. Remember?'

'What are you saying, Elke? That the link with China has something to do with the family deaths?'

'I wouldn't rule it out,' she said. 'Would you?'

'I'm not ruling out anything.'

'Like that whore Viktoria taking over Mikhail's interests. Suppose he dies, Pyotr – think what Mikhail's already made over to her. Don't you realise she's a fortune-hunter?'

'That's Mikhail's problem.'

'If he dies,' she said, 'she may be our problem, darling. She's a poisonous bitch. You have to get rid of her, Pyotr.'

'Don't let her get to you, Elke. Things won't change at Forovaz. I don't think we'll ever again feel safe here in Moscow or anywhere else until we get Grigory's killer.'

'And if you don't?'

'There's no *if* about it,' said Pyotr.

'You have to tighten security in Moscow.'

'That's being done.'

'And ensure every kind of precaution's made to improve control of day-to-day dealings internationally.'

'I'm going to create a shield. I'm going to give Dmitriev a bigger role.'

'We can make Forovaz even greater,' she said. She was stroking Pyotr's hair. 'The family should close ranks now. I want to help you, Pyotr. You know what you should do? You should have Mikhail moved to London. Sideline him. Let Viktoria have him and good riddance. That'll give you a free run in Moscow. It'll make you Number One.'

'As a matter of fact that's crossed my mind already.'

'You think you can persuade him?'

'Leave it to me. Otherwise, nothing else will change.'

'That includes my love for you, Pyotr.'

'And mine for you.' He took her in his arms. 'I need you, Elke.'

'And I need you,' she said. 'I'll always need you.'

27

ACROSS THE KALUGA HIGHWAY
FROM NOVO-SPASSKOYE. MOSCOW

On the move in Moscow, Mitsuko Furyawa left the
Hilton and took a room at the Marco Polo Presnja Hotel
on Spiridonovsky Avenue.

She e-mailed Ono:

> The hotel's some three kilometres from the city
> centre, one of my old haunts not far from the
> Patriarch's Ponds, the setting for the opening
> of one of my favourite novels, Bulgakov's *The
> Master and Margarita*.
>
> I want to see you.

Ono e-mailed back:

> Then come to Athens.
> I want 2 C U 2

From her room in the Marco Polo Presnja, Furyawa
called the Vansburgische Landesbank in the Grand
Duchy and asked to speak to her gnome-like personal

banker. The woman on the switchboard said he was presently in a meeting.

'Then please be good enough to tell him that Dr Pereira is calling from Moscow.'

Almost at once the gnome came on the line. 'I'm relieved to hear you,' he said. 'I've been trying to reach you in Beijing.'

'I'm vacationing in Moscow.'

'You are?' The gnome hesitated. 'Look, I'm with a client. May I call you back?'

'I'll call you.'

'As you wish. Give me two minutes while I go to another office.'

Two minutes later she called again. 'I want to confirm that the way's clear for my associates to hand over the diamonds for safe keeping in Antwerp.'

'All done. Everything is in place.'

'I'll call again when I get there.'

'I look forward to that,' the gnome said. 'Let's meet up.'

'I'd be pleased. Now tell me why you've been trying to get hold of me.'

She heard the hesitation in the gnome's voice. 'Are you alone, is your Somali friend –?'

'I am alone.'

'Listen. I have some disturbing news for you.'

'You have?'

'Yes. It seems that your client accounts are being investigated.'

'By whom?'

'Law enforcement officers.'

'Which law enforcement officers?'

'The FBI.'

Dr Pereira was silent a moment.

The gnome said: 'One of our counter-intelligence people here suspects that your accounts have, as it were, been opened up by the Americans. He made searches and traced the officer involved. A man called Sergei Dmitriev based in Moscow with Forovaz. He has an office at their headquarters building on Gorokhovetsky Street. I don't suppose you're aware of Forovaz?'

'As it happens, I am aware of Forovaz. What evidence has this man got?'

'A considerable amount. He's endeavouring to trace the original source of the capital we've invested for you.'

'Have his people made any approaches to Vansburgische Landesbank?'

'Not as far as I know. What's making matters difficult for our people is that Dmitriev doesn't actually keep the records he's made at the Forovaz offices.'

'Where does he store them?'

'We have a good idea where. How well d'you know Moscow?'

'Well.'

'He lives in a rented house with his wife and daughters across the Kaluga Highway from Novo-Spasskoye. We made some discreet enquiries with the landlords. It seems that, without their permission, Dmitriev installed a wall safe for his private use.'

'Did he now?'

'A very elaborate safe. Our people saw the photo the landlords took of it. I have it here. Wait a minute –'

Pereira waited. Her capacity to keep a cool head was being sorely tested.

'Here – I have it in front of me, with our people's

notes. The safe is what's called a Kombiter Parma Cesare. They say it's Italian, manufactured in Lainate. It has an electronic combination lock. A micro-motor opens the door. Does that mean anything to you?'

'It does, yes. Your man's done well.'

'Actually, it's a woman.'

'No matter,' said Pereira. 'Has your woman had a go at it?'

'No, that wouldn't be in her remit. But we could, of course, with your permission, have some Moscow-based security firm take a look. Unfortunately, as I'm sure you'll appreciate, the job would be both expensive and dangerous. I regret to say that we're not at all enthusiastic about taking it on board.'

'I can understand why not. But we have nothing to be worried about, do we? I mean, our transactions may be confidential but there's not an iota of illegality about them.'

'Correct,' the gnome said. 'But if the CDs this Dmitriev has made were to fall into the wrong hands – I mean, especially in Moscow . . .'

'I wouldn't greatly like that,' Pereira said.

'Believe me, I'm exploring ways of securing their retrieval. We need, as it were, to be forewarned if the FBI is launching an investigation. The idea that the Americans may be looking into our business fills none of us with pleasure.'

'I'm sure it doesn't. How many people at Vansburgische Landesbank know anything about all of this?'

'Me. And my immediate superior and our forensics person.'

'That's how I'd like it to remain. Keep it like that.'

'We will, naturally. And we'd appreciate it if you treated this matter with absolute confidentiality. We have Vansburgische Landesbank's reputation to uphold and indeed, Dr Pereira, your own.'

'Then we're agreed.' Pereira looked at her watch. 'I have one or two contacts with the US embassy here in Moscow of a personal nature. One woman in particular. Think Somali –'

'Ah, yes, I well remember –'

'Leave things with me, my friend. By the way, it'd be useful to know anything else you can tell me about Dmitriev and his family.'

'I can tell you he's Caucasian. Powerfully built. Born in what's now St Petersburg on 19 January 1964. Could be armed.'

'Say again.'

'Could be armed.'

'No. His birthday, when is it?'

'19 January 1964.'

'Is he here in Moscow right now?'

'As a matter of fact, no, he's not. He's away from Moscow. Where, I've no idea.'

'Where are his wife and children?'

'I imagine they're at home. The children attend a school some distance from where they live.'

'Where is it, the house? What's the address?'

'I have it here.'

'Tell me.' Dr Pereira memorised it. 'Do they employ staff?'

'I don't know if they do. I'm sorry to be the bearer of bad news. I wish I could be of greater help.'

Pereira/Furyawa looked at the plan of the city and its

outskirts in the hotel's guidebook to Moscow. She found the location of the Dmitriev house and then checked the taxi and car hire brochure. She rang Hertz on Chernvakhovsy Street; they only had Fords available. She asked them to deliver one to the hotel as soon as possible. She would be waiting in the foyer.

She had to get the evidence on those CDs out of Dmitriev's clutches as soon as possible. To do so, she reckoned she faced two possible courses of action. One was to undertake a discreet preliminary reconnaissance of Dmitriev's family house to calculate what sort of problems she would have to overcome to carry out a break-in later. The other was to make the reconnaissance and undertake the break-in immediately. Whichever one she chose, she had to reckon on Dmitriev's wife and daughters being present; even a servant. The place would be alarmed. And the Kombiter Parma Cesare is a state-of-the-art safe: even for the most highly skilled professional thief, it's a bitch to crack.

The man from Hertz found Furyawa to be attractive and apparently bemused by the business of renting the Ford. He helped her complete the paperwork and make payment by credit card.

'Driving in Moscow's tough,' he told her with obvious pride in his *savoir-faire*. 'Watch out for the traffic inspectors. The highway you're taking is in bad repair. Watch out for car thieves. You're obviously a foreign driver. That's makes you a sitting target. You never stop to help anyone whose car's broken down. He'll be a hijacker. And remove the windscreen-wiper blades, side mirrors and anything else that a thief can take, okay?'

'Thank you.'

'Ring me when you're through with the car. I'll collect it. Or you can leave the keys with reception.'

'I'll do the latter.'

He watched his client draw on a pair of black leather gloves and drive off into the snow.

When Furyawa reached the Dmitriev house, she reduced speed. There were no lights on in the windows. No car in the driveway. She drove past the house twice, parked some distance away down the road and walked back. The house was well clear of the road. If there were neighbours in the nearby houses, there was no sign of them. She decided to break and enter there and then.

Careful to avoid leaving footprints in the snow, she approached a side entrance to the house. There was the smell of a wood fire burning somewhere. She peered through the windows. There was no one in the kitchen. Stepping back, she searched the wall for evidence of a burglar alarm. She had seen no sign of one at the front of the house. She had noticed that several of the other houses in the vicinity had alarm boxes emblazoned with the name of the manufacturer. *Not the Dmitriev house though. A good sign.*

The door at the side entrance was heavily built. Its frame was steel. She looked carefully at the lock. No mortises. A latch. A gap in the wood. She tested the door for give. It gave, only a little, but it gave, and she slipped her nail file into it and the lock clicked. She paused. No alarm. She opened the door and entered the kitchen.

She admired this FBI man Dmitriev. He wouldn't want his house to arouse suspicion about his professional life.

He'd have his possessions thoroughly insured: a thief could help himself to the television, video and DVD player. The gloomy place didn't look like the home of a prosperous family or an undercover snoop.

She wanted to turn on the lights. She didn't. She let her eyes grow accustomed to the gloom and headed through the kitchen to the living room. She felt its walls. Gently raised a few amateur oil paintings from their wall hooks. Looked up and down the wooden floor.

As best she could, she thought herself into Dmitriev's mind. She doubted he would have told his wife of the existence of the safe if it contained something of an official sort. Or would he? Certainly he wouldn't want his children knowing it existed. The children couldn't be relied on to keep its existence a secret. Even though many families hide the family jewellery somewhere in the children's room, this family would be an exception. So that line of thought ruled out a search in the children's room. That left the master bedroom.

She passed two doors painted with signs saying 'Yevgenyia' and 'Elena' and 'Keep Out'. Her foot scuffed a book lying on the floor of the passage: J.K. Rowling's *Garri Potter i filosofskii kamen*.

In the master bedroom she explored the single chest of drawers, rummaging through the contents of each drawer in turn. Silk panties and brassières. The odours of Mme Dmitrieva smelled sweet. Her perfumes were reminiscent of Mei's. She looked at the unmade bed; then knelt on the dirty bedside mat and looked beneath the double bed. *Nothing.* Her eyes explored the room like the lens of a closed-circuit television camera: the row of family photographs on the wall, the door to the bathroom, the high, ornate windows heavily curtained. She looked at the pile of holiday brochures on the floor, opened the drawer to Mme Dmitrieva's dressing table. *Nothing.* She shifted aside the bedside table. There it was.

Kneeling on the carpet she stared at the safe in silence. *Mechanical combination wall safe. One dial. Nine thousand possible combinations. Dial has twenty-six letters. Four digits. I can alter them how I want. I can position them any way I want. Once the combination is set, I can turn the handle and the door opens outwards automatically. Manganese steel anti-drilling shield protects the lock. This bitch has an additional hard plate.* She peered closely at the lock wheel. *Chances are three to one he's used his birthday. I need seven items. This one six figures, one letter.*

Her slim gloved fingers gently stroked the wheel. *Happy birthday? I have* 19 – J – 1964.

Then she heard a click, a *tk*, then the faintest *zz* and a *sssssss* – and she saw the micro-motor open the small door.

Happy birthday! Great Italian safe. Poor choice of code. One chance in three. It's all mine.

The narrow shelf contained one sealed brown manila envelope. Next to it was a gun case. Inside the case was an old-fashioned FN/Browning GP with a magazine containing thirteen rounds. She opened the envelope and found two unlabelled CDs. *Time to go. No hurry. Lock the safe. Leave everything as you found it for the benefit of the next user. Leave quietly by the exit doors. Lock up after.*

Out into the crisp, cold air of the Moscow suburbs and the pleasant smell of burning wood.

Back to the comfort of the Marco Polo Presnja Hotel.
Then, soon enough, in the comfort of my room with a
view, read everything the FBI has to say about me.

When she returned to the Ford she found that the man
from Hertz had been right to warn her about car thieves.
Someone had removed both the car's windscreen wipers
and side mirrors.

28

Mitsuko Furyawa felt over the moon in Eastern Promise, the small shop near Moscow University that does a steady trade in fancy eastern fabrics, furniture and clothing. She bought a saffron robe made of cloth from *panthukula civara* or discarded clothes. The monk to whom the robes had belonged had sewn and dyed the robe himself, a sure sign that he sought to remove all impediments to the solitary life. Mitsuko also bought sandals and a drab woollen hat.

29

MOSCOW TO ANTWERP

Later, Takashi Sakamoto took the Aeroflot flight from Moscow to Antwerp via London; in total, a journey of almost ten hours.

In Antwerp Sakamoto would check the diamonds: the fee for the death and destruction he had so successfully wrought on Gorokhovetsky Street. He also had important meetings in Antwerp.

The first with the two German dealers in antiques.

The second with the person wanted by the FBI and known as Jacques Geddes or Rachelle Pienaar. Arriving from Hong Kong, the South African transsexual would join Sakamoto for the onward journey to Greece and the monastery in the Peloponnese.

The third with the personal banker, the gnome from the Grand Duchy.

In fact, he was headed for a landmark series of gatherings: the summit that would ease the route towards the elimination of Alan Rosslyn.

Some assassinations are both personal and professional. Rosslyn's was personal and the prospect raised a smile of expectation. The lips were moist, the saliva tasted sweet until its purity was polluted by the insertion of the customary tab of Swedish *snuss*, exciting the rush of blood.

30

Assuming the role of chairman, Pyotr Ilyushenko had taken up the reins at Forovaz. He was keen to give the impression that nothing had changed – an impression that everyone knew was untrue. Gone was the formality, the rather schoolmasterly way in which Grigory had run the gatherings. His chair at the head of the table was empty, as was Mikhail's to the right of it. Pyotr began the meeting by saying he had 'good news to report' to the two other senior executives at the meeting, Elke and Konstantin Krivisky:

'Mikhail will be discharged from hospital tomorrow afternoon. The doctors have given the go-ahead for him to be flown to London for further examinations. I've hired a plane equipped with full medical support to take him there. Every possible attempt will be made to restore the use of his legs. Until further notice I'll continue as acting chief executive. Elke, you'll remain deputy chief executive with responsibility for finance, personnel, appointments and administration. Is that okay with you?'

'I'll do anything to help.'

Pyotr turned to Krivisky. 'Mikhail asks that you, Konstantin, act as the conduit of information to him. We will make some arrangement so that you can continue doing so once Mikhail's been established in London. It's also Mikhail's wish that even higher levels of confidentiality be maintained. Even though it may put a strain on manpower, for the time being new appointments will only be made to the board of Forovaz management if and where they're required.' At this juncture, Pyotr took a small white card from his pocket. 'On the other hand, Mikhail has asked me to considerably expand SecurRisks, which will now become a separate entity.'

Elke was watching him closely. This was not something he had told her during pillow talk.

'Mikhail and I have decided to make a new appointment to SecurRisks. It's an in-house appointment. We need a man to handle all our dealings with Beijing and Shanghai, particularly someone who has the trust of Dr Ushi Jiang. This'll be our computer forensics specialist Dmitriev. Zhilin at Allegiance in London approves.'

'Do we really want to promote Dmitriev?' said Krivisky.

'Trust me. He's highly qualified. Down the line, we'll need someone to advise on high-level security at Mikhail's house in London.'

'We already have Metelev there,' said Elke, adding quietly, '– and Viktoria.'

'I know. But we're increasing the level of protection.'

No one could reasonably have offered any objection to the point. Even so, Pyotr felt Krivisky's air of disapproval.

'I know Dmitriev,' Krivisky said. 'With his beautiful wife.'

'What are you saying?' Pyotr asked. 'He may be no use at ice hockey and uninterested in the opera, but I value his turn of mind. Those who make up Dmitriev's expanding raft of clients like his sense of humour. He's made the People's Republic his speciality. He may be academic, secretive even, and rather aloof, but he deserves our respect. And our gratitude. He may have the look of a Russian bull, but never forget he has the mind of a cobra.'

'Does Mikhail really approve of the idea?' Krivisky said.

'I've no doubt that Dr Ushi Jiang will.'

'It's not her business.'

'Maybe not. But Dmitriev and she are close.'

'They've never met.'

'He's made her a very rich woman.'

'Not Dmitriev,' said Krivisky. '*We've* made her a very wealthy woman.'

'And Dmitriev's made her investments watertight. You understand me?'

Elke sighed. 'Let's not quarrel.'

'Konstantin,' Pyotr said, 'I'm the one whose word goes around here now.'

'I know,' said Krivisky, unable to disguise his regret. He had once entertained the idea of acquiring greater power within Forovaz. He'd been Grigory's man. He got on well with Mikhail. Now he was facing the power of the new regime. He didn't think that Pyotr was up to the task. And there was Elke. She had an appetite for control that inspired awe. Her ambition knew no bounds. This was the woman he felt had already assumed a position of frightening influence. And Dmitriev was someone he'd confided in. Now he regretted having told him rather too much during their drinking sessions in Moscow's most fashionable bars.

'You look troubled, Konstantin. Do you mind that I'm Number One here now?'

'We live in troubled times,' Krivisky said. His mouth had dried up and when he cleared his throat, the effort seemed to cause him pain.

Pyotr brought the meeting to an end.

In the corridor outside the conference room, out of earshot of the others, Elke asked: 'What happens to Viktoria?'

'She's Mikhail's responsibility. I can't be bothered with her right now, Elke. She'll do what he wants.'

'And *he'll* do what *she* wants,' she said. 'Perhaps he'll promote her? She only serves one purpose in his life. But now he's, well, paralysed?'

'The doctors say it won't interfere with sex.'

'C'mon, they told you *that*?'

'They did,' said Pyotr. 'Meanwhile, we have to accommodate the man Dmitriev.'

Elke lowered her voice. 'Did you know that Dmitriev is deeply religious?'

'That's his affair. And that's good. What kind of religion are you talking about?'

'He's a devout member of the society of MondoDei.'

'What's that?'

'An Anglo-American group of religious fanatics.'

'You're letting things get to you, Elke. Those people

are harmless idiots. Born-again saints. Look at the US. Don't you worry your little self about those people. We're in the business of making money. Leave saving souls to amateurs and volunteers. I'm just not interested in religion. Science interests me. If Dmitriev is religious I'm happy for him. Why criticise him for it? I mean, anyway, what d'you believe in?'

'Me? Oh, don't you know?' She handed him a slip of folded paper. It was drenched in her perfume.

Pyotr opened it and read:

'*Please*. Come inside me *soon*.'

31

ILYUSHENKO
FAMILY COMPOUND.
MOSCOW

Pyotr was driven to the family compound with the promise of Elke's scented body on his mind. The snow was falling – all too reminiscent of the afternoon of horror in Gorokhovetsky Street.

What Pyotr had not revealed to either Elke or Krivisky was the vow that Mikhail had made to him in secret to find and kill the murderer of Grigory and his wife and daughter.

The vow of vengeance taken against those responsible for the Gorokhovetsky Street assassinations seemed to Pyotr to be a sure sign that Mikhail was fast regaining strength. True, he was to be confined to an American Bounder H-frame wheelchair specially air-freighted to Moscow from 21st Century Scientist Inc of Coeur d'Alene, Idaho. He was also in constant pain, alleviated only by regular doses of morphine-based opioids, inducing hallucinations.

Attended day and night by armed bodyguards and

two London-trained Filipino nurses, Mikhail spent his time in silent contemplation of the icon of St Theophan the Recluse and the photograph of Zen grand master Tzu Yin. Mikhail and Grigory had given substantial donations to the Zen Buddhist order of Tzu Yin. The strict order had attracted disciples and pilgrims from across the world to its secluded walled retreat on a mountainside in the Peloponnese.

Once he was alone with Mikhail, Pyotr rehearsed the day's events at Forovaz. Finally Pyotr asked: 'D'you want me to speak to that journalist? Oleg Chebotarev, the *Moskovsky Komsomolets* man?'

'I know Chebotarev,' Mikhail said.

'You like him, don't you?'

'I don't dislike him – why do you ask about him?'

'Because I promised to call him after Gorokhovetsky Street. We can rely on him. He's always been interested in the Order of Tzu Yin, hasn't he? He has no great love of the police. He might sting them into action. He respects the rule of common justice.'

'I'm not interested in *common* justice,' Mikhail said. 'I am interested in revenge. I've lost my brother. I'm a cripple, Pyotr, look at me. I'm going to make very sure that those who took the lives of Tatyana and Galina lose their lives too. That's the bottom line. I want to know *why* they murdered my kith and kin. I want to watch them die. You understand what I'm telling you?'

Pyotr had told his brother that he understood.

'We will not rely upon the police to advance the progress of their investigations. I have no confidence in them. They're incompetent bastards. They can stew in their own shit.'

Mikhail finally told his brother that he would find a foreign agency to conduct a clandestine investigation and then undertake the killing of those responsible. He made Pyotr take a vow to tell no one.

'If my plan is leaked,' Mikhail told Pyotr, 'no matter who it is, no matter what the cost, I will personally kill them. You know why?'

'I can understand your anger,' said Pyotr.

'I don't think you do understand. You see, I've nothing to lose. Nothing. Leave me alone, Pyotr. I have a lot of business on my hands and, unlike you, I only have one hand.'

Pyotr looked at Mikhail and saw, for the first time in his life, the hatred in his brother's eyes.

'Take care,' said Pyotr.

'You too,' Mikhail replied. 'You never seem to sleep over in your house here any more.'

'I have a lot to do,' Pyotr said.

'Elke?' said Mikhail.

'She's been very supportive of the family.'

'Let's say of your family member, Pyotr.'

'It's not what you're thinking.'

'You have no idea what I think,' said Mikhail. 'But I'll tell you what I know. Be careful with Elke. Be careful how much you trust her.'

'We can trust her,' Pyotr said.

'Trust no one, Pyotr. No one. Not even me.'

'I don't trust you, Mikhail.'

'Get out of my sight.'

As Pyotr left the compound in his chauffeured car, what he saw next reinforced his mistrust of Mikhail. The headlights of a car arriving momentarily blinded him. 'Slow down a bit,' he told his driver. 'Stop at the gates. Check them for anything. Just do as I say – *check* them.'

The driver pulled up at the gates. Pyotr adjusted the driver's mirror and saw the reflected image of the newly arrived car outside the main entrance. The security lights came on automatically. The powerful beams afforded Pyotr a clear view of the man entering his brother's house. He was unmistakable.

That unreliable hack Chebotarev.

But there was worse to come. A second car now passed through the gates. The features of the passenger in the back were as unmistakable as Chebotarev's. They were those of Kiriyenko.

But whereas Chebotarev had entered by the main entrance, Kiriyenko entered by the side entrance used by staff.

Mikhail must have wanted to keep the two men separate and was showing his disrespect for Kiriyenko by making him wait.

Pyotr might have been wondering about the purpose of the two men's visits. One thing was sure: Mikhail had the constitution of an ox. Disabled he might be, but his body was making a remarkable recovery and his spirit and mind were intact as ever.

Mikhail Ilyushenko seldom received visitors to his mansion in secret.

If Chebotarev was surprised by Mikhail's summons, he kept it to himself. He had no sympathy for the oligarchs and little with the Ilyushenko family, except a commitment to the teachings of Tzu Yin and a wish to visit the retreat in the remoteness of the Peloponnese. He knew that the Ilyushenkos had made donations to the Order of Tzu Yin. He also knew that there was no chance whatsoever that his bosses at *Moskovsky Komsomolets* would countenance funding a joyride to Greece. He further doubted that Mikhail Ilyushenko would offer him much in the way of material for an article on the Gorokhovetsky Street outrage.

So why had Mikhail Ilyushenko sent a chauffeur-driven car with a bodyguard to collect him at his home and ferry him through the snow to the family compound? During the past few years the two men had encountered each other several times, mostly at piano and violin recitals in Moscow. He doubted that Mikhail Ilyushenko had asked to see him for a discussion about music.

Mikhail Ilyushenko received Chebotarev's expressions of condolence with grace. Their meeting, Mikhail said, was what he called a felicitous moment.

A convinced abstainer from alcohol and tobacco, Mikhail was generous in his offer of cigars and brandy. When Chebotarev, a tall, stooped and very thin man in his forties with hair cut short, declined both, Mikhail gave his visitor a smile and dismissed his two Filipino nurses and his bodyguard. 'I wonder,' he began, 'do you have current travel papers or a passport, that sort of thing?'

'Yes, I do.'

'The pay at *Moskovsky Komsomolets* – tell me about it. Is it good?'

'I earn a living.'

'I can imagine,' said Mikhail. 'But how much freedom

do you enjoy when it comes to your own movements? I'm thinking especially of foreign travel.'

'As much freedom as I want. But you have to realise that the foreign travel budget is small, very small.'

'Have you ever funded a foreign trip yourself?'

'Only when it comes to vacations. Twice, I think. Once to Paris. Once to Oslo.'

'None in England?'

'No.'

'Where do you have in mind to travel to, say, if money was no object?'

'Greece.'

'Ah, Greece.'

'To the Peloponnese. We have the Order of Tzu Yin in common.'

'We do. We do indeed,' said Mikhail. 'Are you wondering what all this is about, Chebotarev?'

They stared at each other. Two poker players giving nothing away. Mikhail Ilyushenko knowing what he wanted. Chebotarev trying to guess.

'Have you told anyone that I asked to see you?' Mikhail asked.

'No.'

'How can I trust you?'

'I give you my word. That's something I am not prepared to lose.'

'I have nothing to lose. I've lost my brother. His wife and daughter. Two of my trusted staff. I've lost the use of my legs. I've lost an arm and an eye. I'm disfigured. I sit here in an American wheelchair, my blood full of morphine. You might think it's a living hell. Living is an over-statement – I'm half-dead. From the waist down

I'm dead. There's nothing anyone can do to help.'

'I'm very sorry,' said Chebotarev. 'Is there anything *I* can do?'

'Perhaps,' said Mikhail. 'Let us, as it were, work backwards. Let's discuss an idea of payment for what I have in mind. Perhaps you know how much Forovaz is worth?'

'I have no idea exactly.'

'At today's reckoning, let's say . . . somewhere in the region of $65 billion. Give or take a little. I've established a fund exclusively dedicated to the pursuit of those responsible for the deaths of my family members. Money isn't hard for me to come by. If I have a difficulty, it's in finding the necessary total secrecy of its administration. The appointment of those who will do what I wish in absolute confidence. Someone who will report to me in secret. Do you follow what I am saying?'

'I think so,' said Chebotarev. 'But in the first place, isn't it a bit unwise of you to be telling all this to a journalist?'

'In most circumstances you'd be right. But am I not also right in saying that you've received at least six death threats?'

'I can't deny it. Paradoxically, in the present climate, they're less inclined to murder those who have a very public profile. That's my theory. I'm sitting here with you, still alive. So far, wouldn't you say, I've been proved right. Long may it continue. I think it will.'

'So long as someone like myself doesn't offer an extortionate sum of money to have you shot?'

'Naturally. I have to live with the idea,' said Chebotarev.

'So do I, my friend, so do I. We have that and the Order of Tzu Yin in common.'

Chebotarev gave no sign that he feared this intimidation. His voice sounded crisp, almost curt in tone. 'If you need the sort of man to act for you in the way you've described, why not choose your brother Pyotr?'

'Because I need someone outside the family, someone outside Forovaz.'

'Then who exactly do you have in mind?'

'I'm not entirely sure yet,' said Mikhail. 'But I have the idea, let's say as a memorial to my brother, that it's time someone was commissioned to write my biography.'

Chebotarev could scarcely contain his surprise.

'It will, of course, involve an element of trust,' Mikhail said. 'Of, let's say, intimacy. It will also require extensive travel to London, France and Greece. I've trusted you here and now with an extreme confidence. What I want you to do is to go away from here. Keep the confidence. Preserve the trust. And produce a candidate or candidates for authorship. It really is very simple.'

'That shouldn't be too difficult,' Chebotarev said.

'I don't think so either,' said Mikhail. 'I imagine that the prospective writer might expect, say, the equivalent of a few hundred thousand US dollars, plus expenses.'

'He or she shouldn't be too hard to find.'

'The right candidate might receive more,' said Mikhail. 'A sum to be paid into a Swiss bank. I rather think that the amount I have in mind would give the average family man the chance never to have to worry about money for the rest of his life.'

'You're asking me to draw up a list?'

'That's what I'm asking you to do, yes. As soon as possible.'

'How long have I got?'

'Call me first thing in the morning. Any time after six. Oh, and one more thing. As an expression of my gratitude I will be happy to pay for you to visit the Order of Tzu Yin in Greece.'

'Thank you.'

'You only have to say when,' said Mikhail with a look of pain. 'My body is telling me it is time for my medication. If you'd find your own way out, please. My chauffeur and a security man are waiting to take you home.'

'Thank you.'

'Thank you and don't forget to call me tomorrow morning,' said Mikhail, knowing full well that his visitor would remember.

He gave Oleg Chebotarev the smile of the chess master who's sprung the fatal trap and, once Chebotarev was gone, he intoned in the manner of Master Tzu Yin: '*Buddham saranam gacchami* – I go to the Buddha for refuge.'

He wanted Chebotarev to go to the monastery in Greece and commission the man Takashi Sakamoto to avenge the deaths of his brother and his family. That's what Chebotarev would get: enough money to last a lifetime. *To hell with radical journalists. They're human. Like anyone else, they'll take money wherever in the world they can find it.* The biography could wait till hell froze.

32

The British Airways Boeing descended over Antwerp in the winter sunlight.

The Buddhist monk was seated near an emergency exit, eyes closed in contemplation. He felt an inner satisfaction. Intoning to himself: '*Buddham saranam gacchami* – I go to the Buddha for refuge', he conjured up the image of his fellow monks summoned by the pealing of the temple bell to devotions at the *vihara*. It had been a long journey from the snows of Moscow and his mission had been well rewarded by the transfer of his fee to his bank account in Zurich.

Even better, he was in possession of the CDs containing the details of his accounts. He found himself admiring the man Dmitriev's expertise. The evidence was embarrassing in the short term. It might even prove damaging in the long term. The thing is: *Stem the flow*. There was time in hand to see to Dmitriev. Takashi Sakamoto rehearsed a variety of strategies.

The uniformed officer at passport control smiled at the

monk. Unlike the other passengers on the flight from Moscow, the new arrival had no need to collect luggage. All he carried was a bag of shabby cloth containing worn copies of *The Path of Purification* and *The Autobiography of Tzu Yin*, a toothbrush, a nail file and enough euros for the cab fare into Antwerp.

He would enjoy the summit meetings.

Then he would return to the Taigetos Mountains and offer prayers for the dead Russian infidels that their souls might suffer for eternity under the Devil's stewardship.

33

Police Chief Kiriyenko had not so much asked Mikhail who he thought might have been behind the killings; rather, he asked Mikhail to think of who might have gained by them.

'Who would you name?' Mikhail asked.

'Bluntly,' Kiriyenko said, 'if you, given your condition, were to step aside from controlling Forovaz, then it would be Pyotr who took up the reins. He would become one of the most powerful men in Russia.'

'That's supposing I step aside.'

'Alternatively, there's your friend Viktoria Feller.'

'She's not to be involved. She's a business associate.'

'Grigory placed considerable trust in Elke Wedemeier. Grigory told me that she is capable of running Forovaz.'

'Perhaps she is.'

'Then there's the rest of your senior staff, all of whom are privy to Forovaz secret information. It could be sold for vast sums.'

'I don't doubt. But my people only get given one small piece of the jigsaw. A little bit at a time.' Mikhail tapped the side of his head. 'The complete picture is in here.'

'Nonetheless, I'd advise you to look very closely at all your associates in turn. I'll be pleased to help.'

'We'll see,' said Mikhail. 'We'll see. What I want is to have the killer caught and punished. And you haven't produced a single lead.'

'I'm here to tell you that's not strictly true.'

'Then who?'

Kiriyenko was silent.

'You know what? You're no use to me, Kiriyenko.'

'I have tried my best,' Kiriyenko said.

'It isn't good enough.'

'I want your brother's killers.'

'You have a family, Kiriyenko – I don't. So go. Please get out of my sight.'

Kiriyenko gave a slight bow of subservience and left Mikhail Ilyushenko to the gentle ministrations of his Filipino nurses.

Disabled he might be, but Mikhail Ilyushenko was possessed of a frightening aura.

Some time after Kiriyenko's departure, one of Forovaz's private jets brought Viktoria Feller to Moscow in answer to Mikhail's summons.

She arrived with Anna at the Ilyushenko family compound, dressed in a copious sheepskin coat, fur hat, leather boots and dark glasses. It required two of Mikhail's bodyguards to carry mother and daughter's several brand-new suitcases inside the mansion. She had come to help with Mikhail's transportation to London and return there with him.

Mikhail did not see her at once. He was on the telephone to Chebotarev. Just as Mikhail had intended, Chebotarev was offering his own services as biographer. 'That's good,' said Mikhail. 'I will tell you what I need you to do for me in Greece. As to the biography, that will come later. Your fee for acting as my agent in Greece will be paid up front. It will be in line with what I suggested for writing the story of my life. Bear in mind that whatever the book contains must first meet with my approval.'

Chebotarev said that wouldn't be a problem as far as he was concerned.

34

EUSTON ROAD. LONDON

Mei e-mailed Rosslyn:

Alan

If Sergei Dmitriev is the man I think he is, he's a shadowy figure.

He has his fingers in several pies. In Forovaz. In Moscow diplomatic circles. In Beijing. He's what's called a mind-for-hire, a variety artist or something. He travels extensively.

He's also a member of the society of MondoDei.

He has no criminal record. He has a wife Tamara and two daughters living in Moscow.

I'll keep my eye out for more. My friend at Police HQ is very reliable.

Meanwhile, mother and child are doing fine.

We long to see you.

All my love

Mei

Rosslyn replied:

Mei + 1

Thanks for the info on Dmitriev.

Great to hear the news of you two.

Longing to see you.

More later.

I love you both.

Alan

Rosslyn's thinking about Dmitriev was interrupted by a telephone call from Schiff:

'Are you alone? . . . Our friend Dmitriev will meet you somewhere in central London at noon. Is that okay with you? . . . I've spoken to Ron Costley. It's okay with him. But he advises that you now sever your connection with Virtus. You have a meeting with them at nine, right?'

'Ron's told me nothing about severing my connection with them.'

'He's been otherwise engaged,' said Schiff evasively. 'We think it'd be for the best if you consider offering your resignation from the firm.'

'Can you tell me why?'

'Dmitriev will explain why later.'

'Have you talked this over with Costley?'

'Yes, I have. And Costley's doing likewise.'

'He's quitting Allegiance?'

'He's seeing his people this morning. Oh, and if you're wondering about loss of earnings –'

'This is all pretty sudden, Mr Schiff. I haven't had time to think about it, have I?'

'Let me tell you that you have my word that we'll take care of that.'

'We?'

'The money will be paid into your bank account from Geneva.'

'By whom?'

'A charitable foundation.'

'What charity?'

'Would you object if we talk this over in private, face-to-face?'

'No. But this thing isn't the business of any charity. Has Costley agreed?'

'He has, yes.'

Rosslyn was slightly surprised that Costley hadn't already told him the news.

'Is this okay with you?'

'If it means having a shot at Terajima it's okay, yes.'

'I thought you'd take that view. Remember this number, would you? Dmitriev's mobile.'

Rosslyn scribbled down the number.

'He'll be expecting you to call once you've done the business at Virtus. Why not just tell them some story that you're going to Hong Kong to see your girl? She's expecting a baby, isn't she?'

'How do you know that?'

'Costley told me,' Schiff said. 'Listen carefully to what Dmitriev has to say. He can show us the way straight to Terajima. Right now he's the best chance we have of getting to Terajima fast.'

'Hang on a second – this charity, have you run it past Costley?'

'Yes, I have. Didn't I mention it?'

'What's the charity called?'

'Have you heard of MondoDei?'

'Maybe,' said Rosslyn.

'I really have to go now,' Schiff said and hung up.

Rosslyn called Virtus and was put through to Bausch.

'I've been expecting your call, Alan. You'll be wanting to see us, I guess?'

'I'd like a private meeting.'

'We're in early here. Why not come by as soon as convenient?'

35

FITZROY SQUARE. LONDON

In the waiting room at Virtus a variety of clients were waiting to see the Masters. Rosslyn had been told by reception to wait there with them. He recognised the faces – behind dark glasses – of the international rock stars alleged to have purloined charitable funds on a massive scale; the manufacturer of computer chips said to be employing child labour in Taiwan; the Lebanese said to be the third most influential arms dealer; and a former government minister recently released from gaol. Their celebrity was sinking into notoriety and they had beaten a path to Virtus in the belief that the Masters would uncover dirt that could be dumped on the doorsteps of their accusers.

The receptionist escorted Rosslyn to the conference room, where Bausch and the four other Masters were doing their best to preserve an air of dignity and authority. The room was airless. The Masters seemed on edge.

Lincoln Bausch opened the meeting. 'Take a seat, Alan,' he said. He was staring out of the high windows at the fog shrouding Fitzroy Square. 'Coffee?'

Rosslyn declined the offer.

The four other Masters were seated opposite Rosslyn at the conference table. Bausch began the proceedings with an interminable résumé of Rosslyn's career. 'You'd agree with all I've said?' he asked Rosslyn.

'Fine.'

'Alan, the firm's being reconstituted,' said Bausch. He stared at Rosslyn. 'We want to express our thanks for all you've done.' His voice was devoid of gratitude.

'Thank you.'

Bausch bared his teeth. He forced a smile. 'In the new order of things there isn't any place for you here.'

No need to offer the resignation after all. 'If you say so.'

'Nothing personal,' said Valente, the balding eagle. 'Nothing to do with your great abilities as a private investigator.'

'We do what Washington says,' Montana Bogaart said. 'You British may think you're popular guys, but you ain't as popular as you think.'

'If you say so,' said Rosslyn with a shrug. 'Is there a hidden agenda underlying this sudden reconstruction of yours?'

'It's been on the cards for weeks,' said Valente.

'Started with the Feller thing,' said Bausch.

Montana Bogaart drummed his stubby fingers on the polished surface of the table. 'Which is attracting FBI interest.'

'It is?' said Rosslyn.

'We're co-operating with their London people,' said Bausch with a look of distaste.

'They're asking questions around here?' asked Rosslyn.

'That's what they're paid to do,' said Bogaart. 'And we pay Das Gupta to give them answers.'

'To do with Feller?' asked Rosslyn.

'We can't discuss it,' said Bausch.

'You realise he's shown up?' said Rosslyn.

'We know that,' said Bausch. 'We've been fully briefed.'

'Do you mind me asking – briefed by who?' Rosslyn asked quietly.

'Yes, we do mind,' said Bogaart, ignoring the question.

'What happened to Feller isn't totally clear,' said Valente.

'What do you figure happened, Alan?' Bogaart asked.

'God knows.'

'Was he cheating on his wife?' Bogaart asked.

'It was the other way about,' said Rosslyn.

'Happens,' said Bogaart with a grin. 'Isn't she a Russian?'

'I think you know that,' Rosslyn said firmly.

'And we've written off the money he transferred,' said Bausch. 'Given his physical condition. Reasons of compassion.'

'And the fact, Alan . . . that you authorised the withdrawal –' said Valente. He was speaking with extraordinary slowness.

Rosslyn interrupted him: 'I didn't –' and watched the remains of Valente's eyelids droop and twitch.

'We'll let bygones be bygones,' Valente said.

Bogaart cleared his throat loudly. 'Daddy's dong's back in his pants.'

'I never did understand what you meant by that,' said Rosslyn.

'It's what we say in Montana,' said Bogaart.

'I thought you came from –' Rosslyn interrupted.

They were talking across each other. Bogaart was on a very short fuse. 'You screwed up, dude.'

'I don't need to take that from you –'

'You superior –'

'I'm not here to insult you, Bogaart.'

'Asshole.'

Bausch slammed his fist on the file in front of him and stared directly at Rosslyn. 'Stop this, gentlemen. Stop it.'

Only Bogaart's rapid breathing broke the angry silence.

'Thank you,' continued Bausch. 'What we have to decide is what we do about money.'

'We propose payment of three months' salary, Alan.'

'That's okay with me,' said Rosslyn.

'And we're anxious,' Bausch said, 'that you remember you signed an undertaking to maintain secrecy about our operations here at Virtus.'

'I remember.'

'We wouldn't welcome court proceedings against you,' said Bausch.

Rosslyn stared at each of the Masters. As usual, it was the oleaginous Valente who broke the silence. 'There exists the bond of trust. In this business, past is always present.'

Bogaart's reddened nostrils flared. His claw-like fists tightened. 'If you betray our trust, we'll come down on you like a –'

'I've heard all this before,' said Rosslyn.

'This is an agreeable parting of the ways,' said Bausch. 'The usual compensation deal. You'll go to no other agency. No mention of the A word. You took the golden handshake when you joined. You'll find, I guess, that Bernal Schiff'll be showing an interest in you. I wouldn't advise you letting him cultivate you.'

That was it. The sack. The Virtus way.

Goodbye to the sub-species of civilisation they called Foxes, Prey or Vermin. Royals too. *Cracks have appeared in Virtus. They're running scared. Even so-called reconstruction won't save them.*

36

'Did you walk or were you pushed?' Costley asked him. They were heading for their rendezvous with Dmitriev on the steps of the Russell Hotel in Bloomsbury.

'The latter.'

'Me too.'

'I think the roof's fallen in at Virtus,' said Rosslyn.

'Things are grim at Allegiance. The Russians are now pretty much in overall control.'

'The FBI's apparently got its nails into Virtus.'

'I get the impression that control's passing into unseen hands, Alan. We're well out of it.'

'We're not,' said Rosslyn. 'We've been hired by MondoDei, Ron. Schiff says they're paying our salaries from now on.'

'He's right. I've known them for quite a time.'

'You believe in all that stuff, Ron?'

'I believe in morality. It works. We're heading towards Terajima. Schiff thinks Dmitriev is the chance we have of getting at him.'

'Right now he's the only chance we've got.'

Sergei Dmitriev was broad-shouldered and overweight. He had a flat nose set in a ruddy face. His shaven skull looked oddly square. There was an air of the nightclub bouncer about him. When he smiled he showed a gold tooth.

'Mr Schiff gave me photos of you,' the Russian said. They crossed the road and headed for the café in Russell Square.

It was Dmitriev who began the questions. 'You were with special investigations people in Customs and Excise,' he said to Rosslyn. 'Mr Costley, formerly of the Metropolitan Police.'

'You've got us right,' said Rosslyn. 'And you?'

'Me? I was operating as a freelance adviser in computer technology across eastern Europe. SecurRisks, the Forovaz-controlled security firm, approached me. They were looking for someone to handle computer forensics. So I signed up with them. Then I thought, Sergei Dmitriev, why don't you have a word with the Americans? I contacted the embassy. Might they be interested in having someone inside Forovaz? Naturally, they showed interest and that was that. I signed up with them as well. The money's good. I have my wife Tamara and two small daughters to support, you understand. Life in Moscow's getting expensive. Now it seems I can be useful to you gentlemen. With Terajima.'

'What have you got for us?' Rosslyn asked.

Dmitriev looked round the café checking that the conversation wasn't being overheard.

'In the first place, I have access to the details of Forovaz's cross-border mergers and acquisitions intelligence. Patterns of international tax fraud committed by Russian oligarchs in exile. That's led me to a woman called Dr Ushi Jiang.'

Dr Ushi Jiang. At the mention of one of Terajima's aliases, Rosslyn stiffened.

'Terajima?'

'Right.'

'What have you got on him?'

'He's sunk his money into a multitude of offshore banking deals. Some of the dealings have aroused the interest of the Moscow RUOP, the Regional Administration for Organised Crime.'

'How close have they got to him?' Rosslyn asked.

'What I know is that Terajima's transactions embrace money embedded in money laundering networks, suspected criminal syndicates and their illegal use of electronic cash transfer systems.'

'What have you got we can use?'

'Evidence that shows accounts set up within accounts. New banks within existing banks. The secret identities of originators and recipients. As I see it, SecurRisks – and hence Forovaz – is the victim of its own success.'

'How come?' Rosslyn asked.

'Because SecurRisks created a web of problems profoundly compromised by the transnational criminals it services. I've been asked to get hard evidence.'

'By Schiff?' asked Rosslyn.

'Yes. By Mr Schiff. Evidence that Terajima's own financial empire is founded on corruption. He's been hired by enemies of Forovaz to carry out assassinations. Understand that Russian money launderers pay very substantial fees to professional hit men from overseas who employ car bombs, apparently random shootings and the torture and maiming of suspects, including their families.'

'Has the supply of killers in Moscow run out?' said Rosslyn.

'It's more practical for them to use foreigners. You have to realise that it's a secret war of violence, terror and extortion. I'm Schiff's best-placed lookout man. As your colleagues at Virtus would say, I'm the well-hidden Bloodhound. Have you two got away from those kind of people?'

'We're going to, yes,' said Rosslyn.

'That's for the best. You need to get away from Zhilin for one.'

'You know Zhilin?' said Costley.

'Sure I know Zhilin,' said Dmitriev. 'He's savage. He murdered your man Thynne.'

Costley stared, stunned. 'It was suicide.'

'You're wrong,' Dmitriev said. 'I know Zhilin. It was murder.'

Costley looked at the Russian with incredulity. 'So do I know Zhilin.'

'Not as well as I do,' Dmitriev said. 'Zhilin strangled Thynne. You know why? Thynne had assembled too much dirt on the Ilyushenkos. And Zhilin convinced himself that Thynne had to be eliminated. He stole some sort of private journal from Thynne's house. Stole it to cover his tracks. I've seen it.'

'You've seen it?'

'Yes, I have.'

'What did it say?'

Dmitriev reached inside his pocket and handed over photocopies.

'Do you know where Terajima is right now?'

'Not exactly, no.'

'Have you actually met him in person?'

'Not in person,' said Dmitriev. 'Not yet. But Terajima, Dr Ushi Jiang, whatever you want to call him, has made it clear he wants to see me.'

'When's he seeing you?' Costley asked.

'I don't know.'

'So why's he your target?' Rosslyn asked.

'Because my speciality is the People's Republic of China: Chinese international money launderers, the monitoring of China's financial services systems and the links to Russian gangster syndicates. The rapid expansion of China's financial market has spawned myriad banks and holding companies. With few effective counter-measures in place, it's a soft market for criminal penetration. The criminal syndicates have a close working relationship with Vansburgische Landesbank in Luxembourg.'

'You've been looking at all this within Forovaz?'

'Right. I follow the money. For Bernal Schiff.'

Rosslyn saw a smile flicker across Costley's mouth. 'Who are the chief players involved at Forovaz?'

'Until Gorokhovetsky Street it was the Ilyushenkos. And a woman called Elke Wedemeier. She looks after personnel, appointments and administration. She takes a very close interest in my work. She, in turn, reports up to the principal senior partner, now Pyotr Ilyushenko. Ilyushenko delegates most of the routine business to Wedemeier. Wedemeier is Pyotr's mistress.'

'Who else is there?'

'There's another guy called Konstantin Krivisky.

Known as the Artist because his father's some sort of portrait painter. It was Krivisky who wanted me to excite Ushi Jiang about deals in Moscow. He's a drinker. When he's had too much he likes to talk about confidential aspects of the firm's business: his preferences among the staff, those he likes and trusts, those he loathes, especially Elke Wedemeier.'

Rosslyn stretched his arms sideways and then clasped his fingers behind his neck. 'Are you game to help take out Terajima?' For a moment no one spoke.

'I'm familiar with his kind,' said Dmitriev. There was a hint of fear in his voice. 'Schiff's offered me a lot of money to kill him. You two trust Schiff, don't you?'

'We do,' said Costley.

Rosslyn hoped that Costley was right about the American – and perhaps Costley read his mind.

'He's been very good to Feller,' Costley said.

'He has,' said Dmitriev.

'I wouldn't like to see you meet Grant's fate,' said Rosslyn.

Dmitriev made a dismissive gesture with his hands. 'That's the business,' he said. 'Maybe your police'll find the answers. Maybe they're not as numbskull stupid as ours in Moscow.' He grinned. 'Do you play chess?'

'No.'

'I've put it to Schiff that I make a clandestine knight's move. Forwards then sideways, if you understand. I position myself to take him out. First, I have to get in close to him. So I'll let him get close. What you two don't know is that there's a chance of getting to him sooner rather than later. He wants to see me. He wants a face-to-face meeting to review investment strategies. I see him. Then I make a second appointment. That's where you come in. You take him out.'

'Has this got Schiff's approval?'

Dmitriev laughed. 'It was Schiff's idea.'

'You're game?'

'Sure, I'm game. I meet him. I make the second appointment. Times and dates and places to suit you. I call you with my progress, like I call Schiff. And remember that I have a lot to lose.'

'You certainly do, Dmitriev.'

'It's not what you're thinking. I have the evidence from the Forovaz computer. I have it hidden. When I pass it over to Schiff I get a payday. A very big payday. And I get an even bigger one when we have Terajima's skull hanging from the belt.'

'And us,' said Rosslyn. 'What do you want of us?'

'I want you to wait until you hear from me down the line.'

Rosslyn searched Dmitriev's face. For a brief moment he wondered whether Schiff was sending Dmitriev to his death.

The Russian heaved himself to his feet. 'I have a plane to catch. It's been good to talk. We'll speak again soon.'

37

Rosslyn e-mailed Mei:

> Mei + 1
>
> Can you get me anything on a guy called Zhilin, worked with Costley at Allegiance?
>
> Things are moving faster here.
>
> How are you two doing?
>
> All my love
>
> Alan

Mei replied:

> Alan,
>
> We're fine except I'm tired, very tired.
>
> I'll see what I can do about Zhilin for you.
>
> All my love
>
> Mei

38

Antwerp quickened Dr Pereira's pulse. There was the meeting with the Germans in the Café d'Anvers and the enjoyment of hearing how they had dispatched the old *diamantaire* and relieved him of the diamonds.

'You deserve relaxation. You've done well.'

She handed over the small pouch of diamonds, their fee.

The Germans peered into it. They were very grateful. A toast was made and the two men headed off for the Schipperskwartier to take their pick of the flesh for hire.

Then there was the dinner of celebration with the gnome-like personal banker from the Vansburgische Landesbank who had flown in from the Grand Duchy.

He was impressed that she had hired the premier firm of Moscow investigators to open up the safe in Dmitriev's house. 'It must have been an expensive operation.'

'It was. The flow of information's been stemmed. It's a great relief.'

'To me too. Is there anything, absolutely anything, we can do for you, Doctor?'

'One small thing. You said you had an expert in computer forensics. The woman who identified the Kombiter Parma Cesare safe? There's something I'd appreciate her doing for me.'

'You only have to say.'

'I wonder, as a matter of urgency, if she would create a small system for me. I need to take a look at someone's e-mails. I need a way of accessing them without this person knowing.'

'We do it every day of the week.'

'Could you do it for me?'

'With no difficulty.'

'How soon can you set up the arrangement – so that I can access the e-mails?'

'I can do it now.'

'Well, shall we say, in the privacy of my hotel room, as a mark of my gratitude –' Dr Pereira squeezed the gnome's thin thigh '– we might explore ourselves. Would you enjoy that?'

'If it would give *you* pleasure.'

'One day.'

A message was waiting for her at the hotel from Geddes the South African.

Dr Pereira called the number Geddes had given and left instructions to meet for dinner, adding: 'I would like you to leave for Hong Kong tomorrow. Perhaps you'd stand by?'

The gnome from the Vansburgische Landesbank produced a system that allowed her to retrieve the e-mails she wanted with consummate ease.

Dr Pereira began her trawl through addresses and institutions in Hong Kong. Among the several, including the YWCA and the Hong Kong Police HQ, that took her attention was the HKCP, the Hong Kong College of Photography. Dr Pereira remembered Mei saying one day that she'd love to enrol there. *Mei loves photography.*

Well, well, well.

There are hundreds, if not thousands, of Mei Lims in Hong Kong. But the HKCP obviously took pride in their students and posted photographs of them on their website. *It seems they've got a new student there called Mei Lim.* It took Dr Pereira one or two clicks to find herself staring at the photograph of Mei Lim.

Why, how thoughtful of them! The college had even allowed its students to have their own e-mail addresses care of the college system.

She luxuriated in the idea of becoming an unauthorised user.

The system from the Vansburgische Landesbank has a dinky little password-cracking programme. Within just a few seconds it can identify words from the dictionary, common phrases, names. Easy really.

Make a dictionary attack – grab the encryption code employed by the password system.

Encrypt the contents of the dictionary. Just the words, mark you.

Then, according to the Help instructions, I plug in the encrypted words and the bank's system gives me the password match.

If Mei's using a complex password – let's say with symbolic characters, numbers, letters or a mix of all three

– well, there could be a problem. But what does the
HKCP have to hide?
  Let's go get Mei's mails.
  I like to know about the love of my life.

She joined Jacques Geddes in the sauna of the Hyllit
Hotel situated on the Avenue de Keyserlei, near the diamond district in the financial centre of Antwerp.

The naked couple enjoyed a combative yet affection-
ate and playful relationship. Pereira poured cold water
on the heated elements and the room lined with Nordic
whitewood filled with steam. She had many things in
common with the South African pre-operative transsexual. Both were fugitives from justice, each with a high
price on their head. Both pursued professions as academ-
ics which might have allowed them to go straight: the
one as Pastor Leung, renowned in Beijing as the leading
contemporary authority on the *Analects* of Confucius;
the other as a respected authority on state-of-the-art
gynaecological practice, as well as anaesthetics and hallucinatory drugs. Of the two, Geddes was the more talk-
ative. 'You Asians always suffer to be more beautiful,'
Geddes said.

Pereira said, 'If you'd read the Hindu Susruta Samhita,
you'd know that twelve centuries ago adulterous women
whose noses were sliced off as a reminder not to wander
were treated by nose-job experts.'

'My nose is perfect.'

'But the breasts? Gravity can be cruel. They sag. You
should be wary of silicone, Rachelle. Don't touch that
industrial stuff. They dilute it with cod-liver oil.'

'You don't rate my breasts?'

'Not quite so good as the eyes. Who did your ble-pharoplasty?'

'The Beijing Medical Union College's plastic surgery hospital.'

'Never heard of it. But they didn't do too bad a job on you. Was it painful? Tell me about the pain.'

'They did it with local anaesthesia. Didn't feel a thing. A few quick incisions in the skin above the eyelids, inser-tion of tissue. I was back at work in two weeks. South African to Asian. You couldn't tell the difference, could you?'

'You could pass as a Filipina.'

'I often do. But that's not what you want me to do for you, is it?'

'No, it's not.'

'What is it you want?'

'I want my lover back. I have the means to get her. I have the motive.'

'And the opportunity?'

'I think the opportunity is about to present itself and I want to enlist your services.'

'They're expensive.'

'I didn't expect them to be cheap.'

'Most of my capital is invested in California. In the manufacture of guided biopsy systems. Asians don't respond to liposuction. Too much muscle; too little fat. You understand, I have cash-flow problems.'

'I will pay you what you ask.'

'In US dollars.'

'In diamonds.'

Rachelle kissed Dr Pereira on the lips.

'I'll tell you,' said Dr Pereira, 'what I have in mind.'

244

Last Quarter

Rosslyn werd ich's zeigen, Mann
Dem werd ich's stecken, Mann
Sein Hirn spritzt auf die Strasse, Mann
Wie Bruehe
Viel Spass
Das sass
Ein geiler Plan
*Immaculata DeCeption . . .**

* I grooving ged Rosslyn I say yeah
The proving I say yeah
Splasha da brain Rosslyn yeah
Ain't no rain
Stick yo slap
Da eez you rap
Gotcha Immaculata DaConception I say yeah
Gotcha Immaculata DaConception I say yeah
Gotcha Immaculata DaConception I say yeah

39

Ever since his return to Moscow, Sergei Dmitriev had been sleeping badly.

Troubled by nightmares, he had been waking in the mornings at four or five o'clock. He made himself a bowl of strong sweet tea laced with a slug of brandy. Wrapped in his dressing gown and fur slippers he sat gazing at the surface of the kitchen table pondering the tangled circumstances of his life and the questions they posed.

Would there ever be a day, he wondered, when he had amassed enough money to secure his family's future and terminate the arrangements he had with Forovaz and the Americans? The latter's short-term plan to set up Dr Ushi Jiang, to draw her like a fish into the hands of the British so that, with the patronage of Schiff, they could execute their quarry, seemed only a beginning. *The business of killing Jiang is their responsibility, not mine.* For that he was thankful. Killing was not his line. Far from it.

Another doubt formed in his mind: suppose Dr Ushi

Jiang isn't Terajima? The Chinese were highly skilled in adopting false identities, and FBI intelligence on them was well known to be inaccurate and out of date. It was notoriously time-consuming to conduct an effective investigation into the lives and backgrounds of the Chinese criminal fraternity.

What if Dr Ushi Jiang was who she said she was: simply Dr Ushi Jiang, entrepreneur, financial brain, player of the markets with fortunes in secret bank accounts in Luxembourg, Liechtenstein, Geneva and God knows where else? There were plenty of other predators like her swimming in the murk of Far Eastern commerce.

Then, suppose the combined skills of Rosslyn, Costley and Schiff finally succeeded in wiping out Dr Ushi Jiang. Think of the damage to the reputation of Forovaz. It would totally destroy the credibility of the Ilyushenkos and their ruination would not be long in coming. Where would that leave him?

Some time during the most sleepless night since his return, he took two of Tamara's mild sleeping pills, with the result that he overslept by half an hour.

This morning, it would be touch and go whether he would make the start of the meeting at Forovaz.

Showering quickly, he reckoned he would have to leave the house in less than fifteen minutes to reach Gorokhovetsky Street on time. He padded barefoot from the shower to the main bedroom and shaved. He could hear the sound of Tamara's voice above the buzz of his electric razor. She was reading aloud over breakfast to their daughters Yevgenyia and Elena: *Garri Potter i filosofskii kamen.*

Before leaving the bedroom he heaved aside the bedside table to gain access to the Kombiter Parma Cesare wall safe because, later today, he needed to download further encrypted information about Dr Ushi Jiang. His fingers twisted the wheel: 19 – J – 1964. There was a click, a *tk,* then the faintest *zz* and a *ssssss.* The micro-motor opened the small door and he couldn't believe his eyes.

The sealed brown manila envelope had gone. It should have been next to the case that contained the handgun. The gun case was there all right. So was the gun. But the manila envelope with the two computer disks containing highly sensitive and confidential details of private client accounts, including Dr Ushi Jiang's? *Gone.*

The existence of the safe, which he had himself installed, was a secret he shared only with his wife. He had told her that it contained confidential and encrypted papers connected with his research at Forovaz. Tamara had learned not to question him about his well-remunerated work. She was a woman of common sense. She didn't know about the gun, though. It was an old-fashioned FN/Browning GP with a magazine loaded with thirteen 9 x 19mm rounds.

Dmitriev thought back to the last time he had slipped the disks into the envelope and placed the envelope in the safe. *Is my mind deceiving me? Did I slip them into my briefcase without thinking? Some intruder's opened the safe and removed the disks. Why hadn't the intruder taken the gun as well?* He searched his briefcase. *Not here. Or did I mislay them somewhere in the bedroom chest of drawers?* He rummaged through the contents of each drawer in turn. *Not here either.* He knelt on the carpet and looked beneath the double bed. *Nothing.* He shook the sheets and bed covers. *Nothing.* His eyes explored the room: the row of family photographs on the wall, the TV, the door to the bathroom and the windows to the garden. He crossed the bedroom and drew back the curtains. The light from the room illuminated the driving snow.

His mind ran amok. He imagined the intruder taking a line from the door to the bedroom, past the double bed, opening the safe. *The intruder has to have been a professional with inside knowledge. But who?* The safe had cost a small fortune. The unthinkable had happened. The manila envelope and its contents were missing. *Only I know the code to the door of the combination safe.* No longer. *Someone has got in here and stolen the disks.*

He walked quickly back across the bedroom, lifted the pile of holiday brochures and threw open the drawer of his wife's dressing table. The shock of knowing the disks had gone, of imagining that they had been stolen, made him feel frustrated and then angry. And then he felt the grip of panic: the tightening of his stomach muscles, the rapid breathing, the throbbing in the temples. He lifted the gun case and slipped the whole thing, gun and all, inside his briefcase next to the slim metallic flask of vodka (another secret he kept from his wife). *Could Tamara have managed to open the safe? Is she engaged in some deception? If she'd found the gun she'd have protested in a fury, totally lost her rag, unleashed a stream of Russian obscenities. Ranted about Russian males needing guns to camouflage their sexual inadequacies.*

From the open doorway to the sitting room, louder

than he intended, he called out: 'Tamara, I need to talk to you.'

'Wait until I've finished the chapter, okay?' she said.

'No, Tamara. It's urgent. Come here *now*.'

Disentangling herself from their smaller daughter, who was seated on her lap, Tamara stood up. Taller than her husband, with the posture of the ballerina she had once yearned to be, she straightened her bathrobe and approached him with a disgruntled look. He grabbed her hand.

'Sergei, let go of me.' Without releasing his grip, Dmitriev led her into the bedroom and closed the door.

'Sergei, you're hurting me. What the hell is all this?'

His face was ashen. He was staring past the bedside cabinet at the wall safe and its open door. 'Something's missing, Tamara.' He was still clutching her hand.

'What's missing?' she said.

'Two computer disks.'

'What?'

He released his hold. 'Someone has stolen them from the safe.'

'Sergei, listen. I don't know what you're talking about.' She nursed her hand, numb from the power of his grip. 'And don't you hold me like that again!' Walking quickly to the wall safe she knelt on the carpet and looked inside. 'The bloody thing's empty. What are you on about?'

'It contained two packages. One of them contained two disks. The envelope containing those two disks has been removed.'

'What disks?'

'Disks with records of secret bank accounts. They've gone, Tamara. They've gone.'

'The safe's your business, Sergei. This is the first time you've ever really told me about what you keep in there. What secret bank accounts – *your* secret bank accounts?'

Shaking, Dmitriev ignored her questions. 'No one knows the combination code except me. You've never told anyone else of the safe's existence, have you? Okay, if you have, fine. Fine. Please just tell me who you've told.'

'Sergei, I haven't told anyone, for God's sake. Why should I have? You swore me to secrecy, didn't you? It was better I didn't know. That's what you said. I can't remember exactly what you said. I really don't care too much anyway.'

'You've never mentioned its existence to a friend?'

'Why should I have?'

'Or to the kids?'

'No, I most certainly have not. For God's sake, it doesn't matter.'

'It does matter, Tamara. Think back to the dinner party. Did anyone come in here?'

'How could they have got in here? The door was locked. You locked it, didn't you?'

'Could you have left it open – say, just for a second?'

'Sergei, *you* locked the door. You opened the door.'

'I'm talking about the safe.'

'It's a combination safe, isn't it?' Hesitating, she glared at him. 'You don't believe me, do you?'

'All right,' he said. 'I believe you, Tamara. I'm sorry if I shouted at you. But the information on those disks is very sensitive indeed.'

'I wouldn't know,' she said quietly. 'Maybe you took them with you to the office. Maybe you should put on your coat, get to work and check your office.' She gathered up the bedclothes from the floor. 'Didn't you say there were two packages – where's the other one?'

'It's okay. I have it.'

'What's in it?'

'You're not supposed to know.'

'I think you'd better tell me.'

'If you must know, a loaded handgun.'

'I don't believe it. You keep, what, a gun here in our bedroom – and you say it's a secret. What about the kids?'

'It's okay. The safe's locked. No one knows about it except me.'

'Locked? It's open. And you're saying someone's stolen something from it. It isn't a secret any longer, is it? From now on you keep that gun in your office. I don't want it here, Sergei. I don't. Now, if you don't mind, I'm going to get the girls washed and dressed. Unless, of course, you'd like to do it. Would you like to do it, just this once?'

'I'm late for the office,' Dmitriev said.

'Then go – I hope you find your beloved disks.'

'So do I. If someone's stolen them I'm in shit.'

'You'll find a way out of it – you always do. At least come and kiss the girls goodbye.'

He waited until Tamara had left the bedroom before returning the handgun to the safe and locking it. Then he removed a small torch from the shelf beside the door to the bathroom and put it in the briefcase he was taking with him to the office. Disguising the fact that he was now on a personal red alert, that there was the possibility his cover might have been blown.

Contriving to hide the turmoil in his head, he told Tamara that he planned to be home late this evening. He would stay on at the office and take the place apart.

'You haven't forgotten?' Tamara said. 'We have tickets for the theatre.'

'Of course not,' Dmitriev lied.

He kissed Yevgenyia and Elena goodbye, told them to be good and left the warmth of home for the blizzard.

Turning up the collar of his coat, he blundered into the garage where his BMW was parked. The heating system in the garage was faulty and a layer of frozen dirt covered the windscreen. After he had scraped most of the muck away, he shone the torch beneath the car to search for any sign that unseen hands had gained entry and booby-trapped it with an explosive device. The procedure was second nature, but suddenly it seemed to assume even greater importance than usual. He found no suspicious wiring, no lethal package.

He clambered into the car, started the engine and turned up the heater. He didn't set off immediately. Instead, he reached inside his briefcase and took a swig of vodka.

He said a silent prayer, more a desperate plea, that he would find the envelope and the CDs somewhere in his office.

40

GOROKHOVETSKY STREET. MOSCOW

Even beneath the blanket of the snow, the ravages of the bomb blast could still be seen. The weather was restricting the progress of the repair and restoration work. A builder's crane stood there like some black and white tree trunk with no branches. Pathetic piles of bouquets of wilted flowers lay in the snow, their plastic-covered messages of grief flapping in the wind.

Dmitriev crossed the Forovaz reception area without so much as a good morning to the men behind the desk and hit the lift button hard.

Dmitriev's personal assistant Lilya brought him the day's first cup of coffee and handed him the file containing telephone messages. She stood watching him in silence while he checked the messages.

Lilya was short and heavily built with a very fair complexion and natural blonde hair. She wore high heels and rather too much lipstick. Dmitriev thought she resembled a dairymaid in some Social Realist painting. There was a bond of trust between them. Once or twice they had lunched together in a cheap restaurant, where Lilya had confessed that she wanted to leave Moscow and live in London.

The previous Christmas he had given her some expensive perfume, albeit purchased from the duty-free shopping mall at a Middle East airport, and when she opened the gift she had begun to cry. The price tag was still stuck to the box of Dioressence. They talked for about an hour and she told him that she couldn't help it, she knew he was married, but she had become very fond of him. She told him that she was a born-again Christian and that she could, as she put it, 'deal with temptation'. He said something clumsy: 'It's God's gift that thinking people deal with temptation.' It would be for the best, he said, if she told him the truth. He already knew that she was uncannily sensitive to his moods and hadn't been surprised when she said there was nothing she wouldn't do for him. So far he had not taken advantage of her offer. He didn't care to think about what she actually had in mind.

There was routine morning work to be done. Foreign clientele doing business in Russia and Russian clients doing business overseas needed encrypted answers to encrypted questions via e-mail. Encryption was all the rage. 'Give me fifteen minutes on my own,' Dmitriev told Lilya. 'I've a lot to see to before the meeting. No calls. Close the door after you, would you please?'

Instead of checking his e-mails, he searched his office. He reached into the filing cabinet, sifting his way through the files from the backs of the three drawers to the fronts and then back again, swearing at his failure to find what he was seeking. Similarly, he rummaged through the contents of the desk drawers and flipped through sheaves of cuttings from the *FT*, the *Economist, Moscow News, St Petersburg Times* and the *Wall Street Journal*. He sat down, elbows on the surface of his desk, hands cupped under his chin, and breathed deeply. *I'm compromised.* What made it even worse was the realisation that he had no idea who had robbed him of his secrets or how to begin the search for them. His thoughts were in disarray. His ability to focus them had deserted him.

Lilya returned with the reminder that it was time for him to join the other partners.

'Tell them I'll be late,' he said.

'Is something wrong?' she asked.

'Nothing. I don't feel too good.'

'You look terrible, Sergei. Tell me if there's anything I can do to help.'

He wanted to tell her what had happened and, indeed, at this point was just about to do so when caution got the better of him.

'I'm okay, really,' he said, heading for the door. 'No, I'll tell them myself.'

The meeting had already begun in the overheated Forovaz conference room when he took his seat next to Elke Wedemeier. Sweating profusely, Dmitriev apologised for being late.

Pyotr Ilyushenko accepted his apology. 'Are you sure you're okay, Sergei?'

'Fine, thanks,' said Dmitriev, turning over the papers on the table in front of him and settling down to listen to Ilyushenko's brief interpretation of the firm's financial position, which he declared to be profoundly satisfactory.

'Sergei, you had an appointment fixed with Dr Ushi Jiang?'

'Yes.'

'She can't make it,' Ilyushenko said abruptly. 'She asks if you'll introduce yourself to her in Milan.'

'Milan?'

'Milan.'

'Okay,' said Dmitriev. 'I'd like to meet her.'

He thought briefly of Rosslyn, Costley and Bernal Schiff. Ushi Jiang has fallen into my lap.

Elke Wedemeier looked up from the felt-tip doodles on her notepad. 'Can you make it there tonight?'

'Tonight?' Dmitriev asked.

'I took the liberty of having my PA reserve you a seat on the evening flight to Milan,' Wedemeier said. 'Dr Jiang matters to us more than ever.'

'I know.'

'Is that okay with you, Sergei?' asked Ilyushenko.

'Why does she quite so suddenly want to meet me in person?'

Without interrupting her doodling, Wedemeier said: 'She'll have good reasons for wanting to meet you.'

Dmitriev envied her relaxed frame of mind, at this moment so different from his own.

Elke Wedemeier continued: 'I have various plans I think she'd be interested in. It'll be good for you to see her in Milan and hint that we can put important deals to her in greater detail next time she's here in Moscow.'

'Can you brief me before I leave?'

'She'll brief you,' Wedemeier said with a smile.

The meeting fell silent and Dmitriev sensed that an unusual degree of pressure was being applied to get him to fly to Milan. His head was telling him: *I have to solve this problem.* His heart was complaining: *I've no idea what to do about it.* He listened to the voices of his colleagues once more discussing a small point on the agenda. When Pyotr Ilyushenko brought the meeting to an end, Dmitriev failed to realise it was over; or hear what was being said, until he heard his own name mentioned. Ilyushenko was saying: 'Sergei? A word in your ear.'

Ilyushenko steered him towards the windows and out of earshot.

'About Dr Ushi Jiang. Her people at Zubin Harbin Holdings in Hong Kong are very impressed with all you've achieved. They want us to handle new initiatives and I want you to be in sole charge from now on. It'll put you in line for a bonus. A big bonus. You like the idea?'

'Thank you.'

'Entertain her in style. Santini Ristorante on via San Marco's a favourite of mine. I'm pleased for you, Sergei. Treat her with kid gloves. She's a big player. You're the best person to handle her.'

Dmitriev felt quite unable to share in Ilyushenko's mood of encouragement. He hoped his anxiety wasn't showing.

When he returned to his office Lilya confirmed that Wedemeier's PA had booked him on an early evening flight out of Sheremetyevo for Milan. The return ticket would be available for collection at the airport.

Dmitriev called Tamara and told her he would be coming home to pack an overnight case.

'I'm sorry, I can't make the theatre. I have to leave

town. I'll be home again tomorrow night. The boss's orders. I'm sorry.'

Tamara was accustomed to such sudden changes of plan and his leaving Moscow at short notice. As she had many times before, she accepted his apologies with resignation.

'Are you really okay?' she asked indifferently.

'Fine,' he lied.

'Have you found, you know, what you're looking for?'

'No,' he said. 'I don't suppose you have?'

'No,' she said. 'Don't forget I love you, Sergei.'

'I love you too,' he said. 'I'll be back soon.'

'I'll pack your case for you. I love you.'

He glanced up from the Ushi Jiang file on his desk to see Lilya standing in the doorway. 'You don't look too good, Sergei. Are you sure you're well enough to fly to Milan?'

'I've no choice,' he told her.

She closed the door to the office and, leaning against it as though barring his way, said: 'Sergei. You can trust me. I know you so well. There's something torturing you. Is everything okay at home?'

'Yes,' he said. 'Everything's fine at home. But I would value your help with something.'

'Tell me.'

'Not here, Lilya,' he said. 'You could help me later on. Why don't you come with me to Sheremetyevo later?'

They agreed a time.

'Wait for me by my car,' he told her. 'It'll be parked across the street.'

41

ACROSS THE KALUGA HIGHWAY
FROM NOVO-SPASSKOYE. MOSCOW

By the time he reached home, Tamara Dmitrieva had already left for the theatre.

In the hallway, he listened to the sound of his children's laughter. They were playing in the living room with the child-minder.

'Back soon,' he called out. He had already said his goodnights, sweet-dreams and be-goods. Yevgenyia and Elena called out their see-you-in-the-mornings.

On the way out, he noticed the antique umbrella that his wife usually took with her to the theatre. It was unlike her to have forgotten it. Perhaps she thought the blizzard would spoil the umbrella's fabric: snow that might even cancel the departure of the plane for Milan and the appointment with Ushi Jiang.

He called the airport. Planes were subject to delayed departures.

There still remained the need to search his office one last time.

Once again, Dmitriev went to his car, took a swig of

vodka from his flask, and headed off for the city and Gorokhovetsky Street.

42

GOROKHOVETSKY STREET. MOSCOW

The blizzard seemed to have persuaded the staff to leave early and only one of the friendlier security guards was on duty. Oleg the Chechen was seated at the reception desk.

Oleg raised no objection to Dmitriev using a master key to his office, a master key that provided access to all the offices. Since the bomb, one of the new security measures required of all staff – save the Ilyushenkos – was to hand in the keys to their offices when they left the building.

The corridors and office were carpeted, and except for the swish and clank of the opening and closing drawers of his filing cabinet, his search was conducted noiselessly.

Somewhere, though, was a sound, a dull thump, footsteps perhaps, possibly from the floor below. He stood quite still, his eyes unblinking, staring at the open door. The footfalls were heavy, strangely rhythmic. He moved to the door and leaned his head into the corridor.

'Oleg?'

Far down the corridor, a shadow moved.

'Oleg?'

Nothing moved. No shadow. There was a humming, the noise of the lift descending perhaps. He listened, waiting for the hum to cease. Then he telephoned reception.

'Are you sure there's no one else here in the building?'

'No one.'

'Sure?'

'You. Me. No one else is here.'

Dmitriev paused. Oleg's telephone picked up the sounds of someone in the reception area. Or once more, was his mind playing tricks?

'Mr Dmitriev?'

'Oh yes. I'm sorry, I won't be long, Oleg.'

'Don't worry. I'm here all night.'

The search proved futile. He sat on the edge of the desk, legs apart, hands on his thighs and stared at the floor once again rehearsing in the greatest detail all he could remember of events since he'd seen the disks at home. Lost in thought, he was suddenly aware of the figure in the doorway peering at him.

'Mr Dmitriev?'

'Ah, Oleg. I'm leaving now.'

'Can I help you?'

'No. I've finished, thanks.'

'You okay?'

'Fine, Oleg.'

Dmitriev turned out the lights in his office, closed the door and walked slowly along the corridor with Oleg at his side carrying a large black polythene rubbish bag. In his other hand Oleg carried a partially crushed plastic carton. It was unusual for the night security men to leave the reception desk unmanned. Until recently they had performed their duties in pairs. Since the installation of the new CCTV system they kept watch singly. Maybe Oleg sensed Dmitriev's suspicious air.

'I take the shredded paper before midnight and put it in special bins,' Oleg said. He showed Dmitriev the plastic carton. Dmitriev read the label on it, that of a firm of medical equipment suppliers in Orenburg. 'The new regime. New first-aid kits on every floor. This is too heavy for the shredder.'

Dmitriev had never noticed any first-aid kits.

'Are you really okay?' Oleg asked.

'Fine,' said Dmitriev.

'You don't look well.'

'No, I'm fine, Oleg.'

'Take care, Mr Dmitriev.'

'You too, Oleg.'

Lilya was waiting in her car across the street.

43

Lilya drove through the snow to Sheremetyevo. Dmitriev's thoughts were far away. Lilya broke the silence. 'I've been meaning to ask you something for quite a time, Sergei. Will you be honest with me?'

'Of course.'

'People have been asking the questions about you.'

'Who's been asking you questions, Lilya?'

'Wedemeier. Krivisky. Ilyukhin and Dorenko.'

'What questions have they been asking you?'

'Whether you really are a strictly *bona fide* employee of Forovaz.'

Dmitriev's face remained expressionless. 'What did you tell them?'

'Only what Wedemeier had already told me. That I should tell her in private if I noticed you behaving oddly.'

'Like how?'

'Taking confidential material home. Calling London on personal business. Meeting people outside the office whose identity I didn't know. If you had a lover. Visited prostitutes. Anything really that I might think odd.'

'And what did you tell her?'

'There's nothing to tell,' she said with a frown. 'Something's wrong, isn't it? You can tell me, Sergei. You seem to have made enemies. My loyalty's to you and no one else.'

'Thanks, Lilya. It means a lot to me.'

'Are you going to tell me the problem, Sergei?'

'Ilyushenko wouldn't be sending me to Milan to see Ushi Jiang if there was a problem. Listen, you know this bloody city's wild with rumours. Paranoia's endemic. It's in the blood and in the air. Everywhere.'

'Sergei – you've done nothing wrong, have you?'

'There isn't time to tell you everything. I backed up a lot of sensitive material on Ushi Jiang on two disks and put them in my safe at home. They've been stolen.'

Lilya stared at him. '*Stolen* – who's stolen them?'

'I don't know. I have no idea. Matter of fact, I can't believe it. But they've gone.'

'Is someone setting a trap for you?'

'God knows.'

'Are you plotting with one of those security firms, like Kroll?'

'You know about Kroll?'

'It's American. The Americans are very powerful . . .'

'I don't work for Kroll. If I worked for anyone it might be for one of the other main security firms in London. But I don't, see? The people who've been asking you questions about me may think I can cause them trouble.'

'Please.' She was begging him. 'Can I help you?'

'Only by keeping calm and carrying on as usual. Nothing else, Lilya. Just keep your nose clean. Not that you would do otherwise. Let me tell you this. Ruthlessness, treachery, corruption and, above all, mostly dirty money fuel the world we live in. People like you and me don't count.'

They were nearing the Sheremetyevo departures entrance.

'Pull up here,' he said. 'You never know who might have been tailing us. I'd like to take a look.'

He got out of the car and peered at the faces of the people by the entrance.

Lilya said: 'There'll be a car waiting for you at Linate to take you to the Four Seasons.'

'Thanks,' he said. 'Drive home carefully. Look after yourself.'

The Alitalia Boeing departed late from Sheremetyevo.

In the blizzard Moscow was lost from sight.

Maybe I should have alerted London?

44

The car had waited at Milan's Linate airport to take Dmitriev to the Four Seasons, where Ushi Jiang would join him later in the bar. There were messages waiting for him from Moscow in his hotel room. Lilya asked that he call her and had left her home number. There was one from the child-minder and another from Tamara. Elke Wedemeier asked that he call her too.

He called home but the number was engaged. He called Lilya and she answered straight away. She sounded greatly distressed. 'I'm sorry, Sergei. It's bad news. There's been a break-in at your house.'

'Are the children all right?'

'Yes.'

'Tamara?'

'Shocked but okay, yes. She called me to get your number.'

'What was taken?'

'Nothing.'

Dmitriev was staring at the floor.

'Elke Wedemeier wants you to phone her.'

269

'She'll have to wait. I'm late for Dr Ushi Jiang. I'll call you later. And would you mind telling Tamara I'll do the same? Her line's busy.'

'Take care,' Lilya said.

'You too.'

Dr Ushi Jiang was a Eurasian whom Dmitriev judged to be in her late thirties. She was waiting for him at the bar. Dressed in black, heavily scented, slim, with long finger-nails painted dark red, she was a woman of striking good looks. She spoke English with a perfect accent.

She handed Dmitriev her business card, telling him rather grandly that she was making a brief tour of Europe as the senior overseas representative of Zubin Harbin Holdings (ZHH), Hong Kong. She said she wanted to explore one or two new initiatives of a personal kind.

Ushi Jiang looked at him directly. 'I want to speak to you in confidence,' she said. 'There's a proposition of a confidential nature I've been asked to put to you. That's why I asked to meet you in person.' She smiled at him warmly. 'Mind you, I've already done my homework about your background. Nonetheless, perhaps you'd give me your undertaking that this will go no further than the four walls of this room?'

Treat her with kid gloves, the boss man had said. 'Naturally,' said Dmitriev.

'The suddenness of this approach may come as something of a surprise to you,' she said. 'But then I imagine you are not unaccustomed to surprises.'

'If you say so.'

I've had enough surprises today to last me for a life-

time. His mind kept on returning to his fruitless search and now the strange business of the break-in at home. *Maybe someone's used the break-in as a pretext to plant a surveillance system, a bug even?*

'You seem a little anxious,' she said. 'I imagine your work in Moscow is stressful.'

'I enjoy it,' he said.

'We're good at what we enjoy,' she said.

'Most of the time,' he said.

'Suppose,' she said, 'I were to ask you to join the board of ZHH?'

Dmitriev was taken aback. 'It's a very sudden proposition. Is that why you've come here – to ask me that?'

'Among other things,' she said, with a look of amusement.

'Why have you chosen me?'

'We need someone with your experience to head a new office in London.'

'That's flattering,' said Dmitriev. 'But you have to appreciate it's not something I could really square with my people at present. Have you discussed this with Ilyushenko?'

'I haven't. No, I need to sound you out first. I'd like you to consider the offer. Please think about it. I can guarantee your remuneration will be much greater than what you're being paid at present.'

'Money's not the issue,' said Dmitriev.

Quite suddenly he thought he could see a way ahead. *Ushi Jiang's offering me a way of avoiding whatever damage the theft of the disks might inflict.*

'How soon would you want me to join you?'

'As soon as possible – whenever is convenient to you.'

'But if Ilyushenko were to get in the way of my resignation, what then?'

'If he names a price, we'll meet it.'

'I'd like a chance to talk it over with my wife,' Dmitriev said.

'By all means,' said Ushi Jiang. 'Tell her it's a confidential offer. Perhaps you and your wife would like to keep me company for dinner?'

'She's not here with me.'

Ushi Jiang looked surprised. 'You're here in Milan alone?'

'Just for tonight.'

'So it'll be just the two of us then,' said Ushi Jiang. 'We'll have plenty of time to talk about things. I want to know everything about you. Why don't we meet at my apartment suite in La Residenzia Clausen? Here –' She handed him a plastic card. 'The concierge is away sick. I'm afraid you'll have to let yourself in. Do you mind?'

'That's okay with me.'

'The taxi drivers know La Residenzia Clausen. Meet me there at say nine-thirty?' She told him the address. 'Take the lift to the first floor. My apartment's at the end of the corridor. Then we can drive out to the Swiss border and Casinò di Campione. From here it's about sixty kilometres on the A9 *autostrada*. You'll need to bring a *carta d'identità* – a passport will do. The restaurant's good. I'll arrange a car and driver to take us.'

45

The taxi driver delivered him to the entrance of the apartment block La Residenzia Clausen, near old fortifications at the edge of the city.

As she had said, there was no concierge on duty. Dmitriev let himself into the building with the card she had provided. He noticed that the CCTV system was not operating. He crossed the entrance hall to the lift. The apartment, on the first floor, was easy to find, as she had told him.

The corridor was silent. He inserted the plastic card into the slot beside the door handle. The pinprick light flashed green. The door gave a buzz and he stepped inside.

The door opened on to a darkened living room. A single small candle flickered on the glass table. There was a powerful smell of burning incense: powerful, but not strong enough to disguise a strange odour of disinfectant. Stranger still, there seemed to be no one there, and as his eyes became adjusted to the dim light he saw that lengths of heavy polythene covered the carpets and the furniture. 'Hello?' he said quietly. 'Anyone at home?' There was no answer. He began to think he must have entered the wrong apartment.

'Hello?'

There was no reply. He stepped across the polythene floor covering to the kitchen. It looked unused. As good as new. The door to the bedroom was open. He caught sight of a movement across the living room. Just the flickering candle reflected in the screen of the TV set. His knee knocked against a table, dislodging some pamphlets. Stooping down, he collected them together and returned them to the table with his left hand.

'Hello?' he said again, but his question was unanswered.

He switched on the small light fixed to the table on which he had replaced the pamphlets. The light reflected from the bright printed sheets dazzled him. Maybe she had stepped outside. He decided to give her ten minutes.

He switched off the table light. Once again, he allowed his eyes to adjust to the near-darkness. One door remained to be opened. *Must be the door to the bathroom.* He could see a fine line of light coming from beneath it. *She must have left in a hurry without bothering to turn it off.* Suddenly, through the bathroom door, he heard the familiar voice: 'Is that you, Mr Dmitriev?'

The sound of her voice came as a relief. 'I'm sorry,' she called. 'So silly of me. I'm in the bath. Please do me a favour. On my bed. You'll find my robe.'

'I didn't think you were here,' he said, with laughter in his voice.

'I am. I've been listening to music. Rap.'

'You like rap?'

He heard her laugh. The music started from the sound system. *Must be controlling it from inside the bathroom.*

'Bring me my robe, would you please? You don't mind?'

'I don't mind.'

'Find yourself a drink. In the refrigerator. Help yourself.'

The rap beat on.

'You want a drink?' he called.

'Open the Moët.'

He tried the door to the bathroom. *Strange. It's locked.* He hung his overcoat on the chair beside the bed. As she had told him, the champagne was in the fridge. The bottle of Moët and nothing else. He returned to the living room with the bottle in his left hand and the two glasses in his right. He noticed the bathroom light was still on.

'I have the champagne,' he said.

The door opened very suddenly and it can only have taken him a second of stupefying panic to take in what confronted him. The figure dressed head to foot in a white anti-contamination suit and surgical mask. The blur of hands. Latex gloves. The lightweight tent of sterile polythene.

Ushi Jiang drove a blunt instrument up between his legs. The hammer blow forced Dmitriev backwards and downwards.

He cried out, fighting against the pressure of Ushi Jiang's fingers at his neck. He fought to remain conscious, glimpsing the protection mask one moment sucked in and the next blown out by Ushi Jiang's panting.

Ushi Jiang began to talk in a low and very calm voice: 'Tell me you're working for Rosslyn. Tell me, baby.'

Dmitriev's lips were bloodied and swollen. 'Whatever you want.'

'Rosslyn is your controller. He's thick with those asshole Americans at Virtus.'

'I don't know –'

'You don't know?'

'Okay. Yes. Let me go. *Please*.'

'Rosslyn. Rosslyn. Rosslyn.'

The music was blaring out. The rhythm beat through his ears.

Dmitriev felt himself lifted from the floor. The woman seemed possessed of enormous strength. His arms and legs were being spread wide across a low table. The fabric around his crotch was split open. He felt his wrists drawn together and the cuffs fastened around them. He attempted to raise his head, to sink his teeth into her arm. She was ready for him and drove her pointed fingernails deep into his left eye. He fought against the pain, against hyperventilation and the sense of helplessness.

She put her masked mouth close to his face. He felt the breath, the smell of disinfectant. 'This Rosslyn, you know him?'

'I've told you. Yes, I know him.'

'Has he mentioned me?'

'Why should he?'

'Do you know who I am?'

'Dr Ushi Jiang.'

He saw Ushi Jiang switch on the room lights.

Red mist blurred his vision. He thought he saw an

276

open suitcase. Ushi Jiang's black clothes, underwear, a wig. Then he saw the mortician's hammer in Ushi Jiang's hand.

Ushi Jiang brought the hammer down against the bridge of Dmitriev's nose. The short blow shattered the bone and the blood squirted from his nostrils and down his throat. Swallowing blood, he choked.

'I want you to phone Rosslyn and tell him that he and Costley will be dead two weeks from now. I am the writing on the wall. They know who I am.'

Dmitriev made an effort to speak, but instead he threw up the blood. He felt Ushi Jiang cutting away the fabric of his trousers and then his boxer shorts.

'I will – call Rossl –'

'Good boy,' said Ushi Jiang.

'*Plee–sss.*' He felt a tightening in his chest as if his muscles had formed a clamp.

He felt something being pressed against his ear. Somewhere in his mind he heard the sound of water and what seemed to be a dial tone.

'Tell Rosslyn your name. *Speak* your name.'

He heard a voice saying something in English.

'Dmi – triev –'

'Who is this?'

'*Dm* –' The blood engulfed the telephone handset.

The Englishman's voice said: 'You have a wrong number.'

Ushi Jiang screamed: 'Listen!'

She took the mobile phone and, holding it near the speakers, began to dance slowly. A version of an erotic Thai dance. Flapping her hands.

Then Dmitriev saw Ushi Jiang retrieve the telephone.

'The line's dead,' she said. 'Too bad. Now we can begin.'

She pushed the needle deep into an artery in Dmitriev's neck.

Then the scalpel severed his testicles and penis and opened his throat from ear to ear.

Later, Ushi Jiang e-mailed Ono – and Ono e-mailed back:

> Thank you, thank you for that. What did you inject?
>
> I'd have given anything to have done it with you.
>
> Come to me soon.

46

Rosslyn listened to the music being played into the telephone. Mei quite liked rap. He had no taste for it. He imagined some drunk had misdialled from Germany and thought nothing more about it.

Mei e-mailed Rosslyn:

Dear Alan

I'm sorry I haven't written sooner. Don't you worry about this. But I have problems.

I've had some bleeding so I went to the early pregnancy assessment unit. I've had tests. My blood count says I don't have anaemia. I do have a rhesus negative blood group so they gave me an injection to prevent any sort of problem if you get me pregnant after this one! I also had an ultrasound scan showing my uterus and our baby. Brilliant. I saw the heartbeat! It's not really possible to tell if everything's completely okay. I'm having another scan a week from now. But I do have what's called a chromosomal abnormality. So there's a risk of miscarriage.

Bring me up to date with you.

Love Mei

Rosslyn replied:

Mei +1

Please take care of yourselves.

I spoke to my GP, who says these problems aren't unusual. Just keep in close touch with your doctors.

I love you

Alan

47

It was Costley who noticed the murder story briefly featured in the *International Herald Tribune*. Nothing had
been heard from Dmitriev, then the story broke about
the body of a man discovered dead in his bath at the
Meridien Hotel in Moscow. The description of the victim's injuries suggested Terajima's handiwork. The article said that the victim's name was Arkady Venediktov.
A small photograph of Venediktov, reproduced from a
passport mug shot, accompanied the article.

Costley showed it to Rosslyn on their way to the afternoon meeting in Schiff's Holland Park flat. 'Mean anything to you?'

'Looks familiar. Do we know anyone called Arkady
Venediktov?'

'I don't. Do you?'

'No. But I'm sure as hell I've seen that face before
somewhere.'

Rosslyn studied it closely. 'One of your people.
Northern France. You showed me his CV. Plus photograph. We're looking at Nurmukhan.'

Costley started at the newspaper photograph. 'My God.'

Once they reached Schiff's place, Rosslyn was left with the American while Costley closeted himself in a back room and made a series of telephone calls.

Schiff said: 'Our people don't want to make any approaches to the Ilyushenkos. They have their reasons.'

'Like what?'

'They're not telling me what they are.'

'I thought you had full access to FBI intelligence.'

'Even I don't get told everything. One thing I can tell you, though. A courier's on his way here with some photographs. We have to be prepared for bad news about Dmitriev.'

'Where is he?'

'Dmitriev has been in Milan.'

'*Has been* or *is* in Milan?'

'At least let's say he was *last seen* in Milan. He checked into the Four Seasons. Someone there thinks they recall seeing someone resembling Dmitriev with a Eurasian woman at the bar. Anyhow, Dmitriev left the hotel that evening and hasn't been seen since. The hotel people found his passport and personal effects in his room. The bed hadn't been slept in. So they contacted the Russian embassy in Rome. We have a useful contact in the Russian embassy. She spoke with our Consulate General in Milan. The legal attaché has a close working relationship with the Milan police department. The legal attaché went to headquarters and was given sight of the mortuary photographs. And those are what we're going to look at when the courier gets here. The one interesting corpse is of a middle-aged man found in an apartment block called La Residenzia Clausen. The probability is that it's Dmitriev.'

'I hope to hell it isn't.'

'Prepare yourself. What we need to know is: A, are we looking at Dmitriev? B, do the injuries look like Terajima could have inflicted them? and C, just where the hell do we look next?'

A member of his domestic staff brought Schiff a package.

The contents of the envelope included a series of colour photographs of Dmitriev's corpse.

'This is terrible,' said Schiff. 'What sort of animal could even imagine doing that?'

'Animal's too kind a word,' said Rosslyn.

Schiff was looking at some accompanying correspondence when Costley joined them.

'Do you read Italian?' Schiff asked.

'Show me,' said Costley. 'My daughter's taught me a few basics.' He paraphrased slowly: 'They found traces in his blood . . . a great quantity of what could have been . . . diamorphine with traces of other toxic substances. A lethal quantity. He may already have been unconscious when he was cut about.'

'A mercy perhaps,' said Schiff, 'that he didn't feel pain.'

'I'm afraid he will have done,' said Rosslyn. 'Terajima prefers to see his victims die. He enjoys it.' He was replacing the photographs in the envelope when he found the CD. 'What's this?' he asked Schiff. 'You have a laptop?'

'Sure. Let's take a look.'

'It's a *listen*,' Rosslyn said. 'Someone's sent you some music download.'

The three men around the table listened to the rap music.

Once it ended, Schiff said: 'I think I need a translation.'

Rosslyn said, 'Listen to me. I'm going to launch an attack on Terajima. In reverse order. First, I'm going to base myself back at Claverton Street, Ron.'

'Wait a minute,' Costley interrupted.

'There's no *wait* about it, Ron. This is what I'm going to do. I'm going to let Terajima come for me. I'm going to play this by the Terajima rules. Before everything goes from bad to very bad, I'm going to take him out.'

Coming Home

Don't be scared if others
fail to recognise your talents;
rather be fearful if you fail to
recognise theirs.

CONFUCIUS

48

Rosslyn e-mailed Mei:

Mei

Dmitriev's been found murdered in Milan.

It looks like Terajima's handiwork; in fact, I don't doubt that.

I'm going to do the business with the Ilyushenkos. I guess they're looking to control private security in Europe. Who is there to challenge them? They'll get possession of insider intelligence on every major commercial enterprise that matters, to say nothing of what former security service officers bring them. The evidence is narrowing, pointing to Terajima being behind the bomb in Moscow. They'll be running scared that Dmitriev may have talked before he was murdered.

Ron Costley's being really supportive.

I think I'm feeling out the cracks in Terajima's defence.

Tell me how you are. How's the baby?

All my love

Alan

xxx

49

Takashi Sakamato and his companions Merkel, Jortzig and Pienaar reached the monastery in the Taigetos Mountains on a bright winter's afternoon. Brother Søren welcomed them. Something of an amateur meteorologist, he said that storms were expected from the east. The new arrivals should take care when walking in the mountains. Cloud could come down in minutes; visibility would be reduced to zero; search and rescue might prove well nigh impossible.

Together with Rachelle Pienaar, Takashi Sakamoto had brought a collection of diamonds, the fee for his work in Gorokhovetsky Street, to the monastery. Rachelle Pienaar would shortly become the only other person to know where the diamonds would be deposited. A quantity of them constituted the fee for the commission that Sakamoto had in mind for Rachelle.

That night at the monastery, Sakamoto outlined the strategy for the elimination of Alan Rosslyn. There was some division of opinion on matters of general principle. The Germans argued with conviction that it would be better to draw Rosslyn out of London, say to Germany, where they could dispatch him and dispose of his corpse. They suggested an abattoir in Mainz or a sewerage plant outside Hamburg.

Rachelle Pienaar proposed a course of action she had taken once before in Edinburgh, with complete success. She could easily purloin Rosslyn's medical records in London, call him to an appointment for a health check at a temporary consulting room in Harley Street and advise treatment in the Bloemfontein private clinic administered by South Africans in Reading. The treatment would result in the patient meeting his death either by the administration of a lethal anaesthetic or by an injection of the drug Monetl-X to induce fatal haemorrhaging in the brain.

Sakamoto listened to the alternative proposals. He ruled out the German option. He wanted to wait until he had enough intelligence about Rosslyn's present duties and preoccupations before designing the operation to suit the geography. He favoured London as the place of execution. But, at this juncture, he said that his mind was not yet made up. He showed enthusiasm for Rachelle Pienaar's proposal. The essence of the tactic Pienaar had outlined might well be applied – not to Rosslyn, but to Mei Lim. If, he argued, Rachelle could put her proposal into practice, it could be used to take Mei Lim out of Hong Kong as a hostage – a bargaining tool in the event that anything went wrong.

There were discussions about the need to keep constantly on the move, passports, the switch of identities, disguise, the care required to select the most secure telephone communications network, the purchase of a handgun and weapons of destruction, and the collection of the Filipino nurses from northern France. After that they went to their separate quarters in silence. Rachelle Pienaar retired to one of the vacant women's cells; the Germans to the male quarters.

Sakamoto returned to his cell to review his plans in isolation. Much depended on getting inside Rosslyn's mind. To do so he would need Rachelle Pienaar to travel to Hong Kong in the immediate future. There she would achieve the interception of Rosslyn's e-mails to Mei and vice versa. The Germans would have their mission to undertake: the collection of the nurses.

Given the terrorist alerts in the United Kingdom, the collection of explosives involved considerable risk. It would require an approach to a man in Southampton, an employee of Knott Williams, the firm with major MoD contracts. His name was Leonard Christiaan Fredericksen.

Sakamoto decided that he alone would be responsible for the purchase of arms and explosives in London, along with whatever equipment was required for disguise, transport and deception. His initial plan was to take Rosslyn, inject him with a dosage of adulterated Monetl-X and watch him suffer a death that would take between five and six hours. It would be the responsibility of the Germans to dispose of Costley first, thus leaving Rosslyn isolated. What Takashi Sakamoto didn't know at this stage was that a combination of circumstances involving the approaches to be made by Chebotarev and Mikhail Ilyushenko were about to assist him. Like many successful strategists, he was about to receive his share of good luck. In the meantime, there remained an issue of security to be resolved. The diamonds in their chamois leather pouches required storage.

The following morning, therefore, Sakamoto told the two Germans and Brother Søren that he was undertaking a short mountain trek with Rachelle. He made no mention of the route or destination. He requested food and drinking water from the monastery kitchen. He had already confided in Rachelle, saying that they would be making the trek together. Rachelle, for her part, was looking forward to it.

The pair began their trek in wintry conditions.

If all went well, they would reach their destination, the Lirgos Caves, in four hours' time. There was the chance, as Brother Søren had indicated, that the weather might change. A freak blizzard had hit the Taigetos at about this time of the year only two years before. Heavy snowfall had formed drifts of some three metres in depth. Minor, yet still deadly, avalanches had followed. Theirs would be a secret mission, but one which, as Sakamoto wisely realised, required two people to undertake in case one of them was injured. The Germans were stronger and fitter than Rachelle, but she was the only companion he felt he could trust. Along with new boots ordered from Athens, they donned Gore-Tex jackets and down clothing – protection against the ravages of the freezing temperatures.

They forged a path among shattered rocks and across partly frozen streams to a ridge, at the end of which was the low entrance to a cave. Here Sakamoto pushed his way through scrub into darkness.

He directed the beam of his torch upwards to a ledge.

'I love darkness,' Sakamoto said. 'This place was used by guerrillas in the civil war. Deeper down there are the remains of corpses. I am the only person to have seen them.'

Rachelle Pienaar remained silent.

'I have several times brought my flute down here. The burial chambers produce exquisite echoes. You know that Jortzig and Merkel play the flugelhorn. Do you still play a wind instrument?'

'Rarely. My lips are sensitive.'

They were standing on a narrow promontory. The beam from Sakamoto's torch illuminated the overhanging rocks. The only sounds were of dripping water.

'Over there,' said Sakamoto, 'if you want to know, there are other tunnels. They reek of more recent corpses.'

'Whose?'

'Hippies. The creeps venture too far, get lost and starve to death. They die here. I've seen their bodies.'

'Clever of you to have found this place.'

'I know. Look.'

Rachelle Pienaar looked inside the pouches and found herself staring at some of the most beautiful pink diamonds she had ever seen.

'They were taken out of Budapest in 1956. You're looking at a fortune. Your share's in this pouch, Rachelle. If anything untoward were to happen to me, all this –'

'Would be –'

'Yours. Yes.'

Rachelle embraced Sakamoto and kissed his open mouth.

Once Sakamoto had completed the deposit of the diamonds, they made the return journey to the monastery.

The Germans had brought a satellite telephone and laptop computers with them and explained the workings of the secure links of communication between Hong Kong, Greece and London. It was decided that Rachelle would base herself at the Mandarin Oriental in a suite overlooking the harbour. She would check in as Dr Maria Luisa Uy and pay by Uy's platinum American Express card issued in the Philippines.

50

After he opened up the flat in Claverton Street again, the first thing Rosslyn did was to call Ann Chisholm. Without leaving his name on her answering machine, he simply asked to see her. The telephone call she made by return was cryptic. She said: 'It's good to hear your voice after all these years, Mark. I'll send a courier round with the Leonard Cohen CD you lent me in Vienna. Sorry it won't be possible to meet. By the way, I adore "Everybody knows that the dice are loaded."' There the message ended.

The courier who arrived thirty minutes later did indeed bring the Leonard Cohen CD. Inside was an ID card with the name 'Mark Fuller' written in Chisholm's hand and bearing her signature.

There was another note. Written on it was the time of his appointment with Chisholm in University Street.

51

Once she had closed the door of her office, Ann Chisholm began tapping away at the keyboard of her computer. The code produced a stream of what seemed to be static from the loudspeakers: *nnnnrrrrttttssss*. Beneath Chisholm's desk Rufus the spaniel pricked his ears.

'Surveillance repellent,' she said to Rosslyn. 'I've always maintained my work suits the lonely heart. One is never quite alone. There's a question I'd like you to answer for me – how far do you trust Bernal Schiff?'

'You mean you don't?'

'Only that I was paid a private visit yesterday by the Director of Counter Terrorism. A Scots Guards brigadier who rather too politely asked me about Schiff. He asked if I could tell him whether Schiff is running some sort of operation the MoD hasn't been informed about.'

'What did you say to him?'

'That I knew Schiff socially and it would be surprising if Schiff didn't have a few operations of his own that Washington wanted him to keep under wraps. Then he

296

asked me if I knew anything about MondoDei. I said that I know only what I read in the newspapers.'

'Did that make him happy?'

'I don't know. He had a rather impassive manner. Mind you, generations of his family have been in the Brigade. But the brigadier is very much brighter than he looks. And it didn't stop there. I had a visit from two senior officers from the MI6 Russian desk.'

'I don't want them on my back.'

'Neither do I, thank you very much.'

'What did they want from you?'

'They asked me what I thought about the device that was responsible for the deaths on Gorokhovetsky Street in Moscow. I said I knew next to nothing. Presumably, the Moscow police are investigating it. I know one or two of their people in explosives and they're pretty useful analysts. Had I been approached by anyone connected with Forovaz or the Ilyushenkos?'

'What did you say?'

'What do you think I said? No. Did I know anything about the brothers Ilyushenko, particularly Mikhail Ilyushenko? I said I knew he was a Russian oligarch who'd bought just about the most expensive property in the UK. How did I know that? I said I'd read it in the *Daily Mail*. Did I know that the wives of three cabinet ministers are MondoDei? I said that I had indeed heard that MondoDei was rather fashionable in Downing Street. So what's new? So is polenta and feng shui. They were slightly irritated by my observation and I regret having got under their skin. One of them, a pretty Anglo-Chinese, said that there are, I quote, "sensitive personal political issues which Downing Street and the

White House are uncomfortable with to do with the various zones we've asked you about".'

'What were they implying?'

'You tell me. But according to my assiduous study of the *Daily Mail*, I'd say that it's hands-off time re Ilyushenko-Forovaz-MondoDei. Then they asked me what I knew of Virtus and Allegiance. Once again, I referred them to the pages of the *Daily Mail*. Has anyone, they asked, *anyone* from those security firms "accessed any of your personnel here", to which I could only say No. All my personnel know that if anyone starts showing an untoward interest in the work, they report the incident directly to me. A record is placed on the personnel database and passed to MI5.'

'Has any approach been made?'

'No. I showed them the database. Nothing doing.'

'Do you get the feeling they want me stopped in my tracks?'

'Well, your name was never mentioned. But I'll tell you whose name was mentioned – rather, I should say, whose name was shown to me. They asked me to look at that biography of Klaas-Pieter Terajima. Did I know him?'

'You said?'

'What the hell d'you think I said? I certainly do not know anyone of Mr Terajima's description. Why should I? Because, they said, Terajima has used a woman called Dr Ushi Jiang as the "link between Forovaz and megafinance deals with Beijing". Did I know what they might be talking about? I said I was completely in the dark. They were asking questions of the wrong person. And, I am afraid, I lost my cool and told them to get some fresh air.'

'I guess nothing will come of it.'

'Wrong. Then came the *coup de grâce*. MI6 want to review my operations here. They made it clear that my department's personnel have been under surveillance for the past few months. And that puts my head on the block. Yours too, Alan. It means they'll most likely have seen me go to Claverton Street and clocked my meeting with you and Costley. I think you'd better be treading even more carefully than usual. Let's have a farewell cup of coffee.'

'What d'you mean?'

'What I say. From now on I can be of no more use.' She opened the thermos flask on her desk. 'Milk and sugar?'

'Neither, thanks.'

'I should tell you that MI5 surveillance technicians are coming here in two hours from now. The staffers have no idea. They think new software's being installed in their computers. Mind you, the nerds won't get into my office. I'm still Level AA1. No surveillance without written warning countersigned and so on. On the other hand, who believes that? Nonetheless, I have a feeling you didn't come to see little Ann to talk over the finer points of Mr Leonard Cohen. And you never answered my opening question, did you?'

'The answer is that I don't totally trust Bernal Schiff.'

'Watch your backside, Alan,' she said. 'There have been too many unexplained deaths in the world of private security firms in recent months. I'd hate to think you might be added to the list. We all come cheap and the coroners are overworked. None of us is indispensable. Death is one thing the security services are rather good at administering in the national interest. Not that in a million years they'd admit to their successes in the field when it comes to hunting vermin.' She deactivated the static from the loudspeakers.

Rosslyn watched her write a name on a piece of squared paper. She handed it across her desk. 'Would I be right in thinking a friend of ours might offer us a charitable donation – Great Ormond Street Hospital?'

Rosslyn read Nurmukhan. 'That's what I hoped to hear from you.'

'You and I were made for each other, Mark. Ann Fuller has a certain ring about it. Now I have a research and development sub-committee to chair.'

She showed him to the door. 'Don't forget, surrender your ID tag on the way out. Oh, hang on a sec. Here – your *Daily Mail*, take it with you.'

52

Having answered the summons to the mansion in Kensington Palace Gardens, Pyotr Ilyushenko was prepared for his brother to condemn him three times over: for his failure to find the perpetrators of the Gorokhovetsky Street outrage, his failure to preserve the secret dealings with Ushi Jiang that threatened to destroy the Ilyushenko oligarchy, and his failure to find Dmitriev's murderers.

Seated in his wheelchair, Mikhail looked at his brother with silent contempt. Pyotr tried to read the expression in his brother's eye. It seemed to say: *You are the hired hand appointed to run SecurRisks. You stand before me here in my London mansion and you've failed me.* Ever since childhood his brother's silences had struck fear into people.

Mikhail shifted in his wheelchair with what seemed to be an effort to control his anger. Since the bomb attack he had aged. One of his eyes was glass; the one good eye was bloodshot; his head was shaven and the pale skin of his skull showed livid scars, as did his cheeks. His dark-grey suit hung about him, failing to disguise the bulge of the bullet-proof vest beneath his jacket. His left arm was missing, the left sleeve of his jacket folded at the elbow and pinned to the shoulder. In his right hand he held an unlit cigar.

Apart from the Ilyushenko brothers, the only other people present in the gloom of the ornate reception room were the two Filipino nurses who stood either side of Mikhail Ilyushenko's wheelchair. They had parked their patient in the centre of the room.

As a result of exploratory surgery, Mikhail now spoke almost inaudibly. Pyotr was forced to lean close to the damaged face. As he apologised for his failure to combat those conspiring against their financial empire, the muscles near Mikhail's false eye began to twitch, as if this were a sign that his brain found the drift of Pyotr's explanation feeble beyond belief.

Pyotr's broad shoulders were hunched with exhaustion. His bouts of heavy drinking had turned his complexion more florid and his speech was adenoidal from a head cold. When Pyotr finally completed his narrative of the disaster that had now struck the foundations of their fortunes Mikhail asked: 'Dmitriev's computer records have been wiped and you say you have told me all you know?'

'I have,' said Pyotr.

'And only you and I know these so-called facts of yours?'

'Yes.'

'Have you discussed this with anyone else, anyone at all?'

'No.'

'Not even with your Elke?'

'I never talk business with Elke. Only, that is, in the office.'

'Not even after you've mounted her – or can you no longer manage even that?'

Pyotr remained silent, stifling his growing hatred for his brother.

'Always remember you owe everything to me,' Mikhail said. '"Lying is not only saying what isn't true. It is also, in fact especially, saying more than is true and, in the case of the human heart, saying more than one feels. We all do it, every day, to make life simpler." Do you know who said that?'

'No, I don't, Mikhail.'

'Camus. You always were pig-ignorant.'

'How would I know?' said Pyotr, bowing his head in mock contrition.

'What have you got to say to me?' Mikhail said.

'Maybe, Mikhail, the time has come to end our relationship.'

There was a long silence.

'Really, you think so?' Mikhail said. 'Why should I do that, Pyotr?'

'Because you loathe me.'

'Is this the same Pyotr who stood vigil at my bedside? Who has been poisoning your mind? Elke. I am sure it's Elke who puts words in your mouth like some cheap ventriloquist.'

Sweat had matted the hair at Pyotr's temples. 'You're wrong. It's you who's changed, Mikhail. Not me.'

Mikhail laughed – the effort induced a whistling in his

throat. If you were a stranger at a party, I might still cross the room to talk to you. But you seem to forget your incompetence, your failure to protect me.' He allowed his hand to swing against the frame of his wheelchair. 'You're pig-ignorant but you know too much about me. Nothing will defeat me. Nothing will come between us.'

'I haven't forgotten, Mikhail. We agreed that nothing would come between us.'

'I know. I know. That's what we vowed over Mother's grave, Pyotr.' Mikhail hesitated. One of the Filipinos folded an antiseptic tissue and wiped away the mucus that had collected at the corners of his mouth. 'For just how long have you been suspicious of Dmitriev?'

'Only since I ran a routine check on him. I had his house searched.'

'You did?'

'And our man found that he had a private safe. Inside the safe was a handgun and ammunition. I took a risk.'

'What risk, Pyotr?'

'Dmitriev's wife said that her husband had kept computer disks in the safe. That Dmitriev had told her someone had removed them without his knowing.'

'Who was your man who made the search – the Chechen, Oleg?'

'Oleg,' said Pyotr. 'Yes.'

Mikhail stared at his brother. 'Why have you always been so confident about this woman Ushi Jiang? Are you screwing her too?'

Pyotr ignored the taunt.

'Well, are you?'

'A friend of Minister Liu Qichen vouched for her. She has working arrangements with the Ministry of State

Security and has diplomatic immunity. She's totally reliable and the irony is that she thought the world of Dmitriev's work. The two of them never met face to face.'

'Never?' Mikhail said.

'No. They communicated via e-mail and telephone.'

'Except he was going to meet her in Milan.'

'He was, yes.'

'Did they meet?' said Mikhail.

'I don't know. Dmitriev was murdered.'

'You needn't tell me that again. But, Pyotr, what do you really feel about Dr Ushi Jiang?'

'We need her.'

'Does she need us?'

'Beijing needs us,' said Pyotr. 'The Ministry of Finance needs us. She needs the Ministry of State Security – that's if she wants to remain in Beijing without trouble.'

'Do you think you could have the Ministry of State Security cause her trouble?'

'Yes. But –'

'But what, Pyotr?'

'We need her, Mikhail. Look, Beijing's the one place where the money's safe. You realise that, don't you?'

'Yes, I realise that, Pyotr. And you have to realise that if those disks fall into the wrong hands, then the head of state will make our future in Moscow impossible. Why, you could even meet the same fate as friend Khodorkovsky. And for how much longer would I receive the hospitality of the British government here in London? You understand what I am saying?'

'Mikhail, I understand you.'

'But you still have heard nothing from Dr Ushi Jiang?'

'No, I haven't.'

Pyotr scratched his sweating palms. The brothers and their associates had acquired almost unimaginable wealth from their sanctioned looting of Russia's mineral industries. Pyotr was intelligent enough to know that the cracks in the shield of the Ilyushenko empire would render them vulnerable to prosecution, even sentences in gaol. Now it had come to this. Only his brother could instil so powerful a sense of despair in him.

'I don't have to tell you,' Mikhail said, 'that I do not want any cloud hanging over the memorial service for Grigory and his family. You will, of course, be here for it?'

'Of course. If you'd like that.'

'In the present circumstances, it will be best if SecurRisks do not provide the security manpower needed for the ceremony and the protection of the guests. Metelev will see to it.'

'I appreciate that,' said Pyotr. 'Who do you have in mind besides Metelev?'

'I'll personally interview several people here in London. It'll make no difference to SecurRisks. Look, it was my idea to put you in charge of creating the most influential and effective security firm in Moscow. That's what people thought SecurRisks had become – until now.'

'What do you mean,' asked Pyotr, '*until now*?'

Mikhail's arm flapped against the rim of his wheel-chair. 'I mean that this breach of security is the worst thing that's happened to me since Gorokhovetsky Street.'

Pyotr ground his teeth. 'I'm sorry it's come to this, Mikhail.'

'You have every reason to be sorry. SecurRisks is your

baby and I want it to remain that way. SecurRisks protects our interests. I do not, repeat *not*, want it compromised. I do not want any hint, not even the smallest hint,
that SecurRisks is engaged in the sort of violence of ten
years ago. I do not want it said that we have any connection with scum or mob war, bombings and contract
killings. We're no longer boys in leather jackets wearing
gold jewellery.' Surrounded by the trappings of wealth
and respectability, Mikhail Ilyushenko the sentimentalist
liked to recall the past. 'You remember, Pyotr, when we
three practised judo in high school? You remember how
bad Putin was at it?'

'I remember.'

'Never once did he get the better of me. But we owe a
lot to little Putin. I used to tell the kid he should have
worked with me in the Eliseev on Nevsky. Little
Vladimir said he wouldn't be seen dead working in a
supermarket. Just think – suppose he'd found a way of
selling vodka after seven in the evening at quadruple the
price? He'd have gained control of the city markets. We
were the *khozyain*.* Rulers of the *khozyaistvo*.** Who
knows, he might have ended up with us, a phoenix born
of the ashes of the Soviet collapse.'

Pyotr gave his brother a helpless look. 'Sometimes,
Mikhail, I don't understand you.'

'You don't? I am telling you, in simple words, to draw
Ushi Jiang closer to you. Closer to SecurRisks. Finally,
follow the trail of Sergei Dmitriev. Listen, you told me he
has the facts on those computer disks. You told me they

* Rulers, managers or owners of a business conglomerate or territory
** Business empire

are encrypted. You told me that Moscow University's computer guru arranged the encryption.'

'Dmitriev provided his own encryption programme.'

'Then it will take time to unravel the contents. The alternatives are obvious, Pyotr. Either you fail to regain the disks and maybe give the British Home Office reason enough to deport me and the Regional Anti-Organised Crime Directorate reason enough to arrest you. Or you succeed in getting those disks. Have you heard from Kiriyenko?'

'No. He's been questioning Dmitriev's wife and children. You should have treated him better.'

'Don't show your weakness, Pyotr. You hear me?'

'I hear you, Mikhail.' Pyotr Ilyushenko's humiliation was complete. 'I'm sorry it has come to this. If there's anything I can do . . .'

'Never apologise. Now get out of here. Go back to Moscow.'

'Who will deal with Ushi Jiang?'

'I will.'

'*You* will?'

'Leave her to me. Remember what Yeltsin said on the last night in the Kremlin? "Many of our dreams have not materialised." He asked Russia to forgive him. Well, Pyotr, we don't want to go the way of Yeltsin, do we? You're not immune from prosecution.' Pyotr caught the glimmer of the smile on his brother's lips. Mikhail was enjoying every second of Pyotr's humiliation.

'Do you have the resources to deal with the perpetrators of Gorokhovetsky Street?' Mikhail asked.

'To be honest, we don't,' said Pyotr. 'Maybe Metelev could help.'

'Metelev's my right-hand man with plenty enough to do for me here in London. And I don't want it to be a Russian who soils his hands with blood on behalf of the Ilyushenkos. I don't want anyone known in Moscow to do the job. No. We'll have to engage the services of an untouchable. A non-Russian prepared to hit those responsible outside Russia.'

'*Outside* Russia – like where?'

'You'll have to listen to whoever takes on the commission.'

'The assassins on the Index are mostly British.'

'I know,' said Mikhail. 'Don't use the British.'

'That leaves us with little choice.'

'Only five to be exact,' said Mikhail. 'Theodoros Tzoumakas the Greek. The two Germans, Gunther Jortzig and Horst Merkel, Takashi Sakamoto the Japanese and Carlos Naranjo the Costa Rican. There is the problem of availability.'

'Not if the fee is right.'

Mikhail spoke to one of the nurses. 'Leave me my laptop.'

Once she had left the room, Mikhail and Pyotr considered the pros and cons of the available assassins.

'The advantage of Tzoumakas and Jortzig is that we've used both of them before,' said Mikhail. 'Tzoumakas has a hundred per cent record of success. He's also the least expensive. Jortzig is arguably the most efficient killer, master of the hit and run. On the other hand, Tzoumakas is now in his early sixties, nearing the end of his career. Jortzig's speciality is killing in southern Spain, mostly in the employ of British people. The Costa Rican and the other German are unknown quantities. We only have reputation as a yardstick.'

'Why not use one of the two we know?'

'Because, down the line, some connection could be made between one or other of them and us. And neither has proven expertise in corpse and evidence disposal.'

'That leaves us with the Jap.'

'Takashi Sakamoto.'

'I have to say I would find it tough to deal with a Japanese,' said Pyotr.

'Well, if he is the chosen man, you'd better learn – and quickly. Remember that only the two of us here know what needs to be done. That's already one too many. And with Sakamoto that makes three of us. That's why we must complete the business as soon as possible.'

'How much do we pay him?'

'Find out how much he wants. Ask him personally. Do what I tell you. Memorise the details of the contact location. I want you to go to Greece with Chebotarev. You will commission Sakamoto. Chebotarev is researching the Tzu Yin monastery. He will meet you in Athens at the Grande Bretagne hotel. Our associates in Athens will supply you with a handgun. You have a lot to do. If there are problems, speak to me and me alone.' He held out his hand to Pyotr, who took it. 'Your palm's moist. You stink of nerves and stale drink, and you can't afford to be nervous. Go to Greece and enlist Sakamoto. Or would you prefer to stay here for a night's amusement? We're having a soiree. Anna is playing the flute for me.'

'And Viktoria – how is she?'

'She loves me. She sends you her regards. So why not stay tonight?'

'I must get back to Moscow.'

'To Elke?'

'Among other things.'

'I can arrange a woman for you here, Pyotr.'

'That's enough. I do not want to stay here.'

'You don't? I have often wondered why you've never accepted my hospitality, why you've never stayed the night.'

'Mikhail, I have to go.'

'Then get out of here. Call me once contact has been made with the Jap.'

'What do we do if he refuses to work for us?'

'What do you think? Increase his fee. Give him what he asks.'

'And if that fails?'

'Show him your muscle. Tell him SecurRisks have friends in the Regional Anti-Organised Crime Directorate who will be interested to learn of his whereabouts. Mention Kiriyenko. I need my medication. Now go.'

There were no goodbyes. No good luck wishes. Pyotr made his exit alone, through a platoon of servants arranging flowers and dusting silver candelabra, making ready for Mikhail's grand reception later that evening, when the men of influence would touch their forelocks in acknowledgement of the power of the oligarch Mikhail Ilyushenko.

If only the car bomb that exploded on Gorokhovetsky Street had killed him there and then, life would be simpler and it would have been Pyotr Ilyushenko, not Mikhail, whom the ministers would be begging to claim as an intimate.

53

The winter mist blurred the few lights shining from the windows of the barricaded embassies and grand residences either side of Kensington Palace Gardens. The leaves of the plane trees had turned brown and the chill air smelled of rotting foliage. Outside the Embassy of Israel a sign said 'No Photography' and the eyes of CCTV cameras and the armed police officers on diplomatic protection duty followed him until he turned away in the direction of Kensington High Street. Pyotr felt no safer in London than he did in Moscow. Outside the Royal Garden Hotel a six-strong Salvation Army band was playing. One of the women Salvationists was rattling a collection box and gave Pyotr a smile. Ignoring her, Pyotr waved down a black cab and told the driver to take him to Heathrow.

The interior of the taxi was damp; its passenger windows had misted over. The cab driver eyed him in the rear-view mirror.

'Which terminal will it be?' the taxi driver asked.

'I'll tell you shortly.'

He felt as if he had hit a dead end, that Mikhail, the supreme *avtoritet*, had sprung the trap for him. Perhaps he had given orders for those computer disks of Dmitriev's to be made, and then stolen to make him look incompetent. If Mikhail wanted fratricidal war, then fratricidal war he would get. Pyotr wondered how much longer he could resist the urge to kill Mikhail and gain the power that he had craved for so long.

'Where are you from, then?' the taxi driver asked.

'It doesn't matter,' Pyotr said and heard the intercom switched off.

He flipped open his mobile phone and booked the next flight out of Heathrow bound for Athens. Then he called Elke in Moscow. 'I've altered my travel schedule. I want you to come with me to Greece. Take the first plane available to Athens. I'll be waiting for you at the Athens Hilton.'

'I'll be there,' she said. 'How was your meeting?'

'It was bad.'

'What happened?'

'I'll tell you in Athens.'

'Don't let Mikhail get to you.'

'He already has. There has to be an alternative, a better way of life for us.'

'There is, Pyotr. With me. Now's the time to dispense with Mikhail.'

'We'll talk it over in Athens.'

'Yeah,' said Elke, 'we have to.'

'I have a lot to see to. I have to get a gun.'

'Don't discuss it. Later.'

'This is a secure line.'

'There's no such thing.'

'Don't tell anyone where you're going, Elke. If anyone asks, say you have business somewhere in the Balkans.'

'I will, Pyotr. Don't forget I love you.'

He slid the glass partition aside and told the driver to take him to Terminal Three.

54

Even before Rosslyn reached the entrance to the offices of Allegiance in Mayfair he realised that he had been followed from University Street.

There was a man accompanied by two women who were wearing headscarves to disguise earpieces – Rosslyn could see the wires. One of the women, who looked to be in her mid-thirties, was black and carried a baby in a sling across her chest; the other wore a hijab, the Islamic head covering, and was talking to her male companion, who was also wearing Muslim garb.

Rosslyn had first noticed them when he arrived for his meeting with Chisholm in University Street. He had noticed that the man was wearing gold bracelets on his wrist – which the dress code for Muslim males would regard as a solecism. The woman in the hijab seemed to have her dress code right, however.

The watchers had to be one of the less bright surveillance teams from either Special Branch or MI5. Across the street from the entrance to Allegiance Rosslyn saw a black cab parked. The passenger in the back had a small camera pointed at the Allegiance entrance. Even the cab driver had an earpiece of the same type as those the women wore.

There were fifteen minutes to go before the meeting with Costley at Allegiance, so Rosslyn stationed himself at the counter of a nearby sandwich bar. He called Costley and told him about the surveillance team.

Costley knew the sandwich bar and told Rosslyn to ask the Turkish owner if he might leave the bar through the kitchen at the rear of the building.

'Give him a tenner,' said Costley. 'Tell him to lock the delivery door after you, in case your departure excites those watching morons. Then double back and go to the rear of the Allegiance building. You'll see a light brown-painted door with an electronic locking device. Here's the code. Open and enter. I'll join you in about thirty minutes.'

Rosslyn ordered coffee and settled down to read Chisholm's *Daily Mail*. It was then that he found the letter that Chisholm had folded inside the paper:

We have a Russian, Dr Yelena Voloshina, seeking asylum. There's a warrant out for her arrest in Moscow from the Regional Anti-Organised Crime Directorate.

I've had one interview with her in Belmarsh and I've advised the Home Office to let her in.

What's behind her defection is not so much what she's been doing as what's happened to her lover, a man called Nurmukhan, also known as Arkady Venediktov. His body was found in a Moscow hotel. He'd been murdered.

The police, in the shape of a man called Kiriyenko, interrogated Dr Voloshina. Voloshina was charged with conspiracy to murder and detained in Matrosskaya Tishina prison in the TB ward. Then she was transferred to Butyrka prison in northern Moscow.

Voloshina was a senior officer from the state body governing regulation and supervision in the mining industries. Her speciality is explosives. I met her at a conference in St Petersburg last year.

I pressed her about the murder charges, which she said are totally without foundation. The reason for her detention was that Kiriyenko, in charge of the Gorokhovetsky Street investigation, maintains the police found traces of Sibirite explosive on Nurmukhan's clothing.

They also found traces of packaging fibres from detonators from the Murom instrument-making factory linking Nurmukhan to the Gorokhovetsky Street bomb.

The evidence of his being involved is overwhelming. The man Nurmukhan was a sophisticated and apparently rather charming man who travelled widely throughout Europe. She was deeply in love with him; no matter that he appears to have had a very doubtful record.

One speciality of his was easing the way for illegal immigrants, especially Indonesians, to gain entry to the UK.

He had dealings with a man in northern France who Nurmukhan said was a Taiwanese called Liu Jin. The scam being that Nurmukhan was seeking some bogus passports for Indonesians on the run.

Liu Jin warned Nurmukhan that if he talked to anyone – police, informers and suchlike – he'd remove Nurmukhan's eyes with the steel nail file he was carrying.

I also assume you can deduce that Liu Jin is actually Klaas-Pieter Terajima. What I think you perhaps don't know is this. Terajima was commissioned to kill the Ilyushenkos.

From what Dr Voloshina implies, it looks certain that Terajima will be determined to finish the job on Mikhail.

Put it like this, Alan, either Terajima will hit Mikhail Ilyushenko once and for all, or he'll kill you.

I'd say you are up to your neck in shit and <u>you really must watch your back</u>. In the circumstances, MI5, even MI6, and the Special Branch will also seek to bust your balls as well as poor old Ron Costley's. They are protecting someone. In fact, my hunch – for what it's worth and I think it's worth a lot – is that Schiff has been taken off the case. He's not answering calls at his Holland Park flat. Perhaps you know where he is?

I advise you to be very careful. Get out of London NOW. Whatever you do, don't get involved with Mikhail Ilyushenko.

Rosslyn felt the surge of gratitude towards Ann Chisholm transform itself into fear.

With only minutes left before his meeting with Costley, he made a telephone call. Instead of calling Schiff in Holland Park, he put through a call to the

United States embassy and the legal attaché's office. The woman who answered said: 'Who is speaking?'

'It's a personal matter,' Rosslyn said with an Australian accent. 'My name's Dr Ryan Peters. Bernal Schiff is a patient of mine.'

'How can I help you?'

'I have the results of his blood tests. I'm sure I can rely on you to keep the matter confidential.'

'Naturally.'

'Mr Schiff is not answering his telephone at home.'

'Well, perhaps we can forward the test results to him in Washington.'

'In Washington?'

'Yes. He has been recalled. Why don't you mail the results to us? We'll dispatch them overnight. Send them to the Office of the Legal Attaché, United States Embassy, 24 Grosvenor Square, London WIA IAE.'

Schiff had gone; the Americans were backing off – and fast. It was a bad sign.

He had just handed the Turkish owner of the sandwich bar the ten-pound note when he heard a woman's voice calling from the telephone by the cash desk. She was gabbling in Turkish and the only words Rosslyn understood were *Meestah Rosslyn. Phone.*

'There's been a change of plan,' said Costley. 'Get a cab and make for Richmond.' He gave Rosslyn an address in Onslow Road. 'Get there now. Make bloody sure you aren't followed. Things don't look too good.'

He glanced through the sandwich bar's front window. There they were. The black cab. Waiting for him to leave. He stood and watched his pursuers across the street a little longer and shivered.

55

Ron Costley answered the door at the shuttered house on Onslow Road, Richmond-upon-Thames. The hallway was in near-darkness. He double-locked the front door from the inside and said: 'Frances Verity is waiting for us.'

Rosslyn made out photographs of Thynne on the walls of the entrance hall. The place smelled dead. It had been tidied to the point of obsession, as if someone had badly wanted to rid the place of bad memories.

Frances Verity brought a tray into the drawing room. Coffee and a packet of biscuits.

Costley introduced Rosslyn to her.

'The biscuits have seen better days,' she said. 'Help yourselves.'

A melancholy figure in a winter coat and heavy shoes, she stood by the windows gazing at the view of what had once been the manicured garden, now covered with rotting leaves. 'Tell me where you want to begin,' Verity said.

'Begin with Anatoly Zhilin,' said Costley.

'A repulsive individual,' Verity said. 'He's in Moscow. He betrayed everything Mr Thynne stood for and then killed him.' She pointed to the garden shed. 'There. I saw it. He showed me Thynne's body hanging from a hook. Zhilin had strangled him in cold blood and convinced everyone – including the police, including me – it had nothing to do with him. He was the most convincing liar I've ever met.'

'In your own words,' said Rosslyn, 'why did he kill Thynne?'

'Because Mr Thynne had long since realised the Russians who took control of the company were gangsters. The Ilyushenkos. The whole lot of them. It's disgraceful that the government does nothing to get rid of them. Mind you, I never quite understood why Mr Thynne did nothing. I think he must have been terrified of Zhilin, just as he was of Schiff.'

'Why Schiff?'

'It was to do with MondoDei.'

Rosslyn glanced at Costley, who returned the flicker of a smile.

'MondoDei exerts a terrible influence,' Verity continued.

'Tell Mr Rosslyn about Dmitriev,' said Costley.

'From what you said, Ronald, it seems you know as much as I do. He discovered that Forovaz was built on blood money. He knew that capital was flowing into the wrong hands in Beijing. But you see, Mr Dmitriev was a greedy man. He did his deal with the Americans. With Schiff. I dare say he'd have sold his mother's soul if someone had offered him enough dollars. But Mr

Thynne, to give credit where credit's due, was something of a scholar when it came to the human heart. The relationships of a personal kind within the Forovaz headquarters on Gorokhovetsky Street intrigued him. Take the woman Elke Wedemeier, Jean-Pascal Wedemeier's wife.'

'Did Thynne know her?' Rosslyn asked.

'No. But he knew her husband very well indeed. Jean-Pascal is a powerful man. He's a member of Switzerland's Federal Council, the member responsible for finance. Mr Thynne had a meeting with him in Geneva and when he got back he told me that Jean-Pascal was in a perfectly frightful state. His wife had admitted to an affair with Pyotr Ilyushenko. Jean-Pascal said he wanted to see Pyotr Ilyushenko dead. At first Mr Thynne didn't pay too much attention to what Jean-Pascal had said. A week later, Mr Thynne returned to Switzerland, this time to Basel for another meeting with Wedemeier. Jean-Pascal said that he had found someone who would give Pyotr Ilyushenko a very sharp reminder that Elke was someone else's wife. If Ilyushenko didn't leave her alone he'd be given a lesson he wouldn't forget. It never entered Mr Thynne's head that a man of Jean-Pascal's standing would do anything more than send some Russian thugs to Pyotr and deliver a verbal threat. That's what Thynne thought Jean-Pascal intended – what he called a "tongue-lashing".'

'Then what happened?'

'Jean-Pascal made a request. He wanted to give his wife a present. He wanted to give her one, if not two, pink diamonds. Could Mr Thynne find him the name of a reputable dealer? That led Mr Thynne to speak in confidence to Grant Feller, whose family firm you know about. Grant said he'd pick his father's brains. It seemed that his elderly father had already decided to repossess a store of pink diamonds with a view to passing them over to Grant's daughter Anna. He wanted to show them to Grant. All of this Mr Thynne passed on, tragically as it turns out, to Jean-Pascal. Jean-Pascal must have, at some stage, passed the information on to someone else, and the wrong people, the very wrong people, seem to have had little difficulty in tracing the diamonds. My belief is that the same people took possession of the diamonds and murdered Grant's father.'

'Suppose,' said Rosslyn, 'I was to say I don't believe you?'

Verity stiffened. 'I beg your pardon?'

'Suppose what you've told me is a pack of lies?'

Verity looked to Costley for help.

'Tell him,' Costley said.

'I would go straight to the police.'

Rosslyn let the silence hang.

'That's the answer I hoped you'd give me.'

'Why don't you believe me?'

'I do. You're not the only person who's confirmed my worst fears.'

'Who else?' said Costley.

'You think I'm going to tell a paid-up member of MondoDei?'

Rosslyn looked at Verity. 'You're my witness. I'm accusing Mr Costley of being a member of MondoDei.'

'I know,' said Verity. 'It was Mr Thynne's idea he and Ronald join in order to discover all that they're about.'

'She's right, Alan.'

Verity said: 'It turned out that Mr Thynne spent a great deal of money in order to convince them he was a *bona fide* member. But he knew the score, Ronald, wouldn't you say?'

'I'd say that, yes.'

'That's something along the lines of what I'd hoped to hear, Ron.' Rosslyn got to his feet. 'I'm very grateful to you, Frances. If anyone gives you trouble, call me or Ron here straight away.'

'Mr Costley has told me to wait for his signal before I speak to the police.'

'Ron's right. And when you talk to them, make sure it's in the company of a very tough lawyer. I know a shit called Das Gupta who'd fit the bill.'

Rosslyn returned with Costley to London. During the journey, he showed Costley what Chisholm had given him secreted in the pages of the *Daily Mail*.

'Are you going to take her advice or not, Alan?' Costley asked.

'Sure, I'll be careful.'

'Will you get out of London?'

'No.'

'Get a new identity?'

'No.'

'Get involved with Mikhail Ilyushenko?'

'He's going to get involved with me.'

56

The investigative journalist Oleg Chebotarev had left word at the offices of *Moskovsky Komsomolets* that he would be away from his desk for an indefinite period. He explained to his editor why he would be absent. He was sitting on a story about the Ilyushenkos: a worldwide scoop. He, Oleg Chebotarev, was going to act as go-between for Mikhail Ilyushenko and the man Ilyushenko was commissioning to hunt Grigory Ilyushenko's killers. His editor rubbed his hands and wished him bon voyage.

Chebotarev had been unable to sleep on the flight from Moscow and when his source called him and asked him how he was, Chebotarev did not admit to his exhaustion.

'Are you alone?' the man asked.

'I am.'

'Memorise what I say. No recording. No notes. Our contact's left the Tzu Jin monastery in the Taigetos Mountains. He's prepared to see us. I'll meet you at the Grande Bretagne hotel in Athens. The room's booked in the name Levitsky. A woman called Dominique Vedrine will ring you and give you instructions.'

'You think our friend will talk?'

'I don't know. It's up to you to find out.'

'What did you tell him?'

'Nothing. I said I was calling on behalf of a Russian friend who had a commercial proposition in mind. He said he's only prepared to come to the UK. He said his company's services are expensive and he would require payment to be made to a bank in either Switzerland or Liechtenstein. And twice he asked me who my Russian friend was. Naturally, I said he must appreciate that the matter was confidential and that if and when he agrees to meet with my representative he could ask further questions.'

'Could our friend have traced the call to you?'

'No. Our telecommunications are surveillance-proof. I've a great deal to tell you. It'll blow Forovaz sky-high. I look forward to meeting you in Athens.'

57

From her suite in the Mandarin Oriental, Hong Kong, Rachelle Pienaar sent the news of her major discovery to Sakamato. 'I found Mei Lim's present address by means of a trawl through the medical database at the University of Hong Kong Medical Registry. The personal record shows that Mei is pregnant. And there are complications with the pregnancy.'

Following Sakamoto's instruction to visit Mei, Rachelle Pienaar telephoned for an appointment with the deputy registrar of the Department of Obstetrics and Gynaecology.

'The name's Dr Maria Luisa Uy. I'd like to see the registrar about a personal matter.'

'Let me check his diary, Dr Uy. The deputy registrar could see you for ten minutes between meetings with delegations from Beijing. If you'd care to make a note of the time.'

'It's most kind of him,' said Dr Uy.

When Dr Maria Luisa Uy introduced herself, the registrar said that he was always pleased to greet visitors and be of help. 'Tell me what I can do to be of assistance.'

'It's a relatively small matter, but one which is of personal concern to me,' said Dr Uy. 'If regulations forbid it, decline my request. I will perfectly well understand.'

'Tell me what you want,' the registrar said.

'I believe that an out-patient of yours, one Mei Lim, is experiencing some complications with her pregnancy.'

'What interest do you have in patient Lim?'

'We go back a long way. I knew her father Winston in Manila.'

'Ah, yes. I remember reading about his bravery in the *South China News*. A tragic business.'

The registrar, like most keepers of confidential medical records, was a cautious man. 'Let me check patient Lim's records.' Without letting his visitor see what he was doing, he first checked the name of Dr Maria Luisa Uy. There she was: first-class degree from the Institute of Obstetrics and Gynaecology in Manila. He then checked out Mei Lim's patient records. 'Yes, you're quite right. There are problems. But none too serious.' He turned the screen around so Dr Uy could view the records and results of Mei's examinations.

'Could I,' asked Dr Uy, 'pay Mei a visit without crossing professional boundaries?'

The registrar was looking at the computer screen. 'It seems,' he announced, 'that her own consultant is on vacation. In Hawaii. Would you like to speak to her?'

'I don't think it'll be necessary, do you?'

'I agree with you. Anyway, she deserves her vacation. Let's not interrupt it. Patient Lim has been advised that she should telephone the Centre if she suspects any untoward developments. So far she hasn't. So why not pay her a courtesy call?'

'I'd very much appreciate it if you would phone her on my behalf so that she's caused no anxiety.'

The registrar called Mei Lim. She was out. So he left a message on her answering machine. He explained that Dr Maria Luisa Uy would be visiting her.

Then Mei picked up her phone.

The registrar offered Dr Uy the receiver with his hand across it. 'She's showering.'

Dr Uy frowned and fluttered her hands as if to say let her be.

'Ms Lim says why not make your way to her apartment right away?'

'Sure,' said Dr Uy.

The registrar gave Dr Uy Mei's address.

Dr Maria Luisa Uy impressed Mei with her encyclopaedic knowledge of the Hong Kong police service and spoke warmly about her father Winston. When Dr Uy gently asked Mei about her condition, Mei was happy to talk about it in detail.

'And the lucky father is?'

'A man I love called Alan Rosslyn.'

'And where is Alan?'

'In London.'

'What does he do?'

'He's a private investigator.'

'That must be interesting work.'

'It is.'

'Dangerous too, I dare say?'

'Sometimes. He's got a pretty knife-edge investigation on at the moment.'

'I hope it works out well for him.'

'Me too.'

'Is it commercial?'

'No. Criminal. He's hunting down a psychopath. A man called Klaas-Pieter Terajima.'

'The name's familiar. Wasn't that the man who killed your father?'

'He was, yes. I think he's dead.'

'But your Alan doesn't?'

'Right.'

'Well, I gather your consultant Dr Lucy Chang's in Hawaii?'

'Yes, she is. On vacation.'

'Well, I must say you strike me as being very fit and healthy. Would you like me to have a look at the state of things?'

'I'd be very happy if you would. In the bedroom?'

'Wherever's easiest. If you'd remove your clothes.'

While Mei was undressing, Dr Uy moved to Mei's computer and inserted the retrieval system that Dr Pereira had obtained from the Vansburgische Landesbank gnome: the system that would now enable Terajima to read, in total, the e-mails that Rosslyn sent Mei and vice versa.

Dr Uy completed her examination of Mei and said she would like her to undergo some further tests. Dr Uy would arrange for Mei to revisit the treatment centre and supervise matters personally.

'Do you think anything's wrong?'

'I don't expect so,' said Dr Uy. 'Let's see what the tests

tell us. I'll make arrangements with the registrar. I assume you have private health insurance.'

'I do, yes.'

'Good. If you want to talk to me, you can contact me at my hotel. The Mandarin Oriental. I'll be in touch when I have the times for your appointment. I think we should arrange it as soon as possible.'

Mei Lim was worried and after Dr Uy had left she felt a flicker of uncertainty about Dr Uy. To afford the cost of staying at the Mandarin Oriental, Dr Uy had to be one very successful gynaecologist and obstetrician.

On her return to the suite at the Mandarin Oriental, Rachelle Pienaar sent the good news through to Greece. An added bonus was that Dr Uy would be meeting with a senior executive of WaijinAir, the Far Eastern airline charter company specialising in the hire of medically dedicated jet ambulance aircraft.

Rachelle Pienaar asked Terajima for an open budget and Terajima told her to spend whatever WaijinAir required. He expressed his admiration for Pienaar's efficiency. Her planning had been superb and to have gained access to the enemy's innermost thoughts and plans was a masterstroke.

The e-mail correspondence between Rosslyn and Mei Lim made compulsive reading.

58

KENSINGTON PALACE GARDENS.
LONDON

When Rosslyn finally got through to Viktoria Feller at
the Ilyushenko mansion in Kensington, she agreed to see
him the same afternoon. She suggested they meet away
from the mansion in Kensington Palace Gardens. She
told him she would be waiting by the Peter Pan statue.
Her daughter Anna would be with her. It was no surprise
to Rosslyn that Viktoria and Anna Feller turned up with
company.

There was drizzle on the wind and the man who
accompanied Viktoria to the rendezvous was shielding
her with an umbrella. Anna was stroking the sculpted
squirrels, mice and rabbits at the base of the Peter Pan
statue.

Turning the collar of her coat up against the thin rain,
Viktoria stepped away from the cover of the umbrella.
'Alan,' she said, 'it's good to see you again.'

'You too.'

'Let me introduce you to Colonel Metelev.'

The Russian was a squat figure of a man with a pale

face. 'Mr Rosslyn, Igor Metelev.' Metelev's English was fluent with a marked American accent. They shook hands. The Russian's grip was powerful.

Viktoria said: 'Igor is in charge of security at Mikhail's house. Mikhail's been very kind to us. You know that Anna and I are living with Mikhail.'

'I heard that.'

'Virtus is well informed,' said Metelev.

'As a matter of fact I'm no longer working for them.'

'I know,' said Metelev, 'and Ronald Costley has left Allegiance.'

'That's also true,' said Rosslyn, turning to Viktoria. 'Have you seen Grant?'

'I'm afraid there's nothing to be done.'

'How did you get to see Grant?' Rosslyn asked her.

'Mikhail has the ear of the Russian ambassador, who spoke to someone in the Commissioner's office at Scotland Yard. You know how things work. It's a matter of knowing the right people. Mikhail knows everybody. Mind you, Anna and I were accompanied by Special Branch people. They've also been talking to Mikhail about security at his house.'

Anna had rushed up to her mother and was showing her something in the palm of her hand. Rosslyn saw that the girl was holding two snails. 'I think they're beautiful. Like Peter Pan, I play the flute too. You're Daddy's friend, aren't you?'

'Yes, I am.'

'I knew it was you.'

'You did?'

'I've seen a photograph of you. Daddy has one at home.'

Metelev gave Rosslyn a smile. His eyes were dead.

Viktoria said: 'I wasn't going to meet you here except that when I mentioned you to Mikhail he said I should see you. He also wonders if you'd be prepared to call on him. He's very keen to meet you.'

'It's a professional matter,' said Metelev. 'We have something we'd like you to do for us. We would like you to attend the reception at his mansion this evening.'

'I'll be happy to, colonel,' Rosslyn said.

Metelev looked pleased at the mention of his rank. Perhaps it suggested to Metelev that Rosslyn had accepted the position of subordinate.

'I think you'll be interested in what Mr Ilyushenko proposes,' Metelev said. 'The reception is at seven-thirty for eight. Bring identification. Your name will be on the list at the gatehouse.'

'Anna,' said Viktoria, 'time to go home.' She shook Rosslyn's hand and smiled into his eyes wanly. 'So glad you'll get to meet Mikhail at last. We can talk more this evening.' Rosslyn noticed that she was wearing a large diamond ring. Viktoria had followed the direction of his gaze. 'A gift from Mikhail,' she said. 'You know, Mikhail's so loving.'

59

Arriving at the Ilyushenko mansion later than he intended, Rosslyn passed limousines parked the length of Kensington Palace Gardens as far as the junction with High Street Kensington. As Metelev had said, his name was on the list at the gatehouse.

He made his way up the entrance steps. Once he was inside, two guards frisked him; he passed through an X-ray arch and a maidservant took his overcoat.

The main salon was packed. A small orchestra played Tchaikovsky, a compilation of the composer's greatest operatic hits. A group of Chinese stood with their backs to the performers with necks craned to the mouths of interpreters. He felt a tug at his sleeve and found himself looking at Anna Feller.

'Mummy's told me to find you,' she said. 'She's waiting for you in the library.'

'Can you show me the way?'

'Daddy's friends are my friends. I've persuaded Mikhail to let me play my flute with the Salvation Army

335

band from High Street Kensington and have them perform outside the house on Sunday.'

'I look forward to it.'

'Thank you. The Salvationists are about the only friends I've got here. Tell me, do you ever get lonely?'

'Everybody does.'

Two men built like weightlifters stood either side of the library doors. One of them frisked Rosslyn.

'I'm going to the conservatory,' Anna said.

'Have a good time,' Rosslyn said.

'I will. I'm breeding a family of snails in there. They're very much at home.'

The door opened on to an anteroom where a maidservant stood waiting. Viktoria approached him. She was wearing a dress of pale green silk and an emerald brooch on a ribbon of black silk around her neck. Her dark hair had been piled high to show off a diamond tiara. Rosslyn was reminded of a gypsy princess from an Italian movie. She was holding a Sotheby's catalogue.

At the far end of the library Mikhail Ilyushenko was seated in his wheelchair beneath a reading lamp. He was murmuring to a British government minister.

Viktoria held on to Rosslyn's hand. 'Please do what Mikhail says,' she whispered to him.

'Let's see what he wants first.'

She dropped his hand. 'I don't suppose you've got a cigarette?'

'We can ask someone.'

'Smoking's not permitted in this place. I'm the only one who does.'

Rosslyn beckoned to one of the servants. 'Get some cigarettes, please.'

The servant dipped a hand into the pocket of her uniform and handed a packet of cigarettes and her lighter to Viktoria.

Viktoria lit a cigarette. 'He wants to be properly protected. He no longer trusts his brother or any of his people, including Metelev.'

'Do you?'

'I don't know who I trust. I'm living in constant fear.' She began to cough. 'We're on every kind of shit list. Mikhail is blaming Pyotr for what happened on Gorokhovetsky Street. He's convinced his brother's mistress was behind it. He's hell-bent on finding those responsible.'

'You think he's right about who initiated the bombings?'

'I have no idea, Alan. I don't know what to think.'

'Has Mikhail specifically said he thinks Pyotr's mistress was behind it somewhere?'

'Mikhail's silences show what he thinks. He just sits here raging inside, letting everyone else feel guilty for being powerless. We're all to blame. Except me. He loves me.'

'And Anna?'

'She wants her daddy back. Mikhail frightens her. Anna's so vulnerable. She lives in a world of her own. And I'd die rather than lose her. We live here seeing no one. I've no friends left. Only you. I spend my time bidding at Sotheby's and Christie's on the phone. Mikhail's given me an unlimited account. He loves the idea of me spending his money. He wants Anna sent to boarding school in Switzerland. Over my dead body. Anna seems to think I've brought a curse on both of them. On Grant.

On Mikhail. She's been having nightmares that someone's going to kill you too. You know what she's like. If she's not breeding snails, she eavesdrops. Probably got it from Grant.'

'Did she mention any names?'

'She heard Mikhail mentioning a Japanese.'

'A name, though?'

Viktoria inhaled with desperation. 'Look. You didn't get this from me.' She opened her handbag, removed a sheet of paper and slipped it into the catalogue from Sotheby's. 'Take it away. I got it from Mikhail's files. You'll find the details of the man they're hiring to find the people behind the bombing.'

'Does anyone else know?'

She stubbed the cigarette out in the ice surrounding a dish of caviar. 'Alan, we haven't had this conversation.'

The government minister gave Mikhail Ilyushenko a small bow. He might have been in the presence of royalty. The man shambled towards Rosslyn and Viktoria scarcely able to contain his pleasure. 'Just been given a million dollars to help out in Somaliland,' he said, and left without pausing for congratulations.

'Let's see what Mikhail has in mind for me,' said Rosslyn.

The pool of light from the reading lamp illuminated Mikhail like an exhibit in a waxworks. Rosslyn was shocked by the oligarch's condition.

Two Filipino nurses dressed in white stood in silence by his side.

Mikhail Ilyushenko disposed of introductory courtesies and said in a very quiet voice: 'I am wondering, Mr Rosslyn, if you are a married man with children.'

Leaning close, Rosslyn caught a faint smell of lavender water and disinfectant.

Viktoria said: 'Alan's single.'

'No children,' asked Mikhail Ilyushenko, 'no responsibilities?'

'Only personal.'

'To whom?'

'My girl,' said Rosslyn. 'To myself.'

'How many security operations are you running at present?'

'None.'

Mikhail struggled to turn the pages of the file marked 'Confidential' open on his lap. 'You would be busier if this were Moscow.'

One of the nurses offered him assistance with the turning of the pages but Ilyushenko rejected the offer. The only sounds in the library were the turning of the pages, the squeaking of the nurse's rubber shoes on the floor and the ticking of antique clocks beside the mantelpiece.

Eventually, Ilyushenko said: 'For a private investigator your *curriculum vitae* is impressive. Her Majesty's Customs and Excise is a great agency. I see you've had experience of dealing with Greek terrorists and maritime terrorists in South-East Asia. I like what I see of you, Mr Rosslyn. You have an appealing smile. You should know that I have already interviewed two other firms to ensure the protection of my family and my guests when we hold our memorial for Grigory, Tatyana and Galina. My family has enemies. Would you be prepared to oversee the security of this place on Sunday next?'

'I'd be happy to consider it.'

'I'd be happy if you'd give me your decision here and now.'

'You couldn't have chosen a better man,' Viktoria said.

'I know,' said Ilyushenko. 'Perhaps we should agree on a fee?'

'What are you proposing?' said Rosslyn.

'Whatever you say. Simply submit your account to me here. Is there anything else you want to ask me?'

'I'd like one of my colleagues, Ron Costley, to work with me.'

'I know of Costley. Anatoly Zhilin spoke highly of him when he worked with Thynne at Allegiance. By all means bring him aboard.'

Mikhail Ilyushenko turned his head towards the nurse at his immediate left with a look of pain. 'It's time for my medication.'

The nurses wheeled Ilyushenko across the floor to a wall of bookcases. The bookcases slid open to reveal the doors to a lift. Ilyushenko struggled to raise his voice: 'Colonel Metelev will brief you shortly, Mr Rosslyn. Thank you for sparing me your time.' Ilyushenko gestured to one of the nurses to hold the lift doors open. 'You must understand, Mr Rosslyn, that the safety of your friend Mrs Feller and her daughter is of the greatest importance to me.'

Viktoria led him to the anteroom. Metelev was waiting for him. 'Let me show you the layout of the mansion,' said Metelev.

'I'll see you on Sunday,' said Viktoria.

'You will. Thanks for the catalogue.'

'You'll be fascinated by it,' said Viktoria.

Metelev was impatient. 'You've seen the main reception room. One of two reception rooms, not including the ballroom and the banqueting salon. As you can see, this is a big house.'

'How many floors in all?'

'Five.'

'Staircases and lifts?'

'Two staircases. Three lifts. Two for the use of Mr Ilyushenko, Mrs Feller and her daughter. The other for staff. There's a team of six nurses and two physicians. I understand you will offer us assistance with security and protection for the memorial service. Perhaps it will be a routine operation for you.'

'No two security operations are the same.'

'Our primary aim will be to protect Mikhail Ilyushenko – no matter what the cost.'

He led Rosslyn out to the main hall and looked up to the roof of what had been converted into an atrium. Quite suddenly he said: 'Mikhail Ilyushenko has confirmed your people for the job?' There seemed to be a note of reluctance in the Russian's voice.

'Just now, yes,' Rosslyn said. 'I'm looking forward to working with him.'

'With *me*,' Metelev said, as if he were addressing a junior ranking officer. 'I control security.'

'I'll be happy to follow your instructions.'

The Russian smiled. 'No expense has been spared on the refurbishment of the mansion. When it comes to palaces, Russia can teach Great Britain lessons. Look at that staircase.' The main staircase rose behind an Ionic colonnade to a large landing. 'You will have noticed that

341

we've installed metal detectors and X-ray screening facilities. We have CCTV throughout the house and gardens; fire and smoke alarms too, as well as alarms linked to the police. All are tested weekly. There is also an armed police presence surrounding the Israeli embassy and more police across the road at Kensington Palace, in addition to the protection teams outside. Staff have ID swipe cards and we have additional digital and fingerprint ID facilities.'

'Who's responsible for staff vetting?'

'I am. Let me show you the rest of the ground floor.'

The two men strolled across the marble hall, into a dining room, along a wide passage and through two swing doors to a kitchen where a team of mainly women chefs was working. 'Fire regulations mean that the exterior doors to the kitchen here are kept unlocked. No one can get in from the exterior.'

'Who's doing the catering for the reception?'

'Best people from Moscow. Kalitniky Catering Company Kozhevnichevsky Street.'

'Where's the fire escape?'

'To the rear of the house. You'll see it in a moment.'

Metelev said something flirtatious in Russian to a pretty *sous-chef* from the Kalitniky Catering Company, who blushed. 'Through here,' he said to Rosslyn, 'is the entrance to the basement. This is the only way in and the only way out.'

Once they were back in the hallway Metelev paused. 'Do you wish to inspect the upper floors?'

'Only if you want my people to secure them.'

'They are secure. I don't think it's necessary to look at them. There are infra-red alarms and tear-gas facilities. You know the sort of thing.'

'I suppose some of your people are armed?' Rosslyn said.

'They are all armed,' said Metelev.

'You realise,' said Rosslyn, 'that I won't be carrying a handgun?'

'If you need weapons you only have to ask me.'

'That won't be necessary.'

'Some of Mr Ilyushenko's guests have requested armed protection.'

'It'll be better if your people provide it. There's a minimum five-year prison sentence for being in possession of an unlicensed firearm.'

'Then you'll have to use the Queensberry Rules,' said Metelev. 'I suggest we look around the gardens. They're Mikhail's pride and joy.'

Rosslyn could see why. They were manicured like a royal park. Shafts of floodlighting beamed through the winter mist and the colours of the late-flowering shrubs and flowers were vivid. In the distance there was an illuminated conservatory. Even that would not have looked out of place in a city's public gardens.

'Mikhail loves orchids. That's what the conservatory's for. Orchids. You want to take a look at it? Anna's there.'

'Some other time perhaps,' said Rosslyn. 'What else?'

'There's the underground car park. It's being renovated. Entrance beneath a house on Kensington Church Street.'

'Where will the memorial service take place?'

'In the east wing – in the chapel. Mikhail originally wanted the ceremony to take place in the Russian Orthodox church in Ennismore Gardens, the Cathedral

343

of the Dormition of the Mother of God and All Saints.'

'Why the change of location?'

'Because several of Mr Ilyushenko's associates said they'd only attend the ceremony if it took place somewhere with guaranteed maximum protection. You don't have to concern yourself with the chapel, Mr Rosslyn. My people will see to it.'

'What happens after the service in the chapel?'

'There'll be a gathering in the main reception room. After that, our chauffeurs will ferry the guests in bullet- and bomb-proof limousines to the dinner Ilyushenko will be hosting in Oxfordshire. The Oxfordshire constabulary have been alerted. There'll be overhead helicopter protection. Afterwards, the same limousines will take the guests to Heathrow. By midnight most if not all of them will be bound for Geneva in the security of Forovaz private planes. After Geneva they'll be on their own.'

'Let's look at the main entrance gates.'

Rosslyn followed Metelev along the side of the mansion to the heavy entrance gates. The reception guests were leaving. Grey figures stood guard by sleek bulletproof limousines parked in neat ranks. The guards muttered into mobile phones and short-wave radios in English and Russian.

'Tell me about the guests expected on Sunday,' he said to Metelev.

'They'll include some of the wealthiest Russians, who live in fear of their lives. Early in the morning of the ceremony we'll have dogs sniffing around for any traces of high explosive. You'll join us in reviewing identity cards and papers, searching vans delivering foodstuffs and supplies, and conducting body searches of the household staff.'

Rosslyn noticed one of the security guards by the limousines removing an earpiece. The guard approached Metelev and spoke to him in Russian. Metelev glanced sideways through the iron gates, then back at Rosslyn. He said quietly: 'Follow me, please. This way.'

He led Rosslyn alongside the house to the gardens and then to the rear of the conservatory. There was no sign of Anna.

Metelev showed him a narrow steel door in the wall. 'It will be best that you leave by this gate.'

'Something wrong?'

'My people tell me you were followed here.'

'It wouldn't surprise me.'

'There was an unmarked BMW some distance from the main entrance. According to our monitoring system there's now someone else out there showing an interest in your visit. I suggest you leave now. Beyond the gate is an alleyway that leads to another house we own on Kensington Church Street. One of my people will be waiting there. She will take you through the house and show you out. After that, you're on your own. I'd like you to tell me if you have an idea who might be following you.'

'I've no idea.'

'I insist that you make no mention of these shadows to anyone else.'

'I'm not comfortable with this.'

'Neither am I, Mr Rosslyn. Your enemies are our enemies. Leave them to us, please.'

'I don't need telling,' Rosslyn said coldly.

With scarcely disguised contempt the Russian warned: 'Unless there is a change of plan, we'll meet again on Sunday morning at ten o'clock prompt. No record, no further mention of our meeting or anything I've shown you is to be made. Understand? That's an order you will follow. If you choose not to, then matters will take an unpleasant turn. We don't want that, Mr Rosslyn, do we?'

'If you say so.'

'And perhaps you'd hand me that book you have in your hand.'

'Sorry?'

'I said you must give me that book. Nothing of Dr Mikhail Ilyushenko's leaves the mansion.'

'It belongs to Mrs Feller. Tell her she can have it back on Sunday.'

Metelev offered no reply as he unlocked the gate with a swipe card and watched Rosslyn step into the alleyway. Rosslyn heard the metal door close behind him with a thud.

He waved down a cab in Kensington Church Street and told the driver to take him to Claverton Street.

In the cab's warmth he turned on the reading light and opened the Sotheby's catalogue. A single sheet had been inserted, Chisholm-style, on a page describing Lot 17: 'Auden (W.H.), *Epithalamion Commemorating the Marriage of Giuseppe Antonio Borgese and Elizabeth Mann at Princeton, New Jersey, November 23, 1939.* The rarest of Auden's separately published works. Estimate £1000.'

Viktoria Feller must have marriage in her sights.

The slip of paper Viktoria had inserted was worth far

more. Issued in Moscow, it was a copy of the *curriculum vitae* offered by the Regional Anti-Organised Crime Directorate.

Rosslyn only needed to speed-read the document to fathom out the name of the man Ilyushenko was hiring: Takashi Sakamoto. He could well imagine the extreme satisfaction Terajima would derive from being hired to hunt himself.

60

Mei had e-mailed:

> Alan
>
> You may be seeing me sooner than you
> expect.
>
> I've had a visit from a new gynaecologist, a
> Filipino, Dr Maria Luisa Uy, who's very kind
> and knew Dad when he was in Manila. Just
> as well. Maria Luisa says there's a further
> complication. It's some kind of infection that
> needs treatment, something to do with my
> immune system. She says that I'll need to
> have it checked out by someone really reli-
> able. The only really reliable person is a doc-
> tor in London. So I told her that if the baby's
> life is in any way at stake, of course I'd go to
> London. Otherwise, Maria Luisa insists I rest
> at home. Best not to visit the clinic, where I
> could be at risk from some bug or other.

You've read about the 'flu strain that's got hold across Hong Kong. It makes me doubly vulnerable. Don't worry, I'm in good hands.

I'm still taking photos, you remember that competition I entered? My self-portrait won second prize in the Portrait Section. Brilliant! I am going to make a copy of it and send it to you. I didn't send it before because I was superstitious that it might not win. You know me!

As for you-know-who, just you take care and remember everything I told you. He's dead and that's that. Anyway, if he wasn't, why hasn't he called on me?

All my love

Mei
xxx

Rosslyn replied:

Mei

Take the greatest care of yourself and the little one.

Do what Dr Uy says. I'm really relieved you're in the hands of an expert. Remember, if anything hurts, be sure to say.

I will be waiting for you here in London if you need to come over. Make sure the airline offers you the right sort of comfort.

You matter to me more than anything in the world.

By the way, I have proof from three sources that K-P T is on the move.

Costley and I will be overseeing security at the Ilyushenko mansion next Sunday. There's a memorial service being held for the victims of the bomb on Gorokhovetsky Street.

Viktoria's daughter Anna is playing her flute with a Salvation Army band and has persuaded Illy, as she calls him, to let them perform on Sunday next. She's a sweet kid.

Much as I loathe and detest Terajima, I suppose I have to admire his brilliance at deception. But he's met his match, believe you me.

I love you

Always have

Always will

Alan

61

GRANDE BRETAGNE HOTEL.
ATHENS

There was no word from Ono at the hotel. Mitsuko Furyawa's disappointment was alleviated by e-mails from Rachelle Pienaar with copies of Mei's to Rosslyn and vice versa and others from Jortzig and Merkel. The Germans had left Dieppe, bound for London with the *quondam* Filipinos, grateful for their bogus marriage certificates and happy to be at last entering the United Kingdom.

Precautions were in place. There could be no delay.

Now there were appointments to be kept with those who were seeking favours. Oleg Chebotarev, Andrei Levitsky and Pyotr Ilyushenko. There were written messages in sealed envelopes at reception for the clients to announce themselves to his agent, Mitsuko Furyawa. She would see all three together in the refreshment area by the swimming pool.

The only incoming telephone call was from the duty controller of XantisJet asking for the correct spelling of the name of the passenger flying to London Heathrow

351

tonight in one of XantisJet's Cessna Citation VII aircraft. The duty controller carefully noted the name of Ms Tayyiba Al-Nasrallah.

'Yes, Ms Tayyiba Al-Nasrallah will be travelling alone. She will settle her account at Athens airport prior to departure.'

'We will send a limousine to collect her one hour before departure. Will she require duty-free facilities?'

'Ms Tayyiba Al-Nasrallah is a Sunni-Wahhabi Muslim. She will wait for her car in reception.'

Mitsuko Furyawa opened the parcel delivered to her by her bank and ran her fingers across the purchase she had made in the shop near the Al Salam mosque in Neos Kosmos. It contained the *burka*, the full-length, one-piece garment that, along with its soft black veil and metal faceplate, would cover her from head to toe tonight. She was grateful for this Sunni-Wahhabi innovation from Saudi Arabia.

She had plenty of time to don the new one-piece swimsuit and matching bathing cap she had purchased on arrival. Dressed in the robe provided by the hotel, she attended to her make-up, adjusting her false eyelashes, painting her nails and applying her lipstick.

Today was Thursday. According to the plan, it would be Ms Tayyiba Al-Nasrallah who would leave Athens tonight for London, arriving in the afternoon. The following two days would be spent in making purchases: Sunday, sacred to the sun, the day of Armageddon. She felt a certain contentment in the inevitably of Rosslyn's death. The matter of Mei's pregnancy would be easily dealt with. Rachelle Pienaar could perform an abortion as easily as strangling a rat. As fathers look forward to being present at birth, so Terajima looked forward to being present at the miracle of death.

It was in this mood of confidence that Mitsuko Furyawa prepared to receive the prospective clients. They had already checked into the hotel and when the buzzer sounded she went to the door expecting to see the maid who would prepare her suite for the night. Leaving the security chain in place, Furyawa opened it to find a woman facing her.

The woman was holding a loaded handgun aimed directly at Mitsuko Furyawa's chest.

62

In the restaurant of the Goring, Rosslyn and Costley fell out for the first time.

'You're not going to like what I have to tell you, Alan. Now's the time to bring in the anti-terrorist officers.'

Rosslyn leaned back in his chair in the restaurant at the Goring Hotel and looked Costley straight in the eyes. 'Like hell we do.'

'This isn't a job for one man on his own, Alan. You know I'm right.'

'You're wrong.'

'I can't let you take the risk. Terajima's in your sights. You have Chisholm's evidence. Ilyushenko's bringing the bastard to London. The only thing Terajima doesn't know is that, come Sunday, you'll be working for Ilyushenko. You'll be a sitting duck. Maybe Ilyushenko's already told him that. If you think you can trust the Russians, you're very much mistaken. I know what I'm talking about. Look what happened to Thynne. Look what happened to Dmitriev and

Nurmukhan. It has to have been Terajima. Terajima's in a totally different league. Totally. I don't have to tell you. Do you hear me?'

'I hear you, Ron. But I'm not listening.'

Costley pushed his chair back and tossed his table napkin on the table.

'Throwing in the towel, Ron?'

'I'm challenging you, Alan. If you haven't given me word that you've called our friends in the anti-terrorist branch by eight tomorrow morning, I'm going to do it for you.'

'You're really going to do that, Ron?'

'Damn right I am. I'm not sitting on my arse knowing that you're walking into a trap.'

'What the hell's changed your mind?'

'You have.'

'I have?'

'You're obsessed. Mei's right about you. Your obsession's got the better of you.'

'Ron, calm down.'

'I am very calm.'

'You're very tired.'

'You are telling me you're not?'

'I have never felt better.'

'Good, bloody good. And you'll feel even better when you've told Mei you've handed Terajima to the right authorities. If you don't tell her, I will. I'll call in her in Hong Kong.'

'She's not too well. So I'd rather you left Mei alone.'

'Alan, I do not believe I'm hearing this. She's expecting your baby. What does she want to hear from me – that Terajima's blown your brains out?'

'Maybe it'll be easier for her when I tell her I've blown Terajima's brains out.'

Costley opened his wallet. 'Okay, Alan, that's enough. I'm going.' He dropped some ten-pound notes on the table. 'This one's on me,' he added and left the restaurant.

63

TAK HING STREET. HONG KONG

Before checking out of the Mandarin Oriental, Dr Maria
Luisa Uy telephoned Mei and volunteered to bring the
results of the tests in person to Mei's flat in Tak Hing
Street. 'There's nothing to worry about. The baby's fine.
So are you. I've spoken to your gynaecologist in Hawaii
and we both agree that you should have a short course of
medication. I'll give you the pills to start you off when I
see you.'

Mei was overjoyed. She e-mailed Rosslyn with the
news.

Dr Uy arranged to be chauffeured by private ambulance to Mei's apartment. She had left instructions with
the driver and paramedics that the patient would need to
be stretchered to the ambulance.

Mei and Dr Uy reviewed the test results over tea.

'Everything's perfectly normal,' said Dr Uy. 'The medication is American and will provide you with a selection
of necessary vitamins.' She set a phial of pills on the
table. 'We start with a booster injection. It won't take a
second. Would you roll up your sleeve?'

Mei did as Dr Uy asked.

She felt the prick of the needle. Dr Uy had injected her with a powerful dose of anaesthetic.

'Didn't hurt, did it?' said Dr Uy.

'No,' said Mei.

'Just breathe deeply.'

Then she lost consciousness.

Dr Uy went to the desk and retrieved Mei's passport. She also collected Mei's laptop and house keys. Then she telephoned the paramedics.

'Would you join me now, please?'

The paramedics were dressed in white overalls bearing the WaijinAir logo. They took less than five minutes to stretcher Mei Lim out of her flat and load her into the waiting ambulance.

'I don't expect her to regain consciousness for at least three hours,' said Dr Pienaar.

'What did you give her?'

'An intravenous anaesthetic. Xetinol.'

'How are you going to maintain it?'

'I've come prepared.'

The ambulance headed for the airport and the paramedics monitored patient Lim's heart and lungs. Everything was normal. The patient's condition was satisfactory.

64

'Is this Klaas-Pieter Terajima's room?'

Feigning fear, Mitsuko Furyawa was looking into the woman's eyes. She bowed slowly. 'I think you are mistaken.'

'I need to speak with Klaas-Pieter Terajima. Who are you?'

'No one you know. Perhaps you'd remove the bullets, hand the gun to me, the bullets too – or if you wish to continue this conversation, I suggest you come inside and we can talk things over.'

He saw her empty the magazine. She put the bullets in her pocket.

'Perhaps there's another in the chamber?'

Furyawa's observation seemed to panic her. The handbag over her arm fell to the floor of the corridor and the contents spilled out. Furyawa stooped down. Before the woman could retrieve the bag, Furyawa grabbed her passport.

'Give that back.'

359

'We have a kind of stalemate,' Furyawa said. 'I have your passport. You have a loaded gun. You can't get into my room. If you kill me the police will find your passport.'

'Give it back.'

Furyawa flicked the passport open. 'You're Swiss. Your name's Elke Wedemeier. And here's your flight ticket. You have come here from Moscow. I suggest, Ms Wedemeier, you look elsewhere for the man you mentioned.'

Elke Wedemeier looked panic-stricken.

Mitsuko Furyawa handed back the passport. 'I'm going to call reception and ask them to alert the police. *Mocca-mocca su su ama.*'

'What are you saying?'

'I'm going to call reception and ask them to alert the police. It's Japanese: *Mocca-mocca su su ama* – fuck you, bitch. I said fuck you, bitch.'

With that Furyawa slammed the door in Elke's face. Something poisonous had crawled out of the woodwork.

65

SPA.
GRANDE BRETAGNE HOTEL.
ATHENS

Mitsuko Furyawa had completed three lengths of the pool when she saw her clients arrive. She swam to the shallow end, climbed out and draped her robe over her shoulders.

'Hello, gentlemen, I'm Mitsuko Furyawa.'

'Pyotr Ilyushenko.'

'Andrei Levitsky.'

'Oleg Chebotarev.'

'Shall we sit at a table?'

Pyotr Ilyushenko ordered drinks and Chebotarev did the talking. 'We want to hire your friend's services. In principle, can you say if he's available?'

'He may be. What's the nature of the commission?'

The drinks arrived and Chebotarev embarked on the narrative of what had happened in Gorokhovetsky Street.

Mitsuko Furyawa listened without comment. Sometimes she glanced at the entrance to the pool for any sign of the Wedemeier woman. She had realised at once the surprising direction in which Chebotarev's narrative was leading.

When Chebotarev had finished, Furyawa let the silence hang.

Finally she said: 'What is it you need doing?'

'We want your friend to find and kill those responsible for the maiming of Mikhail Ilyushenko and for the murder of all those who died on Gorokhovetsky Street.'

'I hope we can make the deal with you,' said Pyotr Ilyushenko.

'It will be impossible.'

There was another long silence.

Mitsuko Furyawa said: 'Such an operation requires time and careful planning.'

'We understand that,' said Pyotr Ilyushenko.

'We hope to meet your friend in person,' said Chebotarev. 'We understand he can be reached at a retreat in the Peloponnese.'

'You're too late,' said Furyawa. 'He left there some time ago.'

'Do you know how we can reach him?'

'You deal with me.'

'How long will it take you to give us an answer?'

Mitsuko Furyawa was calculating what sum she could realistically ask as a fee. There remained the difference between what she had been offered for the Gorokhovetsky Street commission and what she had received in diamonds. Here was a chance to sink at least another million dollars into her Geneva and Liechtenstein accounts. She wanted a fee of four million US dollars. If pressed, she might settle for three and a half.

'We will have to consider our own position,' she said.

'I can make no promises. We are not anxious to work in Russia at the present time.'

'Have you worked there before?' said Pyotr Ilyushenko.

Mitsuko Furyawa looked at each man in turn. She noticed that the man Levitsky looked uneasy.

'We have not worked in Russia,' said Furyawa.

'We have to leave Athens soon,' said Chebotarev. 'My friend Levitsky and I are going to the Peloponnese in any case.'

'I told you that Takashi Sakamoto has left there.'

'I am interested in the teachings of the Master Tzu Yin,' said Chebotarev. 'I want to see the monastery.'

'We need an answer,' interrupted Pyotr, who now assumed charge of the negotiations.

'The world is always seeking answers,' said Mitsuko Furyawa. 'The best people know how to ask the right question. We will need to know who you people hold responsible for the killings.'

'We don't know who they were.'

'But you must have some idea.'

'The police in Moscow have failed to find a name.'

'They have suspects?'

'None.'

'The killers were non-Russian?'

'Maybe. We don't know. Maybe not.'

'That will make life very hard for us. Where do we start looking?'

'That's what we'll be paying your man to do for us. It's a search, find and kill operation.'

'You should relax, my friends,' said Mitsuko Furyawa. 'We can't hurry. Questions have to be asked. In itself the process will arouse suspicions. We only take on a major operation such as this if we are sure, completely sure, we'll be successful. There's no room for failure. And we've never failed.'

'That's the risk your man will be paid to take.'

'No. We take no risks. We can work in conditions of extreme secrecy. Never trust to circumstance.'

'That's what we'll require of him.'

'I will do my best,' said Mitsuko Furyawa. 'We have two more issues to resolve. I asked you, gentlemen, to bring me your passports and an additional photocopy of each. I require to be certain of your identities. Show them to me.'

The three men did as she had asked.

'May we see yours, please?' Pyotr asked.

'Sure.' Mitsuko Furyawa produced her passport from her handbag and each man examined it in turn.

'What else do you need to know?'

'What fee you're offering.'

'What do you have in mind?'

'You understand we do not bargain.'

'How much?' said Pyotr Ilyushenko.

'I don't think you will be happy with my proposal. The money must be paid in advance and within twenty-four hours of our accepting your commission. It is non-negotiable. If we succeed you will be pleased. If not –'

'How much?' said Pyotr Ilyushenko.

'Five million US dollars.'

Pyotr gave a shallow laugh. 'Three.'

Mitsuko Furyawa shook her head.

'Three and a half,' said Pyotr.

'Four is my last offer. It cannot be done for less than four.'

'Very well,' said Pyotr. 'Four million. But on one condition.'

'There are no conditions.'

'There's one. It has to be met. My brother Mikhail
Ilyushenko demands it.'

'He may ask. He cannot demand.'

'He asks your man to make himself known to him in
person.'

'Where?'

'In London.'

'When?'

'Sunday.'

'Why?'

'We need to know who we'll be dealing with. We need
to see a face. Look, Mitsuko Furyawa, I had someone
check you out. You were paid a visit, weren't you?'

Mitsuko Furyawa thought of the woman with the
gun. Elke Wedemeier. 'No,' she said, 'I do not receive visitors on business. If I had been, I would not have con-
sented to meeting you. I do not appreciate unnecessary
surprises. Our understanding is that we deal with you
alone.'

Pyotr Ilyushenko did not press the matter further. 'We
are close to a deal?'

'We're getting closer. I'll speak to my friend. We'll give
you our answer in about two hours from now. After that
you'll have twenty-four hours to transfer the money to
bank accounts in Geneva and Liechtenstein.' She handed
Pyotr Ilyushenko a printed banker's slip with numbers
on it.

In exchange Pyotr Ilyushenko handed her one of
Mikhail's business cards. 'Your man should be at the

address in Kensington Palace Gardens at noon on Sunday.'

'We will consider your proposal carefully. Please excuse me, I have an appointment in the beauty salon.'

The manicurist removed the existing nail polish and wiped away the traces around the cuticles. She shaped the nails with an emery board.

'Too fast,' said Furyawa. 'The heat will dry my nails and split them. Now push back the cuticle skin – gently.'

The manicurist applied a protective base coat and two coats of polish. The polish dried and it was while she fixed the top coat for extra gloss, a shield against chipping, that a clerk from reception handed over the note addressed to Mitsuko Furyawa:

Waiting for you in the sauna. O.

66

Ono was there alone, naked.

They kissed silently in the steam heat and made love with considerable violence.

'You've remembered how to hurt me,' Ono said. '*Why can't we be clever enough –*'

'*– why should we quarrel ever –*'

'*– never to part.* You've got it wrong.'

'I have not.'

Then they sang together: '*Every time we say goodbye . . . we die a little . . . wonder why a little.*'

'I don't like sentimental songs,' Ono said.

'Come to London with me tonight?'

'I don't have a ticket.'

'I have a private plane.'

Two American women came into the sauna. Ono and Furyawa wrapped towels around themselves and went to the showers.

'When are you leaving?' Ono asked.

'Two hours from now. I'll be in reception.'

'Okay. Here's how it is – if I'm there, I'm there.'

'You'll come?'

'I told you – if I'm there, I'm there.'

'If not?'

'You'll be sad, won't you?'

'No.'

'Kiss me,' Ono said.

'See you in two hours,' said Furyawa. 'You'll see me in the foyer. You'll be looking at someone in a burka. Name of Tayyiba Al-Nasrallah.'

Ono showed no surprise. 'I've done some work on you,' she said. 'I know who you are.'

'You don't.'

Ono laughed. 'I do. That's why I may come to London with you, Tayyiba Al-Nasrallah. Or not –'

With that she pulled on her towelling robe and left the shower room.

67

Two hours later, the XantisJet's chauffeur arrived to collect Ms Tayyiba Al-Nasrallah from reception.

The foyer was packed wall to wall with animated guests arriving for a wedding reception. She told the chauffeur to take her luggage to the waiting limousine. He told her where to find it and she said she would join him shortly.

She left a message without a name for Pyotr Ilyushenko at reception. Once the banks in Geneva and Liechtenstein had received full payment, her friend would present himself to Mikhail Ilyushenko at his mansion in Kensington Park Gardens on Sunday at nine. The deal was struck. There was no turning back.

She skirted the throng of wedding guests. There was no sign of Ono. A barrage of flashlights exploded. She blinked, and at first she had no idea that the man was talking to her.

'Wait,' he said.

She kept on walking.

'One second. Wait. The name Nurmukhan – it means something to you, doesn't it?'

She kept on walking. For a second she thought of calling one of the uniformed men at the exit doors. The wedding guests were shouting in enjoyment. She turned and saw that he was holding two small chamois leather pouches in his hand.

'I've been asked to give these to you,' he said. 'The rest of your fee for Gorokhovetsky Street. We won't meet again unless you end the life of Pyotr Ilyushenko, as you were originally told. You failed the first time. I don't want you to fail again. If you do, your life won't be worth living. Check your bank accounts. I've made complex arrangements concerning a deposit. It's been paid and will be realisable when you kill Ilyushenko. You have no alternative other than to kill him. I take it your silence is your acceptance?'

She took the pouches and held on to them as best she could beneath the drapery of the burka.

'Who are you *really*?' she asked Levitsky.

A group of wedding guests pushed him to one side. 'Nurmukhan was working for me.'

'He was your friend?'

'No. Just a piece of Russian scum who did his job. I know who you are. You killed the wrong man. I want my wife's lover dead.'

'Who *are* you?'

She saw him trying to edge away but the yelling throng barred his way. Some portable hi-fi speakers blared out Greek music. A man had started singing. It was at that moment, after the first few bars of the throbbing accompaniment, that Ms Tayyiba Al-Nasrallah

370

understood who Levitsky was, and then, simultaneously, she saw Ono smiling. She was carrying a shoulder bag.

Ms Al-Nasrallah's eyes took in the hawk eyes of the woman with the gun. The same gun that had been levelled at her at the door to her suite. The woman had squirmed her way towards Levitsky and was standing up close to him.

For a moment Ms Al-Nasrallah held the man's eyes. There was a smile of satisfaction on his face.

Ms Al-Nasrallah heard a woman's voice say, 'Jean-Pascal, it's Elke.'

He was starting to turn round when his face froze, his body shook, his chest arched towards her and his body slumped to the marble floor.

The woman who had fired the single shot was Elke Wedemeier and she had already lost herself in the throng of wedding guests.

Ono pushed her way to Ms Al-Nasrallah and they headed for the exit.

Outside, the chauffeur was waiting at the edge of the crowd.

68

Ms Tayyiba Al-Nasrallah was content to have left the Russians behind – to say nothing of the hawk of a woman with the gun.

The aircraft juddered with the wind.

'*Wasser?*' said the steward, his breath acidic with stale garlic and strong peppermint.

'*Nein,*' said Ms Al-Nasrallah beneath her veil. Ono waved him away.

The steward muttered something in Turkish and Ms Al-Nasrallah made no reply.

She made her way to the lavatory with Ono, taking the chamois leather pouches with her. For several minutes they stared at the diamonds. Levitsky-Wedemeier had kept his word. Ono smiled.

They returned to her seat and Ms Al-Nasrallah summoned the steward.

'I want to make a telephone call,' she said. 'XantisJet told me there are air-to-land facilities.'

'There are,' the steward said. 'I'll set it up for you.'

He activated the telecommunications system and left

372

Ms Al-Nasrallah to make her calls.

She raised the gnome in the Grand Duchy. Ono listened as Dr Pereira asked him to check her reserve accounts. The gnome said it would be easy. Could he call her back in, say, fifteen or twenty minutes?

'No,' she said, 'I'll call you.'

'I'll be waiting.'

Twenty minutes later Dr Pereira was back on the line to the gnome. He was happy to report that the most recent deposits, perhaps the ones she was interested in, were in her account.

It was proving to be a fine payday.

'Are you going to tell me what this is all about?' Ono asked. 'Klaas-Pieter?'

'You first –'

'You're getting forgetful,' Ono said, raising her wrist. 'Snakeskin.'

'You must be one of the newer people.'

'A hired gun,' said Ono.

'The one who murdered the police commissioner in Tokyo?'

'That was a good payday. I come expensive. No more in Japan. You want to discuss a deal?'

'Maybe you won't want to come in with me.'

'Maybe I might,' said Ono. 'Go ahead. Tell me what you want of me.'

69

Seated at the kitchen table in the Euston Road flat, Ron Costley had drunk the remains of the whisky from the bottle he had shared with Rosslyn. The alcohol did little to alleviate his anxiety.

I meant what I said about alerting the anti-terrorist squad.

On the rare occasions when whisky got the better of him, Ron Costley would mutter to himself out loud.

Do we think Rosslyn's a match for Terajima or vice versa? When I was in the ring I'd hit the other man first and hard. Jab to the solar plexus, then uppercut to the chin. The old one-two. Never failed. A series of combination punches. Down they went. Here we have a different contest. Rosslyn has to go on playing the waiting game. Let's face it, he doesn't know what the cobra will look like, won't even know his name. All he'll see is the face. Who'll be quickest to the draw?

He stared at the wall with anger and disappointment. He was disappointed in himself. One thing made him happy: he had received word from Kelly-Jo that she was

374

back in London and showing up some time that night with her friend.

The worse for wear, Costley made up two divans in the other room. Now he heard his own voice telling him to retract the threat he'd made to Rosslyn about calling in the police. He first made a hash of dialling Rosslyn's number and then succeeded, only to find the line busy.

Around midnight the doorbell sounded and he prepared to welcome Kelly-Jo and her friend. He heard the slur in his voice and wished he hadn't drunk so much. He didn't want his daughter to see him like this.

When he listened to the speakerphone he heard unfamiliar voices.

Only one of the residents, a pregnant Indian woman, was at home and it was her voice that he recognised. He went downstairs to see what the fuss was about. The visitors were showing the Indian woman their ID cards. Costley couldn't remember the Indian woman's name. 'Let me take a look,' he said. The man, who had a Polish name, said he was a hygiene inspector from the council. Carrying a small black briefcase, he was attending an emergency with two colleagues in council overalls. The inspector looked sympathetically at the pregnant Indian woman, who was obviously relieved that they weren't police officers or from the immigration services. Costley leaned against the door jamb and let her deal with the inspector. Relieved she may have been, but she was also alarmed to learn that there had been a complaint about rodent infestation on the premises. The inspector was friendly but firm. It seemed rats had swarmed along the sewers from King's Cross. The Indian woman shook her head.

'It's a city-wide problem,' the inspector told her.

'Don't we know?' said Costley, who was unsteady on his feet.

The inspector peered into the narrow hallway. 'May I come in for a moment?'

'Oh yes, please come in.'

Stepping into the hallway the inspector asked: 'How many people live here?'

'About ten in all,' the Indian woman said.

'So many?' Costley said. 'I never knew.'

'Yes, yes,' the Indian woman said.

'Who are they?' the inspector asked.

The Indian woman said: 'There's the Bulgarian girl who works for an optometrist in St John's Wood. Two Turkish girls from the dry cleaners in Cleveland Street and my relations who work in the Rajput Euston restaurant. And Mr –?'

'Costley.'

'There's your friend who keeps himself to himself.'

'He left,' said Costley. 'He bloody left.'

'People come and go,' the Indian woman said gravely.

'Like rats,' the inspector said. 'We're all in the same boat.'

Costley tried to place the inspector's accent. *The Pole has a Polish name. He would have, wouldn't he? Sounds to me more like German.*

The inspector's two colleagues smiled and the Indian woman shivered.

'Don't worry,' the inspector said. 'We're here to get rid of them.' He fingered the pile of mail on the broken ledge in the narrow hallway. 'Can you show me around?'

'I can show you our room,' the Indian woman said.

'But the other residents keep theirs locked.'

'Don't worry,' said the inspector. 'Our job permits us to gain access. I have keys to most basic locks. If you want to call the health department to check our credentials, please feel free to do so.'

'I am frightened of rats,' the woman said.

'They're frightened of you too,' said Costley.

The inspector pointed to the suitcases carried by his assistants. 'We can lay some poison. Can we start at the top of the house?'

'That'll be in Mr Costley's flat.'

'Let's get it done,' said Costley. 'I'm expecting visitors, for God's sake.'

'Shall we go on up?' the inspector said. 'I'll be guided by you, Mr Costley.'

The inspector gave instructions to his assistants. They were to lay poison in the usual fashion. 'Start in the basement,' the inspector said.

The two assistants went about their business and Costley heaved himself upstairs like a mountaineer low on oxygen. 'You know,' he told the inspector, 'don't bloody bother with my flat. It's clean. No vermin. I've laid down poison already.'

'Fine, then – thanks for your help.' The inspector turned to the Indian woman and asked her if she could make him a cup of tea. She happily agreed.

Costley returned to his flat and closed the door. His head was swimming. Kelly-Jo had her own keys. She could let herself in with her friend. He fell face downward on his bed and passed out.

70

From Claverton Street, Rosslyn e-mailed Mei:

Dear Mei

Morale very low tonight. Ron Costley's walked out. The whole thing's finally got to him.

He's going to alert the anti-terrorist people in the morning. I know what I'd do if I were them. I'd tell Ilyushenko to cancel his memorial service. So Terajima won't turn up at the mansion. Or they'll place marksmen all over Kensington Palace Gardens on Sunday morning and take him out. But I don't think the police will want a public showdown. He's much too fly not to be reading their minds. The word'll be out. Chisholm will be forced to turn in her stuff. That'll compromise her as well as me and the one chance we have of getting Terajima will be lost. But I'll be there.

What's kind of curious is that so many people

are scared as shit of Terajima, that it'll be more convenient for them if Terajima's left at large. The Russians and the Americans will get into bed with the Chinese. The British will kowtow to everyone and that will leave us where we started.

If I know Terajima, he'll come swanning in through Heathrow without a care in the world.

Mei, I'm going to try calling you. I want to hear your voice and I want very badly to hear that you and the little one are totally okay. So if you're there and it's your answerphone that picks up, you pick up, okay?

I love you both
Always

Alan

Before pressing the Send key, he reread the text.

Does this read like a paranoid fixation? The thing is, I know I'm reading his mind aright. He knows, I know, it's just so easy to assassinate someone. The art lies in getting away with it. You have to set the scene for deception – days, months, years before. The act, the actual act of killing, takes hardly any time. The dying might last longer.

Fact: the vast majority of people don't like the business.

Fact: if the killer enjoys it, then he's going to be good at it. You cover your tracks. Maybe you arrange for someone else to take the rap. Terajima will have worked

*out exit strategies. In case of trouble, he'll have made
sure he has a bargaining tool, maybe a hostage, maybe
an element of blackmail, anything. He'll have worked
out everything by now. At the selfsame time as Costley is
putting the kibosh on the only chance we have of tri-
umph. Why in God's name has Ron betrayed me?*

He called Mei's number several times and got no
answer. He also called Costley. Costley wasn't answering.

Fully dressed, he lay on his bed and dozed. The second
hand of his wall clock ticked round the dial in the darkness of his room. If he slept, he kept on hearing that ticking. He kept on thinking of passengers arriving at
Heathrow.

*Many by day, fewer by night. How many in a year?
Two or three million? Who knows? One of them
Terajima. In what guise? Under what name?*

When he turned his head on the pillow, he heard his
heart thumping in his ears. His mouth opened; he fought
for breath. His hair was damp with sweat. His eyes were
open and he couldn't see.

Someone had a hand on the doorbell and wasn't letting go of it. His mobile was ringing.

He clambered out of bed. There were two women outside in the dark. He could make out their features, yet
recognised neither.

Then he heard one of the women call out, 'Mr
Rosslyn, *it's Kelly-Jo Costley.*'

'Where have they taken him?' Rosslyn asked.

'University College Hospital.'

Kelly-Jo told him that the explosions had torn the

house in Euston Road apart. An Indian woman had died instantly, and if it hadn't been for the proximity of the fire station at St Pancras, Costley might well have been burned alive. 'We saw it happen,' said Kelly-Jo. 'Un-bloody-believable. The whole front just collapsed, leaving the rear intact and Dad inside wandering about like he'd lost his mind, his face cut to shreds, completely deaf. Why the flying glass didn't blind him, I don't know. It was his lucky night.'

'You call it luck? I don't. You're sure he's okay?'

'Who said he was okay?'

'But he's still alive?'

'Yeah. He's still alive.'

'Who got to him first?'

'What d'you mean?'

'Who found him first? The fire officers, you, the para-medics or the police?'

'The fire officers. Then us.'

'What did he say?'

'*What did he say*? That's why we're here. He gave us your address. He said: "See Rosslyn now. Tell him. Tell him I've changed my mind. Go ahead. Get the bastards. Keep schtum." That's what he said. And that's what we've done. Do you know what it was he was rambling on about? I mean, all this keeping schtum?'

'Yes, I know. I appreciate your saying nothing.'

'We've nothing to say, have we?'

'You didn't see anyone suspicious in the vicinity?'

'No. You know something?' said Kelly-Jo. 'He'd been at the bottle something wicked. He was legless. Maybe that's why he survived. He didn't feel the pain.'

'It's a miracle.'

'I don't believe in miracles.'

'Maybe. Maybe not. Your father's a very strong man.'

'I don't think so,' said Kelly-Jo. 'He's a softie. That's always been his problem. That's why I love him.'

'You're sure he's okay?'

'No. Cuts, severe bruising, maybe a fractured rib. Deaf as a post. Can't hear a bloody thing.'

'Did the police question him?'

'How would I know? They wouldn't have got very far even if they had, would they, what with him being deaf. So you'd better be going ahead with whatever it is that Dad was ranting on about. All I know is that I'm so happy he's still alive.'

'I know how you feel. Is there anything I can do to help you?'

'If you don't mind, we'd like a bed to crash out on for what's left of the night.'

'I only have one spare bed.'

'Better still,' said Kelly-Jo. 'I haven't introduced my partner here – Annoushka.'

The silent Annoushka smiled.

'We've come to London to get married,' Kelly-Jo said.

Rosslyn had tears of relief in his eyes.

'What've you got to cry for, Argentina?' said Kelly-Jo. 'My God – whenever we tell anyone we're getting married they get mad at us or start howling.'

'Have you told your father?'

'What d'you think?'

'Congratulations,' said Rosslyn, pointing them in the direction of the spare room.

71

HEATHROW TO STAINES,
BATTERSEA, TIVERTON,
WARREN STREET AND
HAMPSTEAD. LONDON

Conscious of the need to avoid attracting attention by appearing too flashy, the Germans bought two white camper vans that were ten years old from a garage in Middlesex.

The salesman offered to remove the signs declaring that the previous owner of the vans, an Australian, had been engaged on an evangelical peace crusade to Baghdad in the days before the invasion. The owner was seeking an immediate sale. So was the salesman, who was happy to accept cash payment and happy to remove the stickers.

Jortzig and Merkel test-drove each van and approved their condition.

With the two Indonesian nurses on board, they drove in convoy to Heathrow, pausing only twice, to buy rations at a twenty-four-hour shop and to fill up at a garage.

At Heathrow they met Ms Tayyiba Al-Nasrallah with a change of clothing: a dark-blue blazer, light-brown trousers and polished black shoes with hefty gold buckles, of the sort the proprietor of a Chinese business in Gerrard Street might sport. Terajima introduced them to Ono.

The convoy, now including Terajima and Ono, continued as planned, to collect Dr Rachelle Pienaar and her patient Mei Lim from a modest hotel in Staines. The reunion was low-key. Mei Lim, heavily sedated and semi-conscious, was led to one of the camper vans. From Staines they headed to a warehouse complex south of the river in Battersea that offered facilities to travellers. The warehouse complex did no business at weekends. Apart from the Estonian gateman, they were the only people there. They parked the campers side by side near railway arches.

Cooped up in the van, Terajima brought himself up to date with Rosslyn's e-mails, and then he and Ono pored over a large-scale Ordnance Survey map of Kensington Palace Gardens and the streets in the vicinity of the Ilyushenko mansion. All that now remained was the purchase of *matériel* in the city and then, after nightfall, the exterior transformation of the camper vans.

With these matters on his mind, Terajima took Ono on a foray by cab across south London to the Elephant and Castle. Here they left the cab and made their way on foot to Tiverton Street, not far from the Inner London Crown Court, where they visited the first-floor shop of the Salvation Army.

Terajima told the assistant that he was Dutch and an officer of the Amsterdam Salvation Army staff band's headquarters in Almere. He bought a variety of uniforms: jackets of luxurious navy fleece with full-length zips, epaulettes and Salvation Army logos, lined with a warm quilted padding throughout. He also bought large Salvation Army logos to replace the transfers on his van, which he said were out of date.

From Tiverton Street they travelled northwards across the river, again by cab, to the London Flute Store in Warren Street. Here Terajima bought six grenadilla-wood flutes, each with traditional mouthpieces, and six flute cases. The assistant recommended to him a shop on Tottenham Court Road that sold a variety of instruments, including side drums, tambourines and flugelhorns. From Tottenham Court Road the pair travelled further north to Hampstead, this time by tube, and the Wells Tavern. Terajima's contact there, Leonard Christiaan Fredericksen, a wheelchair user, asked Terajima to help him to the lavatory for the disabled on the ground floor.

At the door to the lavatory, the man in the wheelchair handed Terajima a parcel labelled 'Weiss Cleaning Fluid'. Terajima placed a brown envelope into the plastic bag on the man's lap. Then Terajima and Ono left the Wells Tavern, unnoticed among the crowd of drinkers, returned to the Hampstead underground station and travelled south.

72

Inside the camper van parked at Battersea, Terajima inspected the contents of the bag.

Fredericksen had earned his fee.

Terajima showed Ono the parcel containing a variety of countermeasure flares and decoys, detonators, Shancord and Shaplex demolitions charges and cord, and Norstantz sheet and plastic explosive. The explosive *matériel* would do the job; Fredericksen had also included a handgun and ammunition.

Terajima laid out the *matériel* on the van's kitchen table and, with Ono watching, began his complex construction work. He was turning three of the grenadilla-wood flutes into lethal weapons. The assembly completed, he placed the devices into the flute cases and, together with Ono, joined the others in the second camper van, where he asked them to try on the Salvation Army uniforms.

Later that night they would practise 'Nearer To Thee', parts one and two.

While Rachelle Pienaar prepared supper, Terajima and

Ono went outside in the darkness and affixed the Salvation Army transfer logos on to the exterior of both vans.

Joining the others for supper, they watched the news on BBC-TV. A short item caught Terajima's eye. There had been a shooting at the Athens Hilton as guests crowded the hotel foyer before attending a wedding. One man was dead. He was thought to be Jean-Pascal Wedemeier, of Switzerland's Federal Council. Police had arrested Wedemeier's wife, a Russian journalist and the Russian oligarch Pyotr Ilyushenko. All three were being held in the high-security wing of a prison in central Athens.

He smiled at Ono, who gave a muted laugh.

73

Mikhail Ilyushenko's calls to the embassy of the Russian Federation in Athens proved fruitless. The switchboard operator said that Ambassador Popov was in Salonika and could not be contacted. Mikhail then demanded to be put through to Counsellor Yurkov. Yurkov was unavailable. The operator told him to call back on Monday during opening hours.

From his wheelchair at the library desk, Mikhail also made a stream of calls to Forovaz and SecurRisks in Moscow, to be told that an army of press and television crews were outside the Forovaz building demanding information about what had happened in Athens. Mikhail told his people to formulate appropriate statements on his behalf for immediate release. The statements would say that his brother and his associates were completely innocent of the outrageous charges being levelled against them by the Greeks.

He was on the line to senior partners in Paris and Brussels law firms demanding they dispatch lawyers to

Athens and start negotiating on behalf of Pyotr, Elke Wedemeier and Oleg Chebotarev.

There remained the Russian ambassador in London, who owed the Ilyushenkos favours.

Mikhail was put through to the embassy, but only to a duty officer. The ambassador had already left word that he would be attending the Ilyushenko memorial service next day. The duty officer's voice was reserved and he expressed surprise and regret that Mikhail Ilyushenko had not already been informed.

The people Mikhail regarded as his friends were putting up an iron wall against him. His influence was on the verge of collapse. He realised that the rumours were inflicting irreparable damage on the family name. He could imagine the frenzied press excitement. This was the big story they had waited years to get, the scandal that would thrill readers in their millions. The Ilyushenkos had been caught red-handed murdering a Swiss politician at a wedding reception being held in one of the world's greatest hotels.

Before things could get worse, he called in Colonel Metelev and two secretaries. 'Contact each name on the memorial service invitation list. Make sure they attend . . . draft me a press release . . .'

He remembered the clandestine meeting arranged for nine o'clock tomorrow morning. The meeting now assumed the utmost importance. Nothing could matter more than to find those who had plotted against the family to such effect. Here was the chance to prevent the collapse of the Ilyushenko empire. Revenge was within his grasp.

He would call upon Rosslyn to establish a still greater

level of security at the mansion. The man Costley would also be of help. He had no idea, however, that Costley was at that moment undergoing surgery in University College Hospital.

The other person looking forward to the memorial service was Anna Feller.

The friends she had made among the musicians of the Salvation Army band would have the opportunity to show off their skills. Anna would have the chance to show off hers.

Her mother had promised that some sort of arrangement could be made for the small band to play some time tomorrow morning. It might be a good idea to let them perform for a few minutes in the garden, which would take Mikhail's mind off things. Anna asked if she could play in the garden too. Why not? She played so beautifully.

When Viktoria next saw Mikhail, she did her best to calm him. It was unthinkable, she told him, that Pyotr could have been involved in murder. 'You could invite some journalists to the ceremony. It'll put a good spin on things.'

'I already have. The press will jump at the chance to be here. I will give a press conference.'

'Anna is so looking forward to playing her flute for you with her Salvation Army friends.'

'Make sure they're well received, Viktoria. I want the chapel filled with flowers and a thousand candles. Put your style on things. Now I need my medication.'

74

If Kelly-Jo Costley and her fiancée Annoushka hadn't repaid Rosslyn for his kindness by taking him to the Saturday night Joan Armatrading concert at the Royal Albert Hall, Rosslyn would have received the urgent message from Chisholm earlier.

Chisholm had been called back into her office in University Street a few hours after the bomb blast on the Euston Road. With two of her senior technicians, she had made a prolonged and intensive forensic examination of the debris.

The conclusion was that the devices bore traces of Norstantz explosive that could be traced to Knott Williams of Southampton.

She called a Southampton number and, with the authority of the MoD, insisted that checks be run immediately on the Knott Williams inventories.

Her persistence paid a dividend. There was a query about surplus supplies. Fortunately, the call for Knott

Williams's products in Iraq meant that there was an unusually small quantity of surplus in the underground stores near the Southampton docks. The records on the computer database did not quite tally with what had been checked in the concrete bunkers. The main query related to the Norstantz sheet and plastic explosive. It looked as though a quantity was missing.

'Keep on checking,' Chisholm said.

The Knott Williams chief of security called her back. 'I'm afraid I can confirm that there seems to be an error. The records don't match.'

'Who's had access in the past week?'

'The last person to have had access was our deputy stores executive. A man called Leonard Christiaan Fredericksen.'

'Has he been vetted?'

'Yes. I've got his records in front of me. He's a fine man, a rather religious fellow. Keeps himself to himself. He's a member of something called MondoDei. A single man. Aged fifty-eight. Disabled. Wheelchair user. Lives in a ground-floor flat near the railway station. Has a place in London. A room in the King's Cross area. Used to be his mother's. She died a year ago. No other relatives.'

'You're quite certain no one else has had access to that particular storage area other than this Fredericksen?'

'That's what the records tell me.'

'Could he have removed a quantity of *matériel*?'

'I very much doubt it.'

'You said he's in a wheelchair?'

'Yes. I'm not quite sure for what reason.'

'Are your arrivals and departures at the storage unit monitored?'

'Yes, they are. Body searches. X-ray. The usual thing.'

'CCTV?'

'No.'

'You have photos of him?'

'Yes. In the office on computer.'

'Right. Listen to me. Go to your office. Get on your computer and send them to me now.'

'I'm afraid I'm in the middle of a dinner party.'

'Listen to me, my friend, if you don't send mug shots of this maggot to me now – and I mean now – you'll have every kind of Special Branch and anti-terrorist gorilla arriving at your dinner party and they'll tear it apart. Move yourself. Just before you do, give me Fredericksen's address in – where was it, King's Cross?'

'Have you a pen?'

'Yes, yes. Give me his address.'

Then she called University College Hospital and spoke to the sister in charge of the intensive care ward. She wanted a favour on an urgent personal matter. Could Mr Costley tell her how to contact Alan Rosslyn as soon as possible? The nurse said that Mr Costley's hearing had been damaged and explained the extent of his deafness. Chisholm told the nurse to put the question to Costley in writing. It really was a very serious matter. The sister said she would do what she could to help.

When she came back on the line again, the sister gave Chisholm the number of Kelly-Jo's mobile telephone.

Rosslyn took Chisholm's call outside a pub in Knightsbridge.

Chisholm explained the results of the forensic tests. 'We need to question Fredericksen – and now. One more thing, Alan. I really urge you not, repeat not, to go back to Claverton Street. I know a hotel in Sussex Gardens that's reliable. The Formby.'

Chisholm and Rosslyn arranged to meet outside the main entrance of King's Cross railway station. He called the Formby and booked two rooms. One for himself, the other for Kelly-Jo and Annoushka.

75

The street where Leonard Christiaan Fredericksen had his ground-floor flat had seen better nights. The garbage looked as if it had been delivered rather than collected. Youths with haunted faces glowered beneath tracksuit hoods. A soft-spoken Eurasian in his early twenties answered the door. He was wearing a singlet and leopard-skin-patterned boxer shorts.

'Is Leonard Christiaan Fredericksen in?' Rosslyn asked.

'What if he is?'

Chisholm showed her MoD ID card. 'Police.'

'Nothing serious?' said the Eurasian.

'What if it is?' said Rosslyn and barged past the Eurasian to the door marked Flat B and threw it open.

The man in the wheelchair was dressed in an old-fashioned woman's dressing gown and slippers. The Eurasian took his place behind the wheelchair. He stroked what was left of Fredericksen's hair. 'I'm a qualified NHS nurse,' he said. 'Mr Fredericksen is not to be upset. I must ask you to leave. He's not allowed visitors except on special occasions.'

'This is a special occasion,' said Rosslyn.

'You're not next of kin?'

'Are you?'

Chisholm handed him a ten-pound note.

'Make yourself scarce, Sal. Buzz off and fix your make-up,' said the man in the wheelchair.

'Get out,' said Rosslyn.

'Show some manners,' Fredericksen said.

'Are you Leonard Christiaan Fredericksen?' Chisholm asked.

'No.'

She showed him copies of the mug shots the man at Knott Williams had sent her.

'All right. What if I am?'

'You're looking at a minimum twenty-five years,' said Rosslyn.

'Me?'

'You.'

'What is it you want?'

'We want you to account for all your movements since you left Southampton yesterday.'

'I've been sitting here watching Jane Austen on TV.'

Rosslyn lifted Fredericksen's jacket from the hook at the back of the door. He searched the pockets and produced a wallet.

'This yours?'

'What if it is?'

Rosslyn opened the wallet. Two credit cards. Forty-five pounds in cash. A Lottery ticket. A photo of Sal exposing himself in a baby doll nightie. He unfolded some credit card slips. Fredericksen had purchased some books at Waterstone's in Hampstead. Travel guides to

Thailand. Then he'd gone to the Wells Tavern and bought himself lunch and two glasses of champagne.

'Had a celebration yesterday, did you?'

'What of it?'

'The Wells Tavern?'

'Never heard of it.'

'I suppose you haven't.'

Rosslyn told Chisholm to stay with Fredericksen while he made a call.

Leaving the front door on the latch, he went outside, called directory enquiries and had himself put through to the Wells Tavern. 'Can I speak to the manager, please?'

A pleasant man with an Italian-sounding name answered.

'This is the duty officer at Holborn Police Station,' Rosslyn said. 'I wonder if you could help us?'

'I'll try, yes.'

'Is there anyone there at present who was on bar duty yesterday afternoon?'

'Yes.'

'Who was?'

'Me.'

'Okay, do you recall a man who lunched there in the bar? He was in a wheelchair, white, balding, around fifty-eight years old. Name of Leonard Christiaan Fredericksen?'

'Yes, I remember him.'

'Did he meet anyone there?'

'Yes, briefly.'

'Could you identify this person from a photograph?'

'I might be able to, yes.'

'Did you notice anything about him?'

'He was oriental in appearance. Neatly dressed. He was carrying two carrier bags. One from the Salvation Army. Another from a music store.'

'Are you sure of that?'

'Yes. At one point the oriental man helped his friend in the wheelchair to the toilet for the disabled. The oriental man left the two carrier bags on the settee. I asked someone if they knew who'd left them there. They could've been suspicious or something. And someone said they belonged to the bloke who'd taken his friend to the toilet. When they returned the oriental man took the bags and left. The customer bought himself a second glass of champagne.'

'What did you notice about the man in the wheelchair?'

'Only that I saw him check some package he had in the carrier thing. It sort of made a bulge.'

'Was it there when he came back from the toilet?'

'You know, I don't think it was. I'd seen him with some labels, you know, before his friend arrived and he stuck one or two on the package. One he tore and crunched up and left in an ashtray. It had strong adhesive and I had a bugger of a time getting it off. It had a name on it. Something like "Weiss Cleaning Fluid of Southampton and Gateshead". Or it could've been Portsmouth and Gateshead . . .'

'You sure?'

'Sure as can be.'

'You haven't still got it, have you?'

'I binned it.'

'Listen, would you mind hanging on at the Wells until I get there with a colleague? I very badly need to show you some photographs of these two men.'

'Sure, I'll be here till late. If the door's locked, ring the bell.'

Rosslyn returned to Fredericksen's front room.

He turned up the volume of the TV and called Chisholm to one side.

'Search this place. Give Rufus the signal. We're looking for any labels with the name of "Weiss Cleaning Fluid of Southampton and Gateshead" on them. Turn this shithole inside out.'

Chisholm and Rufus began the search.

'Leonard Christiaan Fredericksen –' Rosslyn put his face in close to Fredericksen's. 'You're in one whole heap of shit.'

'If you say so.'

'If you say that again I'll break your nose.'

'Don't threaten me. I'm disabled. I have rights.'

'You've as many rights as a double-headed hooker. You did a deal with that man at the Wells in Hampstead. You handed over a package.'

'I did not.'

'You removed a lethal quantity of explosives from that firm you work for and you sold the stuff to the man you met at the Wells Tavern.'

'If you –'

Rosslyn grasped the tip of Fredericksen's nose.

'I want you to tell me who the man is.'

'I don't know.'

'You don't know, or you don't want to know, or you know and you don't want to tell me. It doesn't matter a shit because I bloody know who he is. Right now, I can't worry about him. But I'm sure as hell worried about what he might be going to do with that gear you sold him.'

Sweat was pouring from Fredericksen's brow. It dripped across Rosslyn's fingers and still he held on to the man's nose.

'I see you have false teeth, Fredericksen.'

'Dentures.'

'Shame if you were to swallow them.'

Rosslyn let go.

'I want to call the police,' said Fredericksen.

'We are the police, you piece of scum. Don't waste my time, see?'

Chisholm returned to the front room with Rufus. Chisholm was holding a large brown envelope. 'Here's several thousand quid. And, here –' She handed Rosslyn a small roll of adhesive labels. On each was printed 'Weiss Cleaning Fluid of Southampton and Gateshead'.

'Call your people,' Rosslyn told her. 'No need for formalities. Conspiracy to sell explosives. Terrorist activities. Chuck the bucket at this heap of dung.'

Chisholm went outside and made the call.

When she came back, she said: 'They're on the way. Oh, boy, it's a red alert. What do I say to them?'

'Pull rank – have him banged up. Give me the photos of this man.'

He told her to meet him next morning near the Israeli embassy and to bring her sniffer dog. 'If you need me, you know where to find me.'

76

At the Wells Tavern, the man was waiting for him. It took him less than a minute to confirm that the photographs were of the men he'd seen in the bar. One was Leonard Christiaan Fredericksen. The other was Klaas-Pieter Terajima. A young Asian-looking woman had accompanied him.

Rosslyn found a cab on Hampstead High Street and asked the driver to take him to the Formby Hotel in Sussex Gardens.

FOR IMMEDIATE RELEASE

MEMORIAL SERVICE FOR GRIGORY, TATYANA AND GALINA ILYUSHENKO

For your tomorrow they gave their today

The following statement is issued by the press secretary to Mikhail Ilyushenko

The Memorial Service for Grigory Ilyushenko and family will take place on 16 December at 12 noon in the Ilyushenko Chapel, Kensington Palace Gardens, London. The service – to be attended by their Excellences the Ambassadors of the Russian Federation, the People's Republic of China and the Republic of France; Dr Mikhail Ilyushenko, family and friends – will be private.

Messages of Condolence

Condolence books will be open at the Ilyushenko Residence, Kensington Palace Gardens (11.00 to 17.00).

Charitable Donations

People wishing to make charity donations in memory of Grigory Ilyushenko and family may like to contribute to the Ilyushenko Foundation, Gorokhovetsky Street, Moscow.

Press Conference

Mikhail Ilyushenko will hold a press conference in the main salon of the Residence at 11.30 am.

Statement Dr Mikhail Ilyushenko

The Memorial Service at the Ilyushenko Chapel offers a personal way in which we can acknowledge family sacrifice.

The Ilyushenko family is honoured that so many family friends will be present along with British government ministers, members of the diplomatic corps and press and television. In this way a younger generation will become aware of the immense contribution of the Ilyushenko family to international good will and commercial and charitable interests promoting the multi-cultural and multi-racial Britain and Russia of today and the future.

77

Anna Feller woke early.

She opened her bedroom curtains and found that star-shaped crystal patterns had formed on the window-panes. It was still dark, but she could see that more snow had fallen in the night.

She washed and dressed, then strolled through the mansion glancing at the Ilyushenko retainers already hard at work. The Ilyushenko residence reminded her of some modern European hotel she had once stayed in with her mother and father. Chandeliers sparkled above rows of Christmas trees. Aproned women were arranging displays of flowers. Workmen in overalls were unpacking a landscape painting of old Moscow. The sweet lavender smell of furniture polish filled the corridors. A sightless man, his guide dog beside him, was tuning a grand piano. Some girls were laying logs in a fireplace, and she listened to them chattering furtively in broken English. Her meanderings took her to the chapel that adjoined the mansion.

Uniformed cleaners had been at work in the chapel

since the early hours. Anna looked at the gold ornaments and shining marble floors. She had never seen so many flowers. Their heated scents were overwhelming and sickly. Who, she wondered, would light the multitude of candles? Her mother had told her that the antique stone carvings and icons, several of St Theophan the Recluse, were said to be priceless. No expense had been spared on this assembly of holy loot. She stared at the gold-framed photographs of Grigory, Tatyana and little Galina. The smiling Galina was pictured wearing a fairy's outfit. She wondered if she'd have liked Galina and vice versa.

Thoughts of her father intruded on her mood of expectancy, and the rush of sadness she felt made her catch her breath. The fabricated glory of the chapel confused her. She watched men who were testing the bomb-proof steel shutters across the windows and the chapel's entrance.

'Would you let me out of here, please?'

'Wait here. The door shutters will open in a moment.'

Even before they had finished opening, Anna squeezed between them and hurried along the corridors to the breakfast room.

There, three maidservants dressed in black and white pinafores attended her. She asked for the curtains to be drawn aside so that she could see the falling snow, but security grilles like the bars of a prison cell spoiled the view.

Viktoria joined her. She was smoking a cigarette and looked wan. Her bloodshot eyes told of sleeplessness. The telephones had been ringing throughout the night. Mikhail Ilyushenko had complained of pain and it seemed as though the increased doses of morphine were doing little to alleviate it. Haunted by demons, the sleepless Viktoria fretted. Mikhail told her not to worry. She sensed the Ilyushenko empire was threatened and there might be no escape, no promise of a secure life for her. Who could she turn to for support other than her wreck of a lover? Suppose he died? Who would his fortune pass to then? Mikhail sensed her extreme unease. He told her to trust him. He'd been in situations like this before. Well accustomed to conspiracy and violence, the Ilyushenko family was, he said, 'untouchable'. Viktoria had begun to fear the power of the oligarchs: she felt unable to believe her lover. This mansion, this London pile worth millions of pounds, might be secure, but she wasn't. She felt unsafe, unsure – she enjoyed none of the relief afforded to Mikhail by his regular injections of painkillers.

'Is Alan coming?' Anna asked her mother.

'I think so.'

'Is Daddy?'

Viktoria coughed. 'No.'

'Why not?'

'No more questions, Anna. Hurry up and eat your muesli. You'll be late for the hairdresser and beauticians. We're going to have our photos taken.'

'I look awful.'

'The beauticians will change that.' Viktoria raised her voice at one of the maids: 'Where are the Sunday papers?'

'I don't know, ma'am.'

'Go and get them!' Viktoria shouted, stabbing out her cigarette with such force that the dots of hot ash singed the tablecloth. The maids looked at each other and one of them hurried from the dining room. Viktoria tried to recompose herself. She lit yet another cigarette. 'The coffee's shitty.'

'I wish you wouldn't swear, Mummy.'

'Don't talk to me like that . . . Look, Anna, I'm under a lot of stress – don't make it any worse.'

'I don't want your beauticians to touch me. I don't want to go to the service.'

'You'll do as you're told.'

'I hate that chapel . . . it's full of ghosts. It scares me.'

'Please – will you just stop behaving like a baby?'

Anna burst into tears. 'I hate Mikhail . . . He looks horrible . . .'

'Do stop crying. *It destroys me.* Anyway, think how lucky you are. Remember, Mikhail can't help the way he looks –'

'He hates me.'

'Please, Anna –'

'I don't want to stay here.'

'Look, your little band is coming. And lots and lots of people who'll love meeting you. We two have got so much to look forward to together. We love this place. Love it . . .'

'You're lying – like you've always lied . . . to me . . . to Daddy. I want to be with Daddy.'

'Well, you can't be. He won't be living with us again, and that's that. Eat your breakfast, Anna, and stop sulking.'

Anna left her muesli untouched. She jumped to her feet. In floods of tears, she ran from the room, out into the hall, shoving her way past the cleaners and maidservants, up the stairs, along the corridors to her room.

*

Colonel Metelev had been on duty throughout the night, fortified by continual glasses of whisky and water. He had changed into the dark double-breasted suit Yeltsin's tailors had made for him. He had cut his jaw shaving; there were tiny spots of blood on the collar of his new white shirt. Sweating profusely, he checked and rechecked the work of the technicians who had set up the mansion's CCTV cameras together with the monitoring system and screens in the security operations centre.

The operations centre had been established in a small room in the west wing. The TV screens afforded a wide selection of views of the interior and exterior of the residence. Sound engineers were testing the sound system that would relay and record both Mikhail Ilyushenko's press conference and the memorial service. Both would be broadcast to the Forovaz headquarters in Moscow, where relatives of the staff who died in Gorokhovetsky Street and invited dignitaries would gather to bear witness.

Satisfied that the security of the Ilyushenko residence was now impenetrable, Metelev issued handguns, ammunition, holsters and bullet-proof protection vests to three of his deputies from the strong room that adjoined the wine cellar.

It was with a certain sense of pride in a mission accomplished that he presented himself to Mikhail Ilyushenko. He carried with him a spare protection vest and reported that he had personally inspected every corner of the mansion, from the cellars and the underground car park to the roof spaces, the chapel and the exterior of the roof, not to mention the gardens. Counting on his thick fingers, he reeled off a list of names: 'Protection officers are in place . . . they're satisfied with the security . . . the demands of the Russian, Chinese and French ambassadors' security people have been met, as well as those of the American legal attaché. You will find that your Mr Rosslyn will have no complaint.'

Mikhail Ilyushenko had few questions. He asked Metelev to show him the final version of the press release. Metelev handed Mikhail a copy. 'You've made arrangements for the journalists to be admitted to the chapel?'

'They will arrive between eleven and eleven-fifteen. The main salon will be prepared for your press conference. The chapel will be opened thirty minutes before noon. The priest's people are beginning their preparations. They'll explain the order of service to you when you're ready. It will be simple, as you requested. Do you want to check that too?'

'I don't need to check it. I will sit at the front of the chapel . . . allow enough space for my nurses . . . check that they carry my medication. Viktoria and the girl will stand behind me. A chair will be left for Pyotr with his name on it.'

'Pyotr won't be here. A chair –?'

'I said a chair . . . position an empty chair . . . with his name on it in big letters. There are to be no divisions within the family. Make sure the conservatory is open for visitors to admire the blooms.'

'Is there anything else?'

'Yes. The underground car park . . .'

'The underground car park?'

'It will be off limits. I want it reserved for my private visitor.'

'It's not being used . . . it's still being renovated.'

'Don't keep telling me what I know already. You will receive him down there alone. The visitor will give his name as Mr D. You will wait with him until the service is finished. I will see him before attending the reception afterwards. My business will not take long. Tell the priests I will see them later. Pay them cash. Make sure that there is coffee, vodka and champagne for the press people . . .'

'And afterwards?'

'We have talked about this a thousand times, Metelev. You are the person who's responsible for seeing the chauffeurs ferry the guests to Oxfordshire . . . you are responsible for helicopter protection.'

'The snow has reduced visibility.'

'Then think of an alternative. Or cancel, cancel – have the limousines take the guests to Heathrow or Farn-borough or whichever airport is open. Alert our pilots. Take them to Geneva or wherever.' With a great effort, he raised his voice: 'You are responsible. God help you if there is an error.' One of the nurses stroked his forehead with a tissue. 'Attend to Rosslyn, Metelev. Tell Viktoria I want to see her.'

'Can I tell her what you want of her?'

'What do you mean?'

'She has an appointment with her hairdresser.'

'Then go and say that, when she's through, I want her to suck me off.'

Metelev handed the nurse the bullet-proof vest. 'Make sure he wears it,' he said, and added as a whispered afterthought, '– when the woman does what he wants.'

78

In his Formby Hotel room in Sussex Gardens, Rosslyn woke from a fierce nightmare. Terajima was leaning over him. He could even smell his breath. Terajima was holding a cigarette lighter to his eyes. He heard Terajima's thin and brutal voice, saw the smile of victory across the full lips. The bed was on fire and Mei was standing in the doorway, dressed in a kimono open at the waist. He could see the purple veins on the back of Terajima's hand, his long manicured fingernails and raw knuckles, the hands like a vulture's claws. Mei's mouth opened – she'd lost her teeth – she tried to scream and choked on her blood.

That was when he opened his eyes. There was a banging on his door. 'Alan!' It was Kelly-Jo. 'Alan – it's late. Are you okay?'

'Fine . . . wait, I'm awake.' His throat was dry. He must have been screaming. The single grubby sheet was moist with cold sweat.

'We're going to see Dad. The police have spoken to him. Dad says he's kept you out of it.'

411

'Send him my best – tell him everything's fine.'

'I will. Are you sure you're all right, Alan?'

'I'm fine.'

He was far from fine. *The nightmare that it's all too late* –

The warm water that he splashed against his eyes from the grimy basin lessened the terror of the dream. He stretched open his eyes as wide as he could. He had no toothbrush, no razor; there were small curled hairs from a previous guest embedded in the bar of soap. Lipstick marks stained the hand towel.

He threw on his clothes and went downstairs.

The man behind the desk said there was tea and coffee in the machine 'outside the toilets'. Rosslyn paid the bill for two rooms and left.

The snow was falling and, with neither coat nor hat, he had to wait ten minutes for a cab.

79

Ann Chisholm, her head covered in a woollen scarf, was waiting for him outside the Israeli embassy. Dressed against the cold in a dark coat and heavy boots, she was carrying a small attaché case. She had brought Rufus with her, the retired sniffer dog.

'You look frozen, Alan.'

His eyes were lined with weariness. He smiled faintly. 'I am.'

'Still think he'll show up?' she said hesitantly.

Rosslyn could make only a calculated guess. There was neither sound nor sight of Terajima. But he felt him in his bones. The winter cold and the hidden fear of Terajima made him shiver. He was certain now that in a few hours from now, either he or Terajima would die. He looked over his shoulder. 'He may be here already.' The eyes of the armed police officers and the lenses of the CCTV cameras on the walls of the Israeli embassy were on them. 'What's in your case?' he asked Chisholm.

'A miniature trace detector unit. It can very quickly

register the presence of explosive particles on skin or clothing. I also have a packet of Healthy Paws.'

'You have *what*?'

'For Rufus. Holistic dog biscuits. Inside's a loaded handgun. Just in case . . .'

'Is that wise? What happens if they find it?'

'Then they find it, don't they? We'll say we're testing their security.'

Her blood's up, Rosslyn thought. *She's caught the fox's scent.*

Heads bowed, they trudged through the snow to the Ilyushenko mansion's entrance.

Rosslyn told one of the men in the temporary guard hut that they were expected. 'We have an appointment with Colonel Metelev.'

The guard muttered something into a mobile phone. 'Go on in now,' he told Rosslyn. 'Colonel Metelev's waiting for you.'

Mention of Metelev seemed to grant them permission to enter without being searched. Rosslyn clocked this breach of security, but made no mention of it. Metelev approached them just inside the porch. Behind him, the entrance hall was a bustle of activity. Servants were carrying trays of glasses, tablecloths, chairs and candelabra. Metelev looked at Chisholm coolly and gave a little bow. He told a maidservant to take Chisholm's coat and he eyed Rosslyn's wet and slightly steaming clothes and smiled without commenting.

Rosslyn explained that Ron Costley was indisposed and introduced Ann Chisholm and the dog Rufus.

'We don't like animals in the mansion,' Metelev muttered. 'Take it to the gardens.'

414

'It has a name – Rufus – and a vile temper,' said Chisholm. 'Best not make an enemy of him.'

'I need to see Mikhail Ilyushenko,' Rosslyn said.

'That won't be necessary. He says you are to check the place. If there's a problem, you report it to me. Otherwise, you stay on stand-by.'

'We'd like to make a sweep for explosive substances,' said Rosslyn.

'Rufus here,' said Chisholm, 'is fully trained in the detection of explosives.'

'It's been done already,' Metelev snapped.

'Who by?'

'By me. If you have a problem, then tell me.'

'Okay then,' Rosslyn said. 'Where's the guest list?'

Metelev handed over a file and turned away.

'We'll begin with the kitchen,' Rosslyn said to the retreating figure.

'The Colonel seems a little threatened by us,' Chisholm said.

Rosslyn told Chisholm that Metelev had said the exterior doors to the kitchen would be kept unlocked. He glanced at the staff, who were from the Kalitniky Catering Company. 'The fire escape's at the rear of the house,' Rosslyn told her and pointed out the entrance to the basement. 'The only way in – and the only way out.'

Then they returned to the main hallway and climbed the main staircase that rose behind the Ionic colonnade to the landing. Rosslyn told Chisholm about the metal detectors and X-ray screening facilities that had been installed, the CCTV, the fire and smoke alarms, and the alarms linked to the police and police presence surrounding the Israeli embassy and across the road at

Kensington Palace, as well as to the protection teams outside.

On the top floor, Chisholm let the dog off its lead and it wandered round the corridors, poking beneath beds, side tables and chairs and along the edges of Persian rugs. Rosslyn checked the furnishings and windows of the first room, then the second, then the third. The place had been cleaned and decorated with such thoroughness that it seemed almost sterile; it smelled unused, like the least popular areas of a furniture department store. Either the heating or the air-conditioning system filled the silence with a continuous, eerie hum. The top floor, the area Chisholm considered to be the most likely location for a possible bomb, took her and Rufus fifteen to twenty minutes to search. Finally, she pronounced it clean.

They went down to the floor below, where they found Anna Feller standing by a window. Very pale, absorbed in thought and with reddened eyes, she was carrying a fur overcoat and mittens. In her hand she held her flute. Rosslyn introduced her to Chisholm. 'Is Daddy coming?' she asked.

'I don't think so, Anna.'

'I wish he were. I want him to hear me play my flute.'

Rosslyn smiled at her.

She was peering through the window. 'You'll hear me play, Alan? Look. They're here.' Anna rubbed her sleeve across the misted windowpanes. 'My friends.'

Rosslyn followed her stare. Across the road stood a group of Salvation Army musicians wrapped against the snow. Anna ran from the room.

Chisholm moved towards the window to look at the

Salvationists. 'They get everywhere . . . your friend Metelev's down there having a cheroot with the guards . . . you'd think he'd have better things to do.'

Rosslyn glanced at the guest list. 'The bloody thing's in Russian.'

'Give it to me,' Chisholm said. 'I have Russian.'

Reading the names, Chisholm's face darkened. 'Viktor Mavrodi.'

'Who's Mavrodi?'

'A former inmate of Moscow's Butyrka prison . . . held on charges of embezzlement . . . made a fortune speculating in roubles against the dollar.'

'The others?'

'Russian ambassador. Trade representatives. So it goes on . . . masters of *blat*, the peculiarly Russian business of patronage and gangsterism. And there are others – Virtus and Allegiance cronies.'

'Which?'

'Anatoly Zhilin. Lincoln Bausch. Eduardo Valente Jr. Dick Shepperfeld. Montana Bogaart. Das Gupta. Have yourself a happy little Christmas.'

Rosslyn stood for a few moments staring at the list and shifting from foot to foot without saying a word. Even the dog was twitching. The only sound came from the heating system, buzzing like a menacing chorus of angry insects. Beads of cold sweat formed on his forehead and above his upper lip. He staggered back to a chair and slumped into it. 'What the hell are these people coming for – *why*?'

He heard Chisholm's voice: 'Are you okay, Alan?'

'I don't feel too good . . .'

The sea is beautiful. Turquoise. Sparkling tips of tiny

waves. Burning smoke fills the cabin. We'll be burned to death. The rush for the emergency exits.

'Let me get you a glass of water.'

We jump. The deafening whistle in my ears. White spray claws the eyes. Everything's white. Then it all goes black . . . the sea . . . vanishes in a cloud of white spray.

He heard his own voice whispering: 'I can't breathe.'

It's like looking at the sun. Fireballs of yellow, red. There's the stench of burning flesh. Mei is holding me in her arms telling me everything's all right.

He was in Chisholm's arms, his head against her breast.

'Everything's okay, Alan.'

'It isn't.'

She handed him a glass of water.

'Everything's very wrong, Ann. There's a whole lot more to look at. Let's get on with it . . .'

'Alan, you look terrible . . . you're exhausted . . . take it easy . . . there's plenty of time . . .'

'There isn't – and there's the press conference in the main salon.'

'We can watch it in the security operations room.'

'I think we should see Mikhail Ilyushenko first.'

'Look, Alan,' Chisholm said firmly, 'leave Ilyushenko to Metelev. Give or take an hour or two, it'll all be over and done with. The place is secure.'

'Do you honestly believe that, Ann?'

Chisholm offered no answer, and with Rufus in tow, they headed for the lift and the security operations room in the west wing.

It was never quite clear who at the last minute changed

the venue for the press conference from the main salon to the chapel. Perhaps Mikhail Ilyushenko thought the chapel would add extra dignity to the event.

Rosslyn and Chisholm watched the proceedings on the TV screens.

Mikhail Ilyushenko sat in his wheelchair in front of the altar watching the journalists, no more than a dozen of them, arrive and take their positions. There were no seats for them in the chapel. They had to stand.

Once the doors were closed, Ilyushenko introduced himself:

'I am Mikhail Ilyushenko. I am aware that some of you have sought interviews with me, but as you can perhaps see, my physical condition has not allowed me to come before the press until now. You'll appreciate that this is a solemn day for me, and I would be grateful if you'd keep your questions brief and on the subject of the immense contribution of the Ilyushenko family to international good will and commercial and charitable interests promoting the multi-cultural and multi-racial Britain and Russia of today and the future. Thank you.'

The first question was from a man who said he was from the BBC. He held up a microphone. 'Can you tell me whether the Moscow police have made any progress in the hunt for the people who murdered your brother and his wife and child?'

'My people in Moscow are in constant touch with Police Chief Kiriyenko. He also happens to be a personal friend of mine. Kiriyenko assures me that everything possible is being done to bring the murderers to justice.'

A woman from *The Times* asked if he could comment on the arrest of Pyotr Ilyushenko in Athens.

'My brother is assisting the Athens police with enquiries.'

'But he and his colleagues have been accused of the murder.'

'They are innocent of any such thing. It is a misunderstanding. The matter's in the hands of my lawyers. As to Wedemeier, that's a matter for the Swiss authorities.'

A woman from the *Daily Mail* asked if there was any truth in the rumours that the British and American security services were investigating what she called 'the Ilyushenko axis'.

'*Axis* – what axis?'

'Your links to major private security agencies?'

'We have none at all. We are of no interest to intelligence services either here or in the United States.'

'Do you live in fear of your life?' asked a man from ITV News.

'Do you?'

'I'm asking you, Mr Ilyushenko.'

'If I did, you wouldn't be here now.'

'But with respect –'

'I understand the meaning of respect. Your question suggests that you don't. Have you signed the condolence book?'

The question was met with blank stares and a long silence.

'Well, ladies and gentlemen, I have answered your questions. If you won't answer mine, then I have nothing more to say to you.'

Mikhail Ilyushenko glanced up at his nurses. The journalists looked irritable and began to file out of the chapel. Several liveried stewards ushered them towards the refreshments.

'Do you believe any of that?' Chisholm whispered.

'No,' said Rosslyn. He was watching the arrival of the guests on the CCTV system in the security control centre, studying the faces of the men and women being shown to the refreshment area with only a short time left until the start of the memorial service.

'We'll watch the rest from here,' he told Chisholm.

80

BATTERSEA TO
KENSINGTON PALACE GARDENS.
LONDON

The two white camper vans bearing the logo of the Salvation Army had already left Battersea in convoy on their way to their final destination. Terajima was driving the lead vehicle. The explosive *matériel* was on the front seat. Rachelle Pienaar, Ono and the by now semi-conscious Mei were in the back. In the second van, Merkel was at the wheel, Jortzig was in the front passenger seat and the two Indonesian nurses were crouching in the back.

Mei drifted in and out of consciousness. Ono watched Pienaar wipe Mei's face and check her heavy breathing. From Hyde Park Corner the van headed west and the second wagon, following at a discreet distance, did likewise.

'Is she saying anything?' Terajima asked, without turning his head.

'No,' said Pienaar.

'I want her to come round so she can look Rosslyn in

the eyes.' He checked the rear-view mirror, making sure the second van was following.

Outside Kensington High Street tube station, the second van drew up at the kerbside. The Germans and the nurses collected their instruments from the rear and trudged through the snow in the direction of the Royal Garden Hotel and on up Kensington Palace Gardens. If Plan A – Terajima's murder of Rosslyn – went awry and Rosslyn left the house by the front entrance, their job was to kill him and get away as fast as possible.

Terajima drove his van to Kensington Church Street, where he parked it in front of the steel garage doors at the rear of the Ilyushenko mansion. He leaned towards the intercom and gave his name to the guard as Mr D, adding: 'Mikhail Ilyushenko is expecting me.' He heard the guards say a few muffled words in Russian and then tell him: 'The doors will open.'

The electronically controlled doors rose slowly, and the camper van bumped down the short ramp into the garage space and stopped in front of the piles of builder's equipment and materials.

Flickering candles illuminated the Ilyushenko chapel and congregation. The priest conducting the service was newly retired from the Russian Orthodox cathedral in Ennismore Gardens.

He explained that normally he would have been taking the service in Church Slavonic but that today, in view of the international nature of the congregation, he would do so in English. He told them why they were all there, asked them to pray for the souls of the departed and led the saying of the Lord's Prayer.

Viktoria Feller's eyes became moist with emotion as she mouthed the prayer. Apart from Pyotr Ilyushenko, the only other notable absentees were Metelev, who was prowling round the residence, and Anna, who had already gone outside to join the Salvationists.

Mikhail Ilyushenko was watching the ceremony with a kind of magisterial impassivity. It was impossible to tell what thoughts were running through his mind. Near Ilyushenko stood the oligarchs in exile.

The priest said: 'The iconostasis reminds us of our role as pilgrims on the road to the kingdom of heaven. Icons of Christ and the saints show us that, in Christ, we will achieve redemption: "Christ has entered into heaven itself, now to appear in the presence of God on our behalf. Lord, have mercy."'

'*Lord, have mercy.*'

'Grant us this, O Lord.'

'*Grant us this, O Lord.*'

81

Terajima leaned close to Mei in the darkness of the wagon. She was on her back breathing fitfully. Her eyes were shut, her cheeks bruised.

She tried to raise her hands to protect her face. The movement pained her. The effort was too great. When she closed her eyes Terajima's fingers prised them open.

'We will pray together,' he intoned. 'Who is like the beast and able to wage war with him . . .?' There was a manic intensity in his voice. 'For the time of creation nears. The creation of the sacrificial image to the beast, the foetus wounded by the Katana sword.'

Pienaar opened her small surgical equipment case containing the tools of the abortionist as Terajima's voice lowered to a whisper. 'Listen to me, Mei. You're going to see Rosslyn. Together with him, you'll watch Rachelle abort the foetus and she will, very gently, put the foetus to Rosslyn's lips and he will die with it in his mouth. You are honoured, Mei. Honoured. I want to hear your voice . . . speak to me, blossom.'

Instinct said stay silent. Struggling to breathe regularly, she inhaled the sharp aroma of disinfectant and forced her eyes shut again. Now she felt the chill of steel against her head.

Ono was pressing the gun against Mei's temples. Mei could hear the woman's excited giggles and felt Ono press her mouth against hers and then insert her tongue. Mei retched and Ono let her saliva dribble into Mei's mouth. Ono prised Mei's lips wider and stuck the gun in Mei's mouth.

'*Alan is coming*,' Terajima intoned. Mei writhed. Ono withdrew the gun. Terajima snapped his fingers. 'He is coming so I can kill him. He is going to die . . . there will be no mercy. Repeat after me . . . *he is going to die*.'

Mei's lips quivered.

'SAY IT.'

Mei stayed silent and heard Terajima say, 'I will set the timers.' She understood. They were making the final preparations to a bomb.

'Alan is here,' Terajima was chanting. '*Alan is here*.'

Mei felt her legs being raised. Ono smiled at her. Her grip was powerful. The big hands were unfastening the binds that tied her. Ono was peering hard between Mei's legs and Mei fought against Ono's grip but her strength had ebbed away.

Somewhere in the dimness a dot of green light signalled the completion of the preparations.

Mei felt the needle prick a vein in her arm and within seconds was unconscious.

82

THE CHAPEL.
KENSINGTON PALACE GARDENS.
LONDON

The priest blessed *prosfora*, small bread rolls, reciting the names of the living and the dead, inviting the congregation to pray for them. It was at that moment when Mikhail Ilyushenko's head seemed to slump on to his chest.

Viktoria was about to tell the nurses to take him out of the chapel, but the nurses took the initiative themselves and wheeled him slowly out. The congregation looked on sympathetically, believing that the emotional strain had been too much for him to bear. Viktoria followed the wheelchair to the exit, where Mikhail Ilyushenko gestured to her to return to her place in front of the altar.

Accompanied by his nurses, Mikhail Ilyushenko made his way to the lift that would take him down to the garage, where Mr D – the man he knew as Takashi Sakamoto – would be waiting. With the fingers of one hand he was fiddling with the controls of the wheelchair, trying to master them. The lift doors opened. 'I can manage on my own,' he told the nurses, who watched the doors close.

83

Rosslyn had not followed the progress of the service in its entirety. Rather, he had taken advantage of the relative quiet in the mansion to find some coffee at the refreshment tables.

Then, with Chisholm, he returned to the security control unit.

He borrowed a pair of binoculars from one of the Russians and focused on Anna, who had joined the circle of Salvation Army musicians in the snow, her flute to her lips. The girl's cheeks had reddened in the cold but she looked happy and was giving the other musicians smiles of encouragement. It was a rather touching, if not sentimental, scene and reminded Rosslyn of a picture on an old-fashioned Christmas card. Chisholm must have been thinking along the same lines. 'London in the snow looks so beautiful,' she was saying.

Rosslyn looked closely at the group of Salvationists. There was, he felt, something not quite right about them.

He made out that one distinct group wore coats of a different style to the others. Two of the musicians were fiddling with their flutes, clearly either unwilling or unable to play them. The binoculars enabled him to study the features of the two reluctant flautists. He felt increasingly certain that he had seen the two men somewhere before. At one point, both of them turned their faces to the house and he saw that they were talking to each other. Images of faces flickered in his mind. But it was the sight of the stocky musician with three fingers missing from his left hand that triggered his clear memory of the video clip shown him by Sandra Holmes in Schiff's Holland Park flat. The man was the thirty-three-year-old German narcotics distributor, Horst Merkel. He turned his attention to Merkel's companion, the figure with the straight back, the killer wanted for the murder of the judge in Munich.

He asked someone to put him through on the communication speaker link to the guards on the front gates. He told Chisholm to speak to the guards in Russian and ask whether the musicians had shown their ID.

Chisholm spoke briefly to the guard, then to Rosslyn. 'No one's vetted them.'

'Tell them to move the musicians out and away. Now.'

'Are you sure, Alan?'

'Do it.'

Rosslyn left the house and found that the guards had already got wind of what he meant. They were ordering the Salvationists to raise their arms above their heads. An argument had started and Anna was shouting at the guards to let the music continue.

'Let's go back inside, Anna,' Rosslyn told her.

'Go away,' she yelled.

'Anna. It isn't safe.'

'No.'

He grabbed her by the arm and pulled her towards the mansion.

She struggled against his grip. 'You're hurting me.'

'Come on. Something's wrong.'

He succeeded in trapping her arms and carried her back to the house. By now the musicians had disappeared from view.

Back inside the mansion, he dragged Anna into the security control unit.

He was about to tell Chisholm about the altercation outside when the mansion's power went off. 'You stay here, Anna.' He told one of the security guards to keep her safe.

Hurrying with the dog from the security unit, Rosslyn and Chisholm ran across the darkened hallway and along the corridor to the chapel entrance, where some servants were already lighting more candles. They saw Metelev watching the steel doors closing. Rosslyn shouted to him: 'Is Ilyushenko in there?'

'He left –'

'Where is he?'

'Leave him to me –'

'Where's the main power switch?'

'In the garage.'

'Who's authorised to turn it off?'

Offering no reply, Metelev lumbered across the hallway with Rosslyn and Chisholm following. Rosslyn saw the Russian draw a handgun from the holster inside his jacket. Metelev headed for a door marked 'Fire Exit', kicked it open, and ran down the concrete steps.

At the basement level, builder's wooden boards barred his way. Metelev cursed. He gestured to Rosslyn to level a kick at one of the boards and what seemed to be a row of nails. He shouted something in Russian and the two kicked at the wood, splintering it. Two more kicks and the wooden board fell away into the garage.

84

GARAGE.

KENSINGTON PALACE GARDENS.

LONDON

Rosslyn felt the dog brush against his leg. Chisholm was holding on to the dog lead. Rosslyn followed her with Metelev at his side, gun raised. The dog ran toward the camper van.

'Don't move,' yelled Chisholm. 'Don't touch.'

Rosslyn froze. He could hear Chisholm's agitated breathing. He sensed she was opening her device for detecting the presence of explosives. He saw some lights flicker.

'There's a lot of dirt here,' he heard her mutter. 'I need more light.'

Rosslyn walked away from the side of the camper van and his foot struck metal. He called out: 'Metelev?'

There was no answer.

His fingers followed the metal of the wheelchair until they settled on the body. He felt the stump of a shoulder. No arm. He felt his way across the shoulder. His fingers grew sticky. He followed the route to the neck. To the head. He put his face near to the chest. Nothing. He felt his way to the face. The mouth was wide open and warm blood was oozing from it.

'*Metelev – where's the power switch?*' He was about to say he'd found the body of Mikhail Dmitriev Ilyushenko.

'I have it,' Metelev said.

The lights came on.

At the same time, a dull veil of daylight widened across the low ceiling of the garage. Rosslyn made out the snow on the ramp as the garage doors began to rise. Deafening emergency alarm bells rang out.

Then the mechanism of the garage doors seemed to stop working.

There was a large round mirror on the wall placed at an angle to make negotiation of the ramp easier for drivers. In it, he could make out the reflected and distorted figure of Metelev standing there as the doors began to move again, and then began to close.

He saw two indistinct figures moving sideways at an angle. They presented very difficult targets. Rosslyn raised his gun and saw Metelev do likewise. As he did so Metelev began to scream at them in rage and opened fire.

The figures were blurred. One of them seemed to stagger backwards. Metelev was still firing and was stepping back at the same time, in a crouch for cover, when a third figure turned and shot Metelev in the head. More shots followed rapidly. Rosslyn crouched for cover beside the van. He stared hard at the face of the third figure. Even at that distance and in the poor visibility he was, for a terrible second, eyeball to eyeball with Terajima.

434

He raised his gun. It was no use. Terajima had gone. The gunmen had vanished into the falling snow.

The Russian hadn't stood a chance. The other shots had hit him in his shoulder and in his chest, driving his collapsing bulk against the wall. His body seemed momentarily suspended and then, as the doors lowered as if on their own accord, Metelev slumped to the floor, blood pouring from his mouth.

Rosslyn's eyes focused on the body of Mikhail Ilyushenko in the overturned wheelchair. Then he saw Chisholm crouched on her knees inside the van, while the dog squatted near her as if on guard.

He stood motionless and listened to Chisholm's low voice. 'Here,' she said. There was an unfamiliar calmness in her. 'Get in close. Careful. See? The shit's in these flutes and cases. Just above the door here . . . wrapped with industrial adhesive tape . . .'

Inch by inch, she nursed the tip of her long fingernail through the tape, gently unpeeling it.

Rosslyn listened to her whispering: 'The current's from a battery.'

There was a long, what seemed to Rosslyn to be an interminable, pause.

'Relay connection. Electromagnetic switch. Danger of a circuit here collapsing. Could be a short. Okay, it's a small timer. Maybe an adapted alarm clock. Could even be a kitchen timer. I'm going to break the wire.'

She turned to Rosslyn. 'You'd better get out of here before I break it.'

'I'm not moving.'

'Don't tell me I didn't warn you.'

'I won't be here to tell you.'

'Say your prayers.'

Rosslyn watched the movement of her fingers. He saw the wire come away in her hands. Gently, inch by inch, she twisted it so no further contact could be made.

She took a deep breath. 'I think there's a booby trap. There could even be a radio control device. We can't take the risk – let's get out of here.'

Rosslyn was staring inside the van. 'Wait –' he said. There's something . . . someone . . . here. Get the dog in here.'

Chisholm called the dog and it jumped up into the van and headed straight for the bed at the far end of it. 'Alan . . . please . . . we have to get out of here – *now*.'

'Wait,' said Rosslyn.

It was as if he already knew what lay beneath those sheets.

'Get an ambulance . . . *get an ambulance*.'

A piece of paper was stuck to Mei's forehead.

It looked like a label on a corpse in a mortuary. There were syringes on the floor and marks on her inside arms where the needles had been jabbed in her veins and small circles of bruising and dried blood.

The clanging of the alarm bells had stopped.

'Are you okay, Mei? It's me. Alan. I'm here. Keep breathing. You're safe now. It's all over.' He took her in his arms. 'The medics will be here soon. I'll get you to hospital.'

Mei was breathing fitfully. He thought he saw a trace of life flicker in her unseeing eyes. He removed the fragment of paper from her forehead, read his own hand-written message to her, and begged her not to die.

'Speak to me, Mei.'

His pleas went unanswered.

'Mei – *I love you.*'

With tears streaming down his face he cradled her like a child.

85

He set the fragment of paper on the bedside table so it would be the first thing Mei saw when she regained full consciousness.

I want to spend the rest of my life with you.
I love you.
Please will you marry me?

Her head rested on the pillows of the hospital bed. Eyes closed, she looked very frail. The red roses Rosslyn had brought her lay in the washbasin in a corner near the window curtained against the glare of the winter sun.

She looked more beautiful than he had ever seen her. The nurses had washed her hair and it glistened. He was filled with admiration for the way she had survived; admiration tempered by a sense of his own defeat and guilt. He was responsible for this. *If not me, then who?* One thing was still the same. Terajima was still out there.

Costley had persuaded his doctors to let him visit.

Maybe, Rosslyn felt, his friend was on some kind of medication that made him seem so melancholy. The police had begun the lengthy business of assembling forensic evidence and the interrogation of those they considered witnesses. They had taken the credit for the safe and orderly evacuation of the wise and the good from the Ilyushenko mansion. Chisholm had been, as she put it – 'reasonably forthcoming' with the officers from the Special Branch who had no earthly idea who might have dispatched Mikhail Ilyushenko and Colonel Metelev or held Mei Lim prisoner. The discovery of the abortionist's equipment was sickening, the paraphernalia of bomb construction horrifying.

When Costley read aloud the note that Rosslyn had retrieved – *I want to spend the rest of my life with you. I love you. Please will you marry me?* – he handed it back to Rosslyn, the edge of the paper held between the tips of his fingers, as if he had inadvertently touched a crucial piece of forensic evidence. Perhaps that's all it is, Rosslyn felt, one more scrap of evidence – to be subjected to scientific analysis – the note in her jewellery box, the demonstration of the love he felt, the record of the unanswered proposal he had made just before she left. Costley said he should give it to the police. Rosslyn was not inclined to do so.

He received a letter of thanks for '*all you did*' from Viktoria Feller. It had been penned in turquoise ink. '*I'm locked in meetings with lawyers . . . there are problems with the Will . . . God alone knows, I had no idea how much money is involved . . . the police . . . they're searching the mansion – taking for ever . . . their questions are interminable. Their minds are greatly exercised by sam-*

439

ples of blood they found in the snow in Kensington Church Street. Kensington Church Street – I ask you! Anna wants me to take Grant back. He's pitiable. If one day, you could find a way to make it up with him, sort of man-to-man. I mean, perhaps if he regains his mind. Well, I leave all that sort of thing to you. Little Viktoria isn't awfully lucky with men, is she? And poor-poor Grant. Poor all of us. Anna's staying with friends in – either tears or spilled drink had smudged the place name. The sheet of writing paper that bore the address of the Ilyushenko mansion had been smeared with what seemed to be cigarette ash and she had omitted to sign her name.

'Aside from Mei?' Costley asked. 'Are you going to move on?'

'There's unfinished business.'

'Draw a line under it, Alan.'

'I said, Ron. There's unfinished business.'

'I heard you the first time,' said Costley. 'Do you think it's worth pursuing – revenge, is that what you want for Christmas?'

'All I want is peace of mind – pure and simple. That's what I want, Ron. Do you find that so unusual?'

'What I mean is that the shooting's over,' Costley said.

Rosslyn thought of the handgun in the pack of Healthy Paws. Chisholm had insisted he borrow it 'just in case'. It was hidden behind a stack of saucepans at the flat in Claverton Street. Rosslyn reminded himself to return it to Chisholm as soon as possible.

86

The days before Christmas were bitter. The winter sun brought a dull light to the city. The interviews with the police proved less burdensome than he had expected. Three officers from the security service visited him at his flat and showed him papers that had been retrieved from Mikhail Ilyushenko's safe. Among the papers was the Sakamoto CV. Apparently the most senior of the three security service men was a solemn, polite and very thin figure wearing a turban. He told Rosslyn that his people 'wanted to question this notorious fugitive from justice'.

'I'm sure you do,' said Rosslyn.

'Can you help me?'

Quite what he had in mind Rosslyn was unsure. 'The only person who can help you is you,' he said. 'You'll do it. And when you have I'll be waiting for you.'

He suddenly remembered that he was telling them more or less exactly what Mei had told him. He could almost hear her voice: *Alan, the only person who can help you is you. You'll do it. And when you have, I'll be waiting for you.* The man asked him whether he would object to being placed under surveillance.

'Not in the least,' said Rosslyn. 'Thanks for asking anyway. But then if you people are watching me I wouldn't know, would I?'

'I suppose you wouldn't,' the man in the turban said. 'You have to understand that we are dealing with very violent and very dangerous criminals.'

'I understand,' said Rosslyn and the three wise men upped and left.

Mei remained under sedation for what seemed to him an unreasonable length of time. For reasons of psychology, the doctors said, they were anxious that her traumas heal and that she should be left in peace and quiet.

In between his visits to her, Rosslyn began the redecoration of his flat. He stripped the paint from the walls of the front room and the window just below the ceiling as well as the rusted iron bars set into the outside sill. The exterior could wait till the spring. He also replaced the lock to the gate from the street to the stairwell. He painted the interior in the same light and almost luminous grey Mei had chosen. What would have passed as a squash court floor of plain wood he left alone and set to work to defeat the rising damp. The striking photographs, the self-portraits of Mei above his bed, of course remained.

There might be an outside chance, he reckoned, that she might just be strong enough to share Christmas with him. Christmas with Mei and the unborn child who was alive and well. It was something of a forlorn hope. But, just in case, he bought a small Christmas tree, some rows of coloured lights along with sparkling ribbons and set the tree in the window.

For whatever reasons, perhaps these had to do with Christmas, the police and security service people fell silent. On the other hand, there were the occasional signs of a surveillance team in Claverton Street: the black cab parked nearby, its driver ostensibly reading a folded newspaper, his passenger sitting in the back with a studied and vacant stare.

The cab was elsewhere when the carol singers arrived late on a Friday evening. He was first aware of their arrival when they offered the German version of *Silent Night*. Their performance was enhanced by a loud instrumental and choral accompaniment from a portable sound-system.

After one or two verses there was a knock on the door and a woman's voice moaned something like 'Make Poverty History.'

Rosslyn collected a five-pound note from his wallet and opened the door to the stairwell.

A rush of cold air hit his face. He saw the sweep of the gloved hand, the flash of the blade and looked straight into the dark eyes of Klaas-Pieter Terajima. Fear rose in his chest. Terajima's blade opened the skin high in Rosslyn's right cheek, crunching bone, curving towards his nose and then at an angle through his upper lip, the tip of the blade penetrating his gums. The cut seared his nerves; the pain was like a burn from a naked flame.

Terajima kept on coming forward like an animal, as if ecstatic at the sight of so much blood. There was a strange whistling from his flared nostrils. His bared teeth were stained with his recent intake of Swedish *snuss*. He threw his weight against Rosslyn, one knee hammering into Rosslyn's genitals, and struggled to

443

raise the blade high enough to drive it into Rosslyn's throat.

Squirming sideways, blood pouring from his wound, Rosslyn levelled his right hand, pointed his fingers up beneath Terajima's jaw and jammed his nails deep into the folds of skin. Staggering back, Terajima caught his breath and choked. Rosslyn had badly wounded Terajima's Adam's apple.

There was a flash of pained regret in Terajima's eyes. Breathing heavily, the whistling even more pronounced, he heaved himself to his feet attempting once again to stab Rosslyn, this time aiming at the heart. Rosslyn rolled over, slid backwards, his eyes stinging with his own blood and reached to the table for a knife. Instead of the knife his fingers were closing around the handle of a corkscrew when, through a red mist, he saw the tips of black boots – saw a flurry of retreating legs come in and out of focus. There was the distinct crack of gunfire above and outside in the street and the shouts 'Run – *run*.'

He dragged himself across the floor, his hand pressed as hard as he could bear against the open wound, trying to stem the flow of blood, and reached for the pack of Healthy Paws.

'Two have gone,' a voice called out: 'We got one . . .'

Taking Chisholm's borrowed handgun with him, Rosslyn staggered up the steps and peered across the street.

He saw the two bodies lying by the piles of frozen snow. Fighting to clear his eyes, blinking, trying to wipe away his blood, he looked into the first pair of dead eyes, the stare fixed skywards. The first of the three security service men, the one in the turban, lay dead at his feet.

'Mr Rosslyn,' someone was shouting. 'We got him . . .'

Rosslyn lurched towards the second body. People were babbling into mobile phones. 'Terajima,' a voice was saying.

Rosslyn knelt over the prostrate figure. 'You're wrong,' he said. 'This is someone called Rachelle Pienaar.'

'They won't get far, sir. They haven't a chance in hell.'

'You're wrong,' said Rosslyn. 'You're very wrong, they have every chance of getting away.' The pain of the wounds in his face, combined with his loss of blood, pumped waves of nausea through his brain. 'Look – will you go into my flat . . . turn out the lights . . . lock the doors . . . and take me to the nearest hospital?'

'We're waiting for the police.'

'You may be. I'm not. Get me to a hospital.'

'You'd better give me that gun, Mr Rosslyn.'

'Piss off.'

'I might have to ask the police to arrest you for being in possession of –'

Sinking to his knees, his blood dripping down his chest Rosslyn said: 'Do what I say NOW or I might just have to use it.'

The surveillance man, the shadow in the shadows, looked taken aback and set about doing what he'd been told.

It was then that Rosslyn saw the three figures deeper in the gloom. They were moving closer. The streetlight briefly illuminated their features.

He recognised Jortzig, then Merkel. The third was an oriental-looking woman. Rosslyn saw the Germans raise their guns together, almost at the same moment.

He rolled over behind a parked car. The Germans fired. One shot slammed into the body of the car, a second seemed to scream past Rosslyn's ear. As he saw them approaching, he leaned sideways, took brief aim and fired twice. Both shots found their targets. One struck Merkel's chest, wounding him fatally. The other winged Jortzig's shoulder, and as he reeled back, the German screamed. '*Wait Ono . . . Wait.*'

Rosslyn didn't wait. His last shot found Jortzig's head, killing him instantly.

87

UNIVERSITY COLLEGE HOSPITAL. LONDON

He was aware of a dark figure standing over him. The eyes were dark, the hair was lustrous.

'I'm not supposed to be here, Mr Rosslyn.' He felt the hand take his and heard the familiar hesitation in the voice. 'Is there anything I can do to make you more comfortable. Do you want to spend the rest of your life with me?'

Rosslyn raised his hand and touched Mei's moist cheeks.

A nurse brought in a bouquet of roses and a vase. Mei removed the cellophane and began arranging them.

There was an envelope attached to the cellophane.

Mei smiled. 'You have an admirer I don't know about,' she whispered. 'The flowers. They're beautiful. Except – guess what, they're addressed to me. Mei c/o Alan Rosslyn.'

She opened the envelope and the card and read to herself:

I want to spend the rest of my life with you.
I love you.
Please will you marry me?

Klaas-Pieter Terajima

END

TTRAP

B WING

2K18 — 2025

14 YR BIRD

SC. T — TRAAP